Kathy Kaye
Kathleen Scott
Ellie Marvel
Calista Fox

Volume 17

Secrets

Satisfy your desire for more.

SECRETS Volume 17
This is an original publication of Red Sage Publishing and each individual story herein has never before appeared in print. These stories are a collection of fiction and any similarity to actual persons or events is purely coincidental.

Red Sage Publishing, Inc.
P.O. Box 4844
Seminole, FL 33775
727-391-3847
www.redsagepub.com

SECRETS Volume 17
A Red Sage Publishing book
All Rights Reserved/December 2006
Copyright © 2006 by Red Sage Publishing, Inc.

ISBN: 0-9754516-7-7 / ISBN 13: 978-0-9754516-7-0

Published by arrangement with the authors and copyright holders of the individual works as follows:

ROCK HARD CANDY
Copyright © 2006 by Kathy Kaye

FATAL ERROR
Copyright © 2006 by Kathleen Scott

BIRTHDAY
Copyright © 2006 by Ellie Marvel

INTIMATE RENDEZVOUS
Copyright © 2006 by Calista Fox

Photographs:
Cover © 2006 by Tara Kearney; www.tarakearney.com
Cover Model: Summer Colvin and Israel Diaz
Setback cover © 2000 by Greg P. Willis; GgnYbr@aol.com

Printed in the U.S.A.

Book typesetting by:
Quill & Mouse Studios, Inc.
www.quillandmouse.com

Contents

Rock Hard

Candy

by Kathy Kaye

To My Reader:

Let your imagination run wild while you ponder what a desperate woman would do to lure the man of her dreams into her life—and her bed. Now imagine she's the great-great-granddaughter of a voodoo priestess.

I did!

I hope you enjoy *Rock Hard Candy.*

New Orleans is one of my favorite cities. Its majestic grandeur touches my soul with wispy reminders of times past and promises of wondrous things not yet revealed. Hurricane forces may have momentarily staggered this great lady of a city, but not even Mother Nature can keep her down for long.

Chapter One

The clock struck the half-hour. Eight-thirty.

Jessica held her breath. Her heart raced ninety-to-nothing. She glued her gaze to the coffee shop's front door.

If she didn't breathe soon, she'd black out. If Alex didn't show up, she'd die.

If, when he did show up, he stepped around to her side of the counter and kissed her as he had in her dream, she'd come right where she stood.

This morning's damned dream had her wound up and wanting almost to the point of pain. When she moved, her super-sensitized flesh rubbed against her nylon panties, torturing her with a satiny abrasiveness that nearly drove her insane. Yet, when she sat stone-still, the need to relieve that sexual itch between her legs was almost unbearable.

What was it her grandmother used to say? Stuck between a rock and a hard place?

Yeah right. She only wished she was stuck between a rock and Alex Russell's hard place!

How stupid was that? She had to be out of her mind—or more accurately, brain-washed by her long-ignored natural urges—to be this jacked up!

Then again, it wasn't about just getting laid. Any man could ease her sexual itch. No, it was about Alex—and the mystery man hiding behind his emotional barricades. How had she let herself fall in love with a man still in love with his dead wife?

Crap. She was in big trouble here.

The jingle of the tiny silver bell over her coffee shop door jarred Jessica from her lustful thoughts. A combination of relief and excitement washed over her.

Alex stood just inside the door. Alone.

Just like in her dream.

Jessica's heart skipped a beat and her nerve-endings zoomed to full-alert. Maybe dreams did come true.

"Good morning, Alex," Jessica greeted him in the steadiest voice she could manage.

"Good morning." He crossed the small shop to the cash register in long strides.

If he made one move toward the workside of the bar, she'd faint for sure. In her dream, he'd stepped around the register, then pinned her against the counter with his six-foot three body. But he stayed where he was.

In an effort to pull herself from her erotic memories, she took a deep, bracing breath of the here and now, and asked, "Solo today, huh?"

Alex nodded, his dark hair brushing the crisp collar of his dress shirt. "Yep, just me."

They were alone! Well, if she didn't count the shop's other patrons loitering in the corner tables watching their exchange with mild disinterest. Jessica bit her lip to stifle a groan. What was it about this man that flipped her switch with enough power to light up Bourbon Street?

She cleared her throat, hoping he had no idea the X-rated thoughts running through her head. "The usual? One double latte and a chocolate eclair?"

From her dream, his voice resonated in her head. *I'm hungry for cream, Jessica. And not the kind stuffed in an eclair.*

Just the thought of his warm breath against her ear and the husky timbre of his voice when he'd spoken in her dream sent bolts of hot tingles shooting through her core.

"You know me too well," he smiled as he reached in his hip pocket for his billfold.

Jessica was both disappointed and relieved that he didn't reply with her dream-based answer. Mentally sighing, she forced herself to focus on the task at hand.

She wrapped an eclair in pastry paper, then reached for the stack of small white bags beneath the counter. That done, she prepared his latte and pressed the lid securely on his styrofoam cup. She felt his eyes on her all the while.

Doing her best to smile naturally, she handed him his cup. "After you've ordered the same thing every morning for six months, I'd be pretty dense if I hadn't picked up on your patterns."

"Patterns, huh? At least, I like your terminology better than Mitch's." He handed her a five-dollar bill. "According to him, my life is one long, monotonous rut."

The glisten of his gold wedding band contrasted against the black leather wallet he held in his left hand. If only he wasn't still in love with his dead wife, Jessica would fill his nights with pleasure and his heart with joy. The loneliness in his eyes would disappear under her loving touch.

"Does everything in your life fall into this 'long, monotonous rut'?" Why was she prying? He was obviously still grieving, not ready for what she craved.

Alex had never mentioned his late wife. Not once since he'd first starting coming into her shop, not during their past tasting sessions where he and his ever-present sidekick Mitch would sample some new recipe she'd just concocted. And especially, not when they lingered over a cup of coffee or a beer after those taste-testing interludes. Never. That in itself spoke volumes.

"Yeah, pretty much," he answered, pulling her out of her thoughts.

"Do you agree?" Jessica couldn't stop herself from asking as she handed him his change.

Alex chuckled as he replaced his billfold into his pocket. "Yeah, pretty much."

She shrugged. "So do something about it."

"Like what?"

"I don't know. Make some changes." God, she wanted to kick herself. Why couldn't she give him time to work through the painful changes in his life at his own speed? Why was she pushing him?

"Can't." He picked up the small baker's bag and coffee cup she'd placed in front of him. "I'm allergic to change."

"What? You break out in hives?" She smiled back at him.

"Something like that." Alex turned for the door, and suddenly Jessica couldn't just let him go like that, back to his rut.

"Wait. There's a tear in your bag." Jessica held out her hand, hoping he didn't look for the non-existent rip. "Give it to me and I'll give you another one."

Looking confused, he handed his baker's bag back to her.

Jessica retrieved the bag, holding it well out of his reach, as she waved at the pastry counter with her other hand. "Now, pick anything you want—other than an éclair."

Alex gawked at her a moment and then asked, "There's no hole in that sack is there?"

"Nope."

"Then why—"

"Sometimes change is good."

Alex sighed as he swiped his hand down his face. Was that a grin peeking out from behind his fingers? The thought bolstered her resolve to show him change could be a good thing—if only in his choice of morning pastries.

Jessica winked at him and cooed, "If you break out in hives, I'll let you use my Epipen."

"Fine, but if I start itching, you have to scratch the places I can't reach."

That sounded like heaven to Jessica, although she doubted he meant it with the sexual innuendoes she'd applied to his words. "Deal! Now, what will it be?"

"Just a glazed donut."

"Oh, yeah, you're walking on the wild side now," she teased as she slide the back partition of the display case to one side.

"With sprinkles," he added, rising to her taunting.

Laughing, she placed the extra donut in a bag, then held both bags just out of Alex's reach. "You promise to eat both of them?"

"Promise," he said, then winked at her and crossed over to the door. "See you tomorrow morning, Sweetness."

The endearment might have boosted her hopes that he'd actually seen her as anything other than the "coffee girl" across the street from his office building, but she knew better. It wasn't even Alex, but his partner Mitch who had tagged her with the nickname. The first time she'd asked them to be her guinea pigs, Mitch, flirt that he was, declared that anything that came from her fingertips had to be pure sweetness. Alex had agreed. And the name had stuck. Now Alex seemed to use it more often than Mitch, and maybe that meant something.

"I'll be here." Grinning, Jessica wiggled her fingers in a child-like wave. "Same time, same place. Same ole, same ole."

Alex chuckled again as he left. Jessica thought she heard him mumble something about kindred spirits.

She would love to kinder his spirit, she thought as she watched him cross the street to his office. She'd stack so much kindling under him and stoke his fire until they'd both go up in flames!

If only he would give her one spark of interest to fan to life.

Jessica glanced around the deserted coffee shop and sighed. Rush hour was over. All the little minions, AKA her regulars, had filed into her shop—sometimes three and four at a time—commandeered their morning rations of caffeine and sugar, then marched out to do battle in corporate America one more time. Another day, another dollar.

There'd still be a few stragglers. Those who missed their car pool or rolled over for just five more winks of sleep, five minutes that turned into forty-five. And then there were the lucky ones, those who rolled over and found someone they loved in the bed beside them.

Maybe KNOX's disc jockey Randy Dan had interrupted their erotic dreams as he had hers. Maybe when they rolled over, their lover was beneath them ready to turn fantasy into reality. Maybe they kissed and fondled each other until they generated enough fervent need between them that neither cared there was an ass-chewing waiting for them when they finally made it to the office.

Jessica shuddered as a wave of pent-up passion rolled over her. Maybe she needed to go upstairs and take another cold shower. Obviously, the first one this morning hadn't done the trick.

She rubbed her fingertips from the bridge of her nose into her hair line. Her sweaty palm rested against her cheek. She had to get a grip!

Alex Russell was driving her crazy!

When he had first started coming into her shop, he seemed like a nice enough guy. Soon his smooth, southern drawl coupled with his polite manners had her stealing longer glances at the man when he wasn't looking.

It didn't take long to find the wounded man hiding in the Hunky-Hank body. There was a sadness in his eyes, a sense of resignation that this—his life and the way he lived it—was all there was. The best it got—which wasn't all that good.

Pity never entered Jessica's mind. It was just that—well—it was just that she wanted to show him life was good. She wanted to be the one to teach him to enjoy the sunshine, a corny joke, or a rainy Sunday morning in bed.

Less than two weeks after that fateful morning when Alex Russell first stepped foot in her shop, Jessica decided the gold band around Alex's finger didn't mean she couldn't be friendly to him. Just because he was married didn't mean they couldn't be friends.

The next morning she had smiled directly at Alex. He, being a well-bred southern gentleman, smiled back, then grabbed his coffee and eclair and almost ran out the door. Jessica stared after him a good thirty seconds before she turned to his buddy Mitch. "What did I do wrong? I just smiled at him."

Mitch shrugged. "Nothing wrong with that. He just needs to learn how to smile back."

And then he revealed something about Alex that turned Jessica's heart to putty: he was widowed, and he needed to learn to live again.

Suddenly, she was a woman with a mission. She hated to see someone as special as Alex just going through the motions of living. So she planned to teach him how to lighten up and cast off the shackles of mere existence.

After that fateful morning, things got better. They talked casually as she filled the daily order. Sometimes it was just she and Mitch who talked, but Alex smiled and nodded in the appropriate places. Jessica dug and coaxed at Alex for another two weeks before she felt she'd finally cracked the guard shielding the man. They'd become at ease with each other on a casual level.

That's when her real trouble began.

She liked the real Alex lurking beneath his defenses—liked him a lot. He, on the other hand, didn't seem to know she existed outside the realm of her coffee shop.

Suddenly, Jessica began seeing Alex in a different light—candlelight, moonlight, flashing red neon light, hypnotic strobe light. Sometimes he wore tiger print briefs and gyrated his hips to the bump and grind of some primal beat. Sometimes he wore a black leather thong and arched his groin against a stainless-steel, floor-to-ceiling pole. Always he kept his smoldering gaze fixed on her, only her.

And always in her dreams.

As erotic as her sleeping dreams were, her daydreams were just as vivid, just as alluring—and just as scandalous.

Her most recurring, most disturbing, waking fantasy was where she and Alex shared a quiet breakfast together. He'd peek over the edge of his morning paper, wink at her, and then wordlessly return his gaze to his reading. That one telling gesture spoke volumes. He knew she was there. He wanted her there. His attention might be occupied somewhere else at the moment, but she was always in his thoughts.

Unfortunately, even in her dreams, he still wore his wedding ring. Still honored and loved his late wife.

Jessica took a deep breath, then exhaled slowly. She had work to do and sitting around mooning over a man who sooooo obviously had little to no interest in her wasn't going to get it done.

She slid her great-grandmother's age-yellowed recipe book closer to her from across the table. In her time, Grandmère Chloe had been famous throughout New Orleans for her cooking. Desserts and confections were her specialty.

Family rumor had it that Chloe's mother, a quadroon and voodoo priestess, had taught her more than just the art of baking. That extra bit of spicy gossip had always intrigued Jessica as much as finding one of Chloe's fabulous recipes hidden amongst the more recent ones handed down through the generations.

It was always exciting to find an old, forgotten recipe of Chloe's tucked between the brittle pages of Jessica's most prized possession. Just deciphering Chloe's handwriting was a test of ingenuity. Sometimes converting ingredients of her great-grandmother's time into modern-day equivalents could strain the limits of sanity. But Jessica's favorite time spent with the old recipe book was decoding some of Grandmère Chloe's more cryptic instructions.

She'd just found one of the woman's obscure recipes for limp noodles tucked away in the back of the book when Mitch sauntered through the door.

She closed the ancient recipe book and made her way to the row of large brass coffee urns stationed behind the pantry counter. She filled two cups with double-roasted Columbian coffee and then headed back toward the table. She needed the pure caffeine rush that the strong brew would provide. Left unchecked, her mind tended to wonder back to this morning's erotic dream.

Mitch sipped his coffee. "I guess Alex came in this morning. So how was he?"

Jessica bit back the lovesick smile threatening to overtake her lips. "The same— sweet, polite, a little reserved." And sexy as hell!

"Yep, that's Alex—flatlining his way through life."

Jessica laughed. "Actually, your opinion of his lifestyle, or lack thereof, was our topic of conversation."

"Well, do you blame me?" Mitch took another sip of his coffee. "His wife has been dead over three years and he still leads the life of an old married man."

Stunned, Jessica nearly fell out of her chair. Her jaw dropped. She tried to form a coherent thought, but couldn't.

His wife has been dead over three years....

Years? Not months?

His wife has been dead over three years…

All at once her mind was bombarded by unanswered questions. Why had Alex given the impression it had only been a short time since his wife's death? What about the wedding ring he wore? What about...?

Giving herself a mental shake, she tried to assimilate the shocking news. Alex Russell wasn't just recently widowed!

She'd been secretly drooling over him in both her waking and sleeping hours for six months—and he'd been available. Or at least, he should have been available.

She never thought to discreetly ask about his wife's date of death. The gold band on his left hand had told her everything she needed to know.

Only it hadn't been telling her the whole truth.

Nevertheless, if he was still carrying a torch for his late wife...

"Did he love his wife so much?"

"Oh, he loved Annie," Mitch said, "but grief isn't what's holding him back."

Jessica leaned forward, caught her over-anxious gesture, and made herself relax against her chair. "So what is?"

"Habit." Mitch glanced at his watch then chucked down the last of his coffee. "The first six months after Annie's death was horrible on him, but pretty soon, he was in the habit of living alone. You know, the get-up, go-to-work, go-home rut that people get into. Hell," Mitch said as he rose from his chair. "The book Annie was reading the night before she died is still on the night table."

Jessica swallowed against the knot of sympathy in her throat. "That's so sad."

"Oh, he's not sad anymore. He once said he left the book there to remind him that he used to have someone in his life." Mitch reached into his hip pocket for his wallet.

Jessica waved his money away. "On the house."

"Thanks. Well, see you tomorrow night." Jessica barely heard the bell above her door jingle. Her mind whirled with the information she'd just learned.

Alex Russell had been a widower for over three years.

That was long enough, Jessica decided. She'd been holding back, been giving him emotional space to grieve, not pursuing.

But that was over now!

"Mitch!" Jessica shouted as she raced outside. "Wait."

He stopped at the curb and turned back to her. "What's up?"

"About tomorrow night. You know how I invited you and Alex to a taste-testing thing?"

"Yeah?"

"Well, you are uninvited."

It took a minute, but understanding finally dawned on Mitch's face. "Gotcha!"

Chapter Two

Alex's thighs burned as he strained with effort. He drew in deep, ragged breaths of sultry New Orleans air. Sweat dampened his chest, rolled between his shoulder blades. Too bad he'd come to this state by jogging. Great sex was a lot more fun—that is, if memory served him right.

He sighed. Very little that wasn't sexual had crossed his mind today.

And Jessica's playfulness this morning didn't help.

Still, it was more than just sex that was crossing his mind. He missed the softness of a woman's caress, the silent connection of a simple touch.

Keeping an even tempo, one foot pounding the grass in front of the other, he and Mitch headed toward City Park's softball fields.

Alex glanced at the slowly darkening horizon. Low silvery clouds shimmered in a gray sky. In the thickening shadows, even the grass looked a faint shade of gray-green. The chain link fence surrounding the softball dugouts were gray. The wooden benches in the distance were so sun-faded, they, too, looked gray. Shadows from the cloudy dusk sky filtered through the trees, tinting the leaves a pale shade—gray, of course.

When had the world turned gray?

Alex tried to focus on finishing the run. Another fifty yards and he'd have his daily three-mile jog done— although he should run another mile to work off the extra donut Jessica wrangled him into taking this morning.

He finally reached the drinking fountain, stopped, then bent forward to rest his hands on his knees while he drew in another series of deep breaths. Even his jogging shorts were gray.

Hell, his entire life was gray.

Alex paused as realization struck him. No black or white or red or yellow. No greens or blues. No color in his life— just gray.

Thank God the red-hazed world of anger and pain he'd lived in right after Annie died was gone. Only it had been replaced with the bleakness of painful, lonely black—a color that had faded to gray at some point.

When the change had occurred probably wasn't the pertinent question. It was more like, how long had his world been gray? A year? Two years? At the moment, it seemed like forever.

Gray wasn't terrible. It didn't drain him emotionally, not like the red and black worlds of immediate grief. Neither was it as bright as the color-burst of emotions he vaguely remembered on the other side of the spectrum, the ones that had once been a part of his normal life.

"You okay? You're not going to hurl, are you?"

Alex turned to see Mitch frowning. He'd almost forgotten Mitch was running with him today. "I do this every day, remember? Unlike some people…"

"I'm not into torture enough to make this a daily thing. Are you secretly masochistic?"

Leave it to Mitch to put a sexual spin on exercise. "I like jogging. Helps relieve stress. Clears the head." *Relieves sexual frustration. Prevents me from sitting around my gray house completely alone.*

"Sure it does," Mitch agreed. "It also makes you want to chop your legs off they hurt so bad."

Shaking his head, Alex wiped away the sweat at his temples with the hem of his dingy gray shirt and began his cool down stretches. In truth, he had run too fast today, pushed too hard. What was he trying to prove? What was he running from?

Nothing. Nothing spurred him forward. Nothing held him back. Today was just like yesterday. Tomorrow wouldn't be any better—or any worse.

Mentally, he bristled against the concept. All the grayness of his life… it bothered him. But changing it meant… well, change. That he had a tough time with.

But could he live forever with gray?

Jessica's eyes aren't gray. The thought came suddenly, unbidden. No, her eyes were hazel, an intriguing mixture of greens and browns. Cat-green eyes, that's what they were—as exotic and captivating as a New Orleans midnight. Why, when he looked at Jessica, did he see color?

Alex pushed the wayward thought out of his mind. It wasn't the first time in the six months he'd known Jessica that she'd popped into his mind. He was getting good at pushing her out of his thoughts. But then he ought to be; he'd had plenty of practice.

"Hey," Mitch called. "You still planning to help Jessica taste-testing her new menu tomorrow night?"

"What?" Alex dragged his thoughts to his friend's words. "Oh, yeah. Sure."

Accepting meant another opportunity to see Jessica. Even if all he did was fantasize about her afterwards.

"You like her?" Mitch shot him a suggestive smile.

Alex deflected his tone. "She seems like a nice person."

"A nice person with great tits!" Mitch groaned. "Don't you notice this stuff?"

There was no way not to notice a woman like Jessica, but Alex kept that thought to himself. Mitch would only run amok with it. "I appreciate more about a woman than what she puts in her bra."

"And that's what's wrong with you, my friend. You've forgotten how to think with your dick. It's something every man should excel at."

"So we can objectify women?"

"I prefer the term 'worship'. And quit trying change the subject. Don't tell me you haven't noticed Jessica."

Alex braced his hands on his hips, over the waistband of his running shorts. "I noticed, but—"

"Good. I think she's noticed you too. In fact, I think she might be interested in serving you more than coffee." He paused. "She uninvited me to the taste-testing. Wanted to get you alone."

Alex forgot his next breath. Was it true?

Mitch peered at him with a crooked smile. "Is that panic on your face, buddy?"

"Deep thought," he corrected.

He wasn't panicked, not exactly. A little anxious—natural after three years of nothing but solo sex. Excited—a whole hell of a lot, in fact. The thought of Jessica's interest stirred more than his imagination. The question was, what to do? If Jessica was really interested... well. Maybe he ought to stop fighting his attraction long enough to find out if it was reciprocated.

⁂

Alex paused in front of his office building and stared across the street at the empty, yellow and white-canopied shop. He couldn't not go, nor could he just pop his head in and make his excuses. The last thing he wanted to do was disappoint Jessica. Besides, he wanted to go.

What the hell was he doing? He barely knew this woman.

Only he knew that wasn't really true. He did know Jessica—knew her more than was comfortable for his peace of mind.

Over the last six months he and Jessica had been subtly circling each other, waiting for the other to make the first move. A part of him wanted to acquaint himself with every inch of her—the taste of her mouth, the weight of her breasts in his palms, the feel of her slick and hot around him...

Damn it, he wanted—no needed to soak up Jessica's vibrancy for life if only for the few minutes it took to sample her new recipes.

He always enjoyed their time together, whether he was acting as her taste-tester or just coming in for his morning coffee. He couldn't remember when stopping by the coffee shop metamorphed from a convenience to a much-anticipated opportunity to see Jessica.

She intrigued him. He wanted to see her, to decipher that Mona Lisa smile in her eyes, discreetly appreciate the full curve of her breasts. She was the first woman he'd dreamed of touching in three years. If he told the absolute truth, he wanted to touch her—bad. Unfortunately, Jessica had never given him much reason to suspect she was interested in him romantically or sexually. She'd always been friendly, yes. But more? With a grimace, Alex realized he'd been out of the dating scene so long, he wouldn't know a "go" signal if it jumped in his face, flashing green.

Still, if he followed through on his promise to be her taste-tester, it would be just the two of them—alone. Maybe that was a good thing. Maybe he would find out if Jessica wanted him for anything other than a coffee patron.

But it had been a long time since he'd been alone with a woman. What did he say? What did he do?

Hell, what did he want to do? Thoughts of her had the damnedest way of invading his mind without warning. He suddenly felt like the proverbial car-chasing dog—if he caught her, he wouldn't know what to do with her!

Okay, that wasn't totally true. He had a few provocative ideas about what he'd like to do to Jessica—most of which involved her wearing lacy things that didn't quite cover the basics and him stripping them off of her.

Exhaling deeply, he shrugged off the dangerous image and stepped off the curb onto the street. He was probably making too big a thing about this. More than likely, he'd go in, taste a couple of new recipes and then leave. Thirty minutes tops and he'd be back in his solitary home, just him, the remote control, and a nuked pizza.

With a bracing breath, he crossed St. Charles Street in the damp dusk. The smell of the Quarter pervaded—hints of the Mississippi, big city smog, smoke, spices, and sex provided New Orleans with plenty of flavor. Why did thinking of Jessica awaken his senses so? Even the air smelled richer, more beguiling.

At Jessica's door, the yellow blind pulled down over the backside of the etched glass door proclaimed to the world that the shop was closed. Alex jiggled the door handle to test if it was locked. It was. Before he could decide whether to knock or simply leave, the door opened.

And a totally different Jessica than Alex had ever seen before stood in the threshold.

Tight, low-cut jeans encased gracefully curved hips and long legs—the kind of legs that made a man's mouth go dry just thinking about how they'd feel wrapped around him. A strappy, black knit top enhanced the curve of her firm, full breasts more than covered them. Its spaghetti straps, along with the faint imprint of her pert nipples, told him she wasn't wearing a bra.

Lord, the vision made him yearn to touch to her.

Her brownish red hair, which she normally wore pulled back at the nape of neck with a sedate gold clip, now tumbled loosely about her face and shoulders.

Her vivid hazel eyes sparkled with something... excitement? Anticipation? An impish smile played on her wide rosy mouth. Alex fought for his next breath.

Okay, the eyes and the smile were similar, but Lord, the rest of her made all of him stand up and take notice. His cock hardened. Where was her utilitarian white collared shirt and black slacks? Had she considered that if she paraded around half-naked like that he would be beyond tasting a damn thing?

"Hi!" she said, pulling him out of his flustered thoughts. "Come on in."

"Uh—sure, okay," he stammered as he stepped inside, then regained his senses enough to speak. "I've been wondering what you've got cooked up for me tonight."

"Something irresistible—I hope."

He dragged his gaze from the curve of her hips, past her luscious breasts, finally up to her teasing green-brown eyes.

The intensity of her smile magnified another thousand watts, so blinding and beautiful, the urge to grab her and crush her mouth under his seized him.

Obviously, resistance seemed out of his reach at the moment.

Jessica broke into his thoughts. "I know it's just the two of us tonight, but I'm sure we can muddle through."

Suddenly, he really wanted to know her definition of muddling. Hopefully, it involved tangled sheets, sweating bodies, and lots of skin against skin contact... Unlikely, but the idea made every blood cell in his body rush right between his legs, even as it worried him.

"Well, come on in. I've got everything set up in the back."

Alex followed her through the coffee shop. She opened a door in the corner and led him through.

He'd assumed "the back" was a kitchen of some sort. Instead, it looked to be her living area. The place held warmth, reflecting the woman herself. A large kitchen, saturated with scents of cayenne pepper, something fruity, and a hint of seafood came first. A huge silver industrial oven dominated one corner, surrounded by plenty of counter tops, and a sturdy white stove brimming with four metallic pots. To his right, sat a creamy leather couch, a dark green recliner, a coffee table of cypress, accented by a vase brimming with silk flowers, and a TV. Beyond that, a wrought iron staircase wended up. Toward her bedroom?

Hold it. She'd intended all along to invite him to her apartment?

"You live here. I didn't mean to intrude—"

"Don't be silly. I invited you here." Her trickling laughter set him at ease, even as it increased his awareness of her femininity. "Now, come with me."

Jessica put her warm hand inside his and led the way to the soft leather sofa. At her insistence, he sat, sinking into the plush cushion. She pushed a glass of wine into his hand—something dark and red. As she sipped from her glass, he sipped from his own, looking at Jessica over the rim. Damn, she looked beautiful, and that little top... He could still see the faint outline of her nipples. Did she have any idea what that sight did to a man? Or was that the point?

Would sweet, innocent Jessica deliberately entice a man?

Still, Alex wondered what Jessica would do if he set his glass aside, layered his mouth over hers, and took her breast in his palm.

She ran the tip of her finger slowly around the rim of her wineglass, then brought her finger to her lips and sucked it. Every nerve ending in Alex's body hummed in pent-up need.

"Well, go on. Drink," she encouraged.

He cocked a questioning brow at her.

"It will clear your palate," she clarified.

He cleared his throat and sipped, wishing he could clear his lusty thoughts as easily. The wine was dry but sweet. He wasn't much of a wine drinker, but this was good.

"Soup will be right out," she said as she crossed over to the kitchen area.

Alex glanced surreptitiously over his shoulder to watch Jessica work. Her jeans molded to her tight, caress-able ass. He admired her small waist, her creamy, lightly freckled shoulders. Hell, everything about her seemed sexy.

Within minutes, she returned with a serving tray laden with four covered bowls and a black silk scarf. As he caught sight of that scarf, his senses quickened. What was that for? Before he could ask, his stomach rumbled loudly, reminding him he hadn't taken the time to eat anything but a package of crackers for lunch.

Jessica laughed. "I like a man who comes with an appetite."

Alex raised a sharp glance to her. Had he heard a note of suggestion in her voice? His heart began to pick up speed. Her face reflected something playful, certainly, but did she intend anything more?

She sank to the sofa beside him and picked up the black scarf. Folding one end around her palm, she bit her lip and regarded him with a moment's hesitation.

"I need you to trust me. I want your unbiased opinion of each soup's taste. Supposedly, if you take away one sense, it heightens the others." She lifted the scarf toward his face.

She meant to blindfold him!

His heart began chugging faster. A thin layer of sweat broke out along his hairline. She could just be planning on the scarf blindfolding him as he taste-tested the soups, yes. But the possibilities of everything else she could do to him while he could not see raced through his testosterone-soaked brain. Parts south began to throb.

Stop! He ordered himself. She asked for your taste buds, not your cock.

"Will you let me?" she whispered.

Alex ran his fingers through his dark hair. "Ah… sure. No problem."

Her smile thanked him. "You won't regret it."

When she leaned closer and raised her arms to wind about his neck, his last view was of the downy shadow of her cleavage beneath her top's low neckline. Then he felt her fingers in his hair, settling the scarf in place. Already losing sight was heightening his other senses. Her scent, something like warmed sugar and sunshine, rose above the smells of the kitchen. Her breath caressed his cheek. She scooted closer, and her body heat assailed him. Alex's imagination began working overtime. Could he coax her onto his lap? Out of her clothes?

Before he could seriously ponder the question, she pulled back. "Can you see anything?"

"No."

"Promise?" She half laughed, half whispered into his ear, "Even if I danced around the kitchen naked you couldn't see?"

A mental picture of Jessica bare, dark hair swirling about her shoulders, playing hide and seek with her nipples, slammed into him. As she twisted and turned across the kitchen, her sleek, long legs would be perfectly, deliciously bare. He grunted. He only thought he'd been hard before.

"If you tell me you're actually dancing naked in the kitchen, I'm ripping this blindfold off."

The words were out before Alex realized how they sounded: suggestive—no, downright sexual. And if Jessica had wondered exactly what was on his mind... well, she didn't anymore.

"I'm sorry. That was uncalled for," he murmured. "If I've offended you, I can go..."

He rose to his feet and reached for the blindfold. But laughing lightly, Jessica clasped his wrists and urged him back to the sofa.

"I'm hardly offended. At least I know how to get your attention."

Oh, she had his attention, all right.

Alex heard the laughter in her husky voice and released the breath he'd been holding. Until now, he hadn't realized how badly he wanted to stay.

"So are you ready to feed me?" He changed the subject.

"Sure." The clink of metal told Alex she lifted the lid off one of the bowls. "Can't have a man going hungry around here."

Was it his overactive imagination, or was Jessica being intentionally suggestive?

"Open up." Her voice came low and sultry as her fingers fell on his shoulder, steadying him.

Her touch sent a jolt of awareness through him. He knew exactly how close she was, could smell her perfume, feel the heat of her hand through his shirt. Damn, it was hard to ignore the temptation to reach out and touch her.

As soon as he opened his mouth, she eased a warm spoon inside. Rich flavor inundated his mouth. It was a creamy soup with a hint of parsley. He tasted Parmesan cheese and something else. Mushrooms?

"What do you think?"

Alex heard the anxiety in her voice and immediately set her at ease. "Cream of mushroom soup? It's great. If you're wanting to start a lunch business, this will definitely bring people in."

She released a deep breath, as if relieved. Her warm, sweet breath stirred the air between them. Alex could picture her braless breasts lifting and falling...

A quiver of answering heat shuddered through him, then pooled in his lower stomach.

"Yes! I'm thrilled you like it. Ready for the next soup?"

"Do I get to finish that bowl later?"

Jessica laughed. "You can have anything you want."

Her leg brushed his for a moment. Alex smelled that sugary-sunshine scent again. And her replies, even if meant innocently, were the kind to make a man want her hot, naked, utterly open for his taking.

He needed to get out of there soon, preferably before he pounced on her and made an idiot of himself.

"What's next?" he asked.

"I'm not telling." She moved closer, then whispered in his ear. "It's more fun to keep you guessing."

Shit! Guessing at her intent, guessing whether her actions were meant to be sending signals or just friendly banter was driving him nuts. She was too damn close for him to think straight. He needed space, but no way in hell was he budging from his spot on her couch.

"Take a sip of your wine," she said, seeming to be all business again.

Damn it, he was going insane!

She thrust his glass up to his lips and he dutifully swallowed. "Now try this."

Alex opened his mouth again. Another smooth, flavorful soup, but this one was different, a little spicier. Garlic and pepper and paprika blended, danced in his mouth. And seafood—he smelled it now. He found a chunk of meat and bit down. Ah, lobster. She'd made bisque—one of his favorites—and it was heavenly.

"Delicious. You have a talent for soups."

"Thank you. I like to think I have talent at a lot of things." Insinuation rode heavy on her words. Insinuation or imagination? Damn him for not being sure.

Alex was certain she had talent and he was dying to find out exactly where they lay.

"You like my pastries, do you?"

Pastries. Of course. So much for insinuation. "I do."

He really had to stop thinking about sex, despite the fact he wanted nothing more than to grab Jessica and show her everything on his mind.

"Here's another sip of wine and another soup."

Blindly, Alex reached for the wineglass. His hand brushed her full breast instead. Definitely no bra. He mumbled an apology and swallowed—hard.

After he cleared his palate with more wine, Jessica treated him to a spicy Louisiana gumbo. He recognized it from the smell, even before the spoon touched his tongue. She'd made hers with chicken and sausage and a hearty dose of cayenne pepper. It created a pleasant burn as it slid down his throat, as a good gumbo should.

Then again, he burned in more places than his throat and pleasant didn't even begin to cover the scope of the sensations.

"Again, it's wonderful," he praised, trying to refocus his thoughts on the soups. "The lunch crowd will love it."

"Good. Now another sip of wine." She raised the glass to his lips again, and he drank, warmth sliding through his blood.

"Here's the last one," she said. "It's... different. I'm thinking it will be a summer soup, something to ward off the sweltering July heat."

Nodding, he opened his mouth and waited. Rather than warm or spicy, as the others had been, this was cool and rich, creamy and sweet. As soon as the chill of it warmed in his mouth, flavor exploded on his tongue. Strawberry. He bit down on fresh chunks of the fruit and moaned.

Jessica laughed from deep in her throat, husky and enticing. "I like to hear a man moan with pleasure."

Before Alex could respond to that, he felt her body heat move closer, her sweet scent filled his nostrils. She had moved even closer toward him. His breath just about stopped, while his heart pounded double time.

He didn't know how much longer he could go without touching her.

"Oops," she purred.

Jessica touched the corner of his mouth. Lightly, she dragged her fingertip across his lower lip. Hot, indecent tingles slithered across his heated flesh. Alex sucked in a sharp breath. The woman was making him insane.

"I'd gotten some soup on your lip," Jessica explained.

Her voice sounded thicker, richer, even more husky than moments ago.

Again he felt her thigh brush his. She sighed. As she pulled back, her hand gently brushed his upper leg. Sparks shot straight up to his cock.

Damn it, was the woman coming on to him? Double damn himself for being so out of touch that he wasn't sure. But one thing he did know: he wanted her bad.

"Now it's time for dessert." Her whisper was a suggestion—intimate, sensual, and not the kind to make a man think of confections and pastries.

Suddenly, he had to know if she felt an ounce of desire for him.

Alex ripped away the blindfold and tossed it on the floor. In one quick glance, he took in her watchful, doe-eyed expression and the hard nubs of her nipples rasping against her skimpy top. God, he ached to touch her.

"And you're it," he growled as he leaned in and seized the back of her neck in his palm, drawing her to him.

Smothering her silent gasp of surprise, Alex covered her lips with his. Soft, pliable—he catalogued the impressions even as he greedily grasped for more. He sank into the heat of her mouth, urging her lips apart. Quickly, she opened for him, met him halfway. Her tongue grazed his lips, wound around his own in sensuous circles that made him stiff as steel. She was not a shy woman—not with that little sound catching at the back of her throat as she moaned. Damn, she made him feel strong enough to battle the world and weak as a kitten all in the same kiss.

He continued his exploration—hell, who was he kidding?—his possession of her mouth. He didn't merely kiss her; he inhaled her. And she responded, pressing herself against him, hard nipples to his chest, while she filtered her long fingers through the hair at his nape. Desire scorched his veins like a forest fire, raging suddenly and completely out of control. He burned to have her, to be inside her, thrusting his way to her core. He wanted to watch her come.

Would she say no? Should he?

Jessica shifted slightly, draping herself more snugly across his body as though settling in for a prolonged, amorous interlude of carnal exploration. Then she raked the inside of his mouth with her hot little tongue again, and he thought he might lose his mind right then and there. Damn, she was good at driving a man to his edge.

He'd barely gotten his heartbeat throttled back to the safe side of lethal when he felt her fingers around his wrist, leading his hand from her back around… up… over, until—holy shit—his palm covered her breast.

She filled his hand. Her pointed nipple burned his skin, even through her little top. But it wasn't enough. He wanted her bare. He wanted her now.

Was he certifiably insane? Or just temporarily out of his mind with lust?

Jessica snuggled closer to him, the motion branding a searing jolt of pleasure up the stiffest erection he could ever remember having. Her soft flesh, her intoxicating scent, her sensuous throaty moans overtook him until all he could feel—all he was—was her.

Was this really happening?

Afraid the fantasy would disappear if he thought about it too much, Alex thumbed the tip of her breast. She answered with gratifying catches of breath.

Just like that, his lust factor shot farther up the scale.

"Touch me," she whispered in his ear.

A shiver wound its way down his spine. But a moment later, he understood. There was still that annoying layer of cloth between his hand and her breasts.

Alex rectified that situation pronto, shoving the skimpy top up from her waist, under her arms, then over her head.

Suddenly, he had a full, unobstructed view of the most incredible breasts he'd ever seen. Full, ripe, luscious breasts beckoned for his touch, for his kiss. He couldn't stop himself from pulling her closer and fastening his greedy mouth on her nipple.

Instantly, she cried out, arched against him. She tasted good—warm, sweet, and so damned responsive to every flick of his tongue across her nipple. Her pleasure swamped over him, catching him in the undertow of her rapture. He shuddered.

Then she reached for the button of his slacks.

"Alex." Her moan was a husky whisper, a plea, as she slid his zipper down in a slow hiss.

His breath came faster with the realization that she wanted him—right now, right here. Alex started to sweat. Jessica was a woman in need of pleasing. He hadn't worried about satisfying anyone but himself for the last three years.

It was one thing to think about having sex with her. Thinking—fantasizing—was safe. Actually doing it was a whole other thing.

On the other hand, Jessica had clearly put some thought into tonight. And he… Well, damn it, he hadn't had anytime to consider this. Did he want to tangle the sheets with Jessica? Hell, yes. She was a beautiful woman, responsive to his touch in a way he wasn't sure any woman ever had been. Of course he wanted her. But did he want the awkward pauses that would come after? He didn't know her that well. How would he look her in the eyes tomorrow while paying for his chocolate eclair without remembering the fact he'd screwed her?

"Oh, Alex," Jessica whispered as she nibbled on his earlobe. "I've waited for this a long time. We're going to be so good together."

Alex froze. Well, mentally, anyway. He was still on fire physically, but maybe physical wasn't all she wanted.

Was she looking for a relationship? He was not emotionally available—and he didn't intend to make himself that way again.

Alex removed his hungry mouth from her breast and grabbed her wrists.

"Jessica, I—" He felt himself panting, sweating. What should he say?

"Alex. It's okay. I invited you here, hoping that… I invited you here because I want to be with you."

Yeah, her desire was now clear, and it stunned him. This was too much, too fast. He'd lived in isolation for too long. It wasn't something he could suddenly give up, suddenly change. It was part of his life, part of his skin.

He sat up, sliding away from her, buttoned his pants, avoided her stunned gaze and exposed breasts, swollen now thanks to him. He stifled a groan and looked away. "Maybe this isn't such a good idea. I don't want you doing something tonight you'll regret later."

Jessica opened her mouth to speak, but Alex shook his head and spoke over her stunned protests. "Trust me on this, Sweetness, you'd regret this."

"But—" She stood and reached for him.

"I have to go." He deftly dodged her touch then wrapped his fingers around her upper arms. Keeping her at arms-length away from him, he studied her expression. She looked vulnerable, heartbroken. This wasn't just about sex for her.

Who was he kidding, it was more than sex to him, too. If he didn't care about her, he'd simply stay here and fuck her.

Only he couldn't do that to her, not now, with her emotions so clearly etched on her face. "I'm sorry."

Before she could stop him, he released her and bolted out the door, all too conscious of the fact his shirt was mostly untucked and his breathing still hadn't returned to normal. Hell, he wasn't sure anything would be normal again anytime soon.

Outside, the humid New Orleans night bathed him, cloying, insistent. It didn't do a damn thing to cool him off. So he drove home with the air conditioning on max and his radio on full blast.

But neither could distract him enough to stop his churning thoughts. Life without sex had him perpetually horny, but none of that explained why he'd become so aroused by Jessica, then run out on her.

Ten miles down the road, Alex was still confused, overheated, and hard as reinforced steel. Sonofabitch.

He let himself into his house. The warm darkness washed over him as he shut the door behind him. Alex raked his hand through his hair. He ought to eat. But food didn't seem important now. TV. Yeah, that usually distracted him. The mindless laugh tracks of sitcoms would deflate every ounce of sexual energy pumping through him. Still, he didn't move, didn't pick up the remote. He could still picture Jessica on his lap, eyes glazed, lips parted. He could still envision her breasts against his palm, their taste in his mouth.

She had wanted him. And God, had he wanted her.

But he had turned her down. What must she be thinking?

Shit, he was such an idiot! An idiot with a hard-on!

His first shot at sex in a very long time, and he'd turned it down because he didn't want to deal with the bullshit complications or commitments that came with a relationship. And that was what woman like Jessica thought sex was—a commitment on some level, a relationship.

Nobility was a bitch!

How on earth was he going to relieve himself of this staggering need she had created? Even now, lust coursed through him, demanding… something. Closing his eyes in defeat, he headed for the shower.

In quick, angry motions, Alex jerked his clothes off his body and tossed them to the tile floor. He was not happy and not entirely sure what to do about it.

With a deep sigh, he climbed in, let the warm water run down his body in teasing rivulets. Still, Jessica would not leave his mind. Damn it to hell!

He wrapped his hand around his cock. It stood up nearly against his stomach, so hard that the tip looked blue.

He closed his eyes. Jessica was there, hair curling wantonly around her naked shoulders, pert breasts taut, nipples swollen. She straddled him, guided every inch of his hard penis inside her… and then she began to stroke him with her wet, silken sex. Alex thrust away the reality of his own hand as he pictured Jessica gyrating, gasping, moaning, working above him—in and out, in and out—faster, then faster still. The edge came rushing toward him, looming larger and more explosive with every second. His memories provided the taste of Jessica's nipple in his mouth, his imagination gave him the feel of her wet clitoris under his fingers, along with the sounds of her surrender to pleasure. He pictured her coming. Fire raced through his body, collecting low in his belly, bellowing for release.

An instant later, pleasure spiked. Orgasm slammed him. Alex let out a long groan of relief as he rode the tail of the arcing sensation.

A moment later, he dropped his hand to his side and, shoulders slumped, he opened his eyes. Damn, he was still in his shower—where the water was turning cold.

And he was still alone.

Chapter Three

Stunned, Jessica sat and stared at the closed door where Alex had exited at warp speed. Several eerie moments passed before she pulled herself out of the zombie-like trance his sudden departure had hurled her.

What the hell had just happened?

One minute he'd been right there with her—speeding their way to something wonderful, something mutual—and the next, he transformed into an Olympic sprinter giving a hundred and ten percent to break the world record.

Exit, stage—anywhere where she wasn't!

Still dumbfounded, Jessica automatically picked up the tray of soup bowls and headed for the sink. Halfway through the clean-up, she muttered, "Screw this," grabbed the wine bottle and her glass and went back to sit on the couch.

Waves of rejection and pain washed over her, followed by a crashing tide of embarrassment. She gulped down a long swallow of wine, hoping to drown her humiliation. A flood of anger came rolling over her on the heels of her mortification.

What the hell was he thinking? That she'd change her mind and turn him down? Did he think she was a prick tease?

Heat, probably a combination of red wine and outrage, coursed through her veins.

No, he knew what she wanted, what she yearned for from him. So why had he waited so long into the game to call it quits?

Jessica took a deep, calming breath—and another swallow of wine—hoping to smooth her tattered nerves.

Obviously, he'd been there with her physically and loving every minute of it. No way could he ever deny his arousal. No, he had wanted her as much as she had wanted him.

So what the hell happened?

Tonight's fiasco wasn't Alex's fault. He had come by with the intention of helping out a friend, not seducing a woman. Talk about the difference between apples and oranges. Hell, it wasn't her fault, either. It just didn't play out quite like she'd wanted.

Alex had certainly seemed ready physically. She'd felt the heat of his body, the rigidity of his erection. She knew without a doubt he wanted her. His reluctance seemed rooted in his emotional state more than his physical. Maybe they should have taken more time for him to warm up to her emotionally.

Didn't he know she cared about him—as a man, as a person? Probably not. She'd have to make sure he understood her feelings. This new direction she was attempting to take in their up-till-now casual acquaintance was more about making a connection with him than a sexual partnership.

Jessica had no doubt sex with Alex would be incredible. She got all hot and bothered every time he walked into the same room with her. But it was more than just her flaring hormones searing her from the inside out at the mere sight of him. She wanted to know what he thought of world affairs, if he watched football every Sunday. If so, what team did he root for? She wanted to know if he ate asparagus or broccoli. Or if he was strictly a meat and potatoes man.

She wanted to get to know Alex Russell—the man.

She took another long, slow gulp of her wine and sighed. Maybe he needed a stronger nudge of encouragement. What more could she do, walk around naked with a sign around her neck saying, "Screw me 'till I scream!"

Jessica giggled into her wine glass at her silliness. A couple more glasses of wine and the right opportunity and she might consider that wacky course of action.

Restless—and a little fuzzy-headed, she stood to prowl her apartment for something to distract her from her aching emptiness. She paced, she drank, she paced some more—she drank even more.

Finally numb from her downward spiral of adrenaline and an over-indulgence of wine, she curled up on the couch with Chloe's recipe book in hopes of finding some degree of distraction.

With her thoughts still on Alex, she thumbed through the age-crackled pages until she found the until-this-morning undiscovered recipe tucked in the back of the book. The words, "Cure for Limp Noodles" topped the page in Chloe's barely-readable chicken-scratch handwriting. As Jessica read on, reluctant laughter rose in her.

It wasn't a pasta recipe, but an old voodoo aphrodisiac!

How priceless! After what she'd been through the last couple of hours, finding Chloe's recipe for "Limp Noodles" had to be Karma.

Not that Alex's noodle was limp... far from it. But maybe this recipe would help him overcome whatever was holding him back from fully enjoying the benefits of his ... well, his noodle.

Anyway, between Fate and her revved-up hormones, there was no way in hell she could distract herself from Alex Russell. So...

Play time! If she couldn't distract herself, a little therapeutic clowning around might be just what she needed.

After a quick scan of Chloe's recipe, Jessica darted around her apartment, gathering what she needed. Moments later, she placed the items on the altar around her.

Okay, so what if her altar was really her kitchen island and her cauldron a saucepan positioned over her fondue stand. She had candles, cucumber-melon, not pure bee's wax as instructed, and sticky notes instead of parchment. But paper was paper, right?

At least the actual ingredients were fairly common place, even if the combination of them wasn't. Maybe there was some kind of chemical reaction when combining the mismatched components that had convinced Chloe of their magic.

With everything she needed in front of her, Jessica took one more draining draught from the now-empty wine bottle and lit the candle under her "cauldron." As instructed, she stripped naked; then draped a piece of clothing—the scarf she'd tied around Alex's eyes—recently worn by her intended around her neck. Its silky texture teased at her still-sensitive nipples. His scent wafted around her.

A wisp of arousal tickled at her core.

Slowly she added the ingredients into the saucepan, pausing between each one to write Alex's name on a sticky note and then feeding it to the flame beneath the pot.

Her hand froze over the wilted orchid beside her. She was not sure how to proceed. The recipe called for Adam and Eve root. After a quick search through the dictionary, she'd discovered Adam and Eve root was nothing more than the root of an orchid. Still, did she wanted to sacrifice her sickly orchid for a playful evening of voodoo?

Suddenly, she remembered vanilla beans came from orchids! With a silent promise to nurture her puny flower back to life, she scrambled to her spice cabinet and retrieved a jar of whole vanilla beans. Pleased with herself, she returned to her altar/kitchen island.

Once all the ingredients were simmering in her "cauldron," she picked up the pussy-willow branch she'd taken from the dried flower arrangement in her bathroom and began waving it over the pot as she read the incantation from Chloe's book. "I invoke the power and wisdom of Ezili, the spirit of love and desire."

She swallowed back a giggle and continued on. "Help me, Ole Great Ezili. Help me bring my man to great levels of want and lust."

The room grew warm, the air thick and sultry. Her heart rate quickened. She felt alive and needful. Closing her eyes, she allowed herself to fall into the mood and motion of her waving hand as it moved the pussy willow over the boiling pot.

"Lust for me, Alex Russell. Lust for me and only me. Want me with every fiber of body and soul. You are insatiable, yet only I can douse the fire burning in you. You will only be complete and whole when you are with me, inside me. Lust for me, Alex Russell. Ezili demands it!"

As the humming in her ears intensified to a primal roar, still she chanted over and over again, "Lust for me, Alex Russell! Lust for me, Alex Russell! Ezili demands it!"

Long, thick moments passed as Jessica chanted until she thought she could chant no more. Yet she chanted still. Then suddenly, a eerie breeze blew in from some unknown origin and extinguished the flame beneath the cauldron.

Jessica slumped against the kitchen island, exhausted and sweating.

Oh, my God! she thought once the ability to think finally returned to her. What just happened?

Still naked and shaking, she crossed to the refrigerator and retrieved a bottle of water from inside. She was parched, jittery and more than a little spooked.

A half of bottle of water and several moments later, she'd almost convinced herself that her goosebumps and edginess were direct results from too much wine and an overactive imagination. Almost.

Drawn back to the kitchen island, she studied the golden, gooey concoction in the bottom of her best saucepan. Tentatively, she reached out her finger and scooped out a small dollop of warm goo. She brought her finger to her nose and sniffed. It didn't smell horrific. In fact, it smelled sweet, almost seductive. Knowing better, but unable to stop herself, she licked the sticky substance off her finger.

A bolt of carnal need slammed into her with a force that stole her breath. She broke out in a sweat, her heart pounded against her ribs, and a raging fire of lust consumed her from her gut to her core. She gripped the counter's edge, partly to steady herself, partly to fight the urge to touch herself.

Once the initial effect dulled to a slow burn, Jessica breathed deeply and reached for Chloe's recipe. At the very bottom of the page, underlined three times were the words: DO NOT SERVE HOT!

That's probably why the effect had been so intense, so immediate. Why hadn't she seen the warning earlier?

Realization hit her like a knock-out punch. Chloe's voodoo remedy for limp noodles worked!

And Jessica knew just what to do with it!

The next afternoon, Jessica was a woman with a mission—and a secret weapon.

She wouldn't let herself consider that Alex's sudden retreat had anything to do with her. Alex was too mired in the habit of disengagement with the world for his withdrawal to be based on anyone or anything in particular.

If nothing else, Alex's behavior last night had only fortified Jessica's resolve to bring him back into the sunshine of the world.

Last night had been… exhilarating, frustrating and very eye-opening.

It had felt so good to touch Alex, the real flesh and blood Alex. It felt even better for him to touch her.

She'd never imagined how wonderful the warmth of his palm against her breasts could feel, or the intense pleasure that curled in the pit of her stomach when his insistent tongue laved over her taut nipples. Oh, yeah, Alex Russell definitely had the magic touch.

Now it was her turn to do a little magic.

Once she got over the shock and awe of what she'd done with her first attempt of voodoo magic, Jessica racked her brain trying to figure out how she was going to get Alex to eat the potent lust-potion. Then she remembered all the times he'd taste-tested her homemade candies and knew she'd found her answer. She wasn't going to let a little panic and/or fear of intimacy stand between her and Alex's pleasure.

She had a batch of "miracle-grow" spiked bon-bons whipped up before midnight.

The bon-bons were cooled by morning.

Today, armed with her secret weapon, she marched down the hall to his office. She intended to jerk Alex out of his shell whether he liked it or not! It was, after all, for his own good.

Feeling a little uneasy after their last night's encounter, she took a deep, steadying breath and knocked on Alex's office door.

He called, "Come in."

She let herself inside. "Hi."

"Jessica!" Alex leaped to his feet, bashing his knee on his desk as he did so.

"Am I disturbing you?"

"No—no. Actually, I was just thinking about you."

"Really?" Jessica's gaze zeroed in on his crotch area, before she could stop herself. Rude, but very revealing. No limp noodle there! The bulge in his slacks left no doubt where his thoughts had been. "How sweet."

Alex waved at a chair stationed in front of his desk. "Please, have a seat."

"Thanks." She crossed the small office and sat in the offered chair, not bothering to straighten the hem of her sundress, which had hiked to mid-thigh when she crossed her legs.

She caught him gazing at her legs, his attention pausing at her crossed thighs a second longer than was proper. He looked nervous, uncomfortable and very interested all at once.

Poor baby, if he'd just relax and trust her she could expand his horizons to the point he would never return to the bleak, dreary life he existed in now. Somehow she knew he was ready to escape. He just didn't realize it—yet.

Mentally crossing her fingers, she silently sent a prayer heavenward, just in case she'd misread him. Please, please let him be ready to move on with his life.

"What brings you here?" he asked as he reseated himself. Was it nerves or excitement that put that raspy chord in his usually smooth southern drawl?

"I'm catering a meeting for Mr. Phillips on the tenth floor this afternoon, so I thought I'd stop by and say hello while I was in the building."

"I'm glad you did. I was planning on calling you after work this evening." Alex picked up a pencil and nervously tapped it against the edge of his desk. "I—uh—about last night—I—uh—"

As she saw how nervous he was, guilt tugged at her. What if he was not emotionally ready to leave the past in the past? Was she imposing her eagerness to start a relationship over his desire to be left alone? She had to know before she could go any further with her plans.

She broke in, "Alex, I'm sorry about last night."

Alex looked relieved. "It's me who should be apologizing. I shouldn't have left so abruptly. You just took me by surprise."

"You're sure? You don't hate me?"

He smiled at her. "I'm sure—and I'm a long way from hating you, Sweetness."

Reassured she was doing the right thing, Jessica glanced at the clock on the corner of the desk. Three o'clock. According to the bits and pieces she could decipher of the written text below the recipe, it should take about three hours for the aphrodisiac spell to be at its peak of "helpfulness."

Jessica reached into her tote bag and pulled out a plastic bag holding the spiked candy she'd made the night before. "I've been experimenting again. Would you mind—"

"I'd loved to," Alex interrupted her as he reached across his desk for the candy. He seemed anxious to please her, almost as though doing something for her that he'd done a dozen times before would put them back on their previous footing.

He put a bon-bon between his lips and then rolled the chocolate morsel around his mouth with his tongue. Finally, he bit down on the candy. "Hmmm, it tastes like caramel and some kind of nut extract."

Filching another candy from the bag, he popped it in his mouth. He cocked his head while he chewed the second piece. "Yet, there's something else I can't quite pinpoint."

A quiver of excitement shimmered down Jessica's spine. That "something else" was the voodoo magic laced inside the candy nugget.

Jessica smiled and glanced at her watch. "Well, I'd better be going. But I'll be back in a couple hours. I've got to pick up my coffee urn from Mr. Phillips's conference room between five-thirty and six this evening."

Alex licked the last bit of candy off his lips. "Why don't I save you a trip? I'll run up to the tenth-floor conference room, retrieve your coffee urn, and then bring it over to you after work."

The coffee urn had only been an excuse to be at his office about the time the effects of her candy kicked in. Now he was offering to come to her. Jessica fidgeted in her chair. This was too easy. And not the most upstanding thing she'd ever done. But whether or not he would ever believe her, it was in his best interest.

"That would be great. Thanks. So what time do you think you'll be by?"

"Today's Friday, and I have a couple of things to get out before the weekend, so probably around six."

This would work out better anyway. Her apartment was much more private than Alex's office. She'd been more than willing to have sex with him on top of his desk or up against the wall or even in the men's bathroom. Whatever it took to jump-start his re-entry into life. Location wasn't that important. An ambush was an ambush. On the other hand, the privacy of her apartment might lead to a more "freeing" atmosphere.

And ultimately, freeing Alex was what this was all about. Freeing him from his empty world and returning him back to living life to its fullest.

She just wanted to be with him, wanted to give him a taste of being with her, and then let things go from there. If nothing developed between them, so be it. But it wouldn't be because she didn't give Alex the opportunity to see her as something other than the coffee girl across the street.

There was no turning back now. With any luck, in another three hours Alex Russell was going to be a six-feet-three, hundred-and-ninety-pound raging hard-on looking for an outlet.

And she'd conveniently be in his path!

At straight up six o'clock, Jessica looked out her window and saw Alex bound out of his office building with her coffee urn tucked in the crook of his arm.

He looked like hell.

His loosened tie dangled cockeyed around his neck. His shirt clung to his damp chest. Sunlight glistened off his dark brown hair, accenting uneven furrows where he'd repeatedly plowed his fingers through it.

Uncomfortable didn't come close to describing the man marching toward her. He was more than just disheveled in his clothes, he looked ready to jump out of his own skin.

Jessica straightened the discreetly bent blade of the mini blind she'd been keeping vigil behind and stood. She gave herself—and her new come-fuck-me teddy—one last inspection before she laid her hand on the doorknob and waited for Alex's knock.

Okay, the black, lace, barely-there teddy with matching silk stockings, garters and stiletto heels she'd purchased earlier in the afternoon was probably overkill. But she didn't want to leave any doubt in Alex's mind of her intentions or his welcome.

Hopefully, tonight was just the beginning.

And tomorrow? What will you do when the candy spell wears off? a little voice in the back of her mind whispered. She winced and then mentally pushed the thought away. She'd worry about tomorrow—tomorrow.

Alex's brisk knock pulled her out of her thoughts. Taking a deep, calming breath, she opened the door.

"Here's your—Holy shit!"

Jessica stepped back to allow Alex into the coffee shop—and hopefully out of any passer-by's line of vision.

Alex didn't move.

"Don't you want to come—" she paused and waved her hand toward the interior of the shop. "—in?"

He nodded and took three unsteady strides inside.

She closed the door to the outside world and turned the lock into place.

She felt his scalding gaze rake down her barely-clad body. Undaunted by the carnal inferno blazing in his eyes, she returned his gaze. Wordlessly, they stood staring at each other for an eternity of a heartbeat.

Slowly her gaze lowered from his face and slipped downward. Past his broad, tense shoulders, past his heaving chest, past the coffee urn still clutched in the crook of his arm—and then stopped abruptly at the long, hard ridge straining against the zipper of his pants. Jessica swallowed hard against the knot of anticipation suddenly lodged in her throat, but couldn't move her gaze from the sight of his oh-so-obvious interest.

Her eyes still fixed on his magnificent erection, she waved her hand toward the work counter beside him and said, "You can put that wherever you want."

"That's stating the obvious." Alex's husky voice tingled over her super-sensitized skin. "In the mean time, where do you want the coffee pot?"

"On the counter is fine," she answered, too nervous to manage much more than a whisper.

Alex nodded, placed the silver urn on the counter top and then moved toward her. His hands trembled. He seemed to suck a bracing breath into his lungs as he stopped mere inches from her.

His earthy, animal-on-the-prowl scent enveloped her. She breathed deeply, shuddering at the answering excitement his smell evoked in her.

She watched as he struggled against the obvious effect of her voodoo candy. His face tense, his jaw set in determination, he silently fought for control over his body.

"Besides the obvious, what is it you want, Jessica?" he finally growled out from between clenched teeth. "I'm going to be brutally honest. I need to fuck you. I need to fuck you hard."

For a fraction of a second, Jessica forgot how to breathe.

"You. I want you," she answered, too nervous to manage much more than a whisper. "I just want a chance to be with you."

Hesitation clouded his expression. Although he didn't move a muscle, she could almost visibly see him retreating from her.

"No strings attached, Alex, I swear. I just want to know what it's like to be in your arms, to feel your body inside mine. For you to touch my life and know I have touched yours—even if it's just for this moment."

Alex nodded, released a ragged breath, then shoved his fingers through her hair. He held her head in place with a velvet-like vise grip and then devoured her mouth with his.

She moaned with the force of sharp pleasure that sliced through her body. This was what she wanted. Him and her. No walls between them, no more anything between them.

Suddenly, his hands were everywhere—over her breasts, caressing and kneading, digging his fingers into the tender flesh of her butt. He rocked his granite hard erection against her already wet and wanting slit, his pants and her lacy teddy the only barriers between them.

Still, he never released her mouth. His lips possessed hers. His tongue drove into her mouth, invading, demanding and beseeching all at once. She countered with an assault to his tongue and mouth that matched his need. She could be conquered. She could be enslaved. But only after she did so to him.

He moaned and slid his mouth from hers, nibbling and kissing his way to her earlobe. His breath was raspy and harsh—needful—against her ear.

"Jess," he whispered as his lips moved down the column of her neck. "Now. Can't wait."

"Yes, Alex! Please," she barely managed to answer. Slipping her hands down his chest from where she clutched his shoulders, she fumbled with the buttons of his shirt. She had to touch him, had to feel the pounding of his heart against the wall of his chest.

Had to know he ached as much as she did.

He must have had the same need for skin against skin contact. He hooked his fingers under the thin straps of her teddy and yanked downward. Her lace bodice fell to her waist. "My God, you are beautiful."

Before she could draw her next breath, he bent and suckled a breast. Painful pleasure ripped through her.

Clawing her nails down his muscle-rippled arms, she managed to unbuckle his belt, but couldn't maneuver his zipper open for fear of injuring him.

Alex mumbled a curse against her breast, then stepped away. With a deftness that surprised her considering the way his hands shook, he unfastened his pants, let them drop to the floor, removed his shoes and socks and then stepped out of his pants. In one brisk movement, he shucked his shirt.

There he stood in all his glorious nakedness, taking gulps of air into his lungs, trembling with the taut readiness of a predator about to make his move.

Jessica almost exploded into orgasm right then and there. After months of denied midnight fantasies and X-rated dreams, she could barely wait a moment longer. He was going to be hers!

Maybe for just this moment, or this evening, but he was finally going to let her inside his world. It was enough—for now.

She reached for his rock-hard penis jutting toward her. He stopped her before she touched him.

"If you touch me, I'm a goner," he said as he brought her fingers to his lips. "I want to touch you first, feel your slickness, taste your flavor."

Her stomach tightened. Her knees went weak. A arrow of heated response quivered down her already inflamed body. She didn't think a woman could come with only a man's words and the promise in his eyes. But she was real close to finding out!

"Alex, I want—"

"I know what you want." He reached out and hooked his finger under the sheer swath of lace covering her womanly slit and yanked. The fabric ripped away.

Shoving his finger into her wetness, he ground the pad of his thumb against her slick clitoris. She shuddered against him.

He gave no quarter. Layering his mouth over hers, he mimicked the stroke of his finger with his tongue.

The world as Jessica had always known it disappeared. Tingling sensations bit at her outer edges; warmth balled tightly in the pit of her stomach until it burst into a firestorm of raw, burning need. Spirals of red-hot tension swirled tighter and tighter until they merged into one fiery cyclone of urgency. Its intensity grew taut, painful. Orgasm rushed toward her, crested over her last restraints and then erupted from the core of her soul, releasing her from her beautiful pain.

The force of her climax shattered her into a million shimmering pieces.

The soaring of her climax rocketed her into the explosive realm of release, but completion sent her slowly sliding back to reality. Her heart rate lessened as coherent thought nibbled at the edges of her sedated haze. Breathing seemed easier as she slowly descended from her carnal heaven. Something pulled at her consciousness as she struggled to stay in her cocoon of bliss. It was Alex's strained voice asking for something.

"Protection?" he hissed through his clenched teeth.

"Got it," she mumbled as she slipped a foil packet from the top of her gartered stockings. Her hands shook too bad to open it. Alex took it from her.

She watched as he ripped the foil away from the condom then positioned it over the head of his blood-engorged penis. Heated anticipation licked at her core as she watched him roll the thin latex over his thick, hard length. Knowledge that her wait was over, that in just seconds he would be thrusting inside her, filling her, stretching her, demanding that she take all of him, sent a searing blade of expectation slicing through her so pleasurable than it bordered on pain.

Oh, God, finally... finally!

Light-headed, she couldn't seem to catch her breath as she stared at his full erection.

Finally sheathed, he grabbed her by the hips and lifted her to him. "Put your legs around my waist."

She did—and the second she was spread-wide for him, he plunged into her with the force of a jack-hammer.

She gasped. He froze.

Bracing her hands on his shoulders, she lifted herself upward until just the tip of his penis touched the lips of her vagina and then slammed down over him again, taking in every inch of him she could. There was no going back. This was what she wanted—Alex filling her completely. She wanted—she needed—this moment of ultimate connection with him.

Alex grunted. "Yes! Like that. That's how I want it—hot and hard."

Wrapping his arms even more tightly around her, he curled his hands over her shoulders from the back. He crushed his body against hers, wedging her between him and the wall.

He pumped, he pounded—faster and faster. Harder and harder. His breaths were ragged as he sucked great gulps of air between his clenched teeth. A fierceness like nothing Jessica had ever seen in him—or any other man—contorted his features.

Need seared through her—need to urge him on, need to see him reach his peak, need to race to her own fulfillment. His intensity, his desperation fueled hers until she was a burning coil of carnal demand.

"Fuck!" he growled, still pumping himself inside her. "Too fast—too soon—want more!"

Jessica barely heard him over the thundering of blood pounding in her ears. All she knew—all she felt was Alex. He was her universe, the air she breathed and the force driving her closer and closer to the edge of the world.

Alex surged into her and then froze.

"Oh, God, Alex, don't stop now!"

"Wait," he panted. "I'll come if I don't stop."

"I'm right there with you. Please, I need you!"

He took her mouth in a breath-stealing kiss, then impaled her with one last grinding stroke.

She screamed into his mouth as she plunged over the edge of rational thought. A half a heartbeat later, Alex growled a primal cry of completion and slumped against Jessica's limp body. Only the weight of their pressed bodies against the locked door behind them held them upright.

Eons later, or maybe it was just moments, Alex eased their still-entwined bodies to the floor. Exhausted, they sat—Jessica still in his lap—and listened to each other's breathing return to normal.

Finally, Alex broke the silence. "Tell me you have a shower and not just a tub."

Jessica laughed softly, relieved that Alex didn't want to analyze their recent behavior. At least not now. She wasn't sure about anything, except she was right where she wanted to be—in Alex's arms.

"Both. Why?"

He nibbled her neck and shoulder. "I've had some shower fantasies lately that only you can make come true."

Jessica silently laughed. Oh yeah, Chloe's recipe for limp noodles just earned itself the number one spot on the top ten list of all-time recipes!

She finally had Alex in her life—at least for now.

Chapter Four

Alex woke in slow, foggy stages.

Daylight pierced his eyelids. Okay, he thought. Another day.

His bed was softer than he remembered. Curious, but okay. Never one to jump up bright-eyed and bushy-tailed first thing in the morning, confusion often fuzzied his thoughts for a moment or so after waking.

He tried to raise his left arm to rub the sleep from his eyes, but it felt heavy and numb, like he'd lost circulation. Odd, but still okay. It had been years since he'd slept so sound that he'd woken with a numb limb.

Even more odd, his whole left side seemed considerable warmer than his right side. Now that was downright weird.

Still half asleep, he reached to shed the coverings that had his left side overheating. His palm skimmed over something soft and warm—and female. A breast!

Jesus Christ!

Yanked into full awareness, he snatched his hand away and then froze. The red-haired woman draped over his left side grumbled something under her breath, snuggled deeper into his embrace and then seemed to fall back into a deep sleep.

Jessica Hennessy? What in the hell was he doing with her? Buck-ass naked! Both of them—together! In bed!

Shit!

Then the previous night came slamming back to him. His urgent need for Jessica and all the ways she'd satisfied him replayed in his mind.

Only it was more than just sex. It was bigger, more intense than just getting his rocks off.

He knew all about sex for the sake of sex. He'd dated a couple of women after Annie died, but they hadn't been anything more than means to a physical release. So he never had any trouble walking away. That's the way he wanted his sex life now—physically satisfying with no strings or regrets attached.

Unfortunately, he had a real bad feeling things weren't going to work out that way this time. Jessica had promised him "no strings attached" last night and he believed her. It was the possible regrets that were troubling him at the moment—his, not hers.

Something about Jessica, something about holding her, kissing her, watching her come, knocked him off-balance. Like she'd reached inside him to a place where he hadn't allowed anyone else to touch. She wrenched responses out of him that went way past just physical gratification.

And that freaked him out.

Suddenly, the musical chant from a bladder control commercial screamed at his self-preservation. "Gotta go, gotta go, gotta go—right now!"

The urge to jump and run coursed through every nerve ending in his body—and it had nothing to do with his bladder. Taking a slow, deep breath, he willed himself to calm down. He was okay. He just needed to get out of there. Go home where it was nice and quiet. And safe.

Safe? What was he afraid of? Jessica? Did he think she kept a stash of Bride Magazines in her bedside table and a wedding planner in her closet just for situations like this?

Why did he, who knew better than to get involved, let his desire overcome his good sense? Where had last night's out-of-control lust come from?

Alex groaned at his mental rambling.

Hell, he didn't know, didn't care what had triggered his sense of preservation of life as he knew it. What mattered was that he'd heard it loud and clear and intended to act on it ASAP!

Slowly, he eased away from Jessica, careful not to wake her as he slid his arm from beneath her head. She mumbled a weak protest, then rolled onto her back still sound asleep. Barely breathing, moving in slower than slow motion, he moved off the bed.

Once he was a safe distance away, he paused and looked at Jessica's sleeping form. As the morning sun bathed her face, he thought she might be the most beautiful woman in the world, or at least the most beautiful in his world. And certainly the most dangerous. Sunshine filtered through a window, drenching her in a puddle of soft golden light. Red, brown and gold highlights in her hair shimmered in the sunshine. Her pale, creamy skin beckoned for his touch. Her eyes were his favorite feature. They were smokey green, captivating, expressive—and wide open!

So much for avoiding the awkward morning after.

Alex cleared his throat and spoke, "Good morning."

"Good morning to you, too," Jessica replied as she rolled over onto her side to face him. "Are you coming back to bed?"

"Ah, n-no." Alex stammered, suddenly, acutely aware he was standing in a woman's bedroom buck naked. What he wouldn't give for a pair of pants or a towel or even a fig leaf right about now. "I'm going home."

"Oh." Jessica grabbed the sheet from around her waist and drew it up to her chin. She must have picked up on his uneasiness. "I could fix some breakfast before you go, if you want."

"No, thanks." He glanced around the room for his clothes. "I should be going."

Jessica's gaze lowered to his very substantial, very eager morning erection, then dropped the sheet to expose her full beautiful breasts. "Are you sure?"

Alex swallowed a groan. No, he wasn't sure. But if he didn't get out of there pronto there'd be no turning back. And who knew what lay ahead of him if he followed Jessica's offered path?

He wanted to go back to his rut-like existence with no emotional pitfalls or cataclysmic changes to waylay him along the way. He also wanted to have mind-blowing sex with Jessica Hennessy again—and again and again.

When had he turned into a sex-crazed, bi-polar hermit? Not that it mattered, at the moment he just wanted to get the hell out of Dodge. Miss Kitty and her wicked, luscious ways were quickly eroding his determination for a quick getaway.

"No, thanks. I don't want to intrude on your weekend." Alex cleared his throat and then asked, "Have you seen my pants?"

Jessica looked disappointed, and maybe a little hurt. "They're down in the coffee shop."

"Yeah, right." An image of his urgency the night before flashed in his mind's eye. The physical pain of the hardest erection he'd ever had in his life, the frenzied stripping of clothes, his cock violently pumping into Jessica's hot, wet slit and then the savage orgasm that ripped clear through to his soul—and it had all been about his pleasure.

Not that he hadn't noticed she had achieved orgasm; he had. But he'd been so self-absorbed in his own release, he'd missed the chance of making her scream her climax.

So much for finesse. Luckily, he'd showed a little more composure and sexual technique after their first encounter. Still, his level of embarrassment, not to mention his morning woody, ratcheted up another two notches. "Well…"

Damn! How did a man extract himself out of a situation like this gracefully? "Thanks for the fuck—or in this case, fucks?" "I had a great time. Let's do it again real soon?" Alex inched toward the bedroom door, deciding to shut his mouth before he dug an even deeper hole than he already had.

He had to get out of there. Alex mumbled a quick goodbye then turned and left the room.

Last night had been mind-boggling and glorious. A coil of heat seared through the pit of Jessica's stomach just thinking about it, followed by a stabbing pain in the vicinity of her heart.

And this morning sucked!

Alex had damn near broken a speed record when he left.

As Jessica dropped the small metal bowl of Bavarian cream she'd just made into an ice bath, she cursed under her breath. What had she expected? Hearts and flowers? It was the candy that had brought him to her shop last night. Not her.

Maybe she should have thought the whole "candy" thing through a little more before she slipped him a mickey-for-his-dickey. His rejection this morning had hurt more than she had expected—a lot more.

Sighing, she tried to focus on the three as-yet assembled components of a Boston Cream Pie laid out in front of her. She sighed again, louder and longer than seconds ago. Maybe she'd just pinch off a bite of cake, slap on a dollop of Bavarian cream, pop it into her mouth, and then chase it with a spoon full of chocolate icing. A comfort-food shooter of sorts.

Then again, maybe she'd forgo her childhood comfort food and go for straight comfort—Southern Comfort, that is.

Just as she reached for a shot glass, someone knocked on her apartment's private entrance. She crossed the kitchen to the door, looked through the peep hole—and gasped.

Alex stood in the alleyway, finger-combing his ruffled hair. He looked a little disheveled, not as though he'd slept in his clothes—she knew all too well he hadn't done that—just not as starched and polished as he normally presented himself. He seemed slightly off kilter or maybe wound up too tight—edgy.

He looked like hell—and heaven, all at the same time.

Unlocking the deadbolt, Jessica opened the door. "What are you doing here?"

Hell if I know! Alex answered silently, feeling very anxious and a little awkward.

He'd gone straight home this morning and paced the floor until he'd damn near worn a path from one end of his living room to the other. He couldn't get Jessica out of his mind. Although to be honest with himself, it wasn't just about the sex. Granted the sex was great, the best he'd ever had. His dick and balls were actually a little tender from the sexual tournament he and Jessica had participated in last night.

That being the case, Jessica was probably too sore to walk. Maybe that was why he had this burning need to see her again. Maybe he was just concerned about her.

Yeah, right! And Pamela Anderson's tits are real.

He hadn't sped across town and pounded on the Coffee Shop's door for ten minutes because he wanted to check on Jessica's health. It wasn't even the cock and bull "I just want to make sure she'd not angry with me" excuse he'd concocted for himself as he peeled out of his driveway.

Bottom line: he wanted to see her again, wanted to be in the same room with her, wanted to soak up her sunshine.

It was almost as though he was compelled back, as though his life depended upon him returning to Jessica.

But first he had to test the waters to see if his fuck-and-run routine had tainted his welcome.

"Alex?" Jessica waved her hand in front of his face, pulling him out of his confusing thoughts. Once she had his attention, she asked again, "What are you doing here?"

"May I come in?" Alex sidestepped around her and into her apartment without waiting for her to invite him inside. "I knocked on the shop's door, but you didn't answer. I thought you might have a private entrance back here in the alley."

"Most of my patrons are Monday through Friday business people. It doesn't pay to open on Saturdays." Jessica explained as she shut and locked the door behind him. "You didn't answer my question. Why are you here?"

I don't know.

"Are you busy? Am I intruding?" Alex asked, still not answering her question.

She shrugged and headed toward the kitchen island.

Crap! She hadn't thrown herself into his arms—or even opened her arms so he could throw himself into hers. Things weren't looking too welcoming at the moment. Still, she hadn't kicked him out on his ass either—at least not yet.

"Intruding? No. I'm just whipping up a little comfort food," she finally answered, standing with her back to the living room where she'd left him.

Unable to control the urge to be near her, he crossed over to stand just inches away from her, leaned down and whispered in her ear. "Need a little comforting this afternoon?"

She spun around in surprise at his close proximity. Before she could move, he bracketed his hands on either side of her hips, entrapping her between the kitchen island and his body.

"I'm sorry about this morning, the way I left and all."

Jessica shrugged a shoulder, yet obviously still peeved. "It's okay. I understand—probably more than you do."

Alex skimmed his knuckle down her jawline, then spoke softly, "You want to explain it to me, cause I'm not too clear why I was such an asshole."

She shook her head and answered just a hush above a whisper. "No, not really."

"I didn't mean to hurt you, Sweetness." He sighed, allowing his remorse concerning his actions to filter through his words. "Can I make it up to you somehow?"

Her chilly indifference seemed to melt away with his sincerity. Relief washed over him in waves.

He might have gone insane if she'd asked him to leave.

"So about that comfort, know where I can find some?" she cooed as she marched her fingertips up his chest.

He leaned down until his face was even with hers, his mouth a mere breath from hers. "Maybe. If you're a very good girl and do exactly as I tell you."

A spark of anticipation flared in her eyes. "I can be very good, or very bad, or downright naughty, your choice."

X-rated scenarios bombarded Alex's mind, unleashing a primal growl from deep in his chest. Sorely tempted to discover Jessica's definition of naughty, he forced himself to tamp down his self-centered impulses and concentrate on Jessica and her pleasure.

"You be the good girl. I'm in the mood to be bad—very, very bad," he whispered against her lips before he stole her breath away with a searing kiss.

Their kiss became a heated battlefield of tongues, teeth, and lips. Breaths mingled until there was no distinction of one from the other. Soft breasts pressed against rock-hard pecs. One sensuous assault of their senses met and conquered by the other. One wave of hot desire overlapped by the next surge of gnawing hunger. Lust ignited primal instinct into an inferno of raw, aching need.

Alex groaned deep and long, then forced himself to step away from Jessica before he lost complete control. Damn! If this is her being good, he might not live through her being naughty.

Suddenly, he didn't want to be the only one teetering on the edge of carnal madness. Jessica Hennessy had brought him to this precarious state, the least he could do was return the favor.

He wanted to push her to the brink of mindless climax, keep her hovering there until she couldn't the stand the pain of her denied orgasm another second, then watch her shatter into a million pieces before his eyes. But first, he needed to slow the pace and establish control of their sex play, or he would come in his pants before Jessica got wound up good.

"W-What's wrong? Why you'd stop?"

"You in a hurry, Sweetness?" Alex asked as he brushed her hair away from her face.

"No, I guess not." The disappointment in both her eyes and her voice was unmistakable.

Alex suppressed his laughter and silently promised she wouldn't be disappointed for long. Looking around the kitchen/living room area for the best place to launch his attack on her senses, he spotted the bowl of Bavarian cream on the rectangular island counter behind her. Inspiration struck.

Oh yeah, this was going to be good.

He wrapped his left arm around Jessica's waist and pulled her to him for a slow, lingering kiss as he pushed two cake pans and a bowl floating in ice to the other end of the island with his right hand. She squealed when he lifted her up on to the counter top.

She watched his every move as he scooted the bowl of pastry cream closer to him. "Alex?"

"Hmmm?" he answered as he dipped his index finger into the cold creamy mixture.

"What are you doing?"

Scooping a dollop of cream from the bowl, he turned to Jessica and smiled. "Tasting." He smeared the cream over her bottom lip, then leaned in and licked the cream off.

"My turn." She reached down and drug her finger through the cream, then tried to spread some on his lips.

Alex stopped her progress before she could touch him. "Huh-uh. This is about you this time."

Moving her cream-coated finger into his mouth, he sucked it clean, then nibbled at the sensitive pad of her finger. Jessica moaned from deep in her throat. He barely suppressed a moan of his own.

He brushed a lock of hair off of her shoulder, then skimmed his finger over her collarbone, "Let's just see how good you can be—and for how long—when I put my all into being bad."

"Is that a challenge?" she asked as he traced her jawline with his lips.

"Sounds like it to me," he whispered.

Goose bumps popped up on her skin when he nibbled on the space just below her left ear. Ahhh, he'd found one of her sensitive spots.

Jessica started to shiver her reaction to his kisses, then caught herself, but not before Alex noticed.

"What's your definition of 'good'?" she asked.

"You just sit there and enjoy. I'll do the rest."

She reached for him again, but he caught her wrist to stop her touch. "What about you?"

"Trust me." He turned her hand palm up, then sucked and nibbled on the tips of her fingers. "I'm going to enjoy every second of this."

After a moment that seemed like eternity, Jessica nodded her agreement. "Just remember, turnabout is fair play. Are you going to hold out when I have you at my mercy?"

"God, I hope so," he growled as he layered his mouth over hers in a demanding exchange of consent and promise. He savored the taste of her for a lingering moment then eased the pressure of his kiss. There were other tastes, other pleasures he wanted to explore.

Alex skimmed his hands under her pink, midriff tee shirt to confirm his suspicions. She wasn't wearing a bra. Her nipples stood taut and rigid as though they strained for his touch.

Cupping the weight of her breasts in the palms of his hands, he squeezed gently as he grazed his thumbs over her tight, hard nipples. Jessica gnawed at her bottom lip, no doubt trying to bite back her response.

"Sweetness, you're really pretty in pink—" Alex knotted the hem of her pink tee in his fingers, then whip it up and over her head. "—but you're take-my-breath-away gorgeous out of it."

Her startled yelp tapered off into a throaty moan when Alex layered his mouth over one of her puckered nipples.

"Yesss," she encouraged as she shoved her fingers through his hair to hold him in place at her breast.

Alex chuckled against her soft, full bosom, flicked his tongue over her distended nipple, then pulled a hairsbreadth away from her. He shook his head slightly, causing his lips to tickle against her breast. "Huh-uh, no touching, no aggressive movements, no calling the shots. Just lay back, relax and enjoy. Let's see how good a girl you can be."

Dipping his fingers back into the ice-cold pastry cream, he slathered it over both her breasts. Jessica gasped as her nipples pebbled into tight, stiff kernels against the chill of the cream. Lowering his mouth to her left breast, he flicked at her cream-covered nipple with his tongue and then sucked her puckered areola between his lips. With his right hand, he rolled and pinched her right nipple between his index finger and thumb, tugging in the same rhythm as he sucked on her other breast.

Jessica leaned back, bracing herself with her arms slightly behind her, giving him even more access to her breasts. She hummed her pleasure in the back of her throat and let her head loll against her shoulder.

"Feels good?"

"God, yes! More." She opened her eyes, but couldn't manage raising her head from its resting place on her shoulder.

He took the hint and transferred his mouth to her other breast and reclaimed her previously suckled breast with his hand. He flicked a little faster, sucked a little deeper and pinched and tugged a little harder—as she moaned her pleasure a little louder.

Alex's needs simmered at the edge of his control as he worshipped her breasts with his lips and tongue. No woman had ever had him this close to coming by only watching her rapturous responses to his touch. He was teetering on the edge of disgracing himself worse than a teenager watching his first porn flick.

Jessica moaned, then murmured something under her breath he couldn't quite hear. Leaving his hand still playing at her left breast, he kissed and nibbled his way up her neck to her luscious mouth.

Willing himself to slow down, he traced the tip of his tongue around her slightly-parted lips, then layered his mouth over hers. He plunged his tongue into her mouth, mimicking the tugging, squeezing rhythm of his hand on her breast. Exploring mutated into inflamed coaxing, then exploded into pummeling demand. All mutual. Jessica countered his tongue's thrust with eager thrusts of her own. She sucked on his tongue as it retreated from her mouth, and then sucked harder when he drove back into her hot wetness.

God, he was going to lose control before he'd ever got her out of her panties.

Suddenly, Jessica ripped her mouth from his, forced his hand away from her breast and placed it over her denim-covered mound, then whimpered between her clenched teeth, "Touch me or I'll go crazy."

"Be careful what you wish for, Sweetness," Alex warned, as he tugged at the button of her cut-offs. He managed to unfasten the metal button and slid the zipper down without his hands shaken. "Raise your butt."

Jessica braced her bare feet on Alex's thighs, wrapped her arms around his shoulders, then shifted forward until her butt cleared the counter surface. Unceremoniously, Alex yanked her cutoffs to her ankles and then laid her on the counter top with the lower half of her legs dangling over the edge.

A cake pan slid off the other end of the kitchen island. He didn't care as long as the bowl of cream remained within reach. He moved to the long side of the island where he could kiss and touch and torment her with his mouth, his fingers and a bowl of cold pastry cream.

"Alex, please—"

"Shhh, now. I know what you want." He leaned over and gently kissed her trembling lips—then shoved two fingers into her hot, wet slit.

It was hard and fast and Jessica loved it. She moaned against his mouth as her body bucked against his fingers.

She wanted more and she was tried of waiting for it. She reached for the buttons of Alex's fly. He caught her wrist again before she could touch him, just as he'd done twice already.

"No, ma'am, not part of the deal. Not yet."

"I don't care about the deal," Jessica barely managed to say when Alex's thumb circled her clitoris with enough pressure to almost drive her to orgasm. "I'm ready for you!"

"Sorry, I'm not quite ready yet." Alex brought her hand to his mouth to kiss her palm.

"Give me two minutes and my hand back and you will be."

Alex chuckled, grabbed both her hands in his one and then pillowed them behind her head. Her breasts jutted upward and he took full advantage of her offerings. Thank God! He licked, he nibbled, he sucked. He damn near had her coming on his fingers!

"Take a deep breath, baby," he ordered.

Before she could asked him why, he dropped a generous three-fingered scoop of ice cold cream on her bare belly. She closed her eyes and shivered, both from the coldness of the filling and anticipation of what he might do with it.

She felt him draw an icy path from the dollop down her belly, where he dropped a large bead of cream into her belly button. Then she felt the warmth of his tongue as he followed his previous path. Once he'd made his meticulous, agonizing slow way to her naval, he nipped at its edges with his teeth, then licked at the sensitive spots where he'd bitten her. Just about the time she'd had enough of his teasing and was willing to forfeit the challenge, he lapped at the cream filling in her naval with the tip of his tongue. He sucked and licked at her belly until she thought she would die from the pleasure of it.

His fingers pushed into her slit, then slowly withdrew them in tandem with the sucking sensations on her navel. And still, he teased her super-sensitive clit with his thumb. Her body tensed, the muscles in her legs shook with the force of her coming pleasure. A fire ball of heat expanded over itself in the pit of her stomach, over and over it grew until Jessica wanted to rush toward it. She was almost close enough to touch it, to let it engulf her in its power.

And then Alex's mouth and fingers left her body, left her dangling on the edge of completion.

"Damn it! Don't do this to me," she shrieked before she could compose herself.

Alex shook his head and tsked at her. "That's no way for a good girl to talk."

"I don't want to be a good girl. I want to come!"

Alex chuckled, but it sounded strained, raspy and raw.

"Not funny. I ache. Do something." God, she hoped she didn't sound as whiny as she felt.

"I feel your pain, believe me. And I'm not going to leave you wanting, at least not forever."

Jessica looked at Alex for the first time since her outburst. He did look as though he felt her pain. Sweat beaded his forehead, his hands shook and his lips pressed tight to each other as though trying to stave off pain. Oh yeah, he was hurting all right.

Somehow that made her feel better. How sick was that?

"Just remember, it's my turn next."

"Is that a threat?"

"No, just a warning. I pay my debts in full."

"I just bet you do, Sweetness." He leaned down and placed a tender kiss across her quivering lips, then moved around until he stood between her wide spread legs. "You are so beautiful."

He reached for the cream. Jessica stopped his hand as it hovered over the bowl. "Don't do that to me again."

"What? The cream? You don't like the cream?"

"I love the cream." Jessica paused, then looked Alex in the eyes and pleaded. "Please, don't deny me again."

Alex cupped his hand around her neck and pulled her to him for a kiss that nearly singed her eyebrows. "Wouldn't dream of it, Sweetheart. Now, lie back and enjoy."

With that he released her and reached for the chilled pastry filling.

Chapter Five

Jessica snatched the bowl off the counter top, then held it above her head as though playing keep away—only she wasn't smiling. She puckered her brow, the corners of her kiss-swollen lips turned down as she slowly shook her head. "I've changed my mind."

About what? Alex's mind screamed, his body slamming into panic mode. About the cream? About sex? About him?

Oh God, if she kicked him out now, he'd have to crawl to the door. No way in hell he could walk with the raging hard-on throbbing between his legs.

He managed to take a step away from Jessica, then braced his hands on either side of her and clutched the edge of the kitchen island to keep his balance. Ducking his head, he inhaled deeply in an effort to get a better grip on the roaring lust coiled in the pit of his stomach. "W-what?"

"I've changed my mind. I don't want to be good anymore."

Still stooped over her, Alex's head snapped up, his eyes level with hers. "You don't want to be good anymore? But you still want to—huh—you still want me—"

"Oh, yeah, I still want you," she assured him, her voice low, raspy and so damn sultry she had Alex straining against the reins of his control. She brought the bowl of chilled cream down and placed it between them. Never taking her gaze off of Alex's face, she drew figure eights through the thick cream filling with her index finger. "I want you to take your shirt off—slowly."

The surge of relief that rolled over him nearly brought him to his knees.

Alex straightened, then cocked a questioning brow at her. She had a devilish gleam in her eye and a bowl full of erotic fantasies in her lap. What did she have in mind?

She dipped her finger into the creamy pastry goo, then brought her finger to her mouth. The tip of her tongue peeked out from between her luscious, wet lips, then ever so slowly licked and curled around her cream-covered finger.

Suddenly, he knew exactly what she had in mind for him.

How long could he hold out before she had him coming in her hand, or —or in her mouth? No more than one or two good licks and he would be a goner!

Heated lust raged through his veins, then pooled in his more-than-primed cock. No doubt about it, he was going to die. But he was going to be one happy son-of-a-bitch all the way to the cemetery.

What was it about this woman that put a hair-trigger on his control?

Oh yeah, he was definitely doomed to disgrace himself. But then again, from where he stood, doomed looked pretty damned good.

Once she'd licked her finger clean, she pointed at him. "I said, take your shirt off."

"Yes, ma'am," he answered, deciding he'd let her lead for a minute or two—which was about as long as he thought he'd last without grabbing her and tossing her onto the floor and fucking her until they both were babbling idiots.

He yanked his shirt up over his head, damned near giving himself whiplash.

Jessica gave him a playful pout. "What happened to slowly?"

"I'm so revved up, that's about as slow as I could manage."

Smiling at him innocently, she hopped down from the island counter, then nodded toward his jeans. "Now your pants."

He popped the snap of his jeans with his thumb, then careful not to hurt himself, he eased the zipper down over his throbbing erection. What a day to go commando. Not even a thin layer of cotton between him and the metal teeth of his zipper.

Standing naked in front of her, his heart jackhammered against his chest with enough force to explode into a thousand pieces. Anticipation and blinding lust coursed through him. But there was also something more, something much more intimate in his need for her. Something a lot deeper than getting a piece of ass.

A weak alarm sounded on the edge of his awareness. There might be repercussions for what he was about to do. The kind of repercussions he didn't want to deal with.

Alex tamped down his doubts almost as quickly as they had slinked their way into his consciousness. He really didn't have any choice. He was too far gone to walk away from Jessica now.

Just go with the flow, Einstein. Think later. Much later, when your cock isn't going to spontaneously combust if she touches you with her tongue!

"Okay, boss lady, now what?"

Still holding the ice cold metal bowl in front of her, Jessica stepped closer to him. The frigid metal pressed against his stomach, causing him to flinch away from her slightly.

She stepped forward again until the frozen metal touched his bare skin once again. He took another step backward. She moved forward, he inched backward. Her forward, him backward. Forward. Backward. Forward. Backward. Until his back collided against the rough brick of her kitchen wall.

Hell! He'd been pinned against a wall by a piece of ice cold metal and her you're-going-to-love-this promise of a smile. What could be better than this?

Before he could brace himself, she dipped her finger into the cold filling. He gasped as the shock of the icy cream touched his nipples, then lost his breath completely when her hot mouth sucked and licked it away. Need like nothing he'd experienced in his life bolted through his body from his nipples to his balls.

The effort not to come where he stood left him panting for his next breath. Oh yeah, it was going to get a whole lot better than this. He just hoped he lived to enjoy it!

He reached for her. She stepped back and silently shook her head. He understood.

He wanted to touch her, wanted to hold her mouth to his super-sensitized nipple and tell her to suck harder. But he didn't. It was probably for the best anyway. It was taking everything he had to hold on to the thin tether of his control.

"Sure, okay, Sweetness. We'll do it your way. But I'm warning you, you better have a short game plan. I'm primed to go off at any moment."

"Unlike you, I don't think suffering is a stimulant to orgasm." Jessica smiled as she bent and placed the bowl of Bavarian cream on the floor beside his left foot. Then balancing herself on her toes, she layered her mouth over his for a deep, intoxicating kiss that left him light-headed. Easing away from him, she whispered against his lips, "But if that's your thing, I'll try to oblige you."

Alex squeezed his eyes tight against the possibilities. He was so done for. He wouldn't last fifteen seconds if she even attempted half the things flittering through his imagination. Groaning, he opened his eyes to find her kneeling on the floor in front of him, her mouth a mere six inches from his jutting penis.

With just the tip of her fingernail, she traced swirling patterns from his knees up and around his thighs while urging him to spread his legs wider. She gently cupped his aching balls in her hands, then leaned forward and licked them.

Sweat beaded across his chest. The air seem to thicken as he struggled to suck oxygen into his lungs. And she hadn't even gotten to the good part. Not to say that what she was doing at the moment wasn't good. It was. But if this was the prelims, he could hardly wait for the main event.

He leaned his head against the wall and inhaled deeply as he tried to slow down his body's reaction to her touch. She took her hand away from his balls and he braced himself for his pounding erection to be teased and fondled by her warm, wet tongue.

He'd never been this hard, this hot, for a woman before in his life.

"Alex." Her warm breath whispered against his aching cock.

"I can't take much more of this," he warned through clenched teeth.

"Maybe this will help."

"I'm way beyond help. I need—" Alex's breath rushed out of his lungs and then refused to return when she slathered ice-cold pastry cream down the length of his cock. His head snapped forward as he tried to unsuccessfully retreat from the icy coldness encasing his dick. He barely noticed the hard, sharp edges of brick wall digging into his back. "Shit! That's cold!"

"Yeah, that's what I thought, too. But this will make it all worthwhile." That said, she leaned forward and licked the sticky cream off his cock. From root to tip, she traced the pointed tip of her tongue along his hard as steel penis. The wet, warm velvet of her tongue sent a streak of erotic torment searing through him.

What little relief to his urgency the coldness had provided evaporated under the hot, titillating strokes of her tongue.

He bucked against her mouth and reached for her. She pulled away.

She was in control and she wanted to make damn sure he knew it.

"You're playing with fire," he warned as he barely restrained the overpowering urge to ram himself into her mouth.

"Afraid I'll get burned?"

He watched, mesmerized as she scooped another dollop of cream onto her fingers. "Tease me like that again and we'll both go up in flames. I'll make sure of it."

"I'm just getting started," she promised as she circled the purple-tinged head of his dick with the cream. Then she followed the path of her fingers with her tongue, licking and sucking her way around the crown of his penis. His heart pounded in his chest. Pleasure ripped through him, so intense it bordered on pain.

How could this woman make him feel weak as a lamb, and at the same time, strong enough to fight the world if she asked him?

He started to speak, to warn her he'd had enough, when she took his length into her mouth. And sucked—hard.

Whatever words he was about to say deserted him, disintegrated under the intensity of pure pleasure searing through him. Air rushed into his lungs and lodged there.

She curled her tongue around his crown and sucked again, long and hard. Then, with as much of his cock as she could take in her mouth, she layered her tongue along the length of his shaft and begin to pump her mouth up and down his engorged erection. One hand stroked his tight balls while her other hand squeezed and massaged the base of his penis.

Primal instinct took over. Lost in the carnal sensations, he plunged himself inside her mouth, deeper and faster and faster yet—until her heard her soft moan over the roaring in his ears.

No! Not like this! He wanted to come with her.

Blowjobs were all well and good, and he enjoyed the hell out of them, but he'd had his fill of solo releases. He wanted all of her, not just her mouth.

He wanted to come inside her, wanted the contractions of her orgasm to milk him dry. He wanted to hear her scream her release close to his ear, wanted to roar back at her with the force of his own.

"Enough playing!" He pushed her off of him, then snatched her up into his arms. Moving back to the kitchen island, he lifted her up onto the edge of the counter top.

"I want you—all of you. I want to make you scream with the pleasure of my cock pumping inside you," Alex growled between his clenched teeth.

None too gently, he wadded a handful of her hair in his fist, jerked her head back and kissed her with every bit of pent-up passion strumming through his system. He skimmed his other hand down her belly, past her mound and shoved two fingers into her tight vagina. She was wet, hot and slick with her own juices.

She was ready, more than ready for him. That was all he needed to know.

Snatching a condom from his wallet, he covered himself, then stepped between her legs. He impaled her with his strutting cock. He groaned with the pleasure of it, almost to the point of coming.

She was tight and hot, pulsing around him. Molten need, red-hot and insistent, engulfed him. Still, he didn't dare move.

When he thought he could allow himself to proceed without losing control completely, he moved with slow, deep thrusts. Pleasure and yearning doubled over themselves with every thrust.

Jessica moaned a carnal encouragement as his tempo quickened. She wrapped her legs around his body and squeezed, driving him deeper yet into her hot wetness. She fought for breath. He could see her getting closer, feel her contracting around him even as she pleaded, "Now, Alex? Now?"

"Yes, Sweetness! Now!"

"Alex!" she screamed as she reached her peak.

He felt the milking spasms of her orgasm grip him. Felt the world tilt on its axis. Unleashed passion pounded through his bloodstream, throbbed in his cock and seared its way from his balls up. He roared Jessica's name as the explosive eruption of white-hot pleasure ripped through him.

Oh yeah, he thought, as the world slowly began to right itself. If this was doomed, doomed was the place to be!

Jessica sighed contently and cuddled deeper into Alex's embrace. If she was dreaming, she never wanted to wake up.

The weekend had been one big blur of passion, tenderness, and time with the man she loved. And she did love him. She knew that now. Heck, she'd probably loved him for months and just wouldn't let herself go there because she had thought his pain too fresh. She wanted to give him time to grieve his wife.

Three years was long enough.

Lazily, she skimmed her fingertips down Alex's arm that curled around her waist and held her close. He kissed the top of her head, his attention never leaving the car chase careening across the TV screen. Oh yeah, he might be absorbed in

John Grisham's latest legal thriller, but he knew she was there.

That was a good sign, a very good sign. The fact that he still wore his wedding band after the weekend they'd shared was definitely not a good sign.

He'd left earlier to run home and clean up, promising he'd be back with pizza and a movie in a couple of hours. And he had. Pizza, a movie, and that damned wedding ring still super-glued to his finger.

Not that she thought he'd come back showered, shaved and bare-handed, she just hadn't thought it would bother her so much.

Almost without conscious thought, she outlined his fingers with the tips of hers. When she'd made her way around all four fingers, she followed the contour of his knuckles to his ring finger—his occupied ring finger.

His thumb stopped in mid-stroke where he'd been absently caressing the underside of her breast. His eyes may have been focused on the TV, but he was acutely aware of where her meandering touch had wondered.

Jessica mentally shrugged. In for a penny, in for a pound. "You want to talk about it?"

Alex's body went rigid beneath her. His gaze now too conveniently glued to the TV. "Not really."

"Why?"

"There's nothing to talk about."

"Your wife has been dead for three years and you still wear your wedding ring. I'd say that's something to talk about."

"Why?"

"Well, uh, considering this weekend's—er—new development, I thought maybe you'd want to talk about it."

That got his attention.

His gaze shot to her face, he removed his arm from around her and sit up straight on the couch. "Are you're asking me what my intentions are? Is that it?"

He speared her with a mocking glare that had her reconsidering the wisdom of opening this particular Pandora's Box. Yet, something nagged at her.

Grief wasn't what was holding Alex back from life. Mitch had said.

So what was?

"No, I'm asking you where you are emotionally."

Alex stood and walked to the window on the other side of the living room. With his back to her, he seemed enthralled, too enthralled, in the alleyway outside. "Why do I have to be anywhere emotionally? Why can't I just be?"

Jessica came up behind him and laid her hand gently on his arm. "Mitch told me about your wife's death. He told me you weren't still grieving for her and I believe him. If I didn't, this weekend would have never happened."

He glanced over his shoulder to look down at her. "So what's the problem?"

"I'm trying to understand why you still wear your wedding ring. Why you still live in the past."

Alex growled under his breath. "I'm going to kick Mitch's ass for this."

"For what?"

"For ruining… Never mind." He moved away from her. "I've got to go. I'm flying out to Boston early in the morning and I haven't packed yet."

Jessica watched him gather his coat and the movie and then head for the door. Just as he touched the doorknob, she called out to him. "Alex? You're leaving?"

He turned to face her. "I like living in the past. Why do something different? Why take the chance on what tomorrow will bring, when I'm comfortable where I am?"

Jessica opened her mouth to speak, but no words came out. Anxiety and despair swapped over any coherent thought she might have had. He was leaving and she didn't want him to go. She stepped toward him, but he shook his head, stopping her in her tracks.

"See ya, Sweetness," he said a breath above a whisper. Then he left.

"Yeah, see ya," she said to the closed door. Only she probably wouldn't ever see him again. At least, not without a coffee counter between them. She wasn't part of the past he was so determined to stay entrenched in.

The weekend had been beautiful. He'd been tender, attentive and passionate. But it was over.

Oh, God, she hurt. And she had no one to blame but herself.

Chapter Six

Alex pulled out of New Orleans International Airport long-term parking lot, exhausted beyond belief. He'd been gone four days—and three sleepless nights. Every time he'd closed his eyes he saw Jessica naked, could almost feel her responsive body next to his. He couldn't decide which was more disturbing, remembering her eyes smolder with passion when he touched her or seeing them moisten against her hurt feelings when he left her.

She was like a drug to him, always beckoning to him, always craving a little more of her than the time before.

Hell, this is what he got for playing in the here and now instead of staying safely tucked away in the uncomplicated life he'd been living for the last three years. He was definitely out of his comfort zone.

Only the minimal-participation existence he'd adopted since his wife's death didn't sound all that appealing anymore, either.

Groaning, he merged into traffic on I-10 and headed home. His cell phone rang, saving him from his unsettling thoughts.

Flipping his phone open, he answered his personal calls with his professional salutation, just like he'd been doing for the last couple of years. Not that there was that much of a distinction between those two worlds. Business had long ago filled the gaping hole where he'd once had a personal life. "Alex Russell."

"Hey, Buddy. Where you been?" Mitch asked.

"Boston."

"Yeah, yeah, I knew about the big campaign pitch up there. I meant, where were you over the weekend. You went MIA on me."

Flashes of himself pumping and grinding into Jessica's soft, succulent body until they were both too sated to move, blazed across his memory. "I was busy."

"No kidding? Getting a life, are you?"

A spark of anger, or maybe it was just a sudden possessiveness for his privacy, fueled his heated retort. "Fuck off."

Mitch laughed through the connection. "I'll take that as a yes."

Alex grunted into his phone, but refused to answer his friend. A sign loomed over the freeway announcing the St. Charles Street Exit two miles ahead. Jessica's apartment was only another couple of miles up St. Charles Street. He could be there in less than fifteen minutes.

Would she be glad to see him or shut the door in his face? Had he occupied her thoughts this last week as much as she had his? If so, would she strip her clothes off the instant she saw him?

Damn. He hoped so. He was soooo up for that!

"Hey!" Mitch bellowed into his ear. "Earth to Asshole. You still there?"

"Sorry, got distracted. Traffic," Alex lied, hoping he sounded convincing. "What'd you say?"

"I asked if you wanted to come over and have a beer?"

Alex thought of beer's earthy bite of fermented hops and instinctually knew that was not what he craved. He wanted something sweet, maybe something chocolate with a gooey, nutty flavored center. Or maybe he just hungered for the sorceress that bewitched him with her tasty treats.

"Sorry, not this time." Even as he told himself he needed to go straight home—needed to leave Jessica alone, he veered off onto the St. Charles Street exit and headed north toward her apartment. "I've got to make a stop before I go home."

"Alex!" Jessica gasped as she opened her door.

"Hi, Sweetness. I just g—"

Jessica launched herself into his arms, damn near knocking the breath out of him. He laughed, partly at her welcoming antics and partly from sheer relief, then squeezed her tightly against him. "Missed me, huh?"

"Maybe," she said against the crook of his neck.

Yeah, I missed you, too, he thought as he buried his face into her soft, thick hair and inhaled deeply. When he realized what he'd admitted to himself, he braced himself for his defense mechanism to kick in and push Jessica away.

It didn't.

Maybe it was jet-lag or three nights of little to no sleep, but no overpowering urge to turn tail and run swamped him. It didn't feel awkward holding Jessica in his arms. He didn't feel exposed to the world.

He just felt her, snuggling against him. And at the moment, that was plenty good enough for him.

Jessica shifted in his arms as though trying to move away from him. He squeezed her closer, refusing to let her go. A pulse beat later, he released one arm from around her back, placed it beneath her knees, then scooped her up into his arms. She squealed her surprise, then wrapped her arms around his neck and kissed him.

Her soft, sweet mouth pressed against his, her tongue teased at his lower lip.

She moaned and slid her tongue into his mouth the instant he parted his lips. Fire and something more tender mingled in his chest until his heart raced, and his breath caught in his lungs.

Heaven, he thought. He'd found heaven—at least for the moment.

He willed himself to go slow, to enjoy the taste of her, the feel of her in his arms and to wallow in the open warmth of her welcome. And he did—for about five seconds. Then he devoured her with his burning need to show her how much he missed her.

He couldn't say words he didn't mean, couldn't make promises he wouldn't keep, but he could show her how much he wanted her tonight. Without asking—without breaking the demanding kiss that had him damn near dizzy, he carried her to her bedroom.

Gently, he laid her on her bed, then stepped away to remove his clothes. When Jessica reached for the buttons of her shirt, he shook his head and whispered, "Let me."

Her fingers hovered over the tiny buttons for a heartbeat, then moved away. "Okay."

When he was completely naked, he stretched out on the bed beside her. She was so beautiful. He would always remember her like this, her eyes, darkening with desire, begging him to touch her yet willing to wait for his touch because he had asked.

He wasn't able to be a part of her world, not like she wanted him to be, but he couldn't bring himself to leave her alone either. Not yet, at least. He wanted to soak her up, wanted to soak up her happiness, her welcome, her need for him.

Ever so slowly, he plucked her shirt's buttons free of their holes, pausing to kiss her newly revealed skin an inch at a time. Braless beneath her blouse, her breasts beckoned for his touch, his kiss. He didn't deny her or himself as he laved her left nipple with his tongue until it was hard, pointed and swollen from his kisses. Then he tended to her right nipple with as much tender thoroughness as he had given her left.

She moaned in heated response as she threaded her fingers through his hair and tried to hold him in place at her breasts. He lingered a moment longer, then moved lower down her body. He removed her shorts and bikini briefs in one fluid motion. Gazing down at her, naked and needful, he almost lost his breath. "God, you're beautiful."

Then he kissed her with all the pent-up loneliness of the last three years— loneliness he didn't even realize he felt until Jessica touched his world.

A fragment of warning skidded across his mind. This was bad for his peace of mind.

Alex brushed the thought away. Jessica felt too good in his arms to let her go just yet.

He had been told once that life was a capricious balance of good versus bad.

Get too much of one or the other, and your whole world could fall asunder.

He was willing to take that chance—for tonight anyway.

He'd snatch up all the good he could out of tonight's time with Jessica. Then tomorrow or the next day, he'd face the bad, the loneliness of his life. Loneliness magnified by her absence.

Lifting his mouth from hers, he gazed down at the beautiful woman in his arms. A growing part of him wanted to whisk her up and run as far and fast as his legs would carry them. Only he couldn't do that. Where would he run to? What was he running from?

"What are you thinking?" Jessica whispered as she skimmed her finger along his jaw. "You look so sad."

"I'm not sad, Sweetness. I'm in awe of your beauty, both inside and out."

"Oh, Alex. You make me want to cry."

"Don't, I couldn't stand it," he whispered just before he layered his mouth over hers.

She threaded her fingers through his hair and then pulled him closer to her. Her acceptance of his kiss, her craving for his touch ignited his already gnawing hunger into a consuming voracity that only she could appease.

He skimmed his hand down her body, pausing to tease and tug at her nipples until she moaned into his mouth. Continuing over her stomach, he slid his hand to her mound then dipped his finger into her womanly slit. She was wet, hot, slick—for him.

A coil of need, white-hot and writhing, balled in the pit of his stomach. How could she do this to him every time he touched her?

She spread her legs wider in open invitation. And he accepted.

He plunged two fingers into her wetness, quick and hard, and then withdrew them slowly. She lifted her hips as though not willing to forfeit his possession, then groaned her gratification when he re-entered her—this time slowly, very, very slowly.

Circling her clitoris with the pad of his thumb, he applied just enough pressure to extract a husky moan from her. An answering contraction gripped his embedded fingers.

Kissing his way down her throat, he nibbled and licked a path along her body until his mouth closed over her clitoris. He stroked it with his tongue, sending quivers across Jessica's creamy thighs. He loved her response to him, loved the way she seemed to relish his touch.

"Alex," she purred as she squirmed closer to his mouth.

Damn it, she was driving him crazy. But he wasn't going to make that trip alone, he silently promised her.

"That's my girl," he coaxed, then sucked her nub between his teeth, nipping at her gently, then laving his tongue over her to smooth away the sting. He dipped his tongue into her slit, then slowly licked her labia until they glistened with a mixture of his saliva and her luscious juices.

When he flicked her clitoris with the tip of his tongue, she moaned in unbidden pleasure. He sucked, he nibbled, he teased at her until they were both panting with barely held in check passion.

"Alex, please!"

She hadn't touched him, hadn't taken him in her hand or her mouth and primed his lust, yet just the sound of her calling his name in passion had him rushing to the edge of his control. How could she do that to him? And how was he ever going to walk away from her when the time came?

Another erotic quiver rippled through her, her body physically begging for him with as much fervor as she'd just verbally uttered. Her intensity, her obvious need, caused Alex to doubt his own staying power when it came to Jessica.

She always did this to him.

He wanted to take his time, to savor her, but his restraint was wearing thin. He needed her with a fierceness that scared him.

Giving in to their physical demands for completion, he moved up her body. He covered her mouth with his in a demanding kiss that left no doubt of his intense need, then eased away from her just long enough to retrieve a condom from his wallet.

She whispered, "Hurry."

As if he could slow down, even if he wanted to, he thought, as he rolled the latex over his throbbing penis. A sarcastic laugh escaped his lips. "I know, baby. I'm right there with you."

He moved over her, settling himself between her legs. Propping up on his elbows, he took her face in his hands and gazed down at her. An emotion he didn't want to try to label swelled in his chest, clogging his throat until he could barely speak.

"Ah, Sweetness, what kind of magic spell are you spinning over me?" he murmured in a husky whisper a breath before he took her mouth in a passionate kiss—a kiss riddled with unnamed emotions and undeniable demands.

Jessica stiffened, then melted into his kiss.

Then he couldn't stand it any more, couldn't stand not being a part of her. He wanted to feel her slick wetness surround him. Thrusting hard, he buried himself to the hilt in her tight, wet slit.

He forced himself not to move for one long heartbeat, allowing Jessica to adjust to his fullness. Then she tilted her hips slightly forward and rocked against him. He was lost.

Withdrawing until just the tip of him remained inside her, he thrust again—and again—and again. Thrusting hard and withdrawing slowly. Thrusting harder and withdrawing a little faster. Then faster and harder. Faster, harder. Faster, harder. Until he felt like a crazed animal. Still, he couldn't stop himself.

He needed her—all of her. He'd take what she wouldn't give. Demand every ounce of her being. Savage greed rode him hard.

And he rode her hard.

Jessica locked her ankles behind his back and met every pounding thrust with a demanding, driving force of her own. He couldn't get close enough, couldn't get deep enough to seem to satisfy either him or her. Suddenly, she stiffened. The muscles in her legs tensed around him. Her nails dug into his back, sending sweet pain ripping through him.

She screamed her climax.

Alex surged deep inside her one final time then surrendered to the raging beast consuming him. Senses and sensations exploded around him. Everything inside of him shattered into sharp, glistening shards. He lost his bearings in the universe.

Helplessly, he clung to Jessica until his world righted itself. Her essence rushed through him, leaving him breathless. Her sweetness, the beauty of her inner being, the whole of what she was and what she could be steep into every crook and cranny of his soul.

Slowly, reality trickled into his awareness.

He shifted himself onto his elbows to take some of his weight off her, then gazed down into her eyes. She was crying. "Oh God, did I hurt you?"

He had been brutal, pounding into her like a demented wild man. If he'd caused her pain—or God forbid, scared her, he'd never forgive himself.

"No," she murmured as she touched her fingertips to his lips. "That was the most beautiful thing I've ever experienced."

Relief washed over him. He released his breath against her fingers, then softly kissed her love-swollen lips. "Yeah, for me, too."

He moved to her side, then wrapped his arms around her and pulled her near. A moment later, Alex heard the soft purr he'd come to recognize as Jessica's sleeping song.

Without warning, the defense that had laid dormant all evening raised its ugly head and roared at him to run—don't walk—to the nearest exit.

But he didn't move.

Then realization blindsided him. He didn't want to run. He liked it right where he was.

Suddenly, the magnitude of that revelation hit him with the force of a twenty-pound medicine ball directly to his pecs.

What the hell should he do now?

What the hell should she do now? The question pounded against Jessica's conscience for the thousandth time since Alex had left some time during the night.

Unfortunately, she already knew the answer.

She had to tell him the truth about the candy. She had deceived him and now she had to come clean.

God, what would she say? "Sorry, honey bunny, but it was your sweet tooth and not any kind of natural attraction to me that had you knocking on my door every time you got a hard-on."

Jessica groaned and continued to pace a path between her couch and her front door. Why had she done such a stupid, stupid thing?

She'd sold out any chance of a future with the man she loved for an up-against-the-wall quickie!

Okay, maybe it was more like five or six mind-blowing bouts of sex, she conceded. One, two, five—it didn't make any difference. What she and Alex had shared over the last week didn't have a chance at everlasting anything—much less love. As soon as the effects of her voodoo spiked-candy wore off, Alex would refuse to be a part of her life.

Yeah, he'd remember the sex, but without an emotional connection between them, sex was just a physical act. Jessica wanted more. Alex deserved more. If not with her, then with someone else—someone who hadn't cast a spell on him to get him in her bed.

Best case scenario, if he knew the truth, he'd be uncomfortable in her presence to the point he'd quit even coming into the coffee shop. Worst case scenario, he'd be so furious with her for subjecting him to her great-grandmother's voodoo version of the date rape drug he'd have her ass thrown in jail. Not that she didn't deserve some alone time in the pokey for what she had done to him, but she really hoped Alex wouldn't carry things quite that far.

Oh, God! What had she been thinking?

She hadn't. She'd just acted out of selfishness, without a thought for Alex or his feelings. She'd been so wound up over him for months, she hadn't considered what would happen when the candy wore off and he lost interest.

Only the effects of the candy hadn't worn off and Alex hadn't lost interest. And that was worrying her almost as much as how he'd feel about her once he knew the truth. What if the spell could somehow physically harm him? What if the effects never wore off?

He'd looked a little pale, seemed preoccupied, when he left her last night. At one time, she thought she'd heard him arguing with himself over the pros and cons of the color gray.

Maybe it was something to do with one of his ad campaigns. Or maybe all those super-charged testosterone molecules fried a circuit in his brain.

If the effects didn't wear off soon, would he turn into a babbling hard-on for the rest of his life?

Guilt knotted in her stomach, sending a bitter wave of nausea coursing through her. Even knowing that telling Alex the truth would drive him from her life, she knew she had no choice. It was the only fair thing to do.

God! What had she been thinking?

A knock on her door froze her in mid-pace. She turned to look at the clock over her refrigerator. Five thirty. It was Alex.

Bracing herself for what she was about to do, she went to the door and let him in.

He seemed pumped with enthusiasm, genuinely glad to see her. "Hi, Sweetness." Alex leaned down and brushed a quick kiss over her lips as he stepped inside. "I missed you."

Jessica's gaze slid down his body to the bulge in his pants. Duh! Of course, he's glad to see you, dimwit, he has an erection, a condescending voice whined in her mind's ear. "Yeah, I can see that."

Alex noted the direction of her gaze and laughed, "Just the thought of being around you gets me hard."

He drew her into his arms for a proper glad-to-see-ya kiss. Her heart rate kicked into high gear the instant he covered her mouth with his. He teased the seam of her lips with the velvet-soft tip of his tongue. She sighed against his mouth, then parted her lips for his entry. His assault was tender, probing, passionate. It was almost her undoing.

With a strength she didn't realize she had until that moment, she pulled away from him. But, damn, she didn't want to!

She wanted to lose herself in his tender touch. She wanted to lie to herself, wanted to believe Alex cared about her for herself. She wanted to believe that he felt something for her, instead of feeling the effects of her aphrodisiac-spiked candy.

God, she wanted to believe in him!

But she couldn't. Mentally fortifying her resolve to come clean with him about what she'd done, she stepped away from him and closed the door.

"Something wrong?" he asked, his enthusiasm ebbing slightly.

"We need to talk."

"Is it important, or can we talk about it on the way to The Blue Oyster? A bunch of us from the office are going over for happy hour and I wanted you to come with me. You know most of them. Mitch, Dana, Carly, John, Thomas, and a few more. We're celebrating. We bagged that Boston client."

Damn, she didn't want to do this! "It's important."

He walked over to the couch and sit. "Okay, we'll talk here and then we'll go to happy hour."

"I wouldn't count on it," she mumbled under her breath as she walked to the couch, changed her mind about sitting down, then turned and paced back to the spot she'd just left. "I—uh—I… I—uh—I don't know where to start or how to…"

Alex leaned forward, braced his elbows on his knees and frowned. "I don't think I like the way you're pacing. Is something wrong? Did I do or say something to upset you?"

"No! You're perfect!" she rushed to assure him.

"I doubt that, Sweetness, but thanks for the vote of confidence." He smiled, visibly relieved whatever the problem, he was not at fault. "So, what's on your mind?"

"I've done something stupid—really stupid, and you're going to hate me for it." She fought to keep the tears scalding the back of her eyes at bay.

Alex shook his head and grinned at her. "I don't know. It'd have to be something really, really stupid for me to hate you."

He was teasing her, she knew, trying to make her feel better, but it wasn't helping. Hell, it was making her feel worse. He was so good, so caring. He didn't deserve the kind of trick she'd played on him.

"That's because you're under the influence," she blurted out before she lost her courage to tell the truth.

"Of what?" Alex looked completely confused, but not angry—at least not yet. "I haven't had a drop to drink. But if we could hurry this along, I can rectify that."

"Not alcohol. Voodoo."

"What!" Stunned, he stared at her for a heartbeat, then burst into laughter. "Damn, woman! You really had me going for a minute. Now, grab your purse and let's go. There are some people I want you to meet."

"No, Alex. I'm serious."

He stood, still laughing. "Come on, honey. Joke's up and we're late."

Oh, God, she had to make him understand. She wrung her hands, unsure what to say to make him believe her. "Please, Alex, will you just listen to me? I'm not kidding around."

Something in the way she looked at him or maybe the pleading tone of her voice must have gotten through to him. He sobered, nodded, then sat back down on the couch. "Okay, Jess. I'm listening."

"Remember when I asked you to taste-test my newest bon-bon last Friday?"

"Yes."

"Well, it was spiked with an aphrodisiac made by a voodoo spell."

He was laughing again. He was trying to hide it, but she could see the twitch of his lips, the over-bright glisten of laughter in his eyes and the slight shaking of his shoulders.

She rushed on, hoping he would see the truth of what she was telling him soon. "That's why you were about to jump out of your skin when you showed up at my place later that evening."

He shook his head. "I was horny because I'd sat and thought of you the whole damned day. If you remember, the night before had been exhilarating, but unfulfilling. Yeah, you had me wound up tighter than a bowstring, but it was because of the previous night and that come-and-get-me thingie you were wearing. Not some candy you gave me. It was pure and simple biology, Sweetness, not voodoo."

"The previous night had nothing to do with it." Jessica shook her head. "No, that's not true. I wouldn't have done what I did if I hadn't thought you were ready. Your eagerness… Wait! I'm getting ahead of myself." She paused to sniffle against her threatening tears. "This is so hard, a-and you're not making it any easier."

Alex moved to stand beside her, wrapped her in his arms, then apologized, "I'm sorry. I can see this is important to you. Come sit down. I promise I will listen to you without interrupting."

She nodded and let him lead her to the couch. Once they were seated, he kissed her temple and waited for her to speak. Taking a deep, bracing breath, she closed her eyes and sent up a prayer for guidance and clarity.

"Chronological order would probably be best," she whispered, unaware she'd spoken out loud until Alex agreed with her. Nodding, she turned to face Alex. "Okay. I've been in love with you for months."

She waited for a reaction from him, but none came, so she continued, "But I wouldn't let myself act on it because I thought you were recently widowed and needed time to grieve."

She glanced down at his wedding ring, then back to his face. This time he nodded, but still kept his promise to remain silent. "Then one day last week, Mitch nonchalantly mentioned how long ago your wife died, like everyone should know you've been widowed for three years. It was a very pivotal moment for me."

Good Lord, she silently chided herself. She sounded so businesslike, so factual, but maybe that's how Alex needed to hear the story, without her emotions mucking up her words and distracting him from their meaning.

"That's when I came up with the idea of the soup-tasting session. I even got Mitch out of the way that evening. Things were working out just the way I'd hoped, until you abruptly left."

"I'm sorry I ran out of you like that." Alex murmured, then squeezed her hand. "Had I known what you had to offer me, what we had to offer each other, an atomic bomb couldn't have blasted me out of your apartment that night."

Was he talking emotional connection, or just talking out of his voodoo-whammied mind?

God, she'd give anything, everything, if she could believe him! But she couldn't, wouldn't allow herself that fantasy. That wasn't Alex talking, but the aphrodisiac.

"I was so confused when you left. You had been so receptive, so—" She gave herself a mental shake and refocused on telling her story in a factual, forthright manner. "Anyway, when I get upset," she waved her hand in the air, "or whatever, I throw myself into my work. So I picked up an old family cookbook and started thumbing through it."

She took another deep breath, and forged ahead. "This is where the voodoo comes in."

Alex cocked a questioning brow at her. She doubted he even realized he'd done it.

"My great-grandmother, or was she my great-great grandmother?, not that it's important." Okay, her nerves were getting the better of her. She was starting to babble. Not a good thing. She mentally kicked herself for her lack of focus.

She had to get through this. She had to make Alex understand what she'd done and why.

"Let's just say that one of my ancestors was rumored to be a voodoo priestess. I found one of her recipes folded down between the pages of my cookbook. It was for 'limp noodles', only she wasn't talking pasta."

She took a deep breath. "Because of your mixed signals earlier that same evening and the revelation that you weren't still grieving your late wife, I decided you needed a nudge in my direction."

Jessica paused to study his face, to see if she could gauge his reaction from his expression. Nothing. No humor, no anger, no nothing. He was too calm, too blank.

A tingle of uneasiness skittered down her spine.

Finally he spoke, "So what did you do?"

"I—uh—made up a batch of the—uh—stuff, then laced a handful of bon-bons with it. Then I gave you the candy, making sure I'd be around when the effects kicked in."

Alex seemed to relax slightly. "Not that I'm saying I believe in any of this voodoo mumbo-jumbo, but because you obviously do, I'll play along. What harm has come of it? You gave me a nudge, I took it, and we're together. No biggie."

"But we're not together because you want to be. I think you're still under the influence of the candy."

Alex paused, as though trying to think logically through a minor problem. "Is there any way I can convince you that I'm not still 'under the influence'?"

Jessica glanced down at their joined hands. A ray of afternoon sunlight refracted off the gold of his wedding band. That damned ring symbolized his unwillingness to leave the past and rejoin the present. Him still wearing it spoke volumes—loud and clear.

"No."

"Fine, so how long does Great-Granny's aphrodisiac last?"

She hung her head, and admitted, "I don't know."

"You don't know?" Alex's calm veneer slipped slightly. "What was in that stuff?"

"Well, it's hard to say. Some of the phraseology was voodoo-based, not to mention over a hundred years old, so I had to guess at some of the instructions.

And some of the measurements weren't precise. A palm full of something is relative to the size of your hand, you know. So I had to guess at that, too. And then some ingredients in the recipe are not readily available anymore, so I had to substitute with the closest thing I could find."

Alex's demeanor moved a step closer toward agitated. "I want to see the recipe and a list of any adjustments you made."

She nodded and went to retrieve Chloe's cookbook from the bookcase. Moments later, she had the recipe and her adjustments laid out on her coffee table for his inspection.

Wordlessly, he scanned the scribbling on the age-yellowed paper, then stopped to read more intently. His head snapped up, heated shock sizzled in his eyes. "What the hell is Adam and Eve root?"

Jessica wrung her hands for the fiftieth time since Alex had shown up on her doorstep. "It's the root of an orchid, but I didn't use it. I substituted vanilla beans instead."

"Well, shit. I should be relieved, huh?" he quipped, his amused skepticism taking a back seat to his animated temper.

"It isn't the ingredients, but the spell I cast over them that I'm concerned about."

"You cast a spell over me?" he bellowed, outrage searing at the edge of his tone. "As in black magic, kill a rooster and drink his blood?"

Jessica's heart sank deeper into the cavern of her soul. He hated her. And had every right to do so. She willed herself not to cry. "It wasn't like that."

"Then how was it exactly?" Alex growled between his teeth. "Cause from where I'm sitting, it's not too pretty."

"I was playing around, looking for something to distract me from what had happened earlier—you know, when you came over Thursday night."

Alex nodded, but remained silent. Instinct told her his silence was a bad sign, a really bad sign. But she continued, "I didn't take it seriously. None of it, not the chanting, not waving the pussy willow over the cauldron, none of it."

"You have a cauldron?" he shouted.

"It was a saucepan on my fondue stand," Jessica exclaimed in self-defense.

Oh yeah, he was definitely pissed! He probably had macabre images of her dancing naked with a snake coiled around her neck while surrounded by chanting voodoo worshippers. This was bad. "I'm not a practicing voodoo priestess."

Alex retreated slightly, an odd expression crossed over his face.

Fisting her hands at her side, she glared at him. "Damn it, I just got caught up in the moment!"

"Thought you said you were just playing around." He sounded accusatory—and angry, very angry.

"I was but then weird stuff started happening. It was like some kind of mojo or power or something took over my body. I couldn't stop chanting, the room became hot and stuffy, suffocating, and then out of nowhere a puff of air blew out my candle."

"Un-freaking-believable," he spat with enough venom to kill.

"I thought I'd just gotten caught up in the moment until I sampled the concoction I'd brewed."

He cocked an eyebrow at her, but said nothing.

"I dabbed a little onto my finger and then tasted it."

Alex looked furious. "What happened?"

"A stab of sexual need bolted through me that almost knocked me to my knees. I was on fire from the inside out. If you'd been here with me, I don't know if I would have taken 'no' for an answer. I needed you that bad."

Alex paled. "And you gave me that shit to me! After that strong a reaction from just a little dab, you let me eat six large bon-bons full of that shit!"

"I didn't know you were going to eat the rest of them when I left the baggie with you." Jessica rushed to explain. "I know, it was stupid. I just didn't think—"

"Exactly! You didn't think." Alex lunged to his feet.

"I'm sorry, Alex. Really."

"So there was nothing in the candy to make me sick?"

"No, but with voodoo there are worse things than getting sick."

"Worse?" he hollered.

"That's what concerning me now," she admitted. "That's why I decided to tell you what I did."

He took a big, gulping breath then ran his hand over his face. "What is concerning you—exactly?"

"It's been over a week since I gave you the candy, yet you're still—er—lusting after me. I've been over the incantations a dozen times, but I can't figure out how long the effects are going to last or exactly how much of the candy I was suppose to administer."

"Administer? As in, if I hadn't willingly eaten the crap, you would have crammed it down my throat and held my nose until I swallowed it?"

"Please, Alex," she pleaded. "I know you're angry, and you have every right to be, but sarcasm isn't going to help."

"You damn right I'm angry" he growled. "You manipulated me into being your boy toy and expect me to be nice. Well, tough shit, baby. I'm pissed, seriously pissed, and sarcasm is just one of the by-products of the condition!"

Oh, this was not going well, not well at all. But then what did she expect? Grins and giggles?

They fell into a tension-filled silence. Alex paced. Jessica watched him. Every time his pacing took him within ten feet of her front door, she held her breath. She couldn't let him leave, not yet anyway. They needed to come up with a Plan B in case his symptoms didn't go away, or worse, intensified.

Closing her eyes, she tried to tamp down her growing fears. Oh, God! What had she done?

Knowing her next question was only going to infuriate him more, she squared her shoulders and pushed on. "Have you had any other weird urges or side-effects?"

"Like what?" he shot back at her. "Have I humped a pony or grown another dick?"

That did it. No amount of resolve could hold back her tears. She covered her face with her hands and sobbed. "Oh, God, I-I'm so s-sorry."

She heard Alex sigh in what only could be frustration and disgust, and then she heard him plop down into the recliner adjacent to the couch. After a moment, he said, "I'm sorry, too. I over-reacted."

That only made her cry harder.

He let her cry for another couple of minutes before he tried again to calm her. "You know, most drugs only last a few hours. The human body naturally flushes out impurities over time. Maybe voodoo spells work the same way."

She still didn't stop crying.

"Look at me, damn it." He tucked his finger under her chin, then lifted her face upward. "I'm fine. Still pissed at your manipulation, but physically I'm fine."

Gulping back her sobs, Jessica nodded. "I want you to leave."

"What?" By the tone of his voice, his "pissed" had just ratcheted up another couple of notches.

"I want you to leave me alone for at least a month. No dropping by, no calls, no morning coffee—no contact whatsoever."

"Why the hell would I do that?" he roared.

Oh, yeah, now he was way past "pissed". Sonic booms were more subtle than Alex's temper at the moment.

She said, "Maybe whoever you have first contact with after the candy kicks in leaves some kind of spiritual or chemical imprint on your system. Maybe if you're not around me for a while the effects will subside."

"That's ridiculous," he growled.

Ignoring his outburst, she went over to her door and opened it. "Drink plenty of fluids. Just in case it's as simple as flushing out your system."

"You're kicking me out?" He sounded indignant.

She kept her voice even and firm. "I have to do this."

Alex turned on her, spitting sardonic bitterness at his prey. "Don't kid yourself. And don't think you're kidding me."

"We need time apart from each other," she tried to explain one more time.

"All we were to you was a game of manipulation. Pull the strings on the Alex puppet and watch him dance to your tune."

"No, Alex, plea—"

"You played me well. Made me believe there was something between us, and then you fucked me three ways to Sunday." Alex's anger shimmered off of him in hot, fierce waves.

Jessica stared at a point just above his left shoulder. She couldn't stand to see the fury in his eyes. "I'm doing this for you."

"Don't do me any more fucking favors!"

She heard the underlying hurt in his enraged voice. Unable to stop herself, she reached for him.

He sidestepped her, then marched out the open doorway to his car. "Just remember this was your choice, not mine!"

She watched him peel out of the alley way and then tear down the street at twice the speed limit. Oh, God, she'd lost him.

Jessica collapsed to her knees and cried. She cried for what they shared and would never share again. She cried for what they could have been, but would never be.

She cried for the death of a beautiful love that might have been.

Chapter Seven

"What the hell is wrong with you?" Mitch demanded as he flipped on Alex's living room light.

Alex squinted against the brightness and grimaced. "Nothing. Go away."

Mitch ignored the invitation to leave and glanced around the littered room. Empty beer bottles cluttered every flat surface. Potato chip crumbs dusted the coffee table and floor. An opened pizza box occupied one end of the couch, only one slice missing. "Looks like you had a party."

"Yeah, a fucking celebration," Alex sneered just before he chugged his beer.

"And you didn't invite me? That's cold, buddy, real cold."

Alex glared at him as he watched his friend clear a place for himself on the couch. Obviously, he wasn't going anywhere soon.

Shit, Alex thought, he just wanted to be left alone. What was so hard about that?

Once settled on the couch, Mitch dogged on, "Thought you were coming to happy hour with us Friday?"

Alex glared harder at his thick-headed friend. Go away! he silently screamed.

"One minute you're grinning like a choir boy in a whorehouse, promising you'll meet us after you pick up Jessica, then two days later you're having a private pity party in the dark. What happened?"

Alex only grunted at him, then took a long, slow draw of his beer.

"Around nine, when there was no sign of you or Jessica, we took a survey on why we thought y'all were no-shows. Hot, sweaty sex won." Mitch cocked a questioning brow at Alex. All he got was stone, cold silence in answer. "What, the ole Alex Russell charm a little rusty? Couldn't talk her into it?"

Alex sighed in surrender. Mitch wasn't going to give up. It would be less time-consuming just to tell him what was going on, then kick his ass out the door. "Hot, sweaty sex with Jessica isn't the problem. That we did just fine."

"Really?" Mitch smirked, much like a father finding out his son was no longer a virgin. "How did that happen?"

"According to Jessica, voodoo."

The look on Mitch's face was so comical it almost made Alex smile. Almost, but not quite. Smiling took too much energy.

"You're going to have to explain that one."

Yeah, he figured as much. Not bothering to hide his irritation, he braced himself to tell the story.

"Evidently, after you told Jess that I've been widowed for three years, not months like she assumed, she put me on the top of her Men to do list." Alex paused to sip his beer again and explained the soup-tasting ambush to his friend.

Mitch nodded, then prompted, "What's all that got to do with voodoo?"

"Considering my obvious physical eagerness and then sudden departure from the soup ambush—"

Mitch's laughter interrupted Alex's clinical description. "Obvious physical eagerness? Sudden departure? You're not talking to your mother, asshole. Just so I get things clear, you want to put it in man words?"

"Okay, even though I was hard enough to break bricks with my dick that night, I hauled ass out of there. Clear enough for you?"

"Why the hell did you leave? Jess had gone to a lot of trouble. She wouldn't have turned you down."

"I—uh—I— Does it matter?" Alex stood abruptly, then had to wait for the room to quit spinning before heading to the kitchen for another beer. "You want a beer?"

"Yeah," Mitch called after him. "And it does matter why you left, but we'll get back to that later."

Alex came around the corner with two beers, handed one over, then returned to his seat. He looked at Mitch's curious but concerned face. Curiosity and concern clearly dominated his features. Strange, Alex hadn't thought of Mitch as anything more than a work/running buddy in a long time. But he was. He was a true friend, someone who was with him during the good times and the bad. Why—and how—had he forgotten the depth of their friendship?

Had he retreated so far back into his emotionless void that he couldn't connect with the people who cared about him?

He quickly shoved his thoughts away in self-defense. His brain was too muddled with beer and brooding to have such deep, disturbing thoughts.

"I'm not sure how to explain things," he began.

"Start from the beginning," Mitch suggested.

"Yeah, the beginning," Alex echoed. "That's how Jessica told it to me. Chronological order."

And so he did.

Ten minutes later, Mitch sat staring at Alex in dumbstruck disbelief.

Finally Alex couldn't stand it any longer. "Well, say something."

"She did all that for you?" Mitch's tone was almost reverent.

"You mean, to me," Alex corrected, curling his upper lip in a insolent snarl.

"What are you so pissed about?"

"Have you not been listening to me? She manipulated me into being with her!"

"Yeah, and if I were you, I'd be damned flattered."

Alex grunted at his friend. "You would."

Mitch rarely lost his cool, but his heated retort now made Alex flinch. "Do you know how special it is to have a woman want you enough to go to these kind of lengths just to be with you?"

"You sound jealous."

"Damned straight I am! No woman—I mean, absolutely no woman—has ever cared enough about me to do something like this." Mitch took a deep breath, then exhaled it slowly. After a moment, he softened his words and admitted, "I'm Johnny-on-the-spot if a woman wants a one-night stand or a weekend fling, but for any kind of longtime involvement, I suck."

A heavy, uncomfortable hush hung over them as they both groped for something to say. Mitch finally broke the silence. "So what's the problem?"

Alex's anger rolled to the surface again. He gritted his teeth against the searing heat of his fury. "She tricked me."

"You telling me you believe all that voodoo aphrodisiac bullshit?"

"Hell, no."

Mitch cocked an arrogant eyebrow at him, but said nothing.

Alex sighed, then expounded on his comment. "She tricked me into believing... something else."

"Into believing what?"

Alex glared at his friend. He wouldn't allow himself to even put into words what he'd been on the verge of believing. Putting it into words, saying those words out loud would make them real—make them tangible. He couldn't stand the pain of something like that, so he pounced on the first thing that came to mind. "She manipulated me. Isn't that enough?"

Mitch stared at him as though he could see right through him. "You're not mad at Jess. You're mad at yourself."

"Shut the fuck up."

"No, it's true. If you didn't care about her, you wouldn't be a tenth this angry. You're afraid she means something to you and that scares the hell out of you."

Alex leaned forward, braced his forearms on his knees, dropped his chin to his chest, then whispered, "Leave me alone."

"That's your problem, asshole! You've been alone too long. Jessica pulled you back into life and at the first sign of a snag, you bolt and run back into your safe little hidey-hole."

Alex stood, caught his balance, then crossed to the door and opened it. The universal signal for "Get the hell out of here!"

Mitch walked to the door. "You're pissing away a chance at happiness. Pissing it away, because it's easier than fighting for it."

Alex couldn't stand to hear Mitch's browbeating anymore. "Get out."

Mitch stepped through the doorway, then turned and spoke one more time, his words more imploring than angry. "For God's sake, Alex, don't be stupid."

Alex slammed the door behind his friend, flipped the light off, then marched back to his recliner.

He wasn't being stupid. He was being realistic. Jessica had manipulated him into being with her, and then when she got what she wanted from him, she'd cut him loose. He had every right to be mad as hell at the conniving bitch.

Only she wasn't a conniving bitch, a voice in the back of his mind screamed at him. She was Jessica, Sweetness, the woman who pulled him out of the emotionless void he'd been existing in for the last three years.

Granted, he might not have wanted to leave the safety of his emotionless existence, but it was the best thing for him.

Suddenly, Jessica's words came slamming back at him. "I've been in love with you for months. . . You had been so receptive. . . You needed a nudge in my direction. I'm doing this for you."

Damn it. Why had he allowed her to touch him, physically or emotionally?

Core-deep honesty answered his question before he could brace himself from the truth. He'd cared about her for months before he'd ever laid a hand on her, before he'd ever tasted the sweetness of her kiss or basked in the warmth of her love.

Alex squeezed his eyes shut against the pain of reality. He'd let himself love again and now he hurt—again. He hurt real bad.

But the last time he'd lost the woman he loved, fighting back wasn't an option. No one fought Death and won. But Jessica wasn't dead. She was out there, alive and obtainable. She made him feel alive too.

By God, she was his.

No one, not even Jessica herself, was going to take her away from him. He would fight until his dying breath for her.

Two weeks after she'd forced herself to let go of Alex, Jessica stepped into her apartment just as her phone rang. She froze. It was a knee-jerk reaction every time her phone rang or someone came to her door.

What if it was Alex? What if it wasn't?

He'd called at least ten times a day for the first week and half after she'd sent him away. But she wouldn't allow herself to answer her phone. If she heard his voice, she might falter and let him back into her life. That wouldn't be fair to him. Hell, it wouldn't be fair to her either. But she was so lonely for him she could easily talk herself into throwing her scruples out the bedroom window.

But she wouldn't do that to Alex. She loved him too much.

No, she was doing this for him. Living a miserable life without him was her penitence for what she'd done.

He'd even come by her apartment four or five times, but she wouldn't answer the door. That had been the hardest thing she'd ever done, seeing him through the window, knowing he was on the other side of the door, and not going to him. She'd cried for hours after he left.

Then three days ago he quit calling, quit coming around. She could only assume, her helpful nudge must have finally worn off.

And now he hated her.

God, she hurt!

Now the persistent ringing dragged her out of her painful pondering. Slowly, she gained enough composure to check her caller ID.

It was Alex.

She couldn't decide if Alex's call was a good sign or a bad one. Her answering machine played its message while she was still trying to figure out if she should pick up or not.

"Jessica, damn it, answer the phone!" He sounded angry—really angry. She backed away from the phone, putting as much distance between her and his anger.

Alex paused, probably waiting for her to pick up. It wasn't going to happen.

Then he moaned, long and low. Jessica heard agony in his voice, felt his pain rip through her own gut.

"I'm dying and it's your fault." He sounded weak now, like he couldn't fight the pain and still sustain his anger. "Please help me."

Oh, God, what had she done? She stepped forward, her hand outstretched, when the phone line went dead.

Jessica stood motionless while the impact of what Alex had said slammed into her. In the next pulse beat, she exploded into action.

Grabbing Chloe's cookbook and her car keys, she ran out the door. She had to get to Alex.

Oh, please, don't let him be dying!

Jessica pulled to the curb and stared at the gray frame house in front of her. It was the address she gotten from the phonebook, but something wasn't right.

There was painter's scaffolding erected across the front of the house. This couldn't be Alex's address.

He lived and breathed—hell, he bordered on worshipping—the status quo. He was so allergic to change he probably broke out in hives when he changed a light bulb. No way would he make such a drastic change as painting over a perfectly good paint job just for the sake of change.

Obviously, the phonebook was wrong, but maybe who ever lived here knew the correct address.

She leaped from her car and raced up the sidewalk. Trying to tamp down her panic, she knocked on the door.

What if these people didn't know Alex's address? Should she go back to her apartment and wait for him to call again? What if he didn't call back? What if the spell had rendered him unconscious and he couldn't call back?

Frantic, she pounded on the door again.

The door opened and a very healthy, very virile Alex stood grinning down at her. "Hi, Sweetness. It took you long enough to get here."

Relief washed over her with such force she almost staggered. Then fury brought her back to her senses. With Chloe's cookbook still clutched in her hand, she crossed her arms under her breasts and glared at him. "You said you were dying."

"I am."

"You look pretty damn good to me."

He grinned. "Thanks, you look pretty damn good to me, too."

"That's not what I meant and you know it!"

"Come inside so we can talk privately." Alex motioned her inside. When she stood her ground, he shrugged. "Fine, I'm sure the neighbors will enjoy the show."

Jessica grunted her frustration as she stepped inside. She squeezed her eyes closed and tried to remind herself that none of this was his fault. Slowly her temper subsided.

"You want something to drink? A beer or soft drink?" Alex asked as he closed the door behind her.

Suddenly, she remembered the scaffolding outside. "No," she answered. "I want to know— what's going on? Why is there scaffolding outside? Why did you trick me into coming here?"

"Fair enough questions, I suppose." Alex said as he moved past her to squat next to six gallons of paint lined up on a newspaper like tin soldiers. "Though your order of asking leaves a lot to be desired."

He held up his hand for silence when she opened her to mouth to speak. "As for what the scaffolding is for, well, it should be obvious. I'm painting my house. And I tricked you into coming because I need your help."

He systematically popped open the paint lids one by one as he spoke, "I'm tired of living in a gray world. My house is gray, my moods are gray, my life is gray. Gray is always just plain ole simple gray, never changing. The neutral of colors. Kind of how I've been living my life for the last couple of years. In neutral. No ups, no downs, no nothing. One day blending into the next and the next and the next after that."

Alex looked up and grinned at her. There was so much emotion in his eyes, truth, determination, resolve and a tenderness Jessica wouldn't let herself build her hope on.

She almost melted into a puddle right then and there.

"Pick a color, Sweetness." His husky plea sent shivers of longing through her soul.

Jessica looked down at the rainbow of colors Alex had displayed for her. Sunflower yellow, rich cranberry red, terra-cotta orange, seafoam green, caramel brown, and bubble gum pink beamed back at her. All bright, all vibrant, and not a shade of gray or even blue in the bunch.

The poignancy for his gesture formed an emotional lump in Jessica's throat she couldn't speak around. Silence hung between them, thick and uncertain.

Finally, she managed to squeeze a croak past the knot of tears in her throat. "I should choose the pink just to pay you back for tricking me into coming here."

Alex stood, then closed the gap between them. "When I called you, I said I was dying. It wasn't a trick. I've been an emotional zombie for years, that is until I met you. You've brought me back to life. And if I lose you, I'll die all over again."

"That's just the candy talking." Jessica tried to shake her head, but Alex held her firmly in place.

"No, it's not. You've been awakening emotions in me since the day I first met you. Every time I got near you another chunk of the wall around my heart fell away. After six months, there wasn't much barrier left to breach." Alex chuckled low in his throat. "You've been invading my thoughts, hell, my world, for months now. The candy didn't do it. If you'd given me another week on my own, we'd still have become lovers. Deep down I knew it was inevitable. I was just being stubborn-headed about it."

She wanted to believe him. More than she'd ever wanted to believe anything in her whole life, she wanted to believe him now.

He said, "The gray world I lived in is my past. You are my future, my happiness. I want to be with you. Hell, I want to marry you. I want us to be together every day of the rest of our lives, but I'm willing to wait until you're ready for a lifemate." He kissed her forehead, then pulled away from her slightly. "Please note, I said lifemate, not roommate or bed partner. I love you, Sweetness. I refuse to spend another minute without you in my life."

Jessica turned her face toward his left hand to place a kiss in his palm and froze. His wedding ring was gone. A slim, pale mark encircled his bare ring finger.

Could it be true? Could he be speaking from his heart and not parts south of his belt?

Alex lowered his head until he touched his forehead to hers and whispered,

"I said I was dying. I am, I swear, I am. Every minute away from you, knowing I'm not going to be a part of your life, I die a little inside."

Jessica swallowed hard against the knot of tears in her throat, closed her eyes and sent a prayer of thanks heavenward. Alex loved her.

He raised his head and stared at her. The truth of his words, the depth of his emotions plainly stamped across his face. He was scared to death she was going to walk away from him. "For God's sake, Jessica, say something."

"I love you, Alex Russell. I think I loved you the first moment we met. And I will love you until the day that I die."

He crushed her to him, then lowered his mouth to hers and consumed her with his greedy kiss. She sank into him, into his embrace, his kiss, his soul.

Slowly he lessened the pressure of his mouth against hers, then peppered kisses over her entire face. Laughter bubbled up inside him.

"What?"

"If I throw you over my shoulder and head for the bedroom, will you think that damned voodoo candy has kicked in again and doubt my profession of love?"

Looping her arms around his neck, she wrapped her legs around his waist, then rocked against him. "I'll never doubt your love again."

Alex nuzzled her neck and headed toward the bedroom. "God, I can't get enough of you."

Jessica laughed against his shoulder. "And if you ever think that you have had enough of me, I have just the little bon-bon to change your mind!"

About the Author:

Kathy Kaye is a female counterpart of a true Southern-bred good-ol' boy. When she's not busy raising three boys, two she birthed and one she married, she writes both romantic comedies and paranormal romances.

She attributes a goodly amount of her romance-writing success to her family who taught her how to love and how to express that love openly and with enthusiasm. Her husband, however, credits it to her wacky—sometimes warped—sense of humor. But he's an Aggie, so what does he know?

Kathy loves hearing for her readers and can be contacted at: KathyKaye_author@yahoo.com.

Fatal Error

by Kathleen Scott

To My Reader:

Some stories are crafted through blood, sweat, and frustrated tears. Others write themselves. For me, *Fatal Error* was the latter. I hope you enjoy Jesse and Soran's story as much as they enjoyed telling it to me.

Chapter One

The virus was not downloading fast enough. Each movement of the clock drew Jesse closer to danger. Soon the sparse night shift—nine employees for all thirty floors, including six live security guards—would be clocking in, and with them one Soran Roberts.

After denying himself the pleasure for so long, Jesse ached to see Soran again. But now was definitely not the time. The Restoration Brigade was counting on his expertise to plant this cascading virus directly into the computer's gray matter. He owed them his life; he couldn't fail them now.

Sweat rolled from his forehead and dripped into his eyes. The screen before him flashed a warning. He ventured a quick glance around the cramped server room, littered with the connections needed to run the vast computer system. Was it just his imagination or had one of the network cables from the main server just moved?

The screen flashed again. Only fifteen percent more until the download was complete. Too bad this virus wouldn't shut the network down of its own accord. This particular virus needed further commands so it could spread. But those would be given from a remote location with him nowhere around.

Getting into the Complex had not been difficult, what with the stolen access cards and synthetic fingerprints molded from those of a disgruntled employee. But breaking into the brain case of the system had been another matter.

He turned his wrist to look at his watch. Shit. Time was running short. Christ, he didn't want to run into her.

Only a few more moments and the virus would be planted directly into the system, and this would allow the common man to reclaim the country. Jesse tried to tell himself that he was being altruistic in his crusade to reform the government through subversive means. But truthfully, he had only to remember Soran and no other motivation mattered. She was the love of his life, though she never knew it.

Back in college, he would never have dreamed that his life would take such a desperate path. Back in college, he wanted only to help make the world a better place. If he had only understood the consequences of his actions back then, he would not be here now staring at the bare wires of a computer gone rogue.

Darkness flashed from the corner of his eye as something sinister tightened around his torso. Cables yanked him backward toward the gray matter. The computer was defending itself against the viral attack. As the cables squeezed his ribs, a name fell from his lips.

"Soran…"

Soran Roberts stood in the glowing blue lights of her office's outer chamber. Her employee badge glowed brightly as she swiped it in a downward stroke through the security lock and listened for the mechanism to disengage. Self-consciously she looked up into the lens of the security camera. Just like all the other cameras throughout the Complex, this one stood as an unblinking paranoid witness to the comings and going of employees. Even the smallest infraction of the rules and management would exact retribution on the hapless worker. It was no way to work, and a worse way to live.

Finally, the door clicked open, and Soran pushed it the rest of the way and started for her terminal.

Minimal light shone in through the open blinds. Illumination in the windows of nearby office buildings shone like stars twinkling in the urban sky. The city held such beauty at night. From here one could not see the dirt and decay of man's need to over-industrialize his surroundings. The darkness that bathed the streets hid the pollution and made the city appear almost pristine.

Soran removed her jacket and hung it over the back of her chair, then sat and pushed the button to bring her terminal online, looking up at the screen imbedded deep into the partition in front of her. To maintain the Complex's stark appearance, all terminal screens were placed in the walls and covered with a thick plastic cover. The keypads were under the counter surfaces with micro-sensors under each character. The setting reflected the Complex's personality perfectly: cold, distant, and unfeeling. If there hadn't been such a great paycheck and benefits package attached, she would have found less conspicuous work at one of a thousand offices that made their homes in the city.

Soran worked as an account auditor for the Complex. All contracts had to be justified and reconciled before the beginning of the next business day. Any discrepancies had to be cleared on her shift so the drones on the day shift could start fresh at the opening of business. Most nights Soran finished her tasks by one or two a.m. and spent the rest of the shift downloading sample portfolios for the next day. That little extra had not been part of her job description, but her initiative had earned her points with management.

Her hands skimmed efficiently over the keypad, entering the access codes to run the DPP—Discrepancy Profile Program—the screen blinked at her, then shut down. Damn! Now she'd have to reboot the system.

To bring the system back online after a fault required a new sequence of codes. Quickly, Soran keyed in the sequence and waited for the system to run a diagnostic before moving automatically to the DPP.

As programs clicked and whirled by, the terminal bathed her face in a blue glow and strobed her in the panorama of the flashing screens. The DPP sequence began and Soran rubbed her hands together, anxious to get started on her work.

The screen flashed at her a few more times before large letters filled the screen: FATAL ERROR. The terminal shut down for a second time, and Soran groaned.

Never in her five years of employment at the Complex had she ever had so much trouble getting the programs up and running. It was useless to try another staffer's terminal as each keypad verified the assigned user by reading the fingerprints. After the Software Wars, fingerprints had become a hot commodity, leading to the reprehensible act of stealing fingers from corpses to defraud the government.

She sat back in her chair and let out a sigh, looking up at the ceiling in search of an answer. What stared back at her made her breath catch. A camera.

When had that been installed? It hadn't been there last night.

Hair prickled on the back of her neck with the thought of being watched by management. Her memory rushed to recall just one small infraction of the rules she had ever committed, but found none. What had gone on in this office during the day to make security place cameras here? Whatever the reason for the invasion of her sanctum, Soran didn't like it one bit. It wouldn't be the same, working at her terminal and feeling compelled to look up every few minutes into the unblinking lens of the Complex's watchful eye.

Paranoia filled her stomach with unease. Perhaps she should just force herself to get back to work. But the terminal still had not rebooted, and if she had too many discrepancies, she'd be all night reconciling the accounts.

She closed her eyes and drew in a few deep breaths, expanding her lungs fully and exhaling through her nose. The exercise calmed her somewhat—enough to try the next sequence of reboot codes.

These particular codes would lock her into NATNET, the mainframe computer that serviced the entire country. Everything from government agencies to power plants to traffic lights were powered by this mega-network. All major corporations used NATNET to back up their internal networks, and the Complex was no exception to this rule.

She put on the headset that would allow her to communicate with NATNET directly.

It always made Soran uneasy to connect with the central network. NATNET was too infiltrated into the daily life of every citizen. With the touch of a few buttons, the government could pick your pocket and invade your privacy. Everyday millions lived with the knowledge that they were only a few keystrokes away from the total destruction of their business, home, or even life. It only took one operator with a grudge to bring everything you'd worked for crashing down around you.

Before starting college, Soran had never questioned the right of the government to such intimate dealings with the common citizen. The world had always worked in such a way. People went on about their lives and never paid attention to the whispers of a few misguided individuals who fought to change the world. But a few of her college classmates had protested the government's infringements of 'certain inalienable rights'—they had never been seen nor heard from again. Unease moved through her whenever she thought about all the friends she'd lost over the years.

A face came to mind and her heart thudded against her ribs. A sob climbed into her throat. Jesse.

Jesse had been her math finance tutor. He was young and intense, but never talked about the clandestine activities that finally had him arrested by government agents. All she could remember was watching him being hauled off to jail in electronic handcuffs. He looked into the crowd through his thick corrective lenses; his thin frame no match for the large guards on either side of him. Yet he fought on, only to lose in the end.

His incarceration was a lesson to Soran to stay in line no matter what. So, like the sterile, nighttime halls of the Complex, Soran had for many years remained silent and uninteresting to anyone who might be watching her. But that pose was harder and harder to maintain recently. Lately, rebellion against the status quo burned deep in her belly. Years of silence against those who would control every thought and action of the populace shamed her for not taking a stand. She just never knew how she could be of assistance. She had no real power to do anything other than plug along and try to survive the best she could in a world run amok with governmental interference.

The NATNET screen flashed, pulling her from her subversive thoughts.

"Hello, Soran Roberts," said the tinny mechanized voice.

"Hello, NATNET. I'm having problems establishing a link with the Complex mainframe. Can you help?"

"Link established."

Numbers danced across the screen quickly in a ballet of binary code as NATNET sought the problem and tried to correct it.

"Internal contaminant sensed," NATNET said after a few moments.

"What kind?" Soran leaned forward in her chair and watched the screen closely for anything that would indicate a contaminant—a sequence out of order, a break in code, lost information, anything. She saw nothing out of place.

The monitors on the vacant desks whirled to life. Soran's attention left the screen before her to gaze at the monitors that showed the head and shoulders of a man. Interference turned the picture into a series of broken pixels, distorting his image.

His lips moved, but the only sounds Soran could hear were the snap and pop of static. Then faintly, so she had to stand to hear, came a plea, "Help me."

"Internal contaminant in monitoring sector of program."

Soran had no idea what to do, but knew she needed more time to figure it out. "Thank you, NATNET, I think I can work out the problem from here."

"Help me, please. Cables tightening."

Soran looked up at the man as his image faded in and out. Where was he? Would he even hear her if she replied to him?

The monitoring system's controls were part of the Complex's mainframe computer, but if NATNET shut down the system she would have no access to it. Soran glanced at the screen in front of her as it went blank. Too late.

Around her the other monitors showed the man's stark pain. His face contorted into a horrible grimace of agony. What were they doing to him? And who were 'they'? How did the monitors pick up and transmit it to her when they were closed circuit to the Complex proper? Could he be somewhere in the labyrinth of corridors that comprised the Complex?

The screen before her came to life again.

"System purge failed," NATNET informed her.

Soran leaned forward as if talking intimately to a friend. "NATNET, abort purge attempts."

The computer continued to whirl and screens to flash by. "Unable to comply. Contaminant mobile."

She needed override commands, but those particular codes were not available to a low-level operator. Only a government operator had the authority to override actions taken by NATNET to correct a problem. But perhaps she could send NATNET another problem to solve until she could figure out a way to communicate with the man inside the monitoring sector.

"NATNET, run DPP for Complex."

"Unable to locate program at this time."

"Run system diagnostics for Complex."

"Diagnostics running."

The man in the monitor pressed his face against the lens. Sweat beaded his skin and made it stick to the glass. "Can anyone hear me?"

"I can hear you. Please, try to stay calm. I'm trying to help you, but I don't know how." Soran spoke into the microphone, hoping that her voice would be picked up by the system and find its way to him, and that NATNET wouldn't report her for trying to communicate with a *contaminant*.

He curled up a fist and pounded it against the camera. "Help me, please."

The area behind him was comprised of hard wire and circuitry. She searched her memory for any place in the Complex that looked like that. But her orientation tour had included only her office, the restrooms, and snack bar. All other areas had been off limits unless she was accompanied by a member of security or management.

"NATNET, display map of Complex."

"That information is classified."

She snapped, "Fine, then display an index of offices."

Screens passed by her in cyberspace until a legend popped up on the screen. Research and Development was located in the basement. Executive Offices were in the penthouse. Safety and Security was conveniently located in between on the fifteenth floor. But the office listing meant nothing to her, as she had no idea where to look.

A cough and sob grabbed her attention. The man in the monitor slid down pulling the camera with him. From the angle of the lens Soran could see the man's torso confined in tentacles of mechanized cables. Biceps bulged as he tried to pry the tentacles from his lean waist. His face turned red and veins bulged on his forehead as the tentacle squeezed.

She had to act fast or the cables would crush him.

"NATNET, is contaminant still in monitoring sector?"

"Affirmative."

"Where is the monitoring sector located?"

"That information is classified."

Soran blew out a breath and ran her hand through her hair. Of course that information was classified.

"Return control of terminal to manual operator," Soran directed the government mainframe.

"Unable to comply."

"NATNET, kill auxiliary power to monitoring sector."

"Unable to comply."

Soran looked up at the monitors. The man lay quiet and lifeless, his mouth open and jaw slack. She couldn't tell if he had passed out, or if the long arms of technology had finally neutralized him.

The monitor hissed and static covered it once again, obscuring her view of the trapped man.

"NATNET, is contaminant still viable?"

"Affirmative. Contaminant mobile."

Soran breathed a sigh of relief. If he was moving, then he was not hurt as bad as she feared.

"NATNET, can you determine the location of contaminant?"

"Negative." The system blinked again. "Attempting to establish tracking modulator."

Soran didn't know what that was, but it sounded heinous.

A quick glance at the screen showed the man was gone. The monitor reflected

Soran's own face staring back at her.

"Status report."

"Monitored dimensions rerouted. Cannot establish tracking modulator." Was it Soran's imagination, or did the computerized voice sound slightly frustrated?

"NATNET, try establishing link to monitoring systems and route to this terminal."

"Application codes needed for order verification."

"Override application codes."

"Override forbidden."

Soran slammed her fist on the counter and yelled in the headset. "Do you want to find the contaminant or not, you stupid piece of mechanized refuse?"

"Insults unappreciated. Restate command."

"Motherfucker," Soran said under her breath.

"Command designated immoral. Restate command."

Soran shook her head. Here she was trying to save a life, and the damned government mainframe was trying to instill a lesson on moral language.

She suddenly had an idea, and typed the sequence codes into her terminal.

"NATNET, shut down system completely and bring back online in start-up sequence."

"Unable to comply. Full shut down will bypass contaminant tracking modulator attempts."

Soran sighed. "Fine. How long will it take to establish tracking modulator once it becomes operational?"

"Link established instantaneously."

"How close are you to establishing modulator?"

"Still attempting diagnosis."

Soran smiled.

She placed the headset on the counter and rose. While the computer worked on that particular problem, she would work on the other—locating the contaminant.

She couldn't let them kill him.

Chapter Two

Jesse crawled along the floor of what the IT crew called the "Cerebellum." Everything had been on schedule for the Galileo Project, until the computer decided it no longer agreed with the charter. It spit the programming back out declaring the entire team guilty of heresy against the government, then turned the programmers' own work against them. All corrective programming couldn't revert the computer back to manual operations. Jesse had warned his colleagues in college against this very thing. No one listened to him then, and now—well, if he couldn't make it out of the Cerebellum, he wouldn't be able to tell anyone anything again.

He placed a hand to his sore ribs. The damn cable had squeezed him so tightly he knew he had to be bruised. The pain had been so bad he'd lost consciousness for a second or two. Now, it hurt to take a deep breath, and even his slow crawl across the floor caused him immeasurable pain.

The door loomed before him like some metal centurion guarding the gates to paradise. Only a few more feet and he would be home free. Well, with the exception of actually making it out of the Complex alive. This had not been part of the bargain when he agreed to plant the virus directly into the system.

Once he reached the door, Jesse leaned against it to catch his breath and rest. The cables that tried to squeeze the life from him lay lifeless in a pile a few feet away. Their severed circuits gaped from an open wound like the guts of some mechanized sea serpent. His hand slid unconsciously to touch the metallic glass hunting knife he wore on his hip. Thankful fingers gave the weapon a loving caress.

It would only be a short time before the Cerebellum rerouted the command to another set of cables and his life would again be in peril. Painfully, he inched up the door to a standing position and turned the cold metal handle. Nothing happened.

"Shit!"

The computer mainframe must have established new lockout commands for the room. There had to be a manual override box somewhere nearby. Such information should have been given to him beforehand, so he could have cut that power before ever venturing into Cerebellum's matrix. That's what happened when you worked for a group rather than yourself. Important information or details got missed, and then someone ended up either injured or dead. Jesse shook his head as he searched the walls beside the door. He had no one to blame but himself for this fuck up. He should have asked the questions before ever volunteering for the mission. But the temptation to be in the same building as Soran was too intense to ignore, even if he had no intention of seeing her.

The walls appeared clean to inspection, no telltale sign of a lock circuit override box. However, that didn't mean there wasn't one. Jesse moved slowly into a squat, holding his injured ribs with his hand pressed tightly to his side. His eyes slowly scanned the wall in front of him. From his angle, it didn't look as strong as the other walls. Even the paint didn't reflect the sheen from the blue security lights in quite the same manner. Curious, he extended his hand to feel along the floorboards. A very slight, nearly imperceptible breeze teased his fingertips.

Jesse eased the glass knife from the sheath and slid the tip in the seam between wall and floor. The knife was slightly too thick, and he couldn't get much leverage. But maybe he could pry up the edge enough to get a fingerhold on it. As he moved the knife out, he turned it upward as much as he could. Not good enough. The panel would not be budged in so crude a manner.

He sat back on his haunches and blew out a pained breath at the movement. Then he saw it, just off to his left. A small round depression about the size of the tip of a pen nib marred the otherwise uniformity of the wall. Jesse stuck the knife tip into the indentation and smiled when the hiss of locks sounded around the wall panel. Pneumatic hinges slid the section open to reveal not what he had been looking for, but something infinitely better.

Chapter Three

Soran's heels made quick clicking sounds along the deserted corridor. She didn't quite know where she was headed, but figured it would be better to at least get a look around rather than sit in front of the terminal and wait for information that the computer wasn't willing to give up. Provided, of course, that security didn't see her skulking around halls and trying to gain access to offices off-limit to her.

She stopped in front of the elevators and pressed the down button. There was a very good chance she wouldn't be able to access the doors for Research and Development, but that was the most likely place to start.

The metal doors jerked open then tried to close before Soran could enter. She frantically waved her hand in front of the light sensor before stepping into the car. Buttons lined the right side of the interior of the car, but as Soran scanned the list she noticed there wasn't one earmarked for the basement. The basement must be accessible only by another elevator—one reserved for the most trusted employees. Not her.

She could always try the Safety and Security Office. As she reached out to push the button for the fifteenth floor, the car jerked into motion and began a slow ascent.

"What the...?"

Lights blinked on one by one. Twenty-four. Twenty-five. Twenty-six and on.

The elevator stopped in between twenty-nine and thirty, easing to a halt.
Crash!

Something hit the top of the car with force and speed. The car shimmied under the impact, and Soran let out a yelp of surprise. A piece of the roof lifted off, causing Soran to move out of the way and look up in disbelief as a man lowered himself into the car with her. He leaned against the far wall taking in quick shallow breaths. He held his ribs tightly.

Soran recognized the man from the monitor, the one she had come to save. "You!"

The man looked up at her. A look of stark surprise came and went under the flash of his dark lashes. "Sorry. I didn't know this car was occupied."

It took her a moment to collect her thoughts after his reply, but when she did she hurried to him and gave him a quick look up and down. He appeared to be all in one piece, though he favored his ribs quite a bit. His face pulled into a pained grimace when he moved. She stopped her physical assessment of him. "I was coming to rescue you. How did you get away?"

He gave her his own cool up and down appraisal. "You? How?"

"I'm Soran Roberts. I work in accounting. The camera transmitted what was happening in the monitoring sector."

He gave a deep disturbing laugh and shook his head. "An accountant. Figures. Good thing I rescued myself then."

For some reason his attitude rankled. "What? You think accountants incapable of heroic deeds? I kept the computer busy until I could find you."

"Well, you found me all right." He grimaced again then sucked in a breath. He didn't look so happy to be found. But more importantly, who the hell was he, and what was he doing in there in the first place? How did he get passed all the security checkpoints? Soran raised a brow and crossed her arms over her chest, trying to affect her most intimidating pose. "How did you get into the monitoring system in the first place?"

"I just walked in. Now, could you hit the down button so I can get the hell outta here before that damn computer really kills me?"

Soran moved stiffly to punch the down button, wishing ungraciously he had been hurt worse. Here she was, probably putting her job in jeopardy just by being with him, and he wasn't at all grateful. "You know I was trying to locate you while I was jacked into NATNET. The authorities probably already know you're here. Security could stop the elevator before you ever get out of the building."

"I'm sure they'll try." The man rose away from the wall and came towards her. Pain etched lines around his mouth.

She stood her ground. "What were you doing in there?"

"Maintenance."

"Not likely." Fear made her keep the charge of corporate sabotage at bay. Even hurt, he could easily overpower her. "The Complex monitors will feed the information into NATNET's mainframe."

"Christ, lady. That's probably already happened. I mean, who do you think you work for?"

Soran frowned at him, not understanding the question. "I work for the Complex."

"And what do you think the Complex is?"

Suddenly, she caught his meaning as ice ran through her veins. "Are you implying that the Complex and NATNET are the same?"

"Yeah," he said. "It's all one big network. Controlling everything." She shook her head. It couldn't be true. "Since when?"

"For longer than I care to admit to."

She stared at him and said, "Then you're here to—"

Then she stopped. Did she really want to know?

Jesse looked at her shocked face. A face he remembered vividly in dreams while incarcerated. Soran. The Pristine Queen. How in the hell did he get so unlucky as to run into her while she was trying to save him? Still too trusting after all these years. Still so goddamned beautiful. Still so untouchable.

Now her cornflower blue eyes stared at him in patent disbelief, whether over his open appraisal of her or telling her about NATNET, he wasn't sure. Soft pink lips parted. Christ, how he'd fantasized about that mouth—sometimes while she had been sitting next to him in his dorm room. It was an angel's mouth.

Her porcelain skin was still flawless. The tight auburn curls fell down her shoulders and brushed against the curve of her pert breasts.

He swallowed.

Under the fluorescent lights he could clearly see her breasts. She didn't have a thing on under the thin silky fabric of her shirt. They were beautiful, perfectly round breasts, with puffy aureoles and juicy nipples. What he wouldn't give to be able to suck them into his mouth.

He broke off that thought and let his gaze slide down to her footwear. The 'fuck me' boots on her dainty feet made his head spin. Oh damn, he wished this were another time and place. That so many years hadn't separated them. That he hadn't needed to protect her from the activities in his past.

Jesse shifted his weight, feeling the fullness of her gaze on him. No telling what she'd do if she realized she occupied an elevator with a man who had loved her so much, he'd sacrificed everything to make the world safe for her and to right the wrongs he'd committed in his gullible youth.

The sad fact of the matter was even if his thin frame hadn't filled out and he hadn't gone for the cosmetic eye surgery, she probably wouldn't remember him. Pristine women like Soran Roberts never really saw guys like Jesse had been.

Then a thought struck him. "What floor is your office on?"

"Twenty-three. Why?"

He brushed passed her as her perfume ripped his concentration from its moorings. He hit the button for twenty-three with all the sexual frustration he felt at being in close confines with his fantasy woman again. The car started moving down the shaft and he turned to her.

She wouldn't like what he had planned, but his colleagues could use a little more help on their side. And they were about to get it in the unwilling person-age of one Soran Roberts. Her keyboard would prove to be a valuable tool to bring the virus live, and she was the only person who could use it.

She didn't even recognize him. Of course, he didn't want her to recognize him. But still--

The elevator stopped, and he pulled her along with him. Heat radiated through his palm where it touched her skin. The skin on her arm was just as silky as it looked.

"Which direction?" he asked, his voice gruff with overwhelming desire and the need to get them both out of the building before security became aware of the problem within the systems.

"I'm not taking you to my office." She unsuccessfully dug her high heels into the slick linoleum flooring as Jesse began to drag her along.

"I beg to differ."

They reached the door, and he jerked her I.D. from around her neck and held her struggling hand to the plate. The doors hissed open and he shoved her through.

"Which desk?"

He made a quick sweep of the room and found only one with the screen glowing with the Complex's logo as screensaver. Above them, security cameras tracked and recorded their movements. He needed to put the fear of government into the woman beside him, and bind her to him through an action the authorities would never question, to make it clear she was his accomplice—or even more than that.

A smile tilted the corner of his mouth as he reached for her.

"Hey, what do you think you're..."

His mouth came down on hers, filling his head with her taste and scent. Those pink, pouting lips of hers parted in surprise, and Jesse took the advantage by slipping his tongue into the hot recesses of her mouth. He knew she'd taste good, but damnit all she tasted like every carnal thought he'd ever had. Eating her alive wouldn't satisfy his appetite for her now.

Hands pushed against his chest as he settled into the kiss, stroking her tongue with his. He grew hard, half from the long years of fantasies he'd held of her, half from finally having her in his arms. He brushed his throbbing erection against her mound, coaxing all the sensation he could from her. He angled his head to the side for better access, to deepen the contact with her.

A moan filled his mouth, but Jesse couldn't be sure who it came from. Hard nipples pressed into his chest as she stopped fighting him and tried to move closer. How many times had he closed his eyes and imagined this prelude to lovemaking? How many sleepless nights had he lain awake with the dreams of her responsiveness to him flooding his mind and heart?

Jesse moved back slightly, nipping at her juicy bottom lip with his teeth. His hands skimmed up her sides to cup her lovely breasts. Knowledgeable thumbs grazed across the tips. She sucked in a shocked breath and stole air from his body.

Slowly her languid eyes slid open and she looked at him through the haze of desire. Her breath came in small pants between her still parted lips. The heartbeat near his hand remained rapid. Looking at her in such a state, he wondered if she'd ever been kissed like that before. The question sent him into a spiral of longing.

Need seared him. He moved his mouth from hers and took a tight nipple into his mouth, teasing it with his tongue through the filmy shirt. Her hands slid over his shoulders and into his hair to hold him in place. His hand pressed across her back, and she arched into him, thrusting her breast deeper into his mouth.

Better judgment should prevail. He couldn't afford the time right now to make love to her properly. But he would—later—when they were back in the safety of the hideout.

Reluctantly he moved her away from him and pulled his knife from the holder.

Shock made her back up, registering the threat as to her person and not her workstation. Knives such as this were a rarity, and could cut through any substance natural or manufactured. Jesse turned and sent the glass hunting knife deep into the plastic cover of the desktop.

"Oh, my God! What are you doing? Are you crazy?" She tugged at his arm to get him to stop.

"No, I'm quite sane."

"I'm going to get in trouble for this. How could you? I can't work without my terminal."

He looked over his shoulder at her as he sawed the serrated edge through the thick covering. "You'll be able to work, just not here."

"What do you mean?"

He finished cutting the perimeter and lifted the cover off, exposing the touch-sensitive pads beneath. "Come to daddy."

A thin cable attached the keyboard to the monitor and thus the mainframe. Quickly, Jesse disconnected the cable and tucked the keyboard under his arm. "Come on, let's go."

"I'm not going anywhere with you." Soran stuck her chin out at him defiantly and crossed her arms under her breasts. Her impertinent right nipple stuck to the slick fabric of her shirt, wet with his attentions, and undermined her obstinacy.

"Oh, I think you will." He pointed up to the camera above them. "After the way you responded to me, there's no way in hell your superiors aren't going to believe you aren't up to your sweet ass in this with me."

Blood drained from her face. A shaking hand pressed against the swollen lips he had thoroughly ravished only moments before. "You bastard."

He shrugged and started for the door. "You better come with me before this place is swarming with security. The keyboard cable also acts as a silent alarm in case someone tries to make off with them." He held it up slightly away from him for emphasis. "Like me."

Indecision kept her in place for only a moment before she hurried after him and into the deserted corridor.

Chapter Four

Soran watched his back as he moved quickly down the hallway. It was a broad back with the taut muscles emphasized under the stretch of his tight t-shirt. He leaned to the side to protect his hurt ribs, the stolen keyboard tucked up against him. The machine must have hurt him worse than he appeared to be. Worse than he'd appeared a moment before when he'd kissed her.

Self-consciously her hand moved to her mouth again, then plucked her shirt from her breast. Never had she been kissed so thoroughly. He acted as if he were starved for the taste of female flesh. She'd wanted to fight him, really, but his mouth had been magic, his touch electric. Memories of his ridged shaft pressed against her flooded her with heat. Liquid pooled between her nether lips, and the wet fabric of her panties slid against her as she walked.

He turned and pinned her with wicked hazel eyes. "Move faster or I'll leave you to face NATNET security."

She stopped dead in her tracks. "I'll just tell them it was a mistake."

Hazel eyes glared at her, pinning her with accusation. "A mistake? Do you honestly think anyone would believe you now?"

It was true. He'd screwed her chances to talk her way out of trouble but good. It took her only a moment to decide her future. She may not know who he was, or his purpose in invading the NATNET computer, but he definitely seemed capable of getting her out of the building. She'd just have to worry about the rest later.

She picked up the pace as much as she could in her high heels. She would choose tonight of all nights to flaunt convention and wear impractical boots. He stopped at the elevator and held the door for her.

"Not that way," she protested.

"I'm not using the stairs. They're slower, more chances of getting caught."

"But the elevator is obvious. They'll expect us to come down that way."

"Then what do you suggest?" he bit out between tight lips.

"The dumbwaiter." She turned down another hallway and led him to a metal door that rolled upward. The dumbwaiter had been placed in the building to make hauling equipment more efficient and to leave the elevators free for employees.

She pushed the button and the door opened, revealing a sizable metal cage connected to pulleys. The door of the cage swung open, and Soran held her hand out, motioning him to get in first.

He stopped and looked at her. "How are we supposed to work it once we get on?"

"Look, buster, I never claimed it was a good plan, but it's still a hell of a lot better than doing the obvious." She looked at the controls on the outside and to the space between them and the cage. Her arms weren't long enough to reach.

She shooed him into the doorway. "Get on, I'll set the controls and get in behind you." At the far end of the hallway, the other set of elevator doors opened and the sounds of running feet echoed down the corridor. "Go."

She watched him get on the dumbwaiter as she set the controls for the first floor. The heavy door started to roll down and Soran dove for the narrow opening. An arm grabbed her and pulled her forward through the portal, and then he reached over and closed the cage door. Momentum caused her to crash up against him. A quick rush of pain and air came out of him as she hit his chest. She slid down the front of him and onto the floor and stayed there, fighting for breath. Living a life of crime was just not something Soran ever thought she'd be good at, not to mention it was hard on the nerves.

She lay on her back for a moment, getting her breath back. She felt her mini-skirt ride up on her thighs and realized this gave him a clear shot of her white lacey panties. His gaze centered on the fabric and burned her to the spot. A hungry look came into his eyes. This wasn't the time, and it sure wasn't the place, but she felt his need.

She saw his need too. Soran let her gaze caress the front of him, coming to rest on the noticeable bulge in his baggy pants, evidence of his arousal. She couldn't have moved if she wanted to. Did she want to? God, no. She wanted the spell to last, for his unwavering gaze to be replaced by his hands, his mouth. But how could she feel lust for a man who had single-handedly ruined her life and put her on the run? He terrified her at the same time he excited her.

He lifted his eyes to hers. Could he read the hot thoughts that ran through her mind? Their gazes locked and her breath hitched.

The cage began to rattle down the shaft. The motion jarred her, opening her thighs even more, an unintentional invitation that she did not withdraw. She knew he could see the wetness on her crotch. His nostrils flared and pupils dilated.

The cage swung as he knelt to bury his face between her thighs. Teeth nipped at her lips through the soft lace barrier. The curve of his nose nudged against her throbbing clit. She moaned.

A finger hooked under the elastic and skimmed through her drenched folds. "God, I've never smelled anything so good in my life."

Her heart rate doubled. She couldn't breathe properly.

He pulled his finger from her and lifted his eyes to hers as he put the shiny finger in his mouth, licking her juices from it.

"So sweet, too."

"Please." She heard her breath come out to plead with him.

"Please what, baby?"

Oh, she couldn't say it. Couldn't tell him what she wanted him to do to her. He had to know, he was already there and could see the evidence—had tasted the evidence. Christ, she didn't even know his name and yet she was willing to spread her legs and let him go down on her on a dumbwaiter while security was after them. Had she lost her mind?

His clever finger moved back inside her panties. "It drives me crazy knowing you like to keep it hairless down here. It's like you've been waiting for me to taste you all along." The words came out low and awed, and sounded as if he hadn't just met her, and had anticipated just that for longer than the ten minutes of their acquaintance.

The hot words scorched her. His breath puffed against her excited womanhood.

A smile played along his lips. "Say it, baby. I want to hear you say it."

"P... please..." she had to stop and lick her suddenly dry lips. She couldn't just say it right out. She'd never said such things to a man. She could, however, be indirect about it. "P... put your mouth on me."

"Where, baby? I'll put it anywhere you want if you tell me where you want it."

She tried to get her courage up when the car came to a halt on the first floor.

He moaned in frustration as he placed a quick kiss on her crotch and then moved away. The keyboard lay on the floor and he picked it up and shoved it under his arm again before helping her up.

As the door slowly came open, he pulled her to him and spoke against her mouth. "Later."

That's all he said, but he didn't need to say anything more. That one word was both promise and threat.

He took her hand and ushered her out of the dumbwaiter and down a corridor to the side entrance of the Complex.

The alarm had caused all doors to go on lockdown. Soran searched for another way to escape as the few night guards made the lobby and began to fan out. Their voices carried down the hallway.

The man pushed her into a room and shoved the keyboard into her arms. He took a chair from one of the desks and threw it through the window, shattering glass out into the street.

He helped her through the broken window, and then followed her through. The guards banged on the locked door, as lights flashed overhead and an automated voice pronounced an unauthorized intrusion.

The night hadn't gotten any cooler. If anything the air seemed to grow damper. Sweat instantly broke out on her skin in the syrupy heat, plastering the sheer shirt to her body.

The man pulled her down an alley and into the recess of a doorway. Police cruisers, with lights and sirens sped by the open mouth of the alley. Spotlights illuminated the night.

The man pressed her deeper into the doorway, protecting her with his body. Heat radiated from his skin, and Soran longed to touch him. His back was to her, and her hand hovered close to the plane of muscle near his shoulder. There was something about him, something so elemental and intense. Her heart gave another painful jolt as she realized who he reminded her of: Jesse. Her Jesse.

"When we move, we need to hurry. You'll have to take your boots off and go barefoot." He spoke over his shoulder.

The zipper started high on the inside of her thigh. She crouched in the limited space as she neared the ankle. Her head brushed his trim waist. He grew still.

"What's your name?" She asked as she moved up and started on the other boot.

"What?"

"I've let you get me into this predicament, and I don't even know your name."

As she finished pulling the boot off, she leaned against him and felt him stiffen.

"Jesse," he said, and pulled her out into the night.

Chapter Five

Jesse held Soran's hand as they moved through the oppressive night. She hadn't spoken a word since he'd told her his name. He was afraid to know the why of that. Did she finally see him as the geeky college math tutor he'd been, or did she not remember that Jesse at all? Either scenario didn't explain the reason for her sudden silence. He needed to get her talking again. But there were more immediate problems pressing—like getting back to the warehouse at the wharf. However, with so many police about, it was not an easy task. Then there was Soran's outfit.

By now, all the police in the area had been sent pictures of them. While his dark t-shirt and utility pants wouldn't stand out in any crowd, that dick-hardening short skirt and peek-a-boo nipple shirt of hers were sure to get her noticed quickly.

He couldn't take her into any well-lit places, and they needed to avoid all public transportation, like the sky trams. That left cabs, and hoofing it across town. He didn't really relish the idea of making her walk across town in bare feet either. No telling what kind of funky-ass disease she'd end up with then.

"Come on, babe. We need to get to the waterfront."

"We can take my glider."

Figured she'd have a nice piece of personal transportation. He shook his head. "It's registered. They're already looking for us, and you should have no doubt they already know everything about you, including the registration on your glider."

"What about the underground? There's a subway tunnel somewhere around here, isn't there?"

Taking her to the underground held about as much appeal as Jesse's memory of her sucking face with the jerk she dated in college. Forty years ago, the bankrupt transportation department had closed the subway lines in order to save money. Now the underground was a haven for the city's homeless. "Not an option."

"Can you jack a trike?" she asked leading him down another alley.

The trike was the three-thruster equivalent of an old three-wheeled convey-ance, a cheap form of personal transportation that required very little upkeep. They were also very easy to jack. Jesse didn't know if he felt insulted by her insinuation that it may not be a skill he possessed.

"I can jack one. Where is it?"

"There." She pointed to the back entrance of an Asian restaurant. The trike had a sign on it that read: Lucky Fong's Take Out. Poor Fong wouldn't be too lucky tonight.

Then a blaze of flashing lights trapped them in their spot.

The police glider cruised at the second floor level. Another one followed at street level. The police were beginning to sweep the area for them.

The past six months had seen an overwhelming increase in the number of police guarding the streets. The Restoration Brigade had speculated how there came to be so many new cops in such a short time, but hadn't come to any conclusions. But whatever the reason for the increased police presence, Jesse needed to make short work of the trike, and without Soran standing over him, distracting him with her warm breath down his back.

"Wait here. I'll go jack the trike and come for you. The cops are looking for two people, not one. If they see me by the trike, they won't be as suspicious."

"No, you'll ditch me now that we're out of the building."

Who was she kidding? She had spread her legs for him and offered up the ultimate prize to him; he damn sure intended to collect. "Not a chance." He crushed his mouth to hers to reestablish his intent.

Her mouth opened and she slid her tongue against his. Electricity burned his nerve endings, fusing his rigid body to hers. This wasn't serving the cause; it was only serving his selfish need. He had another goal, a better goal. But that plan had shattered the moment he saw her again.

He pulled away from her. "Stay here."

She nodded and made no other comment.

The way to the trike appeared clear. In the crosswalk he could see the flashing lights from the police vehicles bouncing off the slick facades of the buildings. Even at night, crowds began to gather outside the Complex, curiosity pushing their fears of government aside. Jesse smiled in satisfaction. The more people roaming the streets, the less chance they had of being caught.

He moved quickly to the trike. A quick survey showed it was an older model, but well-maintained. The door locks were disengaged, so it took only a moment to reconfigure the programming and start the engine and thrusters.

Five minutes later he pulled into the alley where Soran waited for him. She stood with her shoulder against a building, the keyboard tucked against her body.

He idled the trike and held out his hand to help her on board. She leaned forward, placing the keyboard between them and wrapped her arms tightly around his waist.

His sore ribs still ached, but to have Soran so close, he could stand the discomfort. It would have even been better had she not put the keyboard between them and he could have felt her breasts rubbing against his back. Jesse dismissed the horny thoughts and hit the button to pull the doors down around them. "Hold on, babe. These things may be small, but they rocket."

A cheap thrill moved through him as she tightened her arms as he released the idle and they shot forward through the streets.

Pride screamed through him. Twice tonight he'd gotten away due to Soran's quick thinking. She would definitely be an asset to the organization—if she decided to stay with him. And he couldn't count on that. It was a far cry from saving one's self against immediate threat, to helping to overthrow the government.

Jesse tried not to let the thought of her leaving bring him down from his triumph. Tonight had begun a disaster, but ended a coup. Now all he had to do was to convince her to stay with them and put everything she knew about NATNET to good use. The hard part would be to convince her without ever telling her all he'd done up to this point. Or that they had known each other seven years ago. It stung like hell, but it appeared she didn't remember him after all. And that was for the best.

They reached the waterfront, and Jesse pulled the trike up to the door of the hideout. Once the vehicle was painted and the advertising removed, it would be a much- needed addition to their stockpile of hot, yet useful, items.

He opened the lid of the lockbox and punched in a series of access codes into the outer door of the old warehouse. Slowly, and with protest, the door rattled upward. He climbed back into the trike and rolled it forward, parking it just inside the door.

People hurried over to inspect him and the new vehicle. Then Soran alighted and there was a pointed shift of attention from the male population.

"Hey, who'd you bring back?" Rodger, a technician, asked. His bright blue eyes focused on Soran's breasts.

Jesse stepped between Soran and Rodger's ogling glance. "This is Soran. She helped me escape from the Complex."

Beebo, the IT tech, pointed at her. "What's she holding onto?"

"That's a keyboard for the Complex."

"Holy shit," Beebo muttered. "You've brought back the Holy Grail."

"We'll see. I have my doubts it'll work here. I had to disconnect the cable to the monitor and network." Jesse explained as he took the keyboard from Soran and handed it to Beebo. "I read somewhere that there were some networking capabilities built right into the keys."

"You heard right," Beebo said. "I might be able to patch this into our network and confuse the Cerebellum."

Jesse smiled. That's what he was hoping to hear. Programming was his strong suit. He'd leave the networking and circuitry to Beebo.

A side door opened and Josie, an impossibly tall blonde, emerged from the living quarters. She tilted her head to the side and considered the trike before letting her gaze fall to Soran. A hate-filled look came and went in the blink of an eye. But Jesse took note. He would have to be very careful of leaving Soran unattended. Too bad Josie just happened to be a brilliant programmer.

"Is it in, Jesse?" Josie asked.

"Yeah, it's in."

Malicious eyes slid to Soran again. "What's she doing here?"

"Helping."

"We'll see." With that Josie turned and headed back into the living quarters.

Oh, yeah, this wouldn't be good.

Chapter Six

The hideout was nothing more than a large abandoned warehouse, back away from the city traffic. Most cops and street people didn't even bother with this part of town, as it had fallen so far into decay.

The group sat in a control room of sorts amid the workings of stolen hardware. The keyboard had been accepted as manna from heaven; Soran had not received as warm a welcome—at least not by the woman of the group.

Soran sat on a futon across the room from Jesse as he worked with the tech guru to install the keyboard to one of their computers. When the installation was complete, it would be up to Soran to make the keyboard come to life.

As she watched Jesse, thoughts collided in her mind. There were lots of men named Jesse. It wasn't like it was an uncommon name, but still she wondered. If she focused real hard she could almost see her Jesse's shade visible beneath the body of this obvious alpha male. But if it were her Jesse, what a metamorphosis he'd undergone. Not to mention he would have had to rise like Lazarus from the grave.

Was it possible that her Jesse was still alive? It could be, but surely he couldn't be this man. What happened to the thick corrective lenses and the studious persona?

Oh, he couldn't be her Jesse. Her Jesse would have remembered her, wouldn't he? Of course he did tutor several students in a semester, and maybe her Jesse never even noticed when she was in the room. She would usually catch him staring off into space, twisting a lock of hair between his thumb and forefinger in thought. Many the times were when she would have to call him back to the present, and he always looked pissed that she had. Many was the time she'd wanted to plunge her hands into his thick sable hair to see if it felt as soft as it looked.

He leaned over the counter, his face intense with watching Beebo as the tech twisted wires together in a practiced fashion. That was when she saw it. If she hadn't been thinking about her Jesse, she would have missed this other Jesse's hand as it grabbed a lock of hair at his nape and began to twirl it.

"Jesse!" Soran said in a surprised whisper.

He turned and looked at her.

She stood and came to him. "Are you really *my* Jesse?"

The tech turned from his work and looked up at them, raising a brow.

Soran threw her arms around Jesse's neck. "Oh, God, I thought you were dead. I tried to visit you, but they said…" Sobs tore from her body, as unexpected as they were violent.

A shiver went through him as his arms slowly came around her. "I know. I escaped and they had to save face by saying I was dead. It was just easier letting everyone believe it."

Her arms went around him, and his face came to rest between her breasts. She held him close and kissed his head. Her hot tears fell into his hair. "Why didn't you tell me who you were in the elevator? Didn't you remember me?"

He backed away and looked into her eyes. "I remembered you. I never could have forgotten you." He held her hips in the vice of his hands. "Don't cry, sweetheart. It's all right." Suddenly, he stood and said to the tech, "We'll be in my room if you have any trouble. Otherwise, we'll see you in the morning."

Beebo just waved as they departed.

Jesse didn't say another word as he hurried her to his room and closed the door against intrusion. Then he spun her around so she faced the door, his hands on her hips. Slowly, he raised her skirt, his hands moving to skim once again over the lace covering her.

"I want to make love to you, Soran. I'm going to taste you, and love you, and make you come so many times you'll never question me forgetting you ever again."

He bit her ear for emphasis.

The hot words burned down to the pit of her belly. A shudder moved through her and a moan passed her lips. She breathed as his finger found her wetness again. This time he went straight for the kill and rubbed her clit again and again. Soran rocked her hips against his hand. Heat spiraled up from the contact, as his finger traced circles around the pulse deep in her sex. Pressure built behind her eyelids.

"You like that, don't you?"

"Yes," she whispered.

"Does it feel good?"

"Yes."

"Back in college, every time you left my room, I was as hard as a rock and wanting you to come back so I could make love to you. I made love to you every night in my dreams."

He picked up the stroking pace a little and Soran gasped. She rocked back against him; his hard cock thrust between her butt cheeks.

"Jesse."

"I'm here, baby."

"Please, Jesse."

"Please what?"

"Use your mouth on me."

"Where? You know I want to hear you tell me where."

The words clogged in her throat. She wanted to feel his mouth there, right where his hand stroked so expertly. She wanted his tongue on her clit and up inside her.

"M... my pussy."

Jesse lifted her up and turned her around, laying her down on the bed. He went to his knees in front of her, spreading her legs apart. He grabbed her panties and ripped them off. Then he fell on her like a starving man at an all-you-can-eat buffet.

Sucking noises filled the room along with the smell of her arousal. He moved his tongue over her from back to front then the other way, over and over. He took her clit between his teeth and held it in place as he flicked it with his wicked tongue.

Her hands found his hair, burying in the luxurious mass of it. It felt like silk brushing against the insides of her spread thighs, heightening her awareness of him.

Blood rushed to her ears and pounded in every heartbeat. Her hips lifted higher to meet his mouth. "I'm going to come."

"Don't hold it back, baby."

Tongue movements became quick and direct on her tortured clit, and his fingers slid into her tight passage. Quickly, he pumped them in and out, then eased his thumb into her tight little anus.

Soran flew apart under his expert mouth and fingers. When she stopped convulsing, he kissed her slowly, working his tongue around her, then moved away.

"Christ, that was worth the wait," he said as he continued to stare at her center. "Take off the rest of your clothes. I want to see all of you."

She did as told while he shed his own. He was truly a sight to see.

Muscles rippled down his furred chest and stomach. His thighs were strong and taut. A long thick cock stood up from a patch of thick coarse hair. A pearl of fluid glistened on the tip of it.

Soran couldn't resist the temptation of tasting him as he did her. She leaned forward and took him into her hand and flicked her tongue along the shiny head, tasting the drop of salty fluid. His cock jerked in her hand.

Gentle hands caressed her hair back from her face and held it.

"Please," he said in a harsh whisper.

Soran looked up at him with a raised brow and provocative smile on her mouth. "Please what?"

"Suck my cock."

Jesse certainly had no problem with being direct with what he wanted. And he had definitely called her bluff. She had never done this before. What if he hated what she did? What if she did it wrong?

But what could she possibly do wrong? It was obvious that he liked it when she ran her tongue along the tip. Starting there, she flicked her tongue over him again. He moaned.

Power surged through her. Delicately she let her tongue run around the under side of the head before taking it between her lips for a gentle suck.

He gave a tortured laugh. "Ahhhh, you little tease, you."

Her hand tightened on him and began to move up and down the length of him. With each pass, she took him a little deeper into her mouth. Her other hand moved up to cup and caress his tight balls as she worked.

"God in heaven!" he whispered.

She turned her head so she could look up at him. His thumbs worked around to caress her cheeks.

She skimmed her tongue down the underside of him and sucked his balls into her mouth while still pumping his cock with her hand.

"You're fucking amazing, baby."

His hands gripped her face now and pulled her away. Hazel eyes burned into her. "I've got to get inside you, now."

She fell back on the bed and spread her legs for him. Jesse moved over her, rubbing the head of his cock back and forth, taunting her.

"Tease," she said.

So he thrust into her, bringing her back off the bed. He was embedded so deeply she could feel him knocking against her womb. Pelvic muscles clamped around him. She wanted him to stay put, to stay inside her forever.

Soran wrapped her legs around his thighs and put her hands on his ass, then arched up against him.

A sexy and completely masculine smile captivated her. "You like me inside you, don't you?"

She moved under him again, anxious to feel him grind into her. "Please, fuck me."

The thrusts were long and deep, driving her up on the bed. Insistent fingers dug into the flesh of her hips, holding her in place. His hot mouth found her nipple, rhythmically tugging on her as he thrust harder.

"Ahhhh, Jesse. My Jesse," she moaned and wrapped her body tighter around him, burying her face in his hair.

He lifted his face from her breasts and looked deeply into her eyes. The look on his face was one of wonder and disbelief.

An arch of her back and the tightening of her pelvic muscles sent him over the edge. Hot liquid christened her womb in a spray. She kept milking him with her body. As he came, he increased his speed and depth until Soran couldn't hold back her own orgasm. Ecstasy spasmed in her wet tunnel.

Jesse collapsed on top of Soran.

Hard female nipples pressed into him like sexy daggers. He brushed his chest against her, deliberately irritating them with his crisp chest hair. A sensual arch of her back made him want to growl in triumph.

Reality had put all of his fantasies to shame.

Again, he felt her contract her sweet passage around his cock. She'd driven him crazy with that loving torture.

She'd called him *my Jesse*.

He lifted her hair away from her neck, his thumb tilting her jaw upward so he could capture her mouth in a deep, loving kiss. Her mouth. Christ, her mouth tasted as good as her pussy. Both were plump and inviting and made for a man's loving. But not just any man—him.

He couldn't get enough of her taste. His tongue swirled with hers, trying to extract every minute sensation of pleasure from her.

Soran gave everything to the kiss, and Jesse reveled in the knowledge. His dick responded in kind and hardened inside her.

"Again?" She whispered against his mouth.

"Always," he answered and rolled his hips up into her in a slow, controlled thrust.

He skimmed a hand from her side and down between them. The pearl of her pleasure lay exposed to his questing finger and he found it without error. With every stroke of his shaft inside her, his finger stroked her hard little clit.

The first time with her had been uncontrolled and animal. This time he was able to keep the pace slow and in control.

Those beautiful blue eyes of hers slid shut.

"Look at me, Soran. I want you to look me in the eyes when I make you come again."

Long sable lashes sheltered her eyes as they slowly opened to lock with his.

"Ah, baby, you're so fucking beautiful."

Her hand wound between them and clamped around his member, stroking him as he rode her. It felt like a human cock ring. Looking down between their bodies became a study in eroticism. His eyes closed.

Breath caressed his closed lids. "Look at me while you're fucking me, Jesse."

He never thought anything could feel so overwhelmingly good. So carnal. So perfect.

Her hips arched into his hand, scraping her clit against his finger more vigorously. The pressure built inside him, tightened his balls and prepared for his oncoming orgasm. He picked up the pace of his finger, wanting her to find fulfillment first this time.

"Jesse!" she shouted as he felt the sweet prison of her cunt contracting all around him.

How could he possibly hold back his own under such exquisite agony? He let the deep spasms fill her with him.

Instead of collapsing, this time he bent his forehead against hers and breathed in the musk of their lovemaking. If he lived to be a thousand, he'd never forget the potent scent of their sex.

Finally, he rolled off her and gathered her into his arms, resting her against his chest. His heart beat like a sledgehammer against his battered ribcage. Her hand rested on top of his heart. Tenderly he placed his own on hers, and pressed it into his sweat-drenched flesh.

Silence stretched out for miles before them. For once, Jesse didn't know what to say. For once, he hadn't kicked a woman out of his bed after sex. Maybe that was the problem; he simply didn't know what to say to her.

He thought she had drifted off to sleep when she said, "I almost died when I saw them taking you away."

Caught unaware by her admission, he brushed a hand along her silky arm in comfort. The poor girl had been there that day.

"I wanted to run up to the police and demand your release, but I was too afraid."

Of course she would be. The Pristine Queen had never dirtied her hands in the lives of others, or entertained a subversive thought in her life. Until now.

"Every day, I watched the news reports and read the execution lists." She lifted her head to look at him. Tears filled her eyes, and spilled down her cheeks when she blinked. "I didn't want to believe it when I saw your name on them. What could you have done to make you an enemy of the state?"

He smiled and brushed the tears from her face. "Do you really want to know the answer to that, or do you want to just lie here and be glad I'm still alive and kicking?"

"I want to know everything."

He blew out a long breath and moved her away from him. He sat up on the edge of the bed, a hand cupped to his ribs, and looked around for his pants. Silence set heavy in the room, creating a void between them. Finally, faced with the option of telling her all, he couldn't do it. What if she started hating him for the things he'd done in the name of freedom?

"Don't shut me out," she pleaded. "You used to do that all the time back then."

Soran was right. He did shut her out, but with good reason. She was so clean and good. He wanted to protect her from his treasonous activities, while working to give her, and the rest of the country, a better life—a life that one could now find only in history books.

"There was a reason for that," he said between clenched teeth. She couldn't really understand the nature of what he'd gotten her into, and what he'd tried to protect her from all those years ago.

"I thought we were friends. What reason could you possibly have for shutting out a friend?"

"A good one."

"Is that all I get?" She stood up in all her naked glory, fuming at him from across the bed. "I gave up my entire life tonight, without even knowing your name or what you were doing. I was forced into it really. You at least owe me the courtesy of an explanation."

He replied, "Why? Because I fucked you? Remember you were the one with your legs spread, offering it to me on the dumbwaiter."

She blinked at him a few times, then started to gather her clothes and shove them on her body regardless if they were inside out or not.

What was he doing? Did he lose his mind somewhere between round one and round two of their lovemaking? This was the woman he'd spent his entire adult life dreaming about, and he was pushing her away after having the most mind-blowing sexual experience of his life. Oh, it wasn't as if he hadn't slept with anyone before. On the contrary, he had a laundry list of lovers over the years, some of them even members of the Restoration Brigade. But it wasn't like now.

She didn't look up at him as she put on her discarded boots. When she reached the door, she didn't even give him a backward glance. Her sexy shoulders were back, her head held high.

Guilt bubbled up into his throat. It didn't have to be this way. "Soran, don't leave."

He stood halfway in the hall naked as a Greek statue. "By now the authorities are already at your house picking through everything you own to build a stronger case against you."

Now she turned to him. "Maybe I'll just spread my legs for them and see if they'll forget all about it. After all, it made you forget your contempt for me for a while."

The thought of another man touching her, seeing what should only belong to him, unleashed anger in him. It coursed through his veins like acid. And what did she mean about him having contempt for her?

Josie picked that time to walk down the hallway. It was more of a strut than a walk. She looked from Soran to Jesse and smiled.

"Gee, Jess, if you wanted some fun, all you had to do was ask," she said as she came up to him and brushed her over-generous breasts against him. "I know how much you love to fuck."

He blinked. Hell had just opened up and swallowed him whole. He'd slept with Josie in the past, and couldn't deny she was a skilled and vigorous lover. But he wouldn't sleep with her again. Not with Soran back in his life. But that wouldn't stop Josie from trying to get back into his bed. She was like a freaking barracuda sometimes—all teeth and aggression.

Long red nails scraped down the front of his chest, across the plane of his abdomen, and to his traitorously stiffening shaft. Unfortunately, she'd had plenty of practice on how and where to touch him.

Soran's eyes followed the path of Josie's hand and to the evidence of his new arousal. Pain widened her eyes and set her lovely mouth into a sad line. "I'll leave you two alone."

He pushed Josie away from him and grabbed his pants, hopping into them as he followed Soran down the hall.

"Soran."

"Leave me alone." She picked up the pace as she entered the command center.

Beebo still sat at the computer, and looked up in surprise as she entered the room at full tilt and headed for the newly installed NATNET keyboard.

"Give me back my keyboard."

Beebo looked to him for confirmation. Jesse shook his head and reached for Soran's hand to prevent her from snatching the keyboard from the circuitry and negating all the tech's hard work.

"Soran," Jesse coaxed. "Come on back to the bedroom and I'll tell you everything. After you hear it, if you want to leave, I won't stop you."

Wrong promise. She looked even more hurt than when he'd unintentionally responded to Josie's touch.

"You never told her what we're doing?" Beebo asked in astonishment.

"Shut up and check on Magellan's progress, will you," he barked to the tech.

Jesse gave her captured hand a tug and brought her up to his chest. He put his mouth by her ear. "I only want to protect you like I did before."

He could still smell the lingering scent of her sex on his face, and it drove him crazy. Could still taste her unique flavor on his mouth. This close to her he couldn't deny to her that he wanted her again. Wanted to plunge into her depths and never leave her.

She looked into his face, so close he could taste her breath. "All right. But you better be damn convincing."

Chapter Seven

Body language could tell a myriad of secrets about a person's emotional state. Right now Jesse's body language said he was definitely uncomfortable about sharing this part of his life with her. He'd been more than willing to share the pleasures of his body with her, but not the passions of his heart, or the secrets of his mind, and it showed.

Soran sat on the bed and gazed up at him. He sat on top of a cramped corner desk where a small notebook computer took up most of the available space. His arms were crossed over his chest in a touch-me-not posture reminiscent of how he'd sit during his college days while trying to instill some financial principle into her head.

He didn't seem so eager to start the conversation, even though he'd been pretty insistent that she stay to listen. But she didn't want to start the conversation off with what had resulted in their earlier argument: his inability to share the goals of this band of subversives. So she chose a different topic that may cause her more pain, but obviously he would have no trouble discussing. Their sleeping arrangements.

"If I decide to stay, will it be possible for me to have my own room, or will I have to bunk with the other women?"

He frowned at her. "No on both counts. You'll stay in here with me."

"Aren't you afraid I'll cramp your style?" she retorted. "I mean, I'm not into threesomes, and it's pretty apparent you and the blonde have something going already. I don't want to be a part of that, or come between you and your girlfriend. If I'd have known you had someone, I wouldn't have gone with you." God, she'd been a complete idiot. Jesse had probably wanted to have sex with her back in college and now that he had, he could check her off his list of 'things to do.'

The frown deepened. "You wanted me. You can't deny that."

"Oh, I have no intention of denying it, but I can take pains to not repeat what happened in here earlier." No matter how hard she'd have to work to stick to that promise.

"Josie and I used to have a thing, but not for some time now."

"Did you love her?"

"No, not the way you mean."

Soran gave a snort. "Don't split hairs with me."

"I wouldn't dream of it." He rolled his shoulders as if trying to relieve himself of some great burden without ever having to verbalize it. He lifted his hands to his face and breathed in. "I've got to go wash before we have this talk. I can smell you all over me and it's driving me out of my head."

If she let him leave now, he'd come up with some excuse to not tell her what he'd promised. She stood her ground. "If you leave this room before we talk, I won't be here when you get back."

His gaze penetrated her for a few moments before he crossed his arms again. "In all my dreams of you, I never once gave you credit for a stubborn streak."

"I kind of lose my charm in the real world, huh?"

Jesse shook his head, his eyes hardened. "Oh, no. You'll need that if you stay here."

She started to ask him if she needed her charm or her stubborn streak when he uncoiled from his place like a snake that just finished sunning himself on a warm rock.

"I never loved Josie. I couldn't love her, because I've loved you since you walked into the library and up to the table where I sat and announced I'd been assigned as your tutor." He squatted between her open knees, and brought his hand up under her hair to rub her neck. "God in heaven, you were the sweetest, most guileless person I'd ever met. I couldn't fathom how you'd lived in the world and not been corrupted by it."

"You never said anything about...."

"Do you blame me? I didn't want to alienate you. Look at you. Not only are you sweet beyond imagining, but you're something out of an erotic fantasy. A man would kill for a woman like you." His eyes implored her to understand something. And it hung there between them, suspended in the air, caught in the web of tension. He had killed—for her.

He added, "You deserve to live in a world where you don't have to watch what you say, or censor your feelings because government has run amuck and decided it knows better than you what you want to think and feel."

"Jesse..." she started, but he leaned forward and stopped her words with a loving caress of his lips against hers, stopping her protest where it hovered.

"No. Let me tell you what happened back then. How much did you know about me in college?"

"As much as you let me." She shrugged. "Not much."

Regret pooled in his eyes and he nodded. "During college I worked for a company that promised to build labor-saving software for domestic use."

"I remember," Soran said. "But so far you're not telling me anything earth-shattering. I would think having labor-saving programs in such a vast computer makes perfect sense."

"Sure. Only as the project drew to a close and we began to implement the software, I realized they were jacking the programs into NATNET's brain."

"You mean into the network? Well, we've always known all those supposedly helpful programs are part of the surveillance grid."

"This is more than just surveillance. These programs not only jacked in to the network. They set up housekeeping. And then--"

When he fell silent, she prompted, "And then what?"

"And then the damn program went sentient on us."

She stared at him. "But that could be reversed. "

"Not if the government didn't want to reverse it," he said grimly. "It liked the Machiavellian effects of the machine running everything. Makes sense, from their angle. A computer isn't like senators and presidents. It doesn't have any emotions or ambitions. It can solve problems quickly and efficiently, without needing to play the Washington game or be re-elected."

Soran couldn't believe her ears. "But we elect our officials. I can show you my voter registration card."

"And so can millions of others. Paper tigers. That's all the elected officials are. They do nothing but draw salaries and pontificate on issues they neither care nor know a thing about."

His subversive dissertation brought her world down—but it resonated with so much she—and everyone else in the country—had tried to ignore. A sentient computer running the country instead of the humans elected to govern? It seemed too fantastic, and yet, the truth of it shone in the depths of his troubled eyes. And even as the situation terrified, it also explained so much. If the Complex housed NATNET's mainframe, then tonight Jesse had been in there to correct the problem. He had said he was in there for maintenance, but the computer had fought back. Did the computer refuse help it deemed harmful, or had Jesse meant the mainframe ill? "And what were you doing tonight?"

He blew out a breath. "I planted a virus into NATNET's Cerebellum that will systematically destroy all its programming and return its main functions into a network of separate servers stationed throughout the country. We're taking the nation back, so we can live in freedom again."

Terrifying thoughts of rampant chaos rushed through her mind. What would happen when NATNET went offline? She had always lived in a world where all the computers were serviced by one huge supercomputer. And yet, she had never known that years ago the computer *had* become the government.

"You think destroying NATNET is the best way to guarantee freedom? It's a huge risk."

"I'm not saying I'm helping to create a utopia because I don't believe such an ideal can really exist." He took her hand and squeezed it. "In college, you saw me being pulled away by the guards and my name on the execution lists. Isn't that enough to make you believe me? I did nothing more than disagree with the other programmers."

Soran shook her head, "Seeing you taken away like that had to be the hardest thing I've ever had to stand and watch. Knowing what you faced, and how awful it all must have been, makes me angry. And seeing you again tonight, being strangled by those cables—it's brought it all back. But-- but does that give you a right to be the one to decide the fate of an entire nation?"

Jesse shrugged. "Maybe not, but it doesn't matter. It's done. The virus is implanted. It just needs commands to go live."

Soran lifted her hand and brushed the hair from his brow. "I'm really trying to understand this. All of it. Why have you kept it from me for so long? Why didn't you tell me back in school what was going on?"

"I'd have been damned if I would have let any of it touch you." He lightly caressed her cheek and then mouth with his thumb. "I had to keep everything away from you. I didn't want you to have to lie to the authorities if they ever questioned you about my activities."

"You knew they'd catch you?"

He gave a lopsided smile. "It was only a matter of time. Someone on the project was bound to talk to the authorities about my lack of commitment."

His 'lack of commitment' looked more like change of heart from where she sat. Commitment was not something Jesse lacked. "How did you escape once they caught you?"

Jesse moved in closer to her, his eyes fixated on her lips. "Not now. Let's kiss and make up first. Tell me you're going to stay with me."

After listening to his reasons, how could she leave him? But there were still so many questions left unanswered. Still so much she needed to know before deciding the direction of her life. What Jesse and his friends planned to do held so many dangers, both to those involved, and to all the people living within the U.S. borders who knew nothing of the coming revolution. He didn't just want her to stay. He wanted her to join them. And for that decision, Soran needed more time and more information.

"I'll stay with you. For now. But please don't leave me out in the dark again. If I'm going to keep myself safe, I need to know everything that's going on."

He smiled then, not the predatory half-smiles he'd been giving her, but a full-mouth, tooth-showing smile. He acted like he'd been victorious. Her breath caught in her throat. Jesse was a devastatingly handsome man and after being with him, Soran didn't think she could stand being separated from him any longer. He must have read her thoughts, for he leaned closer and kissed her.

Her thighs went up in flames as his tongue tasted her mouth over and over again. "Let's get you out of these clothes again." He broke away just long enough to look down as he relieved her of her silky blouse.

Excitement slammed into her, and her nipples tightened in anticipation of Jesse's lovemaking.

He ran his thumbs over them. "Your nipples are so damn responsive." With that he began to suck on first one and then the other, laving each with the tip of his hot tongue and sending her to the very edge. She arched her back and eased back onto the bed. Jesse followed her down to the bed still latched onto her.

A hand ran up under her skirt and grabbed one of her bare cheeks. "Mmmm, no panties."

"You ripped them off me that last time."

He raised his head and looked at her. "I like this much better."

"I just bet you do."

With that, he jerked off her skirt and dropped his pants. The full, heavy erection saluted her proudly as he came back down on the bed in front of her.

"We'll leave your boots on this time."

She gave him a self-conscious smile. "Fulfilling another of your dorm room fantasies about me?"

"In a big way." He kneeled between her legs and placed the back of her thighs over his shoulders. Palms flat against the inside of her legs, he ran them up and down, coming so close to touching her where she ached for him before retreating to the tops of her boots again.

After the third pass, he lowered his head and flicked his tongue between her folds, finding her clit and zeroing in on it without mercy.

"I can taste my come all over you, baby."

"Don't stop to talk now," she laughed, almost out of her head with sensations. Truthfully, she loved the way he talked dirty to her while he made love to her. He made her feel beautiful and desirable.

He laughed, and the gust of air made her arch in response. "Oh, did you like that?"

She answered him by lifting her hips higher, and grinding her pelvis against him.

He slid up and in her. The backs of her thighs remained on his shoulders and he pumped into her hard and fast. He wrapped her long hair around his fist and pulled her head back. When he leaned into her neck he bit her, then moved to her shoulder. Each bite was followed by a long lingering kiss.

Harsh breath rushed by her ear. "Tell me you love me."

"I love you, Jesse."

Thrusts became more desperate. "Mean it. Please, mean it."

"I do, Jesse. I love you so much."

The hot rush of his orgasm filled her for the third time that night. This time Soran didn't just feel the physical action, but could feel Jesse's love and protection fill her as well. Emotions carried her along until she too cried out in release, showering him in her own hot fluid.

When they settled back to earth and Soran lay curled up on his chest, she looked up into his face and ran her finger over his closed eyelids.

"What?" He opened his eyes and looked at her.

"I was just thinking that I had never noticed until tonight how green your eyes are."

He took her hand and kissed her fingers. "Implants."

"Really?" She rose up and looked closer. "When?"

"After I escaped. I had to disguise my looks. My vision had never been great, even as a kid, so I took care of two problems at the same time. Seemed like a good idea at the time."

"Where did you have it done?"

A dark brow lifted in question. "You don't think I went into the nearest optometry clinic, do you?"

"You trusted your vision to the butchers on the wharf?"

Jesse kissed the tip of her nose. "I didn't have much choice, now did I? The authorities were looking for someone with inch-thick lenses. That was a dead giveaway."

"You could have gotten colored contacts and been done with it."

He rolled slightly then moved her to spoon in behind her. When he had her where he wanted her, he moved her hair back from her neck and spoke into her ear. "I see I'm going to have to educate you on the finer points of being a fugitive."

"Mmmm," she moaned backing up into his groin. "How do you propose to educate me?"

"We'll start in the morning. Even incredible lovers like me need their sleep on occasion."

Chapter Eight

Jesse woke just before noon with a puff of dark, curly hair in his mouth. He gathered the thick mass of Soran's hair and moved it. Intense love and possessiveness filled him. This is how it should have been all along. He should have been waking up next to her every morning since he escaped. If he had only followed his heart back then, he wouldn't have had to fill his nights with only dreams of her. He wouldn't have had to imagine that all his lovers had long dark hair and the bluest eyes he'd ever seen. But who knew, perhaps she wouldn't have come with him back then. At least she was with him now, and he was determined to keep her here.

The bed jostling caused her to wake, and she popped her head up from the pillow like the pictures of prairie dogs he'd seen—when there had still been prairies in North America.

"What time is it?"

He looked at the clock again just to be sure. "Noon."

Her head plunked down on his pillow again. "Still early."

A perfect round butt stuck up from the twist of bed linens. Jesse ran his hand over it, enjoying the way Soran moved under his touch. "Raise your hips a little," he encouraged.

She glanced over her shoulder as he rolled over and eased in behind her. He nudged her leg with his thigh, giving him a better access to her center.

His morning erection needed instant relief, or he'd get nothing accomplished today. Normally, he took matters into his own hands, but now Soran was lying beside him. Soran! He still couldn't believe it.

Her skin felt incredible next to his. Soft and warm. As he pushed into her, the tight, slick passage grew from warm to hot. "Mmmm, you feel good in the morning."

"I feel sleepy in the morning," she murmured.

"Sleepy? I'm trying to wake you up, woman." He moved his hips in a circle, and Soran moved back against him in response.

"It's working."

Words gave way to animalistic moans. All thoughts ceased. Only the mating mattered. Feeling her sheath all around him, hearing the passionate cries from her throat, made him pump all the harder. He fucked her like his life depended on it. And maybe it did. Thoughts of Soran had sustained him through many lonely hours. Now her love would fortify him against the hardships to come.

"Jesse," she mewed.

"I'm here, sweetheart."

Each sound that issued from her throat sounded more frantic, more intense than the one before until she exploded beneath him. His name fell in a litany from her lips. He thankfully followed her into bliss and when the crisis ended he wrapped his arms tightly around her.

A knock sounded on the door, disrupting them from their post-coital cuddle.

"Jesse, we need you in the tech room," Beebo called through the door.

"Be right there," he called back, then leaned over to whisper in Soran's ear. "I guess we should get up and get dressed."

"He called you, not me," she said.

Jesse slid his hand slowly down her body, while pulling out of her. "Come on, woman."

He moved over and she flipped over onto her back to look at him. "Then can I at least borrow one of your shirts? I can't go out there again in mine."

Jesse gave a slight chuckle, as he bent over to retrieve his pants from the floor. "You're a fugitive now, you can't afford to worry about being seen in the same thing twice."

"Jesse, do you even remember what my shirt looks like?"

That thought brought him up short. "Yeah." That shirt would be embossed on his memory for the rest of his life. He opened the drawer built into the bed frame and threw a black t-shirt at her. That should prevent anyone from seeing what he'd claimed.

"Could I possibly get a shower someplace?"

He pretended imposition. "Geez, lady, next you'll want concierge service."

She leaned over the bed and grabbed him by the waist, pressing her breasts into his back. "Please, just show me where the shower is, and I'll meet you in the tech room when I'm done."

How could he refuse when she was pressed up against him that way? "All right."

⁂

Jesse couldn't resist following Soran into the shower. She looked so delicious with the water and suds sluicing down her beautiful body.

"Let me wash you," he said working the soap between his palms for lather.

"I'm already washed." She cleared water from her eyes and looked at him.

"Ah, but not the really good part." He moved closer to her, pinning her up against the wall.

"What about Beebo?"

"He can wash himself. He's a big boy."

Soran laughed and the sound filled his heart. "No, he's waiting for us. If you start washing my 'good part' you'll want make love to me again and Beebo will come looking for you."

Jesse leaned his forehead against hers. Water ran over his head and then fell onto Soran. He watched it trail down her breasts and make tiny waterfalls off her nipples. The sight mesmerized him.

"Are you listening?"

"How can I possibly listen when you're standing naked and wet in front of me?"

He let his soapy hands trail down her body and caress into her soft folds. He moved his fingers inside her. Sharp nails clutched at his arms to hold her steady against him. "Yep, you're wet all right."

She moved against him, rocking her hips against his hand. A soft moan fell from her lips. Her neck arched back.

Then the shower door opened and Josie stuck her blonde head inside. "We're out there waiting for you to activate the virus, and you're in here acting like Jesse Storm, Freelance Gynecologist. Now, get your hand out of her twat and get moving."

Soran gave a little squeal and buried her face against his shoulder. She started to shake.

Jesse said, "Who I fuck and where I fuck them is none of your damn business, Josie. Don't you know how to knock?"

"It's not like I haven't see your dick before," she rejoined as she gave Soran a cool look up and down. "I thought you liked big tits, Jesse."

Jesse lost his cool. "Get the hell out of here!"

Josie gave an arch of her brow and turned to leave.

He could hear Soran breathing, feel her shaking, but she didn't say a word. Jesse slid his fingers from her and pulled her close to him. "Don't listen to her. You're perfect. Every last inch of you is perfect."

She moved her face from his shoulder and stared into his eyes. "As I've never had any complaints before, I'm not worried about what she said." Water dripped from her eyelashes and nose. She leaned into him and brushed her mouth against his, her eyes sliding shut with a look of complete rapture.

Grateful, Jesse took the offered kiss, letting her know with his firm lips and questing tongue how perfect he found her. Her confidence in her own sexuality turned him on even more.

Jesse broke off the kiss, and held her for a few more moments before moving her away. "Then why did you squeal and shake if you weren't upset?"

Soran laughed at him. "I'd think after last night you'd know it when I come."

Jesse gave her a sly smile and a quick kiss on the tip of her wet nose. "Come on, before someone else decides to tell us when we can make love."

They quickly dried off and donned their clothes. He handed her a pair of green fatigue pants that had belonged to a former member. Nikki wouldn't be needing the clothes anymore – she had gotten captured by police and executed for her ties to the RB. Next he handed Soran a pair of combat boots retrieved from the storage area. "These should fit you. If they don't, we'll get you some that do after you key in the codes."

She looked at him from the floor where she sat pulling on the shoes. "What codes?"

"The ones that will activate the virus."

"I have to do that?"

"It's your keyboard, babe. No one else can use it."

She stood up and moved her feet back and forth testing the boots. "And what would you have done if you hadn't gotten me or the keyboard?"

"We would have worked from one of ours and hoped the Cerebellum was already sick enough to not fight the strange commands." He linked his arm through hers and herded her towards the tech room.

"But now you have mine, so you can rest easy that the Cerebellum will recognize an operator its familiar with."

"Exactly." Jesse paused and looked at her. "Unless, of course, the governmental operators have wiped your link from the memory board."

She gave him an annoyed look. "It's always something with you, isn't it? But they would do that if they thought I had something to do with loading the damn virus. And you made sure they would suspect me, didn't you?" She stopped him mid-stride with a hand to his arm. "Tell me, Jesse, when you came to the Complex last night did you plan to kidnap me and make off with my keyboard? Was I part of the plan?"

He looked at his shoes then back up at her. "No. I went last night wanting to get in and out without ever seeing you."

"But you knew I was in the building at the time?"

"Of course I knew. I've always known where you were."

"And yet you say you love me all this time and obviously have taken pains to stay away when you knew where I was? Why?"

"To protect you." He ran a finger down her face and tucked a strand of her curly hair behind her ear.

"Then why was last night different? What made you decide to take advantage of the situation last night, and bring me here?"

Jesse's chest tightened. A band of unease squeezed him. He couldn't very well admit to being impulsive in his actions, and yet that was exactly what had happened. He'd seen her in the flesh, had been close enough to see, to touch, to smell her again, and he'd not been able to resist the temptation, the need for her that had kept him going for the past seven years.

"Well?" She prompted when he didn't answer.

"Look, maybe I didn't have a right, but damn it, you charged into that elevator to save *me,* and I just couldn't leave you behind this time." Jesse shook his head and started walking again. She could follow or not. He called over his shoulder. "The virus I planted is a smart virus, and it's waiting for your command to go live."

The confession only seemed to trouble her more, but she followed him.

He sat Soran down at the computer. The little room was packed to capacity with the Restoration Brigade waiting anxiously for her to key in the commands that would begin a new future for the country. But now she stared down at the keyboard, and he knew she had questions, the same questions they'd asked themselves. How could this virus change anything? The Restoration Brigade had no power. Wouldn't the virus knock out the infrastructure and possibly collapse the economy?

"Look, I need some more answers before I do this." She turned to Jesse, her shoulders hitching up in defense. "What happens once the grid comes down? Everyone will lose power then. How is that helping people?"

Jesse replied, "It will only be down long enough for us to restore the power through the substation generators across the country."

"So you're replacing one network for another. When the grid comes down and the government topples, you'll become the government. You'll become what you're fighting against."

His eyes bore into her, pleading with her to understand. "Do you honestly think I would allow people to live in suppression as they have been under the old regime?"

She asked, "But what about the prisons? How are you going to keep the criminals inside when the power fails?"

Everyone looked to Jesse for his explanation. He was not the leader of the group, but they all seemed to defer to him now. Heat burned behind his eyes at her accusation. "You mean criminals like me?"

Anguish washed her face at his statement. "No, Jesse. Not like you." She took his hand in hers and kissed his palm. "I believe in you."

He took a deep breath. She meant it. After all these years apart, after all he had done to put her from his life, she truly did believe in him. After all he'd done to protect her, and instead had pulled her into more danger, she believed him. Amazing.

He wished they didn't have a full room of people watching. He wanted her right then and there. Wanted to drive his throbbing self inside her and never leave the safety and warmth of her body.

But just because she said she believed in him didn't mean she believed in his cause. She dropped his hand and said, "But not all the people in prison are there for the same reason you were. Some actually belong there. How are you going to separate them out?"

He had an answer for that at least. "The activation process has a countdown. After you activate the sequence, we'll have about four hours before the virus awakens. By then the prisons should be on lockdown and the automatic locks engaged on the cell doors. If the locks are already engaged, the prisoners won't be able to unlock them."

She didn't give up that easily. "All right, that explains this immediate area. But what about the prisons on the West Coast?"

"Chances are, by the time the prisoners are aware the grid is down, we'll have ours up and running."

"Powered with illegal generators."

"They won't be illegal in a few hours."

"It takes longer than a few hours to establish a new government. And after what you told me about NATNET and the paper tigers, this virus means there won't be anyone trained to perform as a public servant, let alone a governmental body."

"Ah, ye of little faith." Unable to deny himself the taste of her lips a moment longer, he leaned over and kissed her. Pulling away, he smiled into her face and put his bent finger under her chin. "Don't worry. We have already put provisions in place so the people can quickly elect officials who will actually work for their paychecks."

She turned away from him and looked at the screen. Her chest rose and fell as she took in a deep breath and let it out slowly. Finally, to his relief, she nodded. "What do I need to do?"

Beebo slid a card to her, printed with a line of code. "You need to power up like you did before, and access NATNET. Then key in these codes using the keyboard."

"NATNET will be expecting verbal commands."

"Yes, but you'll key these in while giving the verbal commands." He slid over another card. "These are the governmental operator verbal authorization codes."

"How did you get these? I didn't even have these!"

Beebo smiled, showing partial caps of gold on his eyeteeth. "Disgruntled employees come in real handy sometimes."

Soran shook her head and typed in her access codes. The screen flashed by painting the faces of the anxious onlookers in a blue glow. Then a screen popped up that Soran had never seen before. It was a skull and crossbones with the words ACCESS DENIED in black across them.

"Houston, we have a problem," Soran said to Jesse. "It won't let me in. They've already purged my access codes."

"That's all right," Beebo broke in. "You already have a partial link if it can tell you access is denied and put that graphic up. Just key in the codes and jack into the headset and state the verbal commands."

Soran put on the headset and then busily typed as she talked to NATNET. The crackle of static filled the speakers, then the voice came on.

"Soran Roberts, you have been aborted from the program. Cease communication attempts."

Jesse drew in a sharp breath. But Soran said calmly, "Run program marked RB one-twelve." As she said the word she hit the last key. The screen cleared, the voice screamed, and a clock graphic popped up and began the countdown.

Soran threw the headset off and looked up at Jesse. "It sounded so human when it screamed."

Jesse looked down at her. The horrified expression on her face made him uneasy. At least it was too late to balk now. "You did it. Now we wait."

She ran a hand through her hair. "I've never been good at waiting."

He hopped off the table where he sat and held out his hand for her. "Come on then, no sense in waiting around here watching numbers flash by. Let's go to the surplus store and get you some clothes."

Chapter Nine

So they rode through the streets on Fong's stolen trike. It looked nothing like it had last night, Soran noticed. It was now painted silver with a red, white, and blue flag waving across it. How they had managed the paint job overnight she would never know, but it looked great, even if it did make her feel guilty. It was her fault the damn thing was a hot vehicle. She hadn't meant for Jesse to keep it, and had wrongly assumed someone would return it today.

The surplus store was located in an area where the wharf and midtown came together. Soran had pulled her hair up on her head, and didn't have a stitch of make up on. Her reflection in the store windows didn't look like the Soran Roberts who left for work last evening. That Soran Roberts had died in the night, and a new one born in her place. The new one seemed to move differently, as if she were the sexiest woman on the planet. Or at least the sorest.

Muscles she hadn't used in a very long time screamed with agony every time Jesse took a corner. Instinctively, her arms tightened around him. She'd never had such a passionate lover. He couldn't seem to get enough of her, but then he had admitted to loving her since college.

He turned around and smiled over his shoulder at her. Her heart melted into a puddle inside her chest. Love for him poured through her blood, racing out to every cell and molecule of her tingling body. She placed a kiss between his shoulderblades then laid her cheek against him.

She couldn't agree with everything he did, or the methods he and his friends used to affect change, but she did believe in him. There was something intense yet honest about Jesse. There always had been. As they moved through the dirty streets, passing the press of unwashed humanity, Soran realized someone like Jesse could never stand idly by and watch while a sentient computer caused the country to implode, especially since he helped to design the programming for it in the first place.

The trike rolled to a stop, as Jesse guided it into a parking space. He hit the button to raise the cover, and turned to Soran to pull her into his arms. "We'll get you some clothes. They don't have anything as slinky as you had on last night, but the clothes are cheap, and you get a lot for your money here."

As soon as they walked through the doors, Soran saw what he meant. Clothes and other paraphernalia were piled on long folding tables. The piles towered over the tables and looked in danger of falling over onto the worn-out floor.

Soran let her hands run over the thick, scratchy fabrics of the industrial-strength clothing. Though her heart yearned for the silk and lace left behind at her apartment, common sense told her to make do with what was available, especially since they might need to go to ground when the virus became active. And who knew how long it would be before she could venture out to buy more. But then Jesse didn't seem to worry about venturing into the crowded streets driving the star-spangled trike.

She dug her arms up to the elbow in the bin and rummaged through the pile to find her size. There really was no discernible order to the chaos. She just had to dig until she found hidden gold.

Jesse came up behind her and bumped her into the table. She could feel his erection nestled in her backside. Warm breath tickled her neck.

"I promise I'll get you whatever you want after."

"This is fine."

He ran a hand up her arm, and Soran could feel her nipples harden behind the protection of her borrowed shirt. His other arm reached around her and handed her a stack of folded pants. She grabbed them and looked at the first tag. How did he know her size?

"Will they fit?" he asked, stepping back slightly. She immediately missed his warmth against her.

"Yes. But I need shoes and shirts."

He took her by the hand and moved her towards the back of the store. There racks and tables were heaped with more goods unwanted by polite society.

She handed him back the stack of pants then rifled through the shirts. Anything to cover her top half would work. She wasn't going to be particular. As a matter of fact, the soft cotton of Jesse's t-shirt felt good against her sensitive breasts. Every movement caused a sensual feeling to move through her. She smiled a private half-smile, knowing that recently this shirt had been on his body.

"What's that smile for?" His hazel eyes moved over her with the same intensity as his touch.

She shook her head at him. How could she be so happy when her entire life had turned upside down overnight? Because her previous life had been filled with material things and loneliness, that's how.

It struck her while standing there with surplus t-shirts caught in her fists, and wearing boots one size too big, that if Jesse's virus worked she would never again have to worry about being watched by government. Hell, she had committed high treason twice in the last twelve hours, and deep down she didn't feel as bad as she thought she would. If anyone should feel guilt over their actions, it should be those elected officials who remained silent while a machine ran the country for them.

Suddenly, Jesse leaned forward and kissed her between her brows. "You have the fastest changing expressions I've ever seen. One moment you look deliriously happy, the next you're frowning like someone just stepped on your foot."

She shrugged. "I'm just thinking—well, I meant what I said earlier. I do believe in you, Jesse."

His eyes raked over her body again. "Then hurry and shop, woman, so I can take you home and make love to you again."

Soran raised a brow and turned fully to him. "Why wait? Don't they have a dressing room or closet in here somewhere?"

A predatory smile curled his mouth up on one side. "Yeah, I believe they might."

He grabbed her hand with his free one and dragged her through the store, stopping in the back and looking both ways before ducking into a little alcove covered by a thin, wool curtain.

No sooner had Jesse closed the curtain on them then he threw the pants to the floor and pressed Soran against the far corner. His mouth took hers in a wild kiss full of passion and frustration.

"I've wanted to do that since you keyed in the codes." His voice sounded harsh as he let her up for air.

"I wasn't stopping you."

"I know." He attacked her mouth again, this time hurrying to unbutton her fatigues and pull them down to her knees. He dropped down like a supplicant to his goddess and began to lick and tease her wet sex.

Soran pressed her hands into the walls and let her head fall back, biting her lips from crying out in ecstasy. A thick blunt finger stole into her passage. Her body tightened instantly, rocking her down to her shoes with the force and suddenness of her orgasm.

Soran let her body go limp and hung over Jesse's body. Little kisses rained on her femininity.

"I love the way you taste, baby. I can't seem to get enough of you," he breathed against her skin.

"What did you do all those nights after I returned to my room?" she asked into his back.

"Do you want to know?" He moved up her, his hands firm on her ribcage forcing her to stand.

When they were eye to eye, she nodded.

He whispered, "I thought about you until I was crazy with it. Your perfume haunted my room for hours afterward, and I had my nose and mind filled with you. My dick hard, my resolve to protect you even harder."

She pressed her mouth to his, not kissing him, but taking in a deep breath of her scent on his lips. "Did you take matters into your own hands?" she whispered against him lips.

"Many times. Does that turn you on?"

Instead of answering, Soran opened her mouth on his, unfastening his pants as he had done hers moments before.

No more words were exchanged as Soran showered Jesse with all the love and attention he had denied himself all those years ago. For all those times he only dreamed of holding her and making love to her, she rewarded him.

Skinny and unappealing as he had been back then, Soran had still had a secret crush on him. It had been Jesse's inner strength and resolve that had attracted her. For some reason she had seen beyond the surface to the potential man he could become—the man he did become.

Tears squeezed from the corners of her eyes as she thought about the day his name had appeared on the execution notices. She had taken to her room for days, crying and refusing food. She mourned as if they had been lovers. And in the end they had been, even if discreetly behind closed doors and the privacy of their minds.

He moved inside her, stroking her inner walls. She moved her mouth to his ear. "I used to do the same thing back then. I'd go back to my room and pretend you were making love to me."

Jesse moaned into her shoulder and shuddered against her. He bathed her womb in his release. He kissed her neck and fanned her face with hot breath as he tried to get his composure back.

After a few minutes he moved slightly away from her. "We better get dressed before someone decides they need the dressing room."

Soran nodded. Jesse tucked himself back into his pants and fastened them before helping her set herself to rights. He bent over and picked up the new pants and pulled the curtain back for her.

Several people looked at them as they exited the dressing room, but didn't say anything to them. A slight heat filled her cheeks as she headed back to the abandoned pile of shirts she'd been looking through before the sexy interlude.

Jesse followed in her wake, but stopped and stared at something across the room. "There's Beebo. I'm going over to talk to him while you look."

Soran looked up and smiled, and Jesse planted a quick kiss on her mouth before heading off toward Beebo.

She gave them a quick glance before going back to looking through the shirts. Beebo had a worried expression on his face, and Jesse turned to look at Soran just as the doors behind her swung open and uniformed police poured through the doors with impulse pistols pointed at her.

"Soran Roberts," said the helmeted leader of the squad through the cold, inhuman glare of his face shield. "You're under arrest for high treason against the country, and anarchist activities within the public and private sector. You are being remanded to custody where you will await your trial and subsequent execution."

Stunned, Soran raised her hands beside her head as the officers advanced on her. The leader came up behind her and threw her to the ground, forcing her arms behind her back. Cold steel clamped tightly around her wrists, a heavy body pressed a knee into her lower back. With a hiss and click, the electronic handcuffs closed.

A deafening silence loomed over the store. Even her own heartbeat seemed to vanish in the face of the government's long arm of justice. And Jesse? Where was he? Did Beebo see the police enter the store and get Jesse out before they had time to arrest him, too? But no, the police had said only her name. They hadn't even noticed Jesse in the store, nor had he done anything to stop them from taking her.

A quick jerk of a strong hand in the back of her pants brought her to her feet. She twisted around to look behind her, but couldn't see anything but a broad chest covered in the black uniform of repression.

She closed her eyes and prayed Jesse had gotten out of the store. If he was free, he could find a way to rescue her.

Chapter Ten

Jesse looked on in horror as the cop threw Soran to the floor and cuffed her. Shoppers stopped to watch the spectacle of her arrest, up until the hive mentality kicked in and they realized that if they were in the immediate vicinity of a suspected traitor, they too might come under suspicion. The store emptied quickly then, and Beebo pushed Jesse out of the doors along with them.

"You have to think, Jess. Don't react. Not now. If you do, Soran's lost."

Jesse knew Beebo was right, but it ripped his guts out to stand by and watch the woman he loved be carted away cuffed and under armed guard. He swiped a shaking hand down his face. "They'll execute her."

Beebo patted his back. "Not if we can get to her first. Come on, let's follow the squad cars and see where they're taking her."

Yes, Jesse needed to keep his mind focused on freeing Soran and not on the terrible danger she was in. Guilt twisted his gut into a series of naval-worthy knots. If he hadn't stolen her keyboard and bound her to him with that kiss, she would never be under suspicion now. He did this to her. Him. Jesse Storm, the man who professed to love her so much he had denied her in his life for seven years to keep her safe. Now, he'd loved her and lost her within a day's time.

Jesse and Beebo climbed into the trike. The lingering scent of Soran clung to the interior of the vehicle and a painful spear of despair lanced through his heart.

"How did they know where we were?" he asked to the interior of the trike, not expecting Beebo to answer, but when he did the answer chilled him.

"I caught Josie contacting the authorities right after you two left. She turned in Soran, but I didn't hear your name."

"Fucking bitch. I swear to God I'll kill her for this."

He gave the ignition a violent punch, and the trike hurtled off down the busy city streets, following the sounds of the sirens' wails.

"Don't worry, Rodger already kicked her and her gear out of the warehouse," Beebo shouted over the hum of the engine.

"Perfect, now she can go directly to the authorities with everything about us. We'll all be arrested."

"No, he told her if she did, she'd go down with the rest of us. He's got her dead to rights. The woman has been hiding signature codes in her programming. There's no way she could ever deny her involvement with us. Not only that but her fingerprint I.D. is all over financial transactions to our various accounts."

Jesse tried not to feel disappointed that the most they could get from her would be exile from the RB, but he didn't have the time right now to pursue that avenue further. His main priority had to be Soran.

"Hold on, babe, I'm coming for you," he said and pushed down on the accelerator.

∗ৡৢ(ʕ•ʔ)ৣৡ∗

Her arms ached and fear caused her to break out in a cold sweat that ran between her shoulder blades and pooled beneath her breasts. The scent of their lovemaking filled her nostrils whenever she took a breath in, and she was sure from the looks on the cops' faces they noticed too.

The entire booking process had taken less than a minute. They did nothing more than verify her fingerprints on a scanner and take a quick digital image of her retina. Then they removed her shoes and socks. Soran imagined this was to prevent her from hanging herself with her shoelaces before they had the pleasure of killing her in some other fashion. Finally, she was hustled through the corridors with her hands still cuffed behind her back, and shoved into a small, sterile room.

Light glared down from the ceiling, making it impossible to see the faces, or even dim outlines of her guards. The small tinny whine of a microphone and speakers came from all around her. The trial had begun.

"Soran Roberts, you have been accused of treasonous acts against God and country. How do you plead?"

Soran raised her chin, trying not to blink from the bright lights. "I never acted against God. *He* should find no complaints in me."

"You admit to treasonous acts against the government?"

"I admit to attempting to establish equality, and unseat useless officials who have allowed the country to fall into decay and ruin."

"You are found guilty of said crimes and will be detained until execution. So say we all."

We? Soran thought. Not only was the computer a totalitarian, it also now spoke in a royal plural.

Then she realized what else the computer had said.

She hung her head and started to laugh as bitter tears squeezed from her eyes. Too soon. It was too soon after being reunited with Jesse to be ripped from his life in such a way. She had no doubt he was at this very moment devising some way to ensure her release. After all, he had escaped death himself.

The guards grabbed her and pulled her from the chair. They kicked at her feet to get her to move, and were only successful in tripping her.

They took her to a dark room and pushed her in, through a heavy door. The metal lock clicked into place with the pained cry of finality. Even if Jesse were to find her, he would never be able to penetrate that door. The heavy steel stood as a guardian against escape and allowed only a small path of light to enter through the fist-sized window.

In the moment before the door swung closed, Soran hadn't seen any object that would help her gain her freedom. And anyway, the cuffs around her wrists ensured she wouldn't be able to fashion a weapon or tool. The only weapon left to her was the firm belief that Jesse would somehow find her in time to save her.

Chapter Eleven

Jesse parked the trike around the corner, watching as the police pulled Soran from the cruiser and up the stairs of the courthouse/prison. It was the same place they had taken him. He knew the basic layout, but had no way of knowing where they would hold her until the execution.

He looked to the building as she disappeared inside, then glanced at his watch. Only an hour and a half since Soran had activated the virus. They couldn't wait for the virus to go live.

"Call Rodger," Jesse said. "We have to try and speed up the countdown."

"What?" Beebo gave him a strangled look. "We timed this so it would hit the mainframe and backup systems when they switched over for the day. You can't change your mind now."

"Sure I can. I built the damn program. I put in a safeguard just in case we mistimed the switch. The cascade will infect the backup system, just not at the same time the mainframe is hit."

"Unbelievable. Why didn't you say something sooner?" Beebo pulled out his handheld and sent a text to Rodger at the warehouse.

"Because I didn't think we'd need it."

Across the street a jumbo screen flashed by a videostream of Soran's arrest. Jesse's attention turned to the images as it flashed back to the scene captured by the security cameras the night before in the Complex. Soran was in his arms, at first hesitant then she kissed him back with her entire self.

Jesse couldn't look away from the sight of them sharing their first kiss. He watched as his video image slid down Soran's body, kissing her and running his fevered lips across her breasts. Involuntarily, his eyes slid shut. He could still feel the gentle glide of her silk shirt as he moved his mouth over her to catch that sweet nipple in his mouth.

"Damn, Jesse." Beebo said in what sounded like appreciation for the moves. "No wonder she let you have the keyboard."

The videostream stopped short of showing him sucking on her breast through the gossamer fabric. The picture flashed back to the news anchor, but Jesse couldn't hear what was being said and hadn't ever been good at reading lips.

"What's the talking head saying?"

Beebo looked up at the screen. "Who knows. Probably telling lies supplied by the government mouthpiece."

The handheld computer beeped. "Rodger says he'll try to patch us through on the handheld, but he's not optimistic."

"Give me that. You play lookout." Jesse took the handheld from Beebo, and slid to the ground to cradle it on his lap for better stability.

Jesse waited for the computer to show a prompt that would establish a link with the mainframe at the Complex.

"Jesse," Beebo warned. "You better hurry. There are several very big and very armed police coming this way."

"Shit!" Jesse stood and hurried along the wall, back down into the alley. They ducked into a doorway and to a little café.

Jesse moved quickly to the back of the establishment and slid into a dark booth. With any luck the cops wouldn't search in here. Having his image up on the jumbo screen hadn't been conducive to secrecy. But a dark corner booth was infinitely better than sitting out in the open and waiting for the police to happen by and arrest him.

Suspicion and accountability worked both ways. If he were trying to bind Soran to him by use of the Complex's video security, he had certainly bound himself to her. Not that he minded the association; he'd had too many dreams and fantasies about her to care. Matter of fact being linked to Soran for the entire world to see was more like a long overdue declaration for him. He'd staked his claim, and there it was on the jumbo screen in the middle of the city for all to see.

His stomach came up nearly to his throat. If he could just see her out of this mess he'd made of her life, he would be with her for the rest of her days. They'd live and work side by side to rebuild the country into a place they could raise their children and not have to worry about looking over their shoulders their entire lives. And they'd have sex until they were both mindless with passion. He'd never met a woman more passionate, brave, smart or kind in his entire life. He needed her like air and water.

The screen flashed on the handheld. He had a link to the mainframe. The only thing he needed was to access the clock and move it forward on the countdown, nothing more, nothing less.

The screen behind the counter played the video stream of their lovemaking over and over again. Everywhere he looked he saw her face filled with passion as he teased her and promised with his tongue how good their joining would be.

She had pleasured herself while thinking of him! Even back in college when he was a specimen beyond her notice—or so he'd thought—she had wanted him, and he had pined for her and wanted her and denied himself the pleasure of making love to her. The admission had taken him off guard, but had made him come instantly. Just the thought of her soft, delicate hands caressing herself and thinking of him... Oh, he couldn't go there right now. But he wanted to, Jesus

Christ, he wanted to.

He tore his eyes away from the screen and concentrated on his work. Reliving that incredible first kiss wouldn't help to free her, or put her back in his arms where she belonged.

The videostream changed, and Jesse heard Soran's voice strong and defiant. She sat in the middle of a bright room. Her eyes squinted against the light.

"...unseat useless officials who have allowed the country to fall into decay and ruin."

Beebo let out a deep breath. "Man, you sure know how to pick 'em. Talk about going down swinging."

"That's my girl," Jesse whispered. The pride in his voice couldn't be hidden or held in check.

"You are found guilty of said crimes and will be detained until execution. So say we all." A mechanized voice handed down the sentence to Soran, who did nothing more than bow her head and laugh.

Soran heard the locks disengage from her cell door. She sat huddled in the corner waiting quietly for someone to rescue her. Defeatism was not her modus operandi, but she was also smart enough to know when wasting energy to get out of an impossible situation wouldn't serve her. It was better to reserve energy stores until she could find a weak spot, or when they were transporting her to the execution, which could be now.

At least she had known love. Until last night when Jesse blew back into her life like a cyclone she had thought that love would never find her. Now looking death in the eyes, she had to say it was worth every minute. But she wasn't giving up. Jesse would come for her, of that she had no doubt.

Two guards appeared in the doorway. With the light behind them, she could barely make out what they were doing. But the unmistakable sound of zippers being let down spoke loudly of their intent.

Fear put a metallic taste in her mouth. They were going to rape her before they took her to her execution. She drew her legs up tight to her body so she could kick out at them when they attacked. They might be able to overpower her, but she would not let them take what she'd willingly given to Jesse.

"Come on, you little anarchist slut, I'm going to give you the ride of your life."

The guard crouched before her and grabbed for her waistband. Soran brought her leg up, kneeing him squarely in the gonads. He wailed in pain and fell back. The other guard rushed towards her with the impulse gun raised.

The blast hit her full in the chest and dragged her down into blessed blackness.

It took some coaxing to rewrite the code, but finally Jesse had the clock up and reset for five minutes. That would give him time to gain access to the courthouse before the grid came down and knocked out all power in the city. However, they would only have two minutes to get out before the generators kicked in and power came back up. Seven minutes total to save Soran and get the hell out of the strike zone.

It did help to have an IT expert that worked a hack like a magician. Beebo had successfully hacked into the courthouse/prison system and found the area where they were holding Soran. At least Jesse wouldn't have to take time to look for her, if that were the case the rescue would be doomed to fail. He tried not to think of it. He would have Soran back in his arms tonight.

They exited the café, and Beebo ran around the end of the block to get the trike and bring it closer to the courthouse.

Jesse would enter through the south entrance and hope to God no one recognized him as the man making love to Soran on the video stream.

Security was tight.

With an accused traitor in the building, no one would be allowed in or out without identification. Jesse looked down at his fingertips. He shrugged and headed into the line of people waiting to clear security. The small halogen flashlight in his pocket wouldn't pose a problem, but the glass blade in his boot might if it were found.

When his turn arrived, he placed his hand on the pad and waited for the scanners to pass over. The red light started to blink. The officer at that controls looked up at Jesse.

"Please hold your hand firmly on the plate," she said with bored indifference.

He did as instructed and tried to tune out the sound of disgruntled people behind him. If they were disgruntled, he was looking down the barrel of a long-ass impulse gun. He looked at his watch. Only three minutes left until shut down.

The red light blinked again and the officer hit a few buttons on her console. She looked up at him and frowned. He peeked around to read the console screen. It read: Subject deceased.

"Hold out your arms."

He complied and tried to act as if nothing were wrong, as if his entire life didn't depend on getting through the security field in the next minute.

The young officer searched his fingers and arms. Satisfied he hadn't had someone else's fingertips or hands grafted onto his arms, she made him walk around the counter as she held a wand to him, waving it up one side and down the other. When no sound emanated from him she patted him down. She pulled the small flashlight from his back pocket and examined it. Convinced it was no threat, she handed it back to him then let him through the checkpoint.

There wasn't time to take the elevator so he hurried to the stairs and ran down the two flights to the holding area.

Halfway down, time ran out.

"What the fuck?" the guard with the impulse gun asked.

Contrary to her first thought, Soran was not dead, merely momentarily disabled. The impulse gun had not been set to kill, only immobilize. The darkness that filled the room, and the absence of an electrical hum told Soran the grid had gone down early. Surely four hours hadn't passed since she entered the codes.

"Come on, Jeffries, we better find out what's going on." Soran could hear the scrape of boots and a moan of pain as the guard helped the injured one to his feet.

"Wait a minute," Jeffries said taking in a deep breath. "I think the bitch knocked my nuts into my throat."

While they contemplated the status of Jeffries's injured package, Soran used the wall to lever into a standing position. On silent feet she hurried from the room. Quickly, she moved in the opposite direction from which she'd originally come. Chances are the guards would move back up the hallway, rather than farther down.

How would she find her way out of here? The place was a virtual labyrinth of black corridors and eerie silence. If the virus had forced the blackout, then the lights should be coming back on any moment. Soran only had a short time for escape.

A door opened close to her and a flashlight beam bounced, scanning the walls. Then the beam bounced toward her former cell.

Soran sank against the wall. Her heart thundered against her chest wall, and her breath sawed in and out. So close. Too close.

The light stopped at the cell door and shone through the tiny window. "Soran?" Came a harsh whisper from the light bearer.

"Jesse?"

The light beam swung towards her, hitting her directly in the face. Her retina burned from the flash.

He hurried back down the corridor toward her. "Come on, we have less than a minute before the lights come back on."

"How did they go out so soon?"

"I fixed 'em," he said and took her arm. She was still cuffed, so the sudden move made her stumble. "Aw, shit, babe. We can't take the time to remove those now."

"It's all right," she said, her heart pounding in her chest. "Just get us out of here."

He directed her back to the stairwell, but instead of heading up to street level, he moved her lower into the bowels of the building.

When they passed two floors and the lights still hadn't come back on, Soran started to worry. "Jesse?"

"I know."

"Where are you taking us?"

"Shhh," he said as voices came from above and below. Instead of pulling her down another flight, he took her through the door and down another dark corridor. "Hurry."

The sounds of shuffling feet filled the hallway. Flashlight beams bounced sporadically along with the movement of people. If they were very lucky, the light wouldn't catch the shine of her handcuffs or her bare feet.

Jesse swung the light in front of them, and finally an exit sign appeared.

"Hey!" yelled a voice from behind them.

Jesse pulled her faster and her through the door. "Hurry, babe."

The sounds of pursuit grew. The high-pitched whine of impulse guns whizzed by. The air stung with the smell of ozone. A shot grazed Soran's cheek, and she bit her lip to keep from crying out. The hit left her ears ringing, and put her dangerously off-balance.

Jesse came up short and pulled her around to him and said something she couldn't hear. She shrugged her arm from his grasp and continued to move forward. It didn't matter if she had been hit. They would both be down soon if they didn't keep moving. And she was sure the guns were no longer set to immobilize.

They came out of the corridor and into a wide-open space that smelled like death. Rotting flesh, human feces, and axel grease did not make for an aromatic combination. Soran tried to bury her face against her chest to block out the wretched stench and to force the building gorge back down.

"We won't be here very long," Jesse tried to assure her.

"Not if the guys with the guns have anything to say about it."

He moved her behind a displaced piece of metal, probably from an old partition or token booth. "We'll hide here until they pass." He pressed her deeper into the makeshift shelter.

The little beam of light that had guided them, suddenly blinked out and Jesse held his hand over her mouth to keep her quiet. Police covered the area and moved their lights in arcs. Impulse guns continued to rain electrical charges through the air on the off chance it hit one of them.

"Spread out. They can't have gotten far," a deep voice said into the darkness.

Something small and furry chose that moment to run across Soran's bare foot. She prayed to every god real and imagined that the little rodent didn't decide to take a taste.

Jesse's hand moved from her mouth, and she could feel him fumbling for something on the ground. She wondered if the furry little beast had crawled up his pant leg. Suddenly, he turned her away from him and she felt his fingers moving along the links of the cuffs. Both ends pulled taut and dug painfully into her wrists, she supposed to give him room to work without hurting her in the process. Then her hands were mobile. The cuffs were still attached to her wrists like some jailhouse jewelry, but at least she could use her arms.

A dull ache began to spread from hand to shoulder blade. Too long in one position had done nothing to enhance her strength. Then ever so gently, Jesse's lips moved over first one arm and then the other, healing tenderly as he went. She turned to him, moving her sore arms around his neck and holding him close.

Jesse had had a few bad moments there. But now with Soran in his arms again, he began to feel more confident that things would turn around. The lights still had not come back on, but then again in this area of the abandoned subway, there probably hadn't been an electrical feed in decades.

"We'll hide out here until they pass and then we find a way to the surface. Beebo's waiting for us with the trike."

He felt, rather than saw, Soran nod her head at him. Her head was buried under his chin. Longing coiled in his sacrum and spread along his nerve endings. Desperation made him wish they were back at the warehouse where he could make love to her slowly, enter her sweet body and stay there forever.

Footsteps crushed on the refuse near their hiding spot.

Jesse squeezed Soran tighter to keep her quiet. He held his breath. The glass knife remained clutched in his fist, the handle gripped so tightly it grated into his palm.

He needed to turn around, to be ready for a threat. The movement would be heard, but it was necessary. He had come too far to cower in a corner in the dark. Slowly, Jesse took his arms from around Soran and pivoted on his toe.

The cop stepped closer. The flashlight beam penetrated the dark of their sanctum. An impulse gun rose. A finger closed on the trigger.

Jesse lunged. The knife penetrated the thick uniform and entered the chest cavity with little resistance. Blue lightning crackled around the body, and the stench of burnt circuitry filled the tiny space.

"Holy mother…" Jesse whispered in awe. A cyborg. This was a revelation that the Restoration Brigade hadn't counted on, but it did explain the increase in the number of police officers in the city.

Soran let out a breath of surprise then moved past him to the body crumbling before her. She picked up the impulse gun and held it up. "These aren't keyed to fingerprints, are they?" she whispered.

He looked down at the fallen robotic officer and shook his head. In the light of the flashlight, the fingers were covered with black gloves. "No, I don't think you have to worry about that."

Jesse bent over the body and patted it down for more weapons and replacement cartridges for the gun. He came up with several useful items, and filled the pockets of his utility pants.

"Pick up the flashlight. If anyone sees the beam they'll think we're one of them."

"Maybe you, but not me."

"Hold it up higher."

When she picked up the flashlight, he caught a glimpse of her face. She looked pale and tired. Neither of them had taken time to eat today, and he doubted they had even offered her a last meal. A steady diet of adrenaline wore thin after a while.

"I'm sorry," Jesse said, brushing her hair back from her face. "I got you into this, and I'll think of a way to get you out."

She stepped closer to him and cupped his cheek with her palm. "I didn't give up on you when I sat in that black cell waiting to be taken to my execution. I knew you'd come to rescue me. Don't you dare give up on me."

He bowed his forehead to hers. Did he even deserve her? He kissed her then, a long deep kiss of promise. There was no way in hell he'd ever give up on her, but he would understand if after the events of today she wanted to bow out, even if there would be major difficulties in disentangling her from their cause.

"Come on, we need to find the way out of here."

Jesse ducked out from behind their hiding place and checked the area. Lights swayed and bounded going away from them down the long shaft of the abandon tracks.

He took her hand and pulled her along.

They walked along the westbound tracks for about ten minutes. He had to hand it to Soran. Even though she walked barefoot through some of the foulest debris he'd ever encountered, she hadn't uttered a complaint. Her can-do attitude would have made the Marine Corps of old proud.

He glanced over at her. Perhaps he hadn't given her enough credit back in college. His need to protect her had done her an injustice. Jesse had been so caught up in her innocence that he had completely overlooked her strength and fortitude.

Finally, they came to a stairway that had once led up to street level. Iron gates were held in place by rusted screws.

"Can you break them away?" Soran asked.

"I'm gonna try." Jesse tried the gate and found it was only pulled to in an attempt make it look secure. "This stairway must still be used by the undergrounders."

He ushered her through and pulled it back to.

"Why haven't we seen any? Shouldn't we have been accosted by now?"

"Not necessarily. The commotion near the courthouse would have made them scatter. You'll never see them unless they want you to."

They were halfway up to street level when Soran put her hand on his arm and stopped him. "Do you think they'll ever come back above ground to live?"

"Doubt it. They already mistrust society as it is, I don't think it'll change just because the power grid came down."

He hoped that he had been correct that in the subways, they hadn't been able to tell when the new grid kicked back on. Truthfully, he didn't know why the grid hadn't come back on yet, and it worried him in no small measure.

They emerged into the late afternoon sunshine. Heat attacked them from all directions after being in the cool dark confines of the underground. The city had become ground zero for mass chaos. Sky trams filled the air, and people crowded the sidewalks looking up as the infrequent patches of blue became dotted with incoming tactical fighters.

"Jesse..." Soran breathed beside him.

Even in the filtered light of a city day, eeriness invaded the streets. The jumbo screen a few blocks away had gone black and reflected only the invasion from above. Neon lights that touted the wares of various NATNET-owned corporations refused to hum with life.

He pressed his lips together and started to move in the direction of the parked trike. What had happened? He'd been so careful with the programming. Every line of code had been gone over again and again to ensure the success of the switchover. Then it hit him. Josie! If she had encrypted her own signature after he'd done the last check before installation, it could have corrupted the backup system. She'd rolled over on Soran, why not the rest of them?

Troops of police came down the street, impulse rifles at the ready. Jesse pulled her into a doorway, well back from the press of the crowd near the street. He shielded her from view and turned his back to the street. Reflections in store windows told him all he needed to know.

"Damn computerized cops. We need to rally people to take them out."

"Not all of them are computers, Jesse."

He looked down at her, but she wouldn't look at him. "What? How do you know?"

"Because before the grid went down two of them... in my cell... and..." her voice got lower and lower until he could barely hear her, but he didn't need to hear what she said to understand what she meant.

"Did they?" He asked as his arms went around her.

"No."

Tremors started to course through her body. He needed to get her back to the warehouse. She may be tough, but she still had her limits.

Jesse placed a lingering kiss in her hairline. "It'll be all right. We'll figure it all out."

Her hands slid around his waist and ducked into the waistband of his pants. The cuffs prevented them from sliding any farther than her wrists. He really needed to get her back to the trike before anyone noticed the cuffs or her bare dirty feet.

The parade of police seemed endless, clogging Broadway, and choking the side streets. Where were they all coming from?

They tucked into the store, and cut through to the back, coming out a block over. Crowds continued to press into the streets to bear witness to the unfolding events. Jesse wove them in and out between bystanders, keeping a steady pace, and losing themselves to the crowd of humanity.

The trike was parked where Beebo had left it. The man standing outside it looked up like all the other nervous citizens.

"Beebo," Jesse called.

The man let a visible sigh of relief pass over his dark features. He turned and opened the doors of the trike before they could reach him.

Jesse helped Soran get in. "Take her back to the warehouse. I'll be right behind you."

Soran grabbed for him. "What are you doing? You can't leave me again. The last time you did, I got arrested."

Jesse wound a hand around her neck and pulled her to him, placing a rough, demanding kiss on her protesting lips. He pulled back and said, "Go with Beebo, please. We need to split up. It's safer that way."

"I won't leave you behind," she protested and tried to climb back out of the trike.

He picked her up and sat her on the seat. "Please, do as I say."

"Jesse…" Tears filled her eyes.

Dammit. She hadn't complained once, and now she was about to come undone because he was sending her to safety with Beebo.

He cradled her face in his hands as the tears spilled down her cheeks. "Don't do this to me. I love you so much. I just want to know you're safe."

"What about you? I want to know you're safe, too."

He kissed her lips again, wanting to do so much more to her. "I'll see you in fifteen minutes. No more than that."

Jesse looked up as a swarm of the computerized police officers came down the side street. He pressed another kiss on her lips, then stepped back as Beebo pulled the doors down and hit the ignition and thrusters.

They sped off down the street, leaving Jesse staring after them, feeling as if the Grand Canyon had just opened in his chest.

Chapter Twelve

Jesse tucked into the sanctuary of a doorway and watched the trike move through the crowded streets. His heart took a dive. But he didn't want Soran around for what he planned next. It was hard enough keeping her safe on their flight from the Complex the night before. Going back in to dismantle the computer by hand would be dangerous enough by himself. He didn't want to have to worry about her.

His hand curled into a fist as he lost sight of the trike. He rested his head against his arm and took a deep breath. Yesterday, he wouldn't have thought twice about going back into the building to face certain death. But last night, everything had changed. Today, he had an entire future with Soran to look forward to. But in order to have that future, he had to circumvent Josie's treachery. No telling what layers she had added to the program to thwart them. He couldn't even speculate why, after being so faithful to the cause, did she turn her back on them so completely.

"Bitch," he muttered and pushed away from the doorway.

Police were still moving down the streets, marching in some unnamed parade.

Jesse took to the alleys, trying to make his way to the sky tram station. Chances were the fighters hovering above would try to force the sky trams to ground just to keep the populace where the police could watch them.

But there was a ground transport system at the same station. It only ran across midtown, but that would be enough to get him to the Complex building quicker than walking would.

Jesse arrived at the sky tram station with little fanfare in his wake, and yet the entire station had been thrown into the midst of confusion. Someone had taped a large paper banner across the arrivals and departures board that read: Until further notice, all trams are outbound only. The ground transports sat huddled in a parking lot; their drivers needed for the extra runs out to the farthest boroughs.

The citizens were abandoning the city. The need to yell at them for their stupidity and narrow-mindedness burned the back of his throat like acid. He wanted with all his heart to climb atop the ticket station and impress upon them the need to take a chance on a new direction of government.

But he remained still. It would be better if they were away from the city when the final grid came down. The unmanned fighters would fall from the sky and crash to earth. Christ, not even Soran would be safe if a fighter jet fell on the warehouse.

He ran a worried hand down his face and scrubbed around his mouth. No time to think about consequences now, he had committed himself to the deed and he had to follow through. He just had to keep trying to convince himself that Soran would be fine.

He pushed through the crowd to find some conveyance to transport him to the Complex. Then, he spotted it shining like a beacon calling to him from the confines of a designated parking space: the transportation commissioner's company glider. Oh, this would be such a sweet liberation of merchandise. Much sweeter than Fong's delivery trike.

Jesse looked around to ensure all transit personnel were engaged in helping people to embark, then he slid silent as a wraith to stand beside the glider. He made a quick survey of the area and thirty seconds later, against the sensual hum of a stolen vehicle, the glider's engine purred to life. He pulled from the parking lot and eased into traffic—no official wiser in the melee of ten million people evacuating the city.

The glider swished through traffic at the second story level, above the heads of panicked crowds and robot police. Dark windows prevented the curious from seeing inside and giving away his identity. The last thing he needed was to be brought down to street level in a fiery crash, especially one compliments of the city's finest, human or not.

As he neared the Complex, the hair on the back of his neck tingled. Guards had the streets blocked off and a hastily constructed fence surrounded the building. Jesse winced. It wasn't just a fence but generator-powered razor wire. The generator turned the wire like a cotton gin, making it impossible to get a hold of to snip and scale. It most likely also had an electrical charge as well.

"Great, just fucking great," he said to the interior of the glider. Then he smiled. He had a glider with an official city seal on the side, what was he worried about? If the gate patrol happened to scan the bar code on the plate, they would automatically open the gate and he could glide right into the underground parking garage. Of course there was always the chance that with the blackout and last night's break-in there would be heightened security at the entrance. But it was a chance he had to take.

Soran held on to Beebo as the trike sped through the streets. She had never seen so many people out of their offices or apartments. With the oppressive summer heat beating down, the buildings would be like brick ovens.

Something more was going on than just a little mistiming on the part of the program. Jesse was too thorough, too focused, to let something so vital go by unnoticed. No, this was definitely not his doing.

Soran looked up through the windowed trike cover. The tactical fighters continued to fill the sky. They did nothing more than circle the city like a convergence of vultures waiting for the behemoth city to die. Were they trying to keep the peace by flexing the mainframe's muscle? And how were they communicating with the mainframe down? Same with the artificial cops manning the streets. There had to be a secondary defense grid that hadn't come down. But Jesse would have known about it, or one of his friends.

They reached the warehouse without further problems and were soon safely ensconced in the tech room. Soran leaned back on the futon. Was it only last night she'd been in this room? Nervous energy moved through her, pulled her taut enough to snap. Conversely, she also felt as if all her limbs were made of lead.

The energy peaked and spread through her body and she bounced to her feet. "We have to take down the defense grid," she said to Beebo.

Rodger looked at her from under thick blond brows. "Not yet. Let me cut the rest of those fancy cuffs off you and then you can go get cleaned up. Meet us back in here after you've had a shower and something to eat."

Food. How could she possibly think of food when Jesse was out there and in danger? Every moment he stayed away was a moment of agony for her. The deep pit she thought closed upon learning of his narrow escape suddenly loomed open again. She rubbed her chest where her heart felt heavy and incapable of beating.

"I'll let you take off the cuffs, but I can't do anything else until we bring down the defense grid, and Jesse is back here safe."

"You're about to drop..." Rodger started to argue, but Soran held up her hand to stop him. She didn't want sympathy. She just wanted to finish what they started, and to have her man by her side.

"Is there any way we can patch into NATNET with part of the grid down?" she asked Beebo, ignoring Rodger's attempts to get her to relax.

Beebo turned around in his seat and looked at the blank screen in front of him. "I may be able to find a backdoor inside. As long as the gas generator holds. Without our layered power online, it's anyone's guess."

That wasn't comforting. "Well, let's try anyhow. Jesse wouldn't want us just sitting around here waiting for him, I'm sure."

Beebo and Rodger exchanged looks.

"What?" She had the sneaking suspicion that they knew something they weren't telling her. They certainly knew Jesse better than she had over the last seven years.

Beebo stood and took her hand, directing her back to the futon. When the backs of her knees hit the soft foam cushion, she sat.

"There's something you need to understand about Jesse," he began. "If the grid didn't come down as he planned, you better believe he's gone to the Complex to dismantle the Cerebellum himself. He won't allow two failures."

Loyalty made her sit up straighter. "He didn't fail. NATNET must have fought the virus in ways he didn't anticipate. I mean, who could anticipate the actions of a sentient computer? Even someone who programmed it to begin with couldn't possibly think of all the scenarios and problem solving capabilities of such a vast network."

Rodger sat down next to her, his blue eyes troubled. "No, Jesse definitely didn't fail. The program would have gone off without a hitch -- if someone hadn't sabotaged it before he installed it."

"What?" It felt as if all the air had been purged from her lungs. Drawing a breath would be impossible now

"We suspect Josie corrupted the program in some way before he installed it. This morning after you left she called and turned you in to the authorities. She was the reason you were imprisoned."

"My God," Soran whispered. "How could she have worked and lived with you guys for so long and turn completely against you?"

Rodger shook his head. "We'll probably never have the answer to that."

Soran sat back and covered her face. Because of Josie, she could have been executed, and the rest of the Restoration Brigade and their plans were thwarted. How could Josie do such a thing? Turning in Soran could be attributed to jealousy, but the program-tampering had happened before she came back into Jesse's life.

More determined to help Jesse, Soran stood. "Now, more than ever, we need to take that grid down. The security at the Complex is probably pretty heavy today, especially in light of the power failure."

Beebo sat at the terminal once again and began tapping in a series of codes, trying to find a backdoor into NATNET. Soran took a place beside him at the workstation and slid her keyboard towards her. While he tried for a backdoor, she'd try for the front. Even if the main brain of the system had kicked her out that morning, given the virus, NATNET might just latch on to any operator that felt familiar.

She keyed in the start-up sequence that would lock her into NATNET. The program limped onto the screen, running sluggishly as the screen flickered in an attempt to shut down. Her headset lay on the counter, still plugged in and ready for use. She placed it over her ears and turned to Beebo, giving him the thumbs up.

"Are you in?" he asked sliding his chair closer.

"Almost. The program is trying to boot, but it's not guaranteed to connect."

While they tried to get into the system, Rodger pulled out his phone and tried to contact members of the RB still in the field. Soran fervently hoped he would send some to the Complex to help Jesse. The thought of him going in blind and alone made her chest constrict. She hadn't missed the bruises on his ribs from the struggle with the mainframe the night before.

"Hello, Soran Roberts," came the familiar mechanized voice. No trace of the earlier malice remained. The computer sounded rather smug now, as if it knew it would win.

"Hello, NATNET. I'm having trouble connecting to the Complex mainframe. Can you help?"

"Mainframe running at thirty percent efficiency. Attempting to correct problem."

"Have you reached a diagnosis for the problem?" she asked, wondering if the program would actually give her information.

"Virus detected in power grid sector. Rerouting necessary functions to secondary grid."

The defense grid?

"NATNET, if you do that, won't you need more program space? The power grid is a massive program."

Beebo smiled evilly and gave her a thumbs-up. He'd gotten in the back-door.

"Keep him talking," he said.

She looked over his shoulder to see the screen. He was trying to move programs around.

"All other programs essential to mainframe security," the voice said.

Soran punched in a few more lines of code. "NATNET, can you ascertain how long before the power grid is operational again?"

"Unable to determine. Unknown user detected in defense grid. Shut down of link imminent." There was a brief pause then, "Don't leave, Soran Roberts."

A chill ran down her spine. The computer sounded like a frightened child now.

"It's all right, NATNET, I'm here."

"Defense grid down!" Panic rocked through the headset, and the screen flashed in a red warning before going dark again.

A thundering noise shook the warehouse, a scream of metal and propulsion, moments before a loud crash hit the water just off the end of the warehouse.

"You should have given the command to land before you brought down the grid," she said to Beebo. Then she vacated her chair and ran to the door to see how many fighters were falling from the sky outside the warehouse.

As she stood in the doorway, she looked up and whispered, "My God." She only hoped Jesse was safe from the rain of fighters.

Chapter Thirteen

Jesse brought the glider down to street level and eased up to the parking garage gate. The thought of just flying over the gate was a tempting one, but if he tried, he was sure they would shoot him down. He needed papers or something in case they asked to see them. The interior of the glider showed nothing of value, and the storage compartment only held the owner's manual.

"Damn." Nothing. Then from the corner of his eye he saw an official's hat, complete with gold shield.

He grabbed the hat and put it on, then hit the window just enough to show the hat but not enough to give away his identity. It was a bold bluff on his part, but it was all he had. There were too many non-human cops around to even consider crashing the gate and running them down.

"Identification," the guard said without preamble.

"I'm the transportation commissioner," Jesse retorted in feigned affront.

"Identification. Now." The barrel of an impulse gun came in the window, leveled at his head.

"All right." Jesse acted as if he were fumbling to pull his identification out of pocket. The barrel hit the window and the weapon discharged into the glider's interior, narrowly missing his head. "Fucking Christ."

The gun fell away from the window and clattered against the side of the glider. The guard crumpled to the ground. Jesse looked around and noticed the same thing happening all around him. Looking up through the glider's windowed roof, he could see the fighters falling from the sky like paper airplanes at the end of their flight arc.

Not good. Not good at all. He gunned the thrusters and took off through the open gate and into the garage. All over the city, fighters were falling from the heavens and leaving death and destruction in their wake. This was not what the Restoration Brigade wanted, and this was not how Jesse planned the transition of power.

Guilt tried to swamp him, but he fought it back. There would be time to mourn the lost after he dismantled the Cerebellum for good.

A boom sounded behind him, and the percussion rocked the glider forward, bringing the tail end up. Jesse fought for control. But it was useless. The glider crashed nose down.

His head knocked painfully against the navigational stick. Stars swam before his eyes and he shook his head to clear it. Blood ran down over his eye. Hastily, he wiped it away and climbed from the glider.

Human police officers ran down the street trying to restore order and help the victims injured by the falling planes. Sirens wailed in the distance, and alarms screeched in protest. Smoke and debris rolled down the street, covering the area in a blanket of dust.

Jesse hurried to the building wanting to waste no more time than necessary. All he wanted to do was to get back to the warehouse and see Soran, make sure she was all right.

He pressed a hand to his heart. God help him if anything happened to her. How could a group of geniuses have so grossly miscalculated the odds? Jesse should have sensed that Josie would turn on them. He'd made their split too irrevocable. Soran had only been the salt in the wound.

Explosions vibrated the concrete under his feet, and made his ears ring. He moved quickly to the steps and started up the long trek to the Cerebellum. He thought about the elevators longingly. No power, no elevators.

He had to stop several times on the climb up to catch his breath and let the throbbing in his head subside before continuing on. Compared to that, his ribs felt fine. Oh, the joy he'd get from dismantling the fucking computer piece by piece. The damn thing had cost him too much in the past twenty-four hours. It had nearly cost him Soran.

If it hadn't been for the damn program all those years ago, he would have been with her all along. He wouldn't have had to protect her by pushing her away, and maybe, just maybe, they would have both overcome their shyness enough to confess their feelings back then. Now he'd never know because the damn coded governmental interloper had cost him seven years with her. Seven years he'd never get back, and if the planes crashed into the warehouse it would be time he'd never be able to make up with her.

The halls leading to the Cerebellum were littered with the corpses of the computer's automated personal army. He looked around for anyone moving, but found no one. Perhaps the computer had dismissed the human element after they failed to protect it from the virus.

Jesse moved to the door and was unsurprised to note the pneumatic locks had held. He'd have to find a way to release the pressure to get the door open. He pulled his knife and pried open the lock mechanism. It would only take a slice along the pressure lines to let the air hiss out and release the door.

He made short work of that, and the door slid open. The severed cables still lay on the floor where he left them the day before. The notebook he left behind sat among the refuse. He hurried to it and disconnected it; there was no need to leave that behind this time. He set the notebook aside and began the process of disconnecting the computer.

The glass blade sliced through wires, and severed the brain stem of the computer. Once again, cables tried to defend the computer, but with both major grids down and the virus spreading throughout the system, there wasn't much strength.

A twinge of remorse nudged at the back of his mind. It was like killing a doomed animal. He was no longer quite certain if his actions were to help reform the country or put the beast out of its current misery. It couldn't help what it had become. It had no real emotions to judge right from wrong, only code that found the most expedient way to complete its tasks. Unfortunately, those ways were without the need of human service.

Suddenly, a surge of power brought a cable up around his throat, cutting off his air supply. Blood pounded in his head, narrowing his vision to a mere pinprick of consciousness. No. He'd come too far to die this way. It was rather like patricide, the computer trying to kill him.

Given the angle and size of the cable, he couldn't cut it out without slicing his own throat. He spun around and with dwindling strength pulled the cable from the connection. Wires snapped and circuitry screamed.

The noose fell from his neck and hung loosely around his shoulders. His throat burned, the skin broken and chafed.

He set to dismantling the monster. As he pulled the last of the circuitry from its moorings, the lights blinked on and a cool breeze filled the hot room with a rush of air. The RB's servers had finally come online, restoring power to the city.

A low, shaky laugh began in his gut and issued up from his mouth. They'd done it. They had finally done it.

"How long has it been?" Soran asked Beebo as he sat at the computer trying to patch into the other substations in the interior of the country.

"Thirty minutes."

She rolled over on her side to watch the door, pillowing her head on her arm. She should have never allowed him to leave her again. But he had been determined to complete his mission without her. She was sure his only motive was to protect her, but hadn't she proven herself capable of helping?

The fighters had stopped falling from the sky and a good part of the city stood in ruins. Soran had only to close her eyes to imagine the pain and anguish of the populace outside the safe confines of the warehouse. She wanted to help the victims. But she was afraid if Jesse returned while she was gone, he'd go look for her and they would not be able to find one another again. She told herself that when he returned, they would venture out and help those who were injured.

She let her eyes slide shut, for only a moment. Dreams filled her mind with gossamer cobweb images, none of which made sense to her.

The futon depressed under someone's weight as they sat beside her, but Soran didn't have enough strength to open her eyes.

Her nose filled with Jesse's unique scent as warm lips skimmed across her cheeks and pressed into her eyelids. A large calloused hand caressed her arm.

She could feel an involuntary smile lift the corner of her mouth. Even in the twilight between dreams and reality he made her feel so much. No man had ever made her feel as much as Jesse Storm.

Her smile was rewarded with another brief kiss.

"Wake up, babe," he said into her ear.

Oh, she wanted to. She wanted to see his face to confirm he really had returned to the warehouse and was safe next to her.

Arms wrapped around her waist and moved up to cup her breasts. Heat speared her and coalesced low in her belly.

"Jesse," she breathed.

"That's it, wake up."

Palms skimmed over her tight nipples, eliciting a moan from her throat.

"I can't help touching you. I wanted to do this since I found you in the damn prison. I have to feel you, know you're still alive."

"Mmmm," she rolled over onto her back and let her eyes open.

"There's those beautiful eyes I love." His face was so close to hers she could see the little flecks of gold in his eyes.

"How long have you been back?"

"About an hour now."

"I slept that long?" Soran rose up on her elbows, scooting away slightly from him. He tightened his grip on her and pulled her close again.

"You needed it, but I couldn't wait any longer."

A cut ran down his forehead, and a new bruise had formed around his throat. Soran didn't like what either injury implied, but he was safe and whole and in her arms. So she didn't even ask. Instead she ran her hands and lips over him.

A moan rumbled through him and he pushed her deeper into the cushion. His mouth claimed hers, and she drank a promise of forever from his lips.

Slowly, he let her up for air, kissing each corner of her mouth.

She looked around the usually busy room. "Where is everyone?"

"Outside."

"We're alone?"

He smiled lecherously as a hand snuck up under her shirt and claimed a breast. "We are."

Her tight nipple responded to the caress, hardening into a pleasurably painful peak. "Mmmm, I love the feel of your hands on me."

"You know what? So do I." He leaned into her and kissed her deeply. His tongue explored her mouth as if it were the first time. Quick fingers undid the fastenings of her pants and then slid inside to find her wet and eager for him.

"Jesse," she moaned as his long blunt finger slid into her drenched sheath.

She moved her hands between them to help free him from his fabric prison. "I need you inside me."

He slid her pants down her hips and came into her almost in one motion. It felt so incredible having his hard shaft inside her again that Soran couldn't hold back the immediate and powerful orgasm that ripped through her.

Jesse continued to move fast and hard. Her hands settled on his buttocks as they flexed with each movement. Each stroke brought her closer to oblivion. Her mind swam, her eyes watered. Insanity lay only a heartbeat away. And it thundered, beckoning her to sexual madness. But there was no one she wanted to take her there but Jesse Storm.

"I love you," she breathed. "Forever."

"Soran!" He yelled and let his control break and wash over her. The force and heat of his come sent her headlong over the edge again, until the only sensation she felt was at the joining of their bodies.

Soran didn't know how long they lie there panting and gathering their wits after the maelstrom subsided, but it seemed an endless chasm of time. He didn't pull out and she didn't move to dislodge him, but reveled in the feel of him still large and swollen in her passage.

Lips skimmed her neck and breath stirred the sweaty hair at her temple. "Come on," he said rolling off her after a few more moments. "I want to show you something."

"What?"

"You'll see." He stood and tucked himself back into his pants and fastened them. She did likewise then took the hand he held out to her.

Hand in hand they moved through the warehouse, coming out into the garage section. There under the soft glow of the fluorescent lighting sat her glider.

"Jesse! Oh, my God. How did you know which one was mine?" She threw her arms around his neck and held him close.

"It was the only one left in the employee parking deck, and when I got in it smelled like you." He put his arms around her and pulled her close.

"Are you saying I smell?"

"Right now, yeah. You smell like me, but I like that about you." He kissed her neck and then pulled her out to the main door.

"Where are we going now?" He swung the outer door open and stood behind her as she breathed in the smell of smoldering fires. "The city is ruined."

"Not completely." Warm breath bathed her ear. "Look at the lights, Soran. Our grid came up. All the power you see before you belongs to the people, not the system."

"Oh." She let out an awed sigh. "Can we go into the city and help?"

"Beebo and Rodger are putting supplies together as we speak."

Soran nodded. Jesse would make it right. He always did.

About the Author:

Kathleen Scott lives in rural New Jersey with her husband, cat, and a wild imagination that refuses to be tamed.

Birthday

❦❧❦

by Ellie Marvel

To My Reader:

Sometimes we write from the imagination, and sometimes we write from the heart. The best stories happen when we combine to two, which I hope I've done with *Birthday*. Publishing this story will always give me a special zing because my oh-so patient husband (moosh alert, moosh alert!) was my best friend for ten years before I woke up and smelled the hottie. He waited... and waited... and waited... and I guess he bought new cologne or something because one day I realized he was more than my best friend, he was my really hot, sexy best friend, and I should probably marry him.

So I did.

Birthday is about the rush of what it's like to strike out in all the wrong places and find your someone right beside you.

"I've been celibate long enough. I'm getting laid for my birthday if I have to hire somebody to do it." Jasmine Templeton zipped her patent leather black boots with a decisive yank. To complete her fuck-me outfit, she had on a short, tight red dress, a mega push-up bra, and the world's tiniest underpants.

Definitely an outfit to get noticed in. Jaz hoped it got her more than noticed. She glanced through her hair at her two best friends, waiting in Charlie's living room while she adjusted her boots.

Mr. Sensible, otherwise known as Charlie, tipped up his beer and drained it instead of commenting. But Shae, otherwise known as Crazy Wench, laughed and said, "It won't come to that. All you have to do is venture into the Pit and ten different guys will jock you in as many minutes. If you dance with me, you'll get twice as many offers." She blew Jaz a big, wet kiss.

Charlie rinsed his empty and set it upside down in his dish drainer. He opened the fridge and grabbed another beer, his second, which Jaz knew from experience would be his last. "This is a dumb idea. It's not safe to pick up guys in bars."

Jaz tried not to think about the fact he was right. She twisted up her light brown hair and angled her face sideways in the mirror next to Charlie's front door. Should she wear her hair in a scrunch or leave it down? She hadn't danced until dawn since she had been in her mid-twenties, and she'd had short hair then. "Don't be so uptight, Chuck. It's not every day a girl turns thirty-three."

Charlie glared at her for her use of the dreaded nickname. He preferred Charlie—Charles, in fact, which neither Jaz nor Shae had called him since they met in chemistry class at Trinity State College fifteen years ago.

"We haven't seen Lorraine around recently. Thank God," Shae said. "So how long has it been since you've had sex?"

"None of your business." Charlie flipped his bottle top expertly into the trash, avoiding eye contact, and both women snickered.

"Longer than me, I bet," Jaz guessed.

Charlie sipped his drink and eyed her in a way that would have made her nervous if he hadn't been Charlie—just Charlie. "This is really what you want for your birthday?" he asked. "How about we pick you out a vibrator from the Pink Clam?"

Shae cackled and poured herself a jigger of tequila. "Please. I got her one when she turned twenty-five. And thirty. And last year." She gulped the shot down like it was water, slamming it back onto counter with a whoop.

Charlie arched an eyebrow, and Jaz felt blood rush to her face. "I'm a modern woman. I can have as many sex toys as I want. That includes sex toys of the human variety."

"I'm not arguing about the vibrators, just the one night stand you're planning."

Shae poured herself another shot and one for Jaz. "Maybe it won't be one night. Remember Damien? The barely legal with the pierced tongue? I didn't let that poor boy out of my bedroom for two weeks."

"At which point he took off with your stereo," Charlie said. He raised his beer to her. "Good choice."

Shae shrugged. "I needed a new stereo anyway."

Jaz didn't need two weeks, just one long, hard night to get the lust out of her system. A quickie would be like spring cleaning for her libido, and then maybe she could concentrate on her normal life again instead of wondering why she couldn't meet a nice guy.

It's not like anybody would measure up to her dream man, anyway, that mythical creature composed of parts Hugh Jackman and parts—okay, all Hugh Jackman, as Wolverine. So hot, so dangerous, so forceful, and so incredibly able-bodied! Men like that didn't exist in real life, and the ones who came close were scary jerkwads.

Shae handed Jaz a shot glass, toasted her, and they drank. The liquor burned white-hot courage all the way to Jaz's toes, and at 5'10", that was a long way.

"Tell me why you're going to the Pit with Jaz and me again?" Shae asked Charlie.

"Because you invited me." Charlie tucked the hand not holding his beer under his arm, his shoulders broad in his crisp white dress shirt. "And you're right, Lorraine and I broke up."

"Lorraine the Pain," Shae stage-whispered. "Did you end it the way we told you to? Not even Lorraine deserved the jackhole break-up."

"No comment," Charlie said.

Jaz had always thought Charlie was attractive in an academic sort of way, with dark brown hair and electric blue eyes, but he had the world's crappiest taste in women. Shae and Jaz had fixed him up with some of their nicer girlfriends to no avail. She knew a lot of women who were loser magnets; he was the male equivalent, poor guy.

They were all loser magnets, a fact they'd bemoaned in triplicate on many occasions. They all had great jobs—Shae was a real estate agent, Charlie was a pharmacist, and Jaz was a landscape architect. Shae had been married once—to a loser—and Jaz had met a succession of losers until she'd given up and turned nun for the last six months. Besides, not a one of them had resembled the growly, sexy superhero of her dreams.

Then, three weeks ago, she and Shae had been bridesmaids in Charlie's kid sister's wedding. The fact that Nell's tiny, twenty-something ass was going to Fiji on a honeymoon with a handsome doctor when Jaz's last date had been with a guy who couldn't get it up unless he put a dog collar on her—well, it had stirred up feelings she'd been trying to deny for months.

She was horny. And frustrated. And very, very lonely. It was silly to hold every date to the standard of some fantasy man who simply didn't exist.

She'd confessed her gloom to Shae, whose current answer to all problems was hedonism. Naturally, Shae offered to sponsor her at the Pit, a member's only club with a certain reputation and, she promised, a choice selection of hotties. She'd talked Charlie into going as well. Jaz had no idea what Shae had done to convince him to venture this far out of his comfort zone, but Shae could persuade a bald man to buy a hair dryer.

Suddenly apprehensive, Jaz wriggled her toes inside her high heeled boots and slipped her tiny evening bag over her shoulder. "We need to get this sideshow on the road." She twisted her hair again. "Up or down?"

"Up." Shae mimed burning her finger on Jaz's bare arm. "You're gonna get hot tonight."

Charlie studied her, considering her question in his serious way. "I like it down," he decided.

"Okay." As her intent was to attract men, Charlie's was the closest thing to a male's opinion she had. Which was a weird turn of phrase, because Charlie was all man. It's just that she and Shae decided long ago he was off limits, so they didn't think of him as an eligible bedpartner.

Shae deposited her shot glass in the sink—both women knew not to leave dirty glasses sitting around in front of Charlie—and pointed at him. "Do you have to wear the noose?"

He loosened his burgundy silk necktie. "You think I'm dressed too formally for hiding my face while you two lunatics pick up random men at a local sex club?"

"It's not a sex club." Shae picked up her blue purse, which matched her leather skirt and camisole tank, and checked her condom supply, her identification, her money, and her lipstick, in that order. "It's an exclusive dance club that just happens to have a lot of private nooks."

"I bet you've explored two thirds of them," Charlie muttered.

"Give me some credit." Shae uttered a wicked laugh. "I'm only familiar with one or two select nooks. Now take off the tie. We're going to a party, not a board meeting."

Charlie, still muttering, untied his necktie and slid it out of his collar with a long, sinuous motion. The peppery tequila still on her tongue, Jaz fixated on the gesture, the sound of silk on cotton, the slow twist of his fingers as he unbuttoned his collar. Her minidress had buttons down the back. She imagined some man unbuttoning every tiny red button, maybe slicing them off with a knife, placing hot kisses down her spine, until he reached the top of her ass and…

Boy, she was horny. It was either that or the tequila. She poured herself another shot and tossed it back.

When she clinked her glass on Charlie's breakfast bar, he was staring at her mouth. She held up the tequila bottle. "Want some?" she asked him, knowing he'd refuse. He'd had his two beers.

"One shot," Shae added. "It won't even hit before we get to the club."

Charlie frowned. "I'm driving." He placed Jaz's glass and his half-full beer bottle in the sink and grabbed his keys from the pegboard next to the bar. "Let's go."

"Don't forget your promise, Chuckles." Shae punched him in the arm; with the kickboxing classes she took, it was forceful enough to make Charlie flinch.

Shae hurried them out of the apartment before Jaz had a chance to ask about this promise. Plus, Shae kept talking. "You two are both going to have a good time tonight. That's *my* promise."

They exited the apartment and headed down the stairs to Charlie's late model silver SUV, parked on the street. A warm summer night had fallen; the stars were visible despite the lights of the city. Charlie's apartment was close to downtown, in a huge renovated Victorian that used to be a boarding house. Jaz loved it. The neighborhood was safe and eclectic, but they could walk to bars and restaurants and boutiques. However, it was more convenient for her to live in the country, with space for her greenhouse and experimental garden plot.

As Charlie drove exactly the speed limit to the Pit, ignoring Shae's encouragement for him to kick it, Jaz wondered again what he'd promised Shae. Not to be a spoilsport, most likely. Since her divorce, Shae hadn't had a dull week-end. This was the first time the three of them had joined forces since Nell's wedding, when they used to hang together all the time.

Case in point, they'd made a date a couple months ago to see an historical flick at the new theater off Broad, but Shae had stood them up. That left Charlie, Jaz, and an overlarge tub of popcorn side by side, in the dark, as the torrid life of a prostitute in seventeenth century Venice was unveiled in oh so many ways.

That movie had been all kinds of hot. Jaz had found herself crossing her legs as drumbeats of arousal throbbed in her crotch, conscious of the man beside her scented faintly of aftershave and movie theater butter. When she'd reached into his lap for popcorn—and missed—he'd lurched and spilled the whole tub in the floor.

Unless Jaz was mistaken, Charlie had been feeling the movie's vibe as much as she had. Maybe more, though who could tell from one quick brush against his cock?

They'd pretended it hadn't happened, but since then, things had been edgy between them. Jaz didn't really want him along tonight, but Shae invited him and Jaz could hardly uninvite him. She just wasn't comfortable knowing Charlie would witness her attempt to hook up with whichever guy seemed most capable of giving her multiple orgasms.

She just wanted one session of skin and sex, of thrusting and moaning, of sharing her late night with someone besides David Letterman. A couple hours to forget she was thirty-three and lonely and six months ago had let a man buckle a five dollar studded leather collar and leash from PetWorld on her because she wanted to be a good sport.

Well, she'd been a good sport, and what had it gotten her? No superhero and no home run, that's for damn sure. The last thing she needed tonight was big brother Charlie glaring at her from the dug-out because he didn't think she ought to play the field.

He was going to kill her. Shae, not Jasmine. Dragging him along tonight to the Pit to watch Jasmine meet some slimeball and get laid. He'd promised Shae he wouldn't interfere, no matter what happened, but he suspected she was up to something.

Designated driver? Right. From the looks of things, neither of his friends would need a ride home tonight, and taxis were abundant. So why did she want him here? Why did she want him to suffer?

Charlie could dance—he wasn't one of those rhythm-devoid white guys—but he detested the bar scene, even a private club with an expensive cover designed to keep out the riff raff. He stood along the rail of the namesake of the Pit, the huge, dark, sunken dance floor. The air throbbed with electronic drum and bass in a rapid, sensual rhythm, making conversation nearly impossible. Strobes flashed, smoke machines pumped out fog banks that occasionally obscured the pit, and eerie purplish lights bathed the whole scene with otherworldly glamour. There was a lot of leather, a lot of vinyl, a lot of tattoos and outfits much less decent than Jasmine's pretty red dress and Shae's skimpy tank top. For God's sake, they'd had to sign a release form to just get in. It didn't bode well, as far as he was concerned.

Other guys hugged the rail beside Charlie, jostling, catcalling, eyeing the bodies below. Males outnumbered females two to one. The nooks and crannies Shae mentioned—Charlie tried not to look in them. He saw enough foreplay on the dance floor, and maybe some of it wasn't foreplay. Some of it had to be during-play. Christ!

"Dude, check out that chick," said the short guy beside him who'd been directing various remarks to Charlie all night. He pointed at one of the several elevated cages that cornered the pit where more adventurous women displayed their wares. A skinny brunette buried her face in a blonde girl's crotch and exposed half of her thong-strung ass to the crowd. The blonde rocked her pelvis in time to the music and hung on the cage bars. Around their feet in the pit, men turned and cheered.

The guy's friends all noticed, too. "You think she's really eating her out?" one yelled.

"Who cares? I gotta get me some hottie sandwich," the short guy declared before he disappeared.

Like it wasn't enough to gyrate for the entertainment of the drunken masses in the pit. Thank God Shae hadn't dragged Jasmine into one of those barbaric display cases.

As if she knew he was thinking about her, Jasmine cast another glance up at him before letting her long hair hide her face. She'd been doing that all night.

Charlie knew his presence made her self-conscious, but it hadn't restrained her. Several times he'd been tempted to descend the stairs when some jerk got fresh, only he knew that's what she wanted. Most of these guys were clearly the type of horndog Shae and Jasmine claimed they detested, but they allowed various men to try their luck. By some method of silent feminine communication he'd never understood, they dissuaded them after a few sticky gropes.

It was a dance floor, but he wouldn't call what most of its occupants were doing dancing. It was more like an upright orgy; the party-goers groped and kissed the bodies of every person they could reach, in time to music.

Jasmine and Shae drove off another group of guys, and Charlie cursed silently. What was Jasmine waiting for? Why didn't she pick somebody and get it over with? This wasn't a good time for her usual indecisiveness. Shae could take care of herself, but Charlie didn't know how long he could bear the throng of wolves around Jasmine, intent on bringing down their quarry.

Wolves worked in packs. They took turns exhausting their prey until the poor animal collapsed and offered its throat. Only that's not what the wolves were after, and that's not what Jasmine was offering. Maybe she was holding out for her fantasy man, that actor Hugh Jackman, but Charlie didn't think he was going to show, and eventually Jasmine would settle for someone else.

Someone who wasn't Charlie.

Fuck. Fuck, fuck, fuck. He gripped the metal rail so hard it bruised the inside of his knuckles. If Jasmine were so desperate to get laid, why hadn't he offered to take care of her sexual frustration himself? Why didn't he have the balls to make his move when she was obviously panting for it?

Because she was panting for sex, and he didn't want a one-night stand. With Jasmine, he'd want it all. He'd never told her because it would ruin their friendship if she didn't feel the same.

Which she didn't, or she wouldn't let that tall guy fondle her ass and grind her soft body against his crotch. Was that getting her wet? Did she like the way he touched her?

Jasmine craned her head, met his eyes briefly over the guy's shoulder, and Charlie would have given anything to be the man cradled between her thighs.

Damn!

She shook back her hair and laughed. With casual grace, she slung her arms over the guy's shoulders as they did the dirtiest salsa Charlie had witnessed outside of his dreams. Shae, meanwhile, wriggled her butt against the guy's friend and clasped his hands against her tits. A third guy took advantage of the fact Shae's front side was unoccupied and glued himself to her.

The short guy returned, apparently rebuffed by the pseudo-lesbians. "Bitches," he said. His friends guffawed.

Shorty turned his attention back to the floor, seeking his next victim. "The red dress with the black guy? That is one fuckable woman." He elbowed Charlie. "Ya think?"

Charlie did think, but he wasn't about to discuss Jasmine with a troll in a bar.

"She's hot," his friend agreed. "Come on, they're ditching those losers. Let's make a move."

He'd observed Jasmine sample a score of men tonight, but something surged inside him, something primal and fierce. Charlie stepped in their way. "Mine," he growled. As he said it, he knew it for the truth it was.

Jasmine belonged to him; she just didn't know it yet.

Shorty blinked up at him. "Dude, all you had to do was say."

"You can't call shotgun on chicks," protested one of the other guys.

The third guy said, "Yeah, you can. Remember that time…"

Charlie left them squabbling and shouldered his way through the crowd towards the dance floor.

She should have let Shae talk her into coming to the Pit a long, long time ago.

Jaz closed her eyes and rocked to the bass line of the brain-numbing techno, losing herself in the driving beat. It pounded inside her like sex, hot and hard, and almost as good. A hand brushed her ass. Instead of twitching away, she leaned into it, allowed the anonymous caress before it drifted away.

Dancing here, surrounded by hot bodies and lust, was utterly perfect. So perfect and satisfying, she no longer felt the urge to screw some random guy.

Besides, what would Charlie think? He'd been staring at her all night; all night she'd been conscious of his blue gaze condemning her every move. So she moved faster, wilder. His disapproval inspired her more than she'd intended. She'd actually let some guy stick his hand up her skirt. Her g-string hadn't been much of a barrier between his hand and her wet, sensitive flesh. She'd allowed the exploration for a minute, but he'd been clumsy. And she didn't like his cologne.

She drew the line when the dark-eyed woman with the pierced nose wanted more than a smile. How did a woman kiss? Were they softer or sweeter? Shae kissed the woman instead. Jaz watched, fascinated, but felt little impulse to experiment.

Shae's liplock with the woman attracted a lot of masculine attention. Within seconds, they were six deep in men who assumed they'd be getting two for the price of one. The current of the floor ebbed Jaz away, and she flowed with it, enjoying the play of muscles beneath her skin, the sweat, the thick, black-lit smoke that wreathed around everyone's heads and bodies. Her thighs brushed each other in a pulse of sensation, low and sweet, like she could come just from dancing.

Jaz found a space on the floor near the wall and closed her eyes. She let everything fade but the music, the bodies that occasionally brushed against her, the sibilant hiss of the fog machines. She was alone, and for the first time in months she wasn't lonely. She was horny, yeah, but not with that sad, old-maid, never gonna get it frustration.

In a way she was relieved. She'd wanted to have sex but at the same time had her doubts. Once she was in a position to choose a partner, none of them appealed to her, not at the special bone-deep level that whispered of yearning and hunger.

The volume of the music diminished, and the DJ announced something called a foam party tomorrow night. The crowd cheered. That must be when they dumped soap bubbles into the pit and everyone stripped down to their bathing suits or less. Shae'd told her about that. It sounded fun. She wondered what Charlie would do if she and Shae dragged him into a thousand gallons of suds.

"And now," the DJ intoned in his cheesy, broadcaster voice, "comes the countdown to nightfall!"

The crowd screamed. The music resumed a driving beat that shocked through her from the nearby speaker. Her nipples hardened and she laughed out loud. Everyone began chanting down from ten as the black lights and strobes surrounding the pit flickered. When they reached one, all the illumination except the pin lights inside the railing above her head blinked out. She was surrounded by shadows and bodies and heat and music. With the addition of thick fog in the air, Jaz couldn't see where she was or who was beside her.

That's when a pair of strong, male hands slid around her from behind and tucked her against a tall, muscular body.

She stiffened, the anonymity of the darkness heightening her uncertainties, then relaxed. What the hell. She'd dance with this guy a bit and brush him off like the rest. As long as she couldn't see him, she could pretend he was anybody she wanted.

She let him take her hands and spread her arms out to her sides. His breath tickled her shoulder; her dress was sleeveless. He was taller than she was. They swayed to the music, their hips tight, learned one another's rhythm.

And the man had rhythm.

They danced that way for many long, tactile moments, not trying to speak over the throb of the music. In the darkness, Jaz sensed other couples around them centering on one another, embracing, morphing the dance into something else.

The feeling caught her up in its intensity. Her partner felt it too. He released one of her hands and trailed his fingers down her arm. Daringly, he cupped the side of her breast and flicked the nipple.

Jaz stifled a gasp as sensation jolted inside her. She wound her arm backwards around his head and pulled him closer, meshing their bodies. He nuzzled her neck, nipping the skin in tiny, sharp bites that shot down her spine like a mainline of espresso. His hair was short and silky. Smooth shaven jaw. When she turned to catch his profile, he brushed his mouth across hers in an exploratory kiss that blotted out the faint luminescence from the pin lights.

Jaz parted her lips and tasted him. Alcohol and musk. He met the inquisitive touch of her tongue with a sensual sweep that had her melting. She'd kissed men tonight, but none of them had possessed her with such knowing sensuality, commanding her body's full attention.

The embrace turned carnal, fast. Jaz tried to twist in his arms and face him, the better to kiss him, but he prevented the reveal. She struggled and he held her fast. Her insides churned. Against her backside his cock leapt to life, and a sweet, answering ache awoke in her core that had been absent far too long.

Hot lust beaded her nipples, and as they kissed, he palmed one of her breasts. She moaned and squirmed against him, and an answering groan vibrated in his tongue and chest. He squeezed her breast and moved his attention to her nipple, abrading it through the fabric of her dress and thin brassiere. Moisture gushed in her panties, and her knees weakened.

The man half carried, half pushed her forward until she was face to face with the black wall of the pit, decorated with glow in the dark figures that cavorted like erotic cave paintings. The music throbbed around them, hard and deep, and she knew she'd found the man who would be her lover this night.

On one side of them was the speaker. On the other, she could just distinguish a man and woman pressed against the wall, the woman's legs wrapped around his waist as they kissed frantically. Were they…? It was too dark to see details. The woman's foot brushed Jaz's hip, they were that close. The lights in the pit strobed two lighting-bright flashes, and Jaz was blinded.

Her partner took her hands, placed them against the wall, and bit the nape of her neck again, as if he were about to mount her. For all she knew, he was, and that she'd have to stop, at least here. In a minute, she'd stop. Liquid lust dampened her inner thighs. The man smelled of some familiar cologne, but the sweet scent of the fog overwhelmed her senses and kept her from identifying where she'd noticed it before.

He took his hands off hers to cup both her breasts, his body tight against her back. Jaz grabbed his hands, aroused, and he splayed them against the wall again.

"No. Stay," he murmured into her ear, a command she could barely hear over the pounding electronic drumbeats issuing from the speaker next to them.

The couple beside them thrust and uttered wordless moans. Jaz panted. Her body sang as her fingers clenched the wall, as the man's hands explored her body. In a slow, hypnotic roll that echoed every second beat of the music, he moved his hips against her, tempting her to sway along with him in a dance that simulated the hottest sex she'd ever had. It was like he was reading her mind, fulfilling the fantasies she'd never been bold enough to tell a lover. He dropped his hands to her hips and drew her firmly against him, increasing her awareness of his arousal. He licked her neck beneath her ear. At the same time his hand dropped to the hem of her skirt and inched it up.

His fingers against the bare flesh of her thigh made her heartbeat race. This man, this sensual stranger, had her trapped in a dark corner. His hand brushed her pussy, petting, but not probing. He lifted her skirt all the way until she could feel his trousers against her bare ass, his cock a rod of iron riding the cleft.

Jaz whimpered and rolled her head to the side, begging for his touch. She braced herself on the wall and ground against his erection. If he tried to have sex with her, what would she do? She ached. She wanted to be filled. She'd never felt this out of control and gloried in it. He pressed a finger against her clit, and she cried out from the jab of pleasure that surged through her whole body. He pulled her thong aside and skated across her soft flesh. She was wet, and hot, and every wriggle of his finger brought her closer to an earth-shattering climax. She shifted her arm, intending to discover his cock first-hand, and he ended his caress abruptly and smacked her bottom hard enough to hurt.

The sting lashed through her almost like pleasure. Jaz froze in shock. He did it again, his broad hand landing so it sent a frisson of awareness straight into her pussy. The skin of her ass heated and burned.

"No," he said again, and she flattened her hands against the wall, flushed with passion and embarrassment. He stroked the flesh he'd just abused.

Jaz's head whirled, barely able to absorb the contrasts. He shifted abruptly and thrust two fingers into her body. Luckily his other arm was wrapped around her waist and he caught her before she could fall.

His thumb began to manipulate her clit while his fingers twisted deep inside her. She tightened around him, breathing fast, coming so close she almost flew off the wall. But then he'd stop, and she was so close, she couldn't bear it if he stopped, she'd let him do anything he wanted to her if only…

He stopped.

The lights above the pit clicked on with glaring brilliance. Spots swam in her vision. The fog machines hissed on, and the pit filled with eerie soup. The music changed tempo, slowed, and over the beat she could hear the woman beside her cry out in ecstasy.

He turned her around, kissed each eyelid, and tipped her chin with a hand scented of the wild sea. She closed her eyes and clutched her hands at his waist, prepared to beg him to finish what he started.

His jaw brushed her cheek, next to her ear. His tongue flicked her earlobe and she whimpered.

"Look at me."

She knew that voice. Jaz's eyes flew open.

Charlie.

"Oh, God," she said.

"No, it's just me." He smiled. His eyes were black, the pupils dilated, his dark hair slightly mussed on his forehead. She knew his face so well, only she'd never been this close to it, never felt the touch of his magical hands on her pussy, inside her body. Every moment she'd wondered if there could be something more between them whizzed through her mind in a tangle of uncertainty. She throbbed with a need so powerful it was discomfiting.

Charlie seemed to sense this. Without breaking eye contact, he curved his hand down her body and under her dress, caressing her ass almost reverently. His fingers slipped between her cheeks, beneath her thong, and traced a hyper-sensitive line that ended at her clitoris. In three swift, slick strokes, he had her back at the brink.

Jaz gulped for air.

In three more he took her over.

She moaned and sank against the wall, the orgasm rocking through her like fireworks and honey. Charlie slid a finger into her; her sheath clutched him in tight, convulsive bursts of pleasure.

When her pulsations stopped, Charlie bent towards her. Jaz felt herself draw back, away from him. She couldn't kiss Charlie. It was Charlie. Charlie, her best friend.

Hurt flashed across his handsome face so he aimed at her ear instead.

"Happy birthday," he said, and then dug his fingers into her hair and pulled. Immobilized her.

Jaz squeaked at the twinge of pain, and he caught her gasp on his tongue. And she kissed him back, God help her, wrapped her arms around his broad shoulders, pressed against his arousal, and kissed him back.

Triumph surged only briefly in Charlie when Jaz melted into him. Would she have let him embrace her if she'd known it was him? She'd wanted a stranger tonight, some no strings attached bedroom bingo, and instead he'd given her himself.

He explored the sweet inside of her mouth, capturing her sigh and drinking her down in case this was the only time he had this chance. His cock stiffened, and he could only imagine how her soft pussy would feel gripping him. He could get off just thinking about it, but not here, not now.

He kissed her mouth, her neck, her ears, returned to her mouth. Her tongue dueled with his, and they began to dance. The music washed over them like breaking waves. Her body adhered to his, and she twined her fingers behind his neck.

He stroked down her body, curving in and out, and caressed the velvet flesh of her thigh. They should be doing this in private, but she was so passionate, kissing him, moaning—he slipped his hand beneath her dress again. Moisture dampened her thong and turned her pussy to silk. Jasmine pressed harder against him, rubbing her crotch on his leg and trapping his hand between them.

He inched a finger closer and caressed the swollen bud of her clit, rubbing the tiny, hard tip. Her fingers dug into his back and she arched slightly away from his leg to allow him access. He stroked and pulled, her juices coating his fingers and making him desperate to plunge into her with his tongue, his cock.

Her lips moved against his mouth, pleading. He slid two fingers into her sheath; she clenched around him and groaned. His dick and balls ached like they'd been kicked. Okay, not that bad, but almost. He returned to massage her clit, and within a few moments he felt her body become heavier in his arms, as if her knees had given out. He held her tightly with his arm and rubbed her off until she regained her feet.

He couldn't believe he'd brought her to two orgasms in the middle of a crowded dance floor. God, she was so hot and so responsive. If she danced with another man tonight, he'd be inclined to murder. They were going to have to get the hell out of here before he exploded.

The lighting increased. She looked up at him, her chocolate brown eyes confused.

She opened her perfect lips. "I don't think—"

He shushed her with another kiss. He didn't want her to think. Shae and Jaz had always told him he was too good a friend to date, like that was supposed to reassure him. He'd broken one of the unspoken commandments of their friendship by seducing Jaz. When he'd seen her alone, he couldn't resist the primal pull of woman to man. However much pleasure he'd given her, there'd be no going back now.

"Get me a camera!" somebody yelled. It was Shae, one arm draped around the chick he'd seen her kissing and the other around some young dude. Green and blue lights from a mirrored ball overhead flashed across her grinning face. "Gotcha!"

Jaz stepped hastily away from him and rubbed her hand across her lips, as if wiping him off. "It's not what it looks like."

"What?" Shae yelled. She cupped a hand to her ear.

Jaz crossed her arms. "It's not what it looks like!"

Charlie frowned. "Yeah, it was." But nobody, least of all Jaz, heard him.

"You crazy kids!" Shae turned her partners bodily towards the stairs. "Let's get a drink to celebrate."

A mass of people vying for a place on the dance floor stumbled into them in their lovenest beside the speaker. Charlie cursed. His idyll with Jaz was over, and it had been far too short. She was in such a hurry she rudely shouldered several gyrating couples aside, not once glancing back.

He followed. When she reached the stairs, he caught her arm. "Are you running away?" A step above him, her face was slightly higher than his; she was a tall and deliciously statuesque woman—a woman looking anywhere but at him.

"Thirsty!" she yelled, tugging. "Let go."

She was going to act as if it was nothing. It would be like the time when he'd rescued her from that biker bar after an ugly fight with Dirk the Metalhead. Never mentioned again. A nearly indistinguishable lump swept under the carpet.

Frustration surged within him. "I won't let you do this."

"Do what, get a drink?" She feigned ignorance, obviously expecting him to go along with it. Good old Charlie. He goes along with everything. "I'm an adult," she said. "Besides, I only want some water."

"You're blocking the stairs, dude!" Some guys exiting the dance floor yelled at Charlie's back. Cursing, he released her, and she practically ran to catch up to Shae and get away from him and what had passed between them.

As the crowd buffeted him, Charlie mulled over his next step. She'd kissed him back after she'd realized it was him. She'd been willing to explore the electric tension he for one had always been conscious of. That part of her was now aware of him as a man instead of just a friend. That part of her would have a hard time pretending this hadn't happened.

🙰🦑🙰

Shae thrust a brimming shot glass full of clear liquor at Jaz and squealed. "You made out with Charlie! Happy birthday! Shoot this!"

Did Shae think she needed to sterilize the Charlie cooties or something? Jaz accepted the drink but didn't down it. Her hand was shaking a little. Residue from the double orgasm whammy? Kissing Charlie when she knew it was Charlie? Running from Charlie when she realized she wasn't dreaming? All three? It didn't matter; liquid sloshed over the edge of the small glass.

"You're spilling it." Shae snatched it away and poured it down the throat of her male companion, then squeezed a lime down her neck for him to lick. The girl

Jaz had seen her with had disappeared between the dance floor and the bar.

Jaz risked a glance over her shoulder. No tall, dark, annoyed man stalking towards her to demand an explanation. No Charlie. Her stomach clenched.

Shae grabbed Jaz's shoulder and pulled her down so they could hear each other without yelling. "Should I have left you two alone out there?"

"Noooo." She couldn't look Shae in the eye. Shae knew her too well—as well as Charlie did. Her two best friends. Their musketeers dynamic was in for a serious shakeup.

"Are you going to fuck him?"

Jaz choked. "No!"

"When I saw you, I thought you'd finally…" Shae trailed off. "Do you wanna talk about it?"

Jaz shook her head. How could she discuss what she didn't understand?

"If you're not going to hit the mattress with Chuckles," Shae began, and broke off when the bartender returned for her next drink order.

If Shae asked for permission to sleep with Charlie, she'd…oh, that wouldn't do at all. She'd hated every one of Charlie's girlfriends. None of them were smart enough, or nice enough, or funny enough. None of them treated him like he deserved. Shae would chew poor Charlie up and spit him out.

Shae turned back to her, drinks in hand. "Where was I? So if not Charlie, who are you going to do for your birthday? Do you wanna share my new friend?"

Shae's new friend waggled his eyebrows. One of them had a silver hoop in it, and his earlobes had more of the same. He spread his arms in invitation. "Ladies, I am yours to do with what you will."

"I appreciate the offer, but no thanks," Jaz said with what she hoped was a convincing laugh.

Shae handed her another shot glass and lowered her voice. "I'll let this whole kissing Charlie thing slide for now, girlfriend, as long as you aren't so freaked you waste more good tequila."

Medicine. Jaz drank it down. It burned her gullet like shame as she considered Shae's turn of phrase. Never waste good tequila.

Had she just wasted fifteen years of friendship because she'd unleashed her inner slut? Had Charlie even wanted to go there with her? For all she knew, he'd intended to take her up on her offer to dance. As a friend. She'd proceeded to wriggle her tushie against his crotch in a manner that was far beyond friendly. What was he supposed to do, embarrass her by telling her he wasn't interested? Charlie was too nice for that.

He'd have humored her quest to get her rocks off. Yes, that's what he'd do— what he'd done. It's not like he'd asked for anything sexual in return. He hadn't let her touch him. And he'd spanked her! Oh, man. Jaz felt her face heat and her pussy vibrate at the memory. He had seriously disapproved of her birthday plans. This must have been his way of showing it, and she'd liked it way too much.

She'd never be able to face him again. She slammed the glass on the bar. Shae whooped and clapped her on the back. Jaz rubbed her watering eyes, and when she opened them, there was Charlie.

He didn't seem annoyed. More like tall, dark, and...sexually frustrated.

He put his hands on his hips. "Let's go."

"No way," Shae said. "The night is young, and so is my friend." She patted her besotted companion on the ass.

Charlie lowered his brows and glared at her. "I wasn't talking to you."

Shae looked at Jaz and asked an unspoken question. If Jaz gave the slightest sign, Shae would do everything in her power to prevent Charlie from dragging her off.

Should she use Shae as a buffer or find out what Charlie intended? Had he been humoring her or was there more to this?

"Why do you want to go?" she asked him.

With pure masculine obtuseness, Charlie answered, "You know why."

Jaz could think of many reasons. He was hungry. His head hurt. He'd arranged for a midnight double feature of Hugh Jackman movies for her birthday. He hated it here, hated the way she and Shae were behaving. He wanted to yell at her. He wanted to lock her in her bedroom. He wanted to lock her in his bedroom.

And most objectionable and most likely, he wanted to discuss what had just transpired.

"I can catch a ride home with Shae if you're tired," she hedged. She backed up until she hit the bar.

He crossed his arms. "I brought you here, I'll take you home. It's not a problem."

"Jaz, the man wants to take you home." Shae, the treacherous bitch, pushed her towards Charlie.

"Go for it, dude," said Shae's young friend. He swung up his hand to high five Charlie, who tossed him a look that would have withered anyone less oblivious.

Alone in the car with Charlie? She wasn't ready to handle that. "What if I'm not ready to go?"

Charlie smiled slowly. Jaz tensed. He got that smile whenever he trounced them at poker. "You mean, because you're still looking for—what was it—a man who can give you multiple orgasms?"

Jaz opened her mouth but no sound came out. He was daring her, challenging her to find anybody who could pleasure her more than he had. This was a side of Charlie she'd never witnessed. Hell, Shae thought there was only a smooch involved; she'd never believe what he'd done to Jaz on the dance floor. She could scarcely believe it herself.

This wasn't her Charlie, except it was, a deeper layer that settled into the whole as seamlessly as if she'd always known he had it in him.

Charlie tapped his chin with a finger. "Hmm. How can you tell which men are like that? What do you think, Shae? Don't you have to screw them first? By then, like you always tell me, it's too late." He shook his head with mock regret.

Shae, her eyebrows arched, did not respond. Nor did Jaz. Shae's friend, however, wriggled his tongue for their inspection. "You can tell by this. It's their lucky night. I'm double jointed."

"Sweetie, your tongue doesn't have joints." Shae dragged him to the dance floor, leaving Jaz and Charlie staring at one another, the air between them sizzling like fajitas.

Without another word, Charlie grabbed her hand and led her out of the club to his SUV. Jaz followed in a daze. She couldn't shake free of the spell his knowing gaze and even more knowing touch had placed her under. He unlocked her door and waited for her to slide into the leather seat.

"Jasmine, I..." He cleared his throat. "Are you ticked off at me?"

His gentlemanly action, his uncertainty, his return to the Charlie she knew, freed Jaz from her stupor. "You dragged me out of there like I was a disobedient teenager. Of course I'm mad," she lied. Mad didn't begin to describe her churning emotions.

He ran a hand through his hair before shutting her door. In another moment, he slid into the driver's side. "Sorry. I couldn't stand to be there another minute."

"You hate clubs. Why did you come with us?" Maybe they could skip the torturous discussion about her multiple orgasms and go back to being friends. Just friends. Jaz crossed her legs, awaking her still-sensitive pussy.

And maybe not.

He started the motor and pulled into the street. "Shae invited me. I told you. And I didn't hate everything about it." He glanced at her meaningfully, but was prevented from any prolonged stare by the need to keep his eyes on the road.

Jaz tried to laugh it off. "I enjoyed myself. I'd like to go back. That foam party sounds like fun."

"I don't think so."

"You don't have to come."

He tightened his lips. "Obviously."

Jaz straightened; her seatbelt bit into her shoulder. "What's that supposed to mean?"

"Don't try to pretend nothing happened between us, Jasmine."

"I'm not. It was...interesting. Oh, look, the "B" is still missing from the Bass and Guitar Store billboard. Aren't they tired of being called the Ass Store?" *Please please don't make me talk about it*, she chanted in her head. *Please don't make me relive it. Please don't make me confess.*

She could practically hear Charlie grit his teeth. Patience was one of his many virtues. "Jasmine," he said, "I do not want to talk about neon signs. I want to talk about us."

She stared out the window. She'd be honest with him. "Well, I don't."

"Why?"

"It makes me uncomfortable. I'm embarrassed."

Charlie white-knuckled the steering wheel. "Why is it okay for a hundred guys you don't know to cop a feel, but it's embarrassing for me to kiss you? You kissed me back, Jaz."

Jaz's stomach flip-flopped. He'd hit the nail on the head. Why was she uncomfortable? Why was the one thing tolerable when the other caused her massive anxiety?

For one, it hadn't been just a kiss. For another, she had no idea where he stood, and she was scared to find out why he'd seduced her. Had he been mocking her wish to feel a little less lonely, just for a night? He might despise her. She valued Charlie's opinion more than he knew. More than she'd realized.

"You're a good kisser," she said finally. "I guess I was feeling a little crazy tonight. I'm sorry. I hope it doesn't screw up our friendship."

"You hope it doesn't screw up our friendship." He took a corner a little fast, for him, and the SUV's tires cheeped. He must be upset with her. Really upset. She'd messed everything up.

She squirmed around in her seat. "I'm so sorry. Can we blame the alcohol? Please?"

"You're not drunk." He pulled off the street, and Jaz realized they'd reached his apartment. Not hers. He shut off the vehicle. "How about we don't blame it on anything?"

"What do you mean?"

He leaned across the console and traced her cheek with one finger. Jaz's breath caught in her throat. "Let's just see where it leads."

"Um." She licked her lips nervously. "I don't think so, Charlie. If it didn't work out… We're both terrible at relationships."

He placed his thumb on her bottom lip. "It would be so good between us."

Jaz expelled a breath. "Uh." She was not her usual eloquent self. "That's just sex."

"And?" His thumb tipped between her lips, rubbed her tongue tip. She tasted salt. Her salt.

Charlie smiled. The street lights did little to illuminate the interior of the SUV, and in the gloom he looked almost dangerous. Sexual. A man who'd do as he pleased with her body and make her like it. Add longer sideburns and a few knives, and he'd be a dead ringer for…

Oh, man. Her nipples peaked. Her breathing came fast. She couldn't let this happen.

"Charlie." She caught his hand and held it away from her perfidious body. "No."

"Jasmine." His other hand fell near the juncture of her thighs. "Yes."

"It won't work. You're too nice. You know, a beta male. You're steady and calm and patient and...nice. Safe." She babbled, describing the Charlie she'd always known, not the Charlie who'd sent her to the moon. Who looked very much like he wanted to fly with her to the stars. "You'll make somebody a great boyfriend, but not me. I'm not good enough for you."

His eyebrow arched. His fingers brushed high on her leg. "You don't deserve a nice guy? You and Shae say you want nice guys and complain about what jerks most of us are."

"No, I mean, yes." Jaz's heart fluttered like a captive bird. The warmth of his hand seeped through her thin dress, and her core jolted to life with a familiar ache. In desperation, she said something she wasn't sure was true. "I don't think of you that way."

"After you found out it was me, why didn't you—"

Jaz threw up her hands. "I don't know!"

"What if Shae hadn't interrupted us?"

"I don't know," Jaz repeated, then lied again. Maybe. "I don't want to know. Charlie, you're not my type, and I'm not your type. It's not worth losing my best friend."

"Your type?" Charlie laughed harshly, almost a cough. "Your type is assholes who drag you to biker bars and threaten to smack you around. Who cheat on you. Who don't respect you. Who treat you like a dirty whore. Are you a dirty whore, Jasmine?"

"No." Jaz's eyes grew hot. He was giving her no credit. She broke up with those guys when she found out they were jerks. It was just that they all turned out to be jerks.

He fell back in his seat. Unless her eyes deceived her, an erection tented his slacks. "I'm glad you realize that, at least."

"I'm so sorry." This was crazy. Pain, disappointment, some weird kind of grief, ripped through her. Charlie had never talked to her like this. She hadn't known what he really thought about her, and now she did.

"I am too."

It was nearly midnight. She was turning into a pumpkin. No, a witch. She'd wounded him badly, and she smarted with the sting of it as well. *Please, please don't let this ruin the friendship. Dammit, Jasmine Templeton, why did you have to be such a slag?*

"I'll take you home," he said in a robotic voice. "By the way, your present's under your seat."

The SUV purred to life and Charlie drove down the street without glancing her way again. After a few minutes of awkward silence, Jaz bent over and scrounged under the seat. She pulled out a slim, gift-wrapped box with a fancy, sparkly ribbon.

"I thought we agreed no presents," she murmured, not expecting him to answer. He didn't. She opened the box to reveal a soft cotton nightshirt. It was ruby red, with a spade and shovel and the phrase "Plays in the dirt" in bold black letters. It was the exact nightshirt she'd noticed in a catalogue at Shae's several months ago. He'd been there, and remembered. He always remembered.

The card read, "To Jasmine. Love, Charlie."

She waited until he dropped her at home—no small feat, considering it was a twenty minute drive—to cry.

Charlie wondered if it was possible for a perfectly healthy, thirty-something guy to be so frustrated he had a heart attack and keeled over.

He cursed and unlocked his door, cursed and pelted his jacket onto his couch, cursed and slammed the door behind him. It rattled the wall so hard the stupid mirror he bought Jasmine and Shae to check their make-up in the "good light" fell off its hook and shattered.

He knew the feeling. Not her type. What bullshit.

Charlie stared at the floor, at his scowl reflected in a hundred different pieces of ragged glass. A few large hunks dangled in the frame, which lay propped against a small bookcase. Normally he'd vacuum the pieces immediately, but right now he didn't feel much like being himself.

If he were somebody else, somebody more her type, maybe tonight would have gone differently. However, her type of guy hadn't brought her any measure of happiness over the years. He knew. His hands were the ones that patted her back every time another scumbag revealed his true colors. He was the one who assured her it wasn't her fault. Granted, it had happened less and less the older she got, and he'd started to think maybe, just maybe, she'd come to her senses.

Certain types of guy—her type of guy—weren't relationship material.

Charlie stalked across his living room, away from the broken glass, and into the bedroom, thinking about the immortal words of Ben Franklin. If you kept doing the same things over and over and expected different results, that was the definition of insanity. If you wanted different results, say, in your love life, you had to try different things. Different types.

He unbuttoned his shirt and kicked off his shoes and pants, leaving them in a crumpled heap beside the bathroom door instead of placing them in the hamper. How could somebody he loved so much be so dense? What did that make him, consumed by such hopeless longing he couldn't invest himself in relationships with other women?

She complained about being lonely. He was lonely, too. He wanted kids, a family, a life partner. It was her fault he couldn't find it.

No, that was ridiculous. Charlie threw himself on the bed with a groan and rubbed his face. The air conditioner blew chilly drafts over his half-naked body, but he didn't bother getting under the covers. It was his own fault for refusing to confront the fact she didn't love him and move on with his life.

He grunted as that thought struck him in the gut like a bowling ball. He'd tainted everything tonight, and he needed to decide what to do next. Continue on like nothing had happened? Jasmine would prefer that, but what if their relationship was already irrevocably altered? She'd been right about that, if nothing else—attempting a romance would end their previous friendship in one way or another.

He could consider this the end and give up on Jasmine. But how could he force himself to quit loving her?

God, this was stupid. Weak. Gutless. Everything—everything she thought he was.

Fury and frustration mounted in him again as he recalled her insistence he was too nice, all the while claiming she wanted to meet a nice guy for an adult relationship.

He wasn't a quitter. Since the friendship was already damaged, it was time to take a chance. Go out with a grand gesture. She might assume he'd take the gentlemanly course of action. She might think he'd limp away like the "beta male" she saw him as.

He would not let it end this way. Now that the ice had been broken, he was determined to melt the rest of Glacier Jasmine. They were great friends; they could be better lovers. He'd liquefied her tonight, and if Shae hadn't interrupted, he wouldn't be here alone right now, frustration curling around him like snakes. Convincing her to let him in shouldn't be impossible, as long as he kept her hot to the point of boiling.

She had fears about ruining their friendship, but she responded to his touch. Did she ever! Her susceptibility proved she felt less sisterly than she claimed. Sexual aggressiveness might not be the route he'd assumed he'd take with a serious love interest, but her feelings were already simmering and her body was practically a volcano.

Too nice, was he? Too good a friend to lose? Fifteen years of listening to her and Shae talk about men and sexual fantasies would not go to waste. He knew just how to give her what she thought she wanted.

Jasmine had no jobs, no yardwork, no errands, no anything planned the whole weekend. She'd intended to be naked and blissed out with some hot young stud the whole time. Alas, she didn't even have a hang-over to show for her thirty-third birthday, just a supersized helping of shame, weirdness and titillation. And a new red sleep shirt, courtesy of Charlie.

Mr. Thoughtful. Mr. Sensible. Mr. Magic Hands. She couldn't remember the last time a guy had gotten her off with his fingers. Jasmine sighed at the memory. How had he learned to do that, Lorraine the Pain? No man could figure out a clitoris without intense tutoring. She couldn't imagine whiny, sulky Lorraine training Charlie how to pat the bunny.

Ick. Ick! The thought of Charlie stroking Lorraine to orgasm, catching her come-cry in his mouth, was absolutely nauseating.

Suddenly too hot, Jasmine kicked off her blankets and beat her fists on the mattress. She had to quit thinking about this!

The day already sucked. It wasn't even eight, and she was wide awake. The least her body could have done was sleep in, but no. Up with some of the later rising birds. Maybe she should have taken Shae up on her offer to share that kid with the...tongue. And maybe she should count herself lucky she was sprawled in bed alone. Considering how much of an idiot she'd been with Charlie, who knows what her crazed mood of the night before would have driven her to next?

Only, hadn't that been the point? There shouldn't be a sneaky sense of relief hiding among all her other conflicting emotions, like a stem of lemon mint in a bed of nettles. She wondered what time Shae would call so they could talk about...

No. This was something she wasn't ready to discuss with Shae. It was private. She needed to wrap her own head around it first, and she could only do that alone. She certainly couldn't do it with Charlie.

Oh, Lord. The thought of doing it with Charlie made her pussy moisten and ache. If he was that good with his hands, what would he be like in bed? How would he want a woman to touch his lean, smooth body, the one he kept hidden beneath loose khaki pants and button down shirts? She'd put sunscreen on his back before, but now she thought of rubbing his chest with massage oil and sliding his underwear slowly down his taut hips.

Wow. The fantasy aroused her so much, she was tempted to reach for her little motorized friend in the bedside table.

What the hell. She didn't generally picture real guys when she masturbated, but just this once she'd give herself a treat.

Jasmine rolled to the edge of the bed and opened the bottom drawer where she kept her single gal's necessities beneath a couple pillowcases. It's not like sex toys embarrassed her, or the hopeful box of condoms and lube, but they, like her mixed up feelings about Charlie, were private.

She pulled out her vibrator and fell against the pillows with a racing heart. Closed her eyes and imagined Charlie crawling up her body from the foot of the bed. Telling her what he was going to do to her, how and where he'd kiss and stroke her before fucking her until she begged for relief. He'd hold her down if she struggled but always, always, satisfy the emptiness she felt inside. She should feel ashamed that she, a modern independent woman, wanted to be dominated, but this wasn't real, this was fantasy.

Mercy! Jaz flicked on the vibrator and rubbed it across her mons, the electric purr teasing her pussy through the thin cotton of her panties. Mmm, she'd like it if Charlie caressed her belly and thighs, awakened her with silken kisses that slowly inched toward her core. Maybe he'd tie her wrists with leather restraints to teach her a lesson about refusing him.

Jaz shoved her panties down her hips and off one leg and parted herself with the tip of the cream colored vibrator. Medium sized, straight, selected more for the buzz than the heft. Turned it up another click as the hot pulses took her closer to the edge. Spirals of pleasure rippled from her pussy to her hips and thighs. She was wet, nearly as wet as last night when Charlie introduced her to exhibitionism.

He'd be so good, just like he said. She wouldn't have to worry he'd leave her high and dry after pumping her a few times, snorting like a bulldog. Not Charlie. He'd treasure her and pleasure her and hold back until he felt her sheath clench around his cock before...

The bells on Jaz's front door chimed as someone opened it. Jaz squeaked, thrust the vibrator under her comforter, and scrambled to find her panties.

"Shae!" she yelled. "I'm gonna take that key away from you, woman. You could have called first. Are you alone?"

What was her friend doing here this early? Jaz gave up on the panties and yanked her new sleepshirt over her naked fanny before padding barefoot down the hallway. No Shae in the living room. Jaz frowned and headed for the kitchen. Cool air brushed across her pussy, and she resolved to give Shae a really snarky lecture about dropping by unannounced.

Not that she'd ever cared before, but being caught masturbating, even by your understanding friend, was a jolt to the system.

A tall man in a fitted black T-shirt, faded jeans, and motorcycle boots stood at her sink, cutting something. Muscles bunched in tan biceps. Dark hair in wild, tousled curls, broad shoulders, tight ass.

Nobody she knew, and nobody she'd given a key to her house. Shae's latest? "Who..." Jaz began.

He turned around.

"Holy shit, Charlie!" Jaz hopped backwards, and her hands fisted in the hem of the short sleepshirt. "What are you doing here?"

Charlie raised an eyebrow and held up a large knife. "Preparing breakfast."

"Break... breakfast," Jaz stammered. His jeans had stains on them. Frayed hems. A hole in his tight T-shirt. What the hell?

Charlie's amused gaze dropped to her nipples. "Yes, breakfast. I see that excites you."

"How did you get in?" Her buckies were a sleep shirt away from full exposure. Charlie was in her kitchen wearing somebody else's clothes. Jaz's stomach clenched and her mouth dried.

"You keep your spare key in the same place." He turned back to his task, coring and slicing an apple and adding it to a bowl with what she could now see was other fruit.

In her current state of arousal, she didn't know if she could handle Charlie in snug jeans. She had to get rid of him, and fast. "This is not a good time."

He stirred the fruit salad with an economy of movement. The sweet odor of strawberries wafted towards her. "If you want to go back to bed, I'll bring the food to you there."

Charlie in her bedroom, with breakfast, and her trusty vibrator still under the comforter.

"No!" she exclaimed, a little too loudly. She stepped back, away from Charlie. "I'll go get dressed."

He half-turned and gestured with the knife. "Come here first."

"Are you threatening me?" she joked.

"I want you to taste this." He turned the rest of the way and angled the knife so she could see the pale pink substance glistening on the blade.

Slowly, Charlie raised the blade to his mouth and licked one side of it, savoring the fruit salad dressing. "It might be too tart."

Jaz could barely tear her eyes off his lips and tongue, imagining them on her body. On parts that were still wet, still alert, from her interrupted self-pleasuring session. Charlie held out the blade enticingly.

"I know you like sweets, Jasmine. Taste this and tell me if it's too tart so I can add more ice cream."

Jaz took a hesitant step forward, then another. What was she afraid of, that Charlie would leap on her and force her to eat fruit salad for breakfast? This was probably his way of apologizing for his behavior last night, his way of letting her know they could still be friends. He didn't look like he wanted to lick whipped cream from every inch of her body. In many respects he just looked normal and unruffled.

Then again he didn't. Ripped jeans? The Charlie she knew wore slacks or new denims. The Charlie she knew had never let himself into her house on a Saturday morning and fixed her breakfast.

Charlie hadn't budged from where he lounged against the counter. Pink dressing dripped off the blade, and he caught it on his palm. Without breaking eye contact, he licked it off.

"It's good," he said. "Now you try."

Jaz shuffled two more steps closer to Charlie, very aware of her secret state of undress. If he knew… But he just proffered the blade toward her mouth. She licked, careful not to cut her tongue on the sharp edge.

Sweet. Tart. A mixture of orange juice and ice cream, maybe, with a hint of strawberries. "It's fine," she said.

Charlie's hand, the one without the knife, snaked out and grabbed her wrist, drawing her towards him. As if by accident, the knife came to rest close to her chest, pointing at her neck.

Jasmine yelped and tried to duck out of Charlie's sneak attack, but his grip was like iron. He twirled her until she was between him and the countertop, her back to him. His body, now so close to hers, didn't press her; he confined her lightly, casually, as if he held knives to her throat on a daily basis.

"Quit squirming, you'll cut yourself. I just want you to try this fruit salad," he chided. The cold knife pressed her collarbone. Charlie's hand brushed the top of her breast.

Panic, and something hotter, rushed through her. "I said it was fine," she managed, her gaze on the blade. The remaining dressing spotted her T-shirt; her struggles had drawn its hem dangerously close to the curve of her bottom and her bare, wet pussy.

Jaz froze, afraid she'd expose herself. She and Shae occasionally joked about the fantasy of a man so overwhelmed with desire he cornered them and compelled them to make love, demonstrating great sexual expertise as he did so, of course. Not a rape fantasy but not your typical wine and candlelight, either.

Of course, Charlie wasn't, so far as she could tell, overwhelmed by desire. He just wanted her to taste the damn fruit salad. Strawberries, orange segments, grapes, and apple slices mounded in the bowl, coated with more of the same pink drizzle.

"You're being weird," she said. She snatched up a grape and popped it in her mouth. "Happy now?"

Charlie closed the gap between them and wiped the flat of the broad knife blade down her chest until it reached her nipples. Her hard nipples. Jaz nearly choked on the grape as longing stirred in her. She'd been wrong about his state of desire; his arousal nudged her and his breath tickled her neck. Her nightshirt hitched up, much like her dress in the Pit last night.

"I could be happier," he whispered in her ear.

Jaz flushed hot, then cold, then hot again. She'd turned him down last night, but here he was anyway, and she was pretty certain, from the feel of the erection, what he had in mind.

It wasn't an apology for his behavior. It was an encore.

Her stomach hollowed, the better to make room for all those butterflies.

She couldn't let this happen. She had to stop him, but he felt so warm and intense behind her, and he was holding a knife to her throat and offering her breakfast. A rather appetizing breakfast that didn't look store-bought.

A random thought occurred to her, so she babbled it, hoping to distract him. This morning Shae wasn't around to interrupt and save her from her own brainless lust.

"That's a nice fruit salad." Her voice was high and a little breathless. "You've only been here a couple minutes. How did you get this cut up so fast?"

"It tastes even better than it looks."

He slid the knife over her nipples, the long blade covering them both and dampening the fabric. With great precision, he rubbed the wide blade up and down, stimulating her through the now soggy shirt, yet not cutting the cloth with the sharp edge. It was so bizarre, and so sensual, Jasmine was mesmerized. The silver blade against the damp red of her shirt. The rigid, cool sensation of the metal on her nipples. The strong hand gripping the handle, the muscular body pinning her to the counter. The faint smell of cologne and soap she associated with Charlie, along with the sugary tang of fruit.

"Most of it I prepared at my house," Charlie said in a conversational tone, as if he weren't polishing her breasts with a carving knife. "I came here for the finishing touches." He dropped her wrist and laid his palm on her abdomen. "And the apple."

Jasmine tried not to pant aloud from the sensations he inspired. She fought the urge to thrust her buttocks against him and beg him to take her from behind, fast and brutal, no questions asked. She fought another urge to grab a handful of fruit salad and mash it in his face so he'd drop the knife and she could escape the dangerous circle of his arms.

Her third urge, the most terrifying one, was to wind her arms around his neck and kiss him slowly, lingeringly, in the bright summer daylight of her kitchen, no shadows or alcohol to hide behind. That urge had little to do with scratching a lusty itch and everything to do with her best friend Charlie.

He placed the knife on the counter and dipped his fingers into the bowl of fruit salad. He painted the side of her neck and lowered his mouth to lick it off. Jaz shook her head.

"Charlie, don't." He nibbled the sensitive skin beneath her ear. "Stop it."

She could feel him smile against her neck. The hand on her ribcage shifted to cup one of her breasts. His thumb flickered over her nipple and pleasure shocked through her.

Jaz bit off a moan, embarrassed by her body's response. Her pussy flooded with a warm ache. His breath tingled her ear, and he inserted a syrupy finger between her lips. She tasted orange, strawberry, cream.

Next he placed a slice of strawberry on her tongue. The tart-sweet dressing complemented it perfectly. His fingers continued to flick and squeeze her nipple and breast. Her heart pounded in her chest and her knees trembled.

"I said stop," she managed. She didn't want him to stop, but there was only one possible conclusion to this heady delight, and it would ruin their friendship. It could never work between them, not the way Charlie was with women and she was with men. Why would they be any different with one another? He would close her out and she would—she didn't know what she'd do with a man like Charlie.

"Aren't you hungry?" He trailed a slice of apple down her neck, followed it with a hot tongue. "Would you prefer to feed yourself?"

"Yes," she breathed.

Charlie fed her a tart orange; the juices dripped down her chin. He caressed her breast one last time and palmed down the contours of her body to rest low on her hip. His long fingers brushed her ass, naked beneath the skimpy shirt. Two more inches and he'd know how close he was to having her. She should stop him, but his hands and words had woven a haze of lust that diluted her willpower like a morning mist in the sun.

"Yes, you're hungry?" he prompted.

"You've got to stop." She tried to push away from him but only succeeded in making matters worse. He shifted, spooning her body with his. Her height put their hips nearly on a level. She lurched away from the counter, the globes of her ass hugging his erection, and he slipped his hand around her body to cup her mons.

"Well, well, well," he whispered. She sagged against him and closed her eyes. "Let me see if I can remember that discussion. Shae sleeps nude, I sleep in my boxers, and you—you wear nightshirts. Like the one I got you for your birthday. Panties, too. What were you doing when I got here, Jasmine?"

"Nothing," she moaned. His fingers entered her creamy cleft, stroked her clit.

"Were you thinking about last night? About what I did to you?"

He pinched her clit and suckled her neck. Slowly, he rotated his hips, his erection, against her bottom, reminding her in no uncertain terms how vulnerable she was to him.

How open.

With a hard twist, he thrust two fingers inside her sheath, and she gasped. God, the ache! It wasn't enough, she wanted more. "What are you thinking right now, Jasmine?"

Her head fell against his shoulder. "We said we wouldn't do this." She wanted to turn in his arms. She wanted to kiss him. She wanted to taste strawberries on his tongue. She wanted to hop onto the counter, wrap her legs around his hips, and bring him home.

He shrugged. "You said some stuff. I didn't agree to it."

"You're not my type." And right now, she didn't care.

"Yeah, that's a shame." He swiveled his fingers inside her until his thumb rested against her clit. In and out, in and out, each time he pressed into her body, he slid across her clit in heightening pleasure. If only his was cock buried inside her, if only he'd kiss her and hold her and tell her…. She tightened around his fingers as an orgasm built inside her.

Like last night, he sensed when she neared her ultimate pleasure, and he halted. Jasmine whimpered.

"I'm too nice and passive to fuck you when you said no, even though I can tell how bad you want it."

He stepped away and a chilly draft seeped up her backside. Jasmine nearly collapsed. First he interrupted her masturbation, and now this? Her core pulsated with disappointment, and moisture slickened her inner thighs.

She whirled on him, furious and aroused and humiliated. "Damn you!"

He raised an eyebrow. She lashed out, caught him on the chin with a glancing fist. He caught her next poorly aimed flail, and the next, until he restrained her arms. She shifted her weight and went for the knee in the crotch, but he danced away, laughing. She tried to kick him and bruised her bare toe on his stupid boots.

Cursing, she yanked her hands; he was far stronger and she couldn't wriggle free. Tauntingly, inexorably, he immobilized her against the counter. She'd never wrestled with Charlie, not even in jest, and hadn't realized how muscled he was. His blue eyes twinkled, but he didn't seem particularly amused. His hair fell in disarray across his forehead. A deep line creased his eyebrows, proof positive of his anger.

Jasmine gave one last tug of her hands. He resisted. She glared up at him. "What the hell has gotten into you? When did you turn into such an asshole?"

Charlie laughed. "Who, me? I'm a nice guy. Too nice. You said so yourself."

"I was wrong." She wondered if she'd brought this on herself, behaving the way she had last night, leading him on and then telling him he was too good a friend to be romantic with. He had every right to be mad at her. But it was no reason to treat her like trash.

"If I weren't such a beta male, you know what I'd do to you?"

"Force your way into my house and feel me up even when I already told you I wasn't interested?" she quipped nastily.

"You have an interesting definition of not interested, Jasmine."

She winced. "Shut up. I can't help a physical response to certain stimulation."

"You and Shae told me that for women, it's more about the touchy-feely than the sex. 'It's all about the romance, Charlie. You have to appeal to a woman's mind, Charlie.' How many times have I heard that?" He chuckled. "If I weren't such a nice guy, I'd prove you wrong. I'd fuck you right here on your kitchen counter."

That stopped Jasmine cold. "What?"

Charlie leaned a little closer, until she could see the striations of blue in his eyes. His dilated pupils. His little half-smile, the dangerous one. His five o'clock shadow. "First I'd hoist you onto the counter and part your legs until I could see your pussy spread out like a flower. All pink and moist and soft. I'd lick you from your ass to your clit until I memorized how sweet you taste. After that I'd slide my cock right into your hot pussy. Right up to the hilt. Then I'd bring you to at least two orgasms before I turned you around and fucked you from behind. And that's not romance, sweetheart. That's just sex."

Jasmine nearly gaped when Charlie described the exact fantasy she'd envisioned. Only he said it would be pure sex and nothing else.

But even in her little fantasy this morning, she'd imagined something more. If it was just sex between them, they'd have had it last night. She'd have jumped his bones years ago. It's not like she hadn't thought about him sexually, at least in passing. She assumed Charlie wasn't that kind of guy. She counted on him to be different, to be more. To be…what? The kind of man she'd eventually settle down with?

This was still Charlie, even if he was acting like the kind of jerk she normally dated, if truth be told, all the while hoping he'd turn into somebody like Charlie.

Holy hell. How long had she felt this way?

She didn't want to put anybody on a pedestal, much less a man who seemed contemptuous of her. Did he want to scare her? Punish her? Whatever it was, she didn't appreciate it. He probably thought he was teaching her a lesson about one night stands or how dangerous men were. About the differences between fantasy and reality, or whatever twisted impulse for revenge had consumed him last night.

"Speechless, Jasmine?" Charlie asked. "Isn't that what you want a real man to do?"

"You left out one part." She grabbed the bowl of fruit salad behind her.

"What's that?"

She hurled the bowl at him. The contents bounced against his stomach. Fruit and sauce splashed in every direction, smearing across her kitchen in long pink strings and red and orange chunks. The bowl clattered to the ground. Charlie didn't move a muscle.

"The part where I call your bluff." She stripped off her shirt and flung it on the ground. Naked, she stood before him and pointed at the counter. "Fuck me."

Charlie expected her to be angry, he'd expected her to be resistant and suspicious, but he hadn't expected her to rip off her clothes like a Playboy fantasy letter.

Man, she was gorgeous. Not too small and not too big. Athletic and tall without losing her softness, and beautiful, round breasts with dark pink nipples he really wanted to taste. She had a trim waist, a gentle curve to her stomach and hips; her pussy was hidden by neat, dark hair. Shae had discussed, *ad nauseum*, shaving or waxing her privates, trying to convince her friends to go bare, but admiring Jasmine's creamy, natural body, he was thankful she hadn't given in.

She was as perfect as he'd always imagined.

"Are you done looking?" she demanded, her face flushed.

He wanted to reach for her. Instead, he let his gaze travel insolently up and down her body in a way she complained men always did. They spoke to her tits instead of her face and imagined her naked. Well, she was already naked, so he imagined how her pussy would taste, how her nipples would harden beneath his tongue. The thought sent a rush of blood to his cock. For the moment, he'd savor the sight and make her sweat.

Willpower, Charlie. Willpower. He said nothing and she turned even redder. He'd seen her angry a number of times, but not at him. She'd forgive him in the end—wouldn't she?

Charlie finished his inspection and met her eyes, as if he had no more interest in ogling the naked chick three steps away from him. Then he gave a little shrug with one shoulder.

Her jaw dropped. He flinched inwardly, but his goal was to piss her off as much as her other boyfriends did. Treat her like they did. Every time he'd seen her with one of those goons, they acted like they could do better—they checked out other women, took her for granted. The stuff she bitched about that they did in private was even worse.

But those were the guys she chose, when she chose to date.

Jasmine closed her mouth and frowned. The only sound was the sauce dripping off him and onto her floor. One part of him itched to clean it up before it dried, but he wasn't here to be that Charlie.

He was here to be the other guy. The one Jasmine wanted to fuck.

Jasmine broke first. "Are you going to say anything or are you going stand there like a weirdo?"

"I'm not the one who ripped his clothes off," he pointed out. "Who's the weirdo?"

"God, you're so..." She let out a little screech, her head falling back and her long hair brushing her breasts. Her nipples peeked out between honey brown strands. His balls began to ache, he was so hard. "I can't believe this."

"I can't believe you ruined breakfast." Especially not after he'd planned to feed it to her like that sexy movie they'd seen. "What else have you got?" In a supreme effort, he turned away from her succulent body and opened her fridge.

Jasmine stepped up behind him. He could smell her faint coconut shampoo. "Do you know what I was doing when you got here?" she asked in a low voice.

"Sleeping?" He shoved aside a take-out carton to check the milk. She probably had cereal somewhere. It wasn't the stimulating breakfast he'd planned, but they did have to eat.

"I was pleasuring myself. Masturbating."

Charlie was glad his back was to her; no way could she miss his erection now. The thought of her touching herself, moaning, inserting her fingers into her vagina, using her vibrator. "Is that right?" he said. He fumbled with the milk jug, nearly knocking it over.

"I was thinking of you, Charlie. Our unfinished business." She slipped a hand up his spine, caressing the back of his neck.

At that, he uttered a bark of unforced laughter. "Yeah, right. Come on, Jasmine. You're just horny right now. I'm too nice to take advantage of that. You said so yourself."

"You're the one who worked me up."

"Not me. All I did was ask you to taste the fruit topping."

She grabbed his arm and jerked him away from the fridge. "Hey," Charlie managed before she dragged his face down and placed a lush kiss on his mouth.

She was sweet. Hot. Charlie kicked the fridge shut with one foot and buried his fingers in her silky hair. She wound her arms around his shoulders; their tongues explored and tangled. With a groan, he cupped her rounded ass and dragged her body against him. Her skin was velvet under his palms. She sighed into his mouth, gasped when he squeezed, moaned when he rubbed his straining cock against her supple belly. Her tits rubbed him through his thin T-shirt.

He lifted. Two steps brought them to the counter, and he returned to nestle between her legs, their heads on a level. He bent to kiss her breasts, drawing one nipple firmly into his mouth. She rested her head against the upper cabinet, her eyes closed and her breath coming fast between parted lips.

She tasted of spice and woman. He palmed her other breast and twisted the nipple to match the actions of his lips. She ground her pelvis against him. "Jesus, Charlie," she panted. "What are you doing to me?"

He thought that was obvious, so he didn't answer. He dropped one hand between her thighs and stroked her downy, moist curls. She whimpered. Her legs were spread. He could easily finger her in this position, so he did, his thumb brushing the knob of her aroused clit.

He could tell by the little arrhythmic jerks her hips made as he probed she wasn't too far from coming. Her pussy was slick and tight. She squeezed around his fingers; her legs drew up to encircle his hips.

"Take off your pants," she begged.

With a shake of his head, Charlie drew his fingers out of her body then plunged them back in, enjoying the light sheen of sweat that filmed her. He licked and suckled her neck and breasts and slowed his hand so she wouldn't come. Not yet. He reached deep inside her, curling his fingers for the magic spot.

She inhaled deeply and grabbed his wrist, stilling his invasion. She looked him deeply in the eyes before kissing him. "I want you inside me," she said against his lips. "Charlie, please. Make love to me."

Without a word, Charlie scooped her up and carried her to the bedroom, their tongues dueling the whole way. He tossed her onto the bed, where she sprawled like a pin-up. A wanton. Her lips were swollen and red from his kisses. Her nipples stood at attention and her pussy gleamed with dew. Her hair fanned onto the bed and she held up her arms.

He took his time removing his shirt, knowing that she saw him for the first time in a new light. As a lover. Her gaze caught on his chest, followed his movements avidly when he stripped out of his pants. She bit her lip when his dick emerged, straight and rigid. Her eyes widened before she blinked several times, and he felt an absurd flush of masculine pleasure.

"Condoms are in the drawer beside the bed," she said, still staring at his dick.

After complying with her request, Charlie knelt on the bed and crawled up it, hovering over her body but careful not to touch her. Her hands clenched the sheets and she shifted her legs restlessly. He paused over her middle, bent, and licked the crease of her hip. The scent of her pussy made his mouth water. He kissed her lower belly, her navel, rubbed his whiskers across her breasts and nipples. She spread her legs and chafed her calves against his thighs, inviting him to continue. He nuzzled her throat and sipped her earlobes before kissing her lips and rediscovering the sweet recesses of her mouth. His hips perched over hers, his cock close enough to sense the warmth of her entrance.

The paradise of her slick juices and tight slit engulfing his dick could wait. He'd been acting like an ass and planned to continue it—outside the bedroom. Again, he hearkened back to her complaints. The typical guy never waited, never made it good for her.

"Charlie," Jasmine breathed. She tilted her hips and wrapped her legs around him. Her hands molded the contours of his back, kneaded his buttocks. She slipped one hand around to feather across his stomach and brush his cock.

He lowered himself onto her, effectively trapping her hand between them. "Don't touch me," he said, knowing he sounded abrasive but also knowing she could undo him. He couldn't tell her that; it would ruin the image he was trying to project.

Hurt flashed across her face. "I want to." She struggled to remove her arm and dragged it free. She massaged his back.

He shifted his hips so his cock slid through her wet slit, effectively distracting her. Her eyelids fluttered and closed. He continued to stimulate her, tease her by entering only the thick head into her sheath before withdrawing. In minutes he had her gasping and begging. He had to grit his teeth not to plunge into her eager pussy like a jackhammer.

"Please. Please, Charlie." Her hands, anxious, pulled at his buttocks and hips. "You're making me crazy."

Finally he entered her, one slow inch at a time. Deeper. Deeper. She shuddered and sighed until he was inside her to the hilt. He adjusted her hips, pushed her thighs up to achieve even deeper penetration. Connection.

He felt as if they'd locked together. He didn't move. He just waited, suspended, until she opened her eyes.

Holding her gaze, he began to thrust. He wanted her to be completely aware this was her nice friend Charlie fucking her brains out. He pulled almost all the way out and reentered, unhurried, enjoying every centimeter of glossy, silken contact. It wasn't experimental, and it wasn't kinky, but it was eminently satisfying. He pinned her to the bed as he plunged in and out of her welcoming body. Her hands fluttered across his back and ass like frantic birds.

"Faster," she breathed. "It's so good, I can't... I can't..."

She could. He'd make sure she did.

Charlie raised himself and inserted a hand between them. He flicked her clit with a finger, rubbed the juices of her cunt over and over the hard nub. He penetrated shallowly and gave her the speed she begged for. When he felt the telltale tremors build and her passage tighten, he rammed home several wicked times. She cried out and convulsed around him.

As she shuddered, he paused so she could catch her breath. Her cunt squeezed him, and his balls tightened dangerously. He moved his hand from her clit to pinch the base of his cock. Down, boy.

She opened her eyes again. "Did you?"

He shook his head and smiled. "It's not time."

Once his urgency passed he began to thrust again, rebuilding her climb to orgasm. He suckled her nipples fiercely, which made her wild, so he kept doing it, increasing the speed of his thrusts. He felt his own climax approach like a tidal wave. Lifting her buttocks and squeezing, he ground into her, pressing her clit, and she exploded around him. He took that as his signal and released his pent-up desires, throwing back his head as he rode the wave.

Jasmine trembled underneath him. He could feel her hands, still on his back, and now tentative. He rested his face on the pillow beside her head and didn't look at her, though he longed to. He wanted to do all those corny things like gaze into her eyes and tell her he loved her.

But he couldn't. She didn't want a nice guy.

He rolled off her damp, well-pleasured body. She murmured something that sounded disappointed and tossed an arm across his chest, snuggling against him. "That was wonderful," she said softly.

How often had he dreamed of this? Charlie's throat tightened, and he replied with a foolish grunt. He pretended to go to sleep. Eventually her breathing evened out.

After that he did the hardest thing he'd ever done in his life.

He left her.

Jasmine woke and realized she was completely naked beneath the sheet. What was... Oh, yeah. Charlie. Fruit salad. Orgasms. She slitted her eyes, but she didn't see him beside her in bed. She concentrated on the sounds of her house so she could figure out where he was.

She didn't hear any deep breathing on the other side of her. It was more than just an absence of snoring; it was an absence of Charlie.

She didn't hear anybody in the kitchen, washing up the mess from her little temper tantrum.

She didn't hear anybody on the couch, flicking through channels on the television.

She sat up. The extra pillow was in the floor instead of dented with the imprint of Charlie's head. There was no pile of clothes—faded jeans, black T-shirt. The house was silent. It was after one o'clock.

"Charlie?" she called out. "Where are you?"

Puzzled, she grabbed a robe off the closet door and went into the living room, looking for signs of her incredibly well-hung friend. Lover. Whatever he was, he wasn't anywhere in the house, and his car wasn't in the driveway.

Had she fallen asleep while masturbating and dreamed the sex? She almost wanted to believe that because of the upheaval in her life she knew was to come. One kiss she could have laughed off as a birthday fling. Maybe. But she couldn't laugh this off. This morning was the best sex she'd ever had, bar none.

It couldn't have been real. Not with Charlie. He was her solid, trustworthy friend. He gave good financial advice. He was disapproving of her boyfriends. He was like an older brother, minus the phase where she followed him around and hero-worshipped him.

Who was she kidding? Her feelings weren't sisterly. She'd refused to acknowledge her growing curiosity about him for months. The movie. She'd known after the movie she was interested.

And he fucked like a god. Telltale wetness dripped down her leg.

She definitely hadn't dreamed it.

Nor did she dream that, during the following week, he didn't return her calls.

"It's me, and I just want you to know this is the last time I'm going to call you. Ever. Bye."

Charlie turned off his answering machine and dug his fingers into his carefully styled hair, tousled like he'd been on a motorbike all day. He'd had to maintain

his Neanderthal facade at work in case she showed up, and the other pharma-
cists were starting to eye him strangely. Not to mention some of his long-time
customers. "You need a shave, boy." He'd heard that one a few times this week,
but he'd only smiled.

He'd thought, hoped, after his desertion she'd get a full head of steam and
come after him. He could use that steam to his advantage, and ultimately, hers.
She had a tendency to drop by a phone-phobic boyfriend's house to kick his ass
and pick up her stuff.

Over the years, Jasmine had left quite a few things at his place. Music, books,
some weird herbal stuff, a pair of shoes, lipstick, small kitchen appliances. But
so far, no Jasmine. Did he not even rate a break-up visit after his behavior? God,
he missed her. Missed talking to her. Missed her scent, her face, her laugh.

He could hardly sleep at night, thinking about her. For the first time since
he was a teen, he jacked off every day, remembering the perfect depth of her
body, her legs wrapped around him, her lips calling out his name. She'd known
who was making her come, no doubt about it, but she had to be taken aback that
good ole Charlie had screwed and scurried.

Which was just the way her type of guy conducted a relationship. They'd
meet, the guy would pursue her until she succumbed, and then he'd start treating
her like dirt. And now Charlie had behaved the same way.

Acting like scum felt so wrong, he was sick inside. How long would he have
to deny his basic impulse to treat her like his favorite person in the world? The
whole point of this was to get her to admit—to realize—the person she'd always
described as her dream man was not who she thought he was. She looked for
excuses to shove men into categories, but human beings weren't that simple. Or
cooperative. The whole dark, dangerous thing she and Shae sighed over—who
was the guy they wanted, anyway, besides a guy who'd take control in the bedroom
with orgasmic results? He could give her that, plus respect, love, and security.
She didn't have to swallow rude behavior for a chance at great sex.

And he'd heard them discuss the sex. Incessantly. According to them, it usually wasn't worth the trouble the jerks put them through.

He couldn't let this pretense go on much longer. He'd already called the
florist three times to order a vase of her favorite lilies of the valley. Three times
he'd hung up before they answered. He needed to talk to her face to face, and he
wasn't afraid to confront her, but maybe he should wait. Maybe she was about
to crack. Wouldn't it be better if she came to him?

If she entered his territory, it would put him in a position of strength for
phase two of his plan, the one where he made her sexual fantasies come true.
This one would be the big fantasy, not just "Breakfast in Bed". The one where
she'd be totally in his power and dependent on him. Part of the reason he'd had
to jack off all week was because he'd been thinking about satisfying Jasmine's
fantasy, the one she'd talked about with Shae, oblivious to his presence. He'd

been researching it. Planning it.

The stage was set in case she visited unexpectedly, but the mountain, she wasn't budging. In fact, she'd only called three times, each message she left more distant than the last.

He may have royally screwed things up.

After he ate a bland microwave dinner, the phone rang again, and caller ID said it was Shae. He picked up.

"Asshole!"

"Who is this?" He honestly couldn't tell. Was it Jasmine on Shae's cell or Shae herself, about to rip him a new one?

"You know who it is, you fucking chicken shit son of a bitch."

"Hello, Shae."

"What did you do to her?" He could hear the sounds of a street behind her, a dog barking.

"Nothing." He cringed inside, like a little boy in the principal's office.

"She says she hates you." Shae's pronouncement was emphasized by the rumble of a car in the background.

"Uh."

"Why don't you call her?"

"I've been busy." Busy forcing himself not to beg her forgiveness yet. Busy haunting a few fascinating Internet sites and making a few purchases.

"Why are you such a fucker?"

He wanted to say it wasn't him, but instead he said, "I'm the same as I've always been."

"Are you crazy? She won't tell me what you did, man, but I know you kissed her at the Pit, and she's been freaky ever since. I can make some guesses."

"Then you tell me what I did." Trying to explain his convoluted plans to Shae, knowing they'd go straight to Jasmine, would definitely not fit into the alpha male persona he was trying to project. It was one thing to fool a woman, but another to fool her friends. Yet another piece of advice Shae and Jasmine had gifted him with over the years.

"She wants me to get her cds and blender from your place."

Oh, boy. Jasmine he desperately wanted to see. Shae might rip off his balls. "No dice. Tell her if she wants them to come get them herself. Tell her I, ah, want to see her."

"Tell her yourself, jackass." Click.

Charlie blinked and put the phone on the cradle. In another minute, a knock thundered on the door.

Good thing he'd done the bulk of his preparations ahead of time.

When they realized Charlie was home, Shae anchored Jasmine's arm and wouldn't let her run. On the other side of the door. Her Charlie. Sex god Charlie. She followed Shae's side of the conversation with sick fascination, her mouth dropping open when Shae said Jasmine hated him.

In fact, she'd told Shae she didn't hate him. At all. And she was worried her newfound interest in him had transformed him into every other guy in the world instead of the Charlie they'd always known and...loved.

Shae clicked off her phone and smirked at Jasmine. "Bet he's wearing khakis. I don't believe you about the jeans."

"Shut up, shut up!" Jasmine straightened and stuck out her chest. Her low-cut blue blouse, technically Shae's blouse, accentuated her bosom. It was also the exact color of Charlie's eyes.

Anything to knock him off guard, including Shae, who'd helped her plan this sneak attack. Normally she could handle the retrieval of the possessions solo, but this time she didn't want it to lead to a break-up. She hoped it would lead to an explanation. A confession. A heart to heart.

But, despite the provocative blouse, no sex. Definitely no sex. Charlie, like so many men before, had gone wonky after she slept with him. Even Charlie.

"You're sure you don't want me to punch him in the face?" Shae caressed her knuckles as they waited in the hallway, politely not using their keys. They'd waited here so many times during their long friendship, and Jasmine studied the floorboards of the foyer hallway.

"Just keep me from doing anything stupid." She hadn't told Shae about the sex, exactly, but Shae had tossed her a knowing look when Jasmine claimed Charlie left after she threw the fruit salad at him.

They heard the deadbolt snick and Charlie opened the door.

He was not wearing khakis and an oxford. In fact, he wasn't wearing much at all.

"Who's your daddy!" Shae exclaimed. Jasmine blinked hard and gulped.

"I was about to get in the shower." Charlie glowered at them. His jeans clung to his hips like they were very fond of his body, and the top two buttons were undone. His tan didn't quite extend to his privates, so a faint line of pale skin at the beltline drew the eye like a magnet. His chest was bare, and Jasmine noticed the black etch of a large tattoo on his arm. Tattoo? His dark, shining hair fell over his forehead in disorderly curls, and what looked like a week's worth of stubble darkened his chin and cheeks. His sideburns had filled in, and he looked, quite frankly, dangerous.

Holy Hannah! Jasmine felt a huge flutter of interest in her pelvic region. Nervously, she shoved a lock of hair that had escaped her chignon behind her ear.

"Is Charlie here?" Shae asked. "We're looking for Charlie, not his unwashed twin."

"What do you want?"

"My... my..." Jasmine couldn't tear her eyes off his ripped abdomen, the hollows beside his hipbones. *My dignity back.* "My blender."

"Are you going to put a bunny in it?"

"Hey!" Shae pushed past him into the apartment. "Nobody here is psycho but you, pal."

"I think I left some CDs here, too." Jasmine tried to follow Shae, but he blocked her. She ended up nose to nose with this outlandish version of Charlie. Nose to throat.

He smelled exactly the same. He'd probably taste exactly the same.

Their eyes locked. Charlie's were so dark in the dimly lit hallway she couldn't distinguish the blue of their irises.

"I can see your tits down that blouse," he commented. "Is that for me?"

"Don't be an ass. We're going out after this," Jasmine improvised. Behind Charlie, Shae raised her eyebrows and made a "You tell him!" face. "You're not invited."

Charlie grabbed her arm and pulled her into the apartment, slamming the door behind her. "You're not going anywhere."

"She can do what she wants, Charlie." Shae threw up her hands. "Do you see a ring on her finger?"

Charlie let Jasmine go and whirled on Shae. He pointed at the door. "Leave."

Shae crossed her arms. "No."

"We're both leaving after I get my things." Jasmine tried to slip past Charlie, but he snaked an arm around her shoulders until she was flush against his chest. His bare skin was like hot silk against her cheek.

"Jasmine and I have a long overdue appointment." Charlie reached behind him and opened the door he so recently slammed. "Scram."

"Don't listen to him. He and I have nothing to discuss." Jasmine pushed against Charlie's chest, more of her hair escaping its bonds, but his arm was a band of steel. "Jesus, Charlie." To her dismay, her heart began to race and her pussy jumpstarted with a delicious little throb.

Shae looked between Charlie and Jasmine, a considering expression on her face. "I'll leave on one condition."

"What's that?" Charlie said. His fingers inched between her arm and her breasts and wiggled. Jasmine's nipples hardened.

"You name your firstborn after me."

"Shae!" Jasmine yelled, aghast. She tried again to break Charlie's hold on her, and this time he used his free hand to pop her on the ass.

"I'm going, I'm going. Don't spank her on my account, unless that's what she likes."

"Don't you dare leave me," Jasmine said to Shae's retreating form. "You promised."

Shae waved a hand without turning her head. "See you crazy kids later."

Charlie closed the door, more softly. He flicked all the locks shut and looked down at her. His hand rested on the curve of her butt. "Is that what you like, Jasmine?"

Her face burned. "I'd like you to let me go." When he didn't, she dug her nails into his arm, and he released her with a low chuckle.

He made no move to pursue her when she hastened to the middle of the living room. They eyed one another. A little smile played across Charlie's sensual lips, and Jasmine remembered how they'd felt on her breasts.

"What's up with the tattoo?" she asked. She wanted to ask, and the attitude, the sideburns, and the split personality, but she'd settle for the tattoo.

He flexed his bicep. "You like? The ink lady said it was hot." It was a band of Celtic knotwork, not flashy but not Charlie, either. It didn't look like a fresh tattoo. The skin around it wasn't reddened or pale. Had it been there Saturday? The only thing she could remember from Saturday was his big cock and his washboard abs.

"Where's my stuff?" She crossed her arms. She wanted this over with, and fast. How could Shae have deserted her, especially with Charlie looking and acting like a caveman? The rumored change in their friend had swayed Shae to accompany her tonight—the chance to see Charlie behave like a typical man.

She hadn't believed it, but Jasmine bet she did now.

The caveman, his bare chest gleaming in the mellow illumination of the lamps beside the couch, gestured, palm up. "Probably in my bedroom. Would you care to check between my sheets?"

"Oh, that's funny." She backed up to his television and stereo bank and pretended to glance around for her CDs. She noticed his apartment was not the picture of meticulous order as the last time she'd been here. Nearly every other time she'd been here. A few crumpled beer cans were on the floor beside the couch. A girlie magazine lay open on the coffee table, beside a pizza box. The brocade throw on the back of his couch she'd helped him choose at Pottery Barn was crumpled at the end of the sofa. His tennies and several athletic socks surrounded the recliner.

And horror of horrors, there was dust on his high definition television screen!

Jasmine wrinkled her nose. "Enjoying a little party for one tonight?"

Charlie shrugged. "That was last night. Good articles in there. Better pictures."

"Gross." Jaz traced her finger across the dust on the television and waggled it. In reality, she was terrified to turn her back on him. What if he took off his pants and invited her to soap him up in his interrupted shower? She'd be a fool to turn that down.

She was a fool already, coming here. Friday night, Charlie said he wanted to see what would happen if they let themselves be more than friends. She'd said no, too afraid to take the chance. Then Saturday, he'd insisted. He'd taken her to bed. If he wanted to deepen their friendship, wouldn't he have stayed? Wouldn't he have returned her calls? Wouldn't he have behaved like the Charlie she knew?

What if, after trying her out, he'd decided they'd never suit sexually? Maybe he thought she was boring in bed. Unattractive. Funny smelling. Yikes!

Something hot and achy welled in her throat, the bubble of confusion and shame that had tormented her all week.

"Take off your clothes," Charlie said in a conversational tone.

Jasmine blinked, not sure she'd heard him correctly. "What? No!"

He advanced on her. In three strides, his palms were on her shoulders. He fisted his hands in the fabric and ripped. Buttons flew in every direction.

"Charlie!" Jasmine's jaw dropped and her hands flew instinctively to cover her chest and the blue push-up bra she'd donned to give her confidence a much needed boost.

"I didn't feel like asking again." He threw Shae's ruined shirt to the ground with barely restrained violence. "You don't come here wearing a top like that because you're going out afterwards."

Jasmine's heartbeat accelerated. Around bizarro world Charlie, she had no idea how to act. "That wasn't my blouse," she said, her voice a pitch higher than normal. "It was Shae's."

Charlie's teeth flashed in a wicked grin. "I know." He leaned closer, holding her gaze with his own. Her lips parted, but he bypassed them and whispered in her ear, "If you don't want me to treat the rest of your clothing the same way, I suggest you take it off yourself."

Then he let her go and stepped back. He crossed his arms over his broad chest and waited.

Jasmine had on a knee length black skirt and pair of pretty blue panties that matched her bra. No hose, strappy blue and silver sandals. The silver matched the chain around her neck with the small Chinese symbol that meant "Earth", Charlie's birthday gift to her last year. Her hair had already fallen halfway out of the bun; she'd been so nervous when she arranged it, she hadn't secured it well.

"I'm waiting." Charlie drummed his fingers on his arm.

Jasmine took a deep breath. "You first."

He dropped his hands slowly to his waist and fiddled with his buttons. Jaz licked her lips. She'd been envisioning this encounter all week—but mostly the conversation. What would she say to him? How would she get him to open up? If he undressed before clearing the air, was she willing to have sex with him?

Frightening thought. It had apparently been sexual contact with her that drove her friend over the edge. After another night with her, would he rush out and rob a bank?

Then he laughed and rested his hands on his hips. "Nah. I'm too shy. You're the stripper, not me."

"What do you mean, no? You...you ripped off my shirt!" Jasmine spread her arms. "I can't believe you did this!"

Charlie openly inspected her breasts. "I didn't undress you last weekend, sweetheart."

Mortification weakened Jasmine's composure as she recalled her maneuver Saturday with her sleepshirt—a maneuver that led straight to the bedroom. A new understanding of events dawned on her. It was possible he hadn't purposefully seduced her. It was possible he'd only taken what she offered, Friday night and Saturday too.

Was that what this was all about? Did he think, after so many years, she'd suddenly expect him to be friends with benefits, just because he was male and she was horny?

Bedamned if she offered herself to him again! They'd have to work their issues out over the phone, if she could freaking get him to answer it, because real life Charlie was as prickly and difficult and distracting and sexy and his abs were so lickable and...

Jasmine stomped her foot like a little girl, mostly to snap herself out of her mounting lust. "Get me a shirt. And my blender. I, um, have a date."

"No, you don't. But we can pretend we just got back from dinner and a movie. I treated, by the way. And the movie did *not* have that idiot Hugh Jackman in it."

"What does he have to do with anything?" This was so miserable. Why were they sniping at each other, arguing like children? Jasmine sighed. "Charlie, let's not do this."

Charlie stepped toward her until he was close enough to touch. She could feel the anger, the heat, throbbing off him. "Oh, let's." And then he picked her up, tossed her over his shoulder with a lot less effort than she'd have expected, and carried her towards his bedroom like a half-dressed sack of flour.

Jasmine squealed and thumped his back with her fists. Her sandals, which had no ankle straps, clunked to the floor. "What the hell are you doing? Put me down!" Blood rushed to her head and pounded in her ears. Her hair fell out of its chignon and dangled past his buttocks.

Charlie stuck his hand up her skirt and snapped the elastic on her panties. "You're wearing drawers. I guess you weren't thinking about me today, huh."

This had to be a joke. "If you don't put me down, I'm going to call the police."

He kicked his bedroom door closed and twirled. She got dizzy, fast. "How can you do that if there's no phone in my bedroom?

"I'll go to the living room. Put me... whoa!"

Charlie dropped her onto his tall four-poster bed, and she bounced, landing sprawled and breathless somewhere close to the middle. Her skirt wrinkled up her legs, nearly exposing her crotch. The plaid comforter she and Shae bought him two Christmases ago was missing; in its place were red satin sheets.

Jasmine started to scrabble off the bed, but quick as a whip, Charlie pounced on her and pinned her down. His thighs straddled her hips. He pressed her wrists into the soft mattress and grinned. Her heart practically stopped beating.

"How can you go back to the living room if you're tied to my bed?"

Jasmine's voice came out as a ridiculous squeak. "If I'm what?"

Charlie leaned·in until their noses were almost touching. Gently, he brushed his lips across hers. Jasmine sighed and parted her lips, inviting him in, but he drew back and whispered, "If you fight, I'll enjoy it more."

Jasmine fought. She twisted and bucked, but everything she did only served to bump and grind their hips together like wild sex. He held her down and laughed, and she got hotter under the collar. In her panties. She couldn't whip her legs up and strangle him, because his weight trapped her thighs. Her skirt rode up around her waist. She tried to smash her head against his and missed. Tried to knee his crotch, but he wedged himself between her legs. Through his jeans, the ridge of his aroused cock rubbed her pussy, and a quick, mortifying heat sizzled through her, top to bottom.

Both of them breathing hard, he wrestled her to the top of the bed and secured her right hand to the bedpost with a soft cloth restraint. Too convenient—it had to have been waiting there for... for her? What was going on? She yanked his hair with her left, desperate, and he winced.

"Ow!"

"Oh!" She stopped pulling. "Sorry, I—"

He took advantage of her cease fire to straighten her left arm and secure it in another restraint. She tugged her arms, agitation ratcheting through her, and he rested his full mass on her body. Her hips cradled him. She had to resist the urge to curl her legs around him and rub against him in blatant invitation.

Charlie smiled, as if he knew what she was thinking. "Now for the ankles."

"Don't." For a moment, they lay, body to body, and she turned her head. She caught the faint scent of candle wax, the flicker of gentle flames against the burgundy wallpaper of his bedroom. A dark blue robe draped off one wooden post. A Chinese print satin box rested on his bedside table, closed and mysterious. A thin scarf draped over the lamp, coloring the glow red.

This was not Charlie's bedroom. This was a...boudoir. He'd prepared for this. The candles and restraints spoke of planning. Deliberation. Effort.

Charlie kissed her jaw, her neck, his whiskers rasping her skin. "The ankles are important. You have very strong thighs." As he talked, his hands maneuvered up and down her sides, caressing her ribs, the underside of her arms, her hips. "If I were to, say, put my head between them, what's to keep you from strangling me?"

"Oh, God." The image of Charlie licking and suckling her pussy with her tied to the bed flooded her senses like an orgasm.

He rotated his hips against her moistening folds. "I want to taste you, Jasmine. Will you let me?"

Yes. Yes. Every part of her screamed yes, please, yes, but Jasmine closed her eyes and gulped air. "Have you always been into S&M? Lorraine never mentioned."

Charlie arched an eyebrow. "You want to talk about my ex?"

"No." A flush skated across her face. "But I do think we should talk about this."

"Are you frightened? I wasn't going to involve any floggers and clamps tonight, but bondage and discipline involves trust. And a safe word."

He reached above her, shuffling beside the headboard. He came back down with a strip of black silk. A blindfold. "Do you trust me?"

"Hell, no." But she did. Even this uncivilized Charlie, she'd trust with her life. She just wasn't sure about trusting him with her body. Her heart.

Charlie nuzzled her ear, and tingles of delight branched through her. "Do you want a safe word?" he said, his breath hot against her skin. "Something that, if you say it, I'll stop whatever I'm doing immediately?"

"I want you to stop right now," she lied. "We need to talk." She could feel her pussy dampen, soften, prime for him. Her clit prickled. She didn't want a special word—she didn't want to be safe from him.

He pushed up from her body and stroked both her thighs, hip to knee, with the satin blindfold. It sent an ache of desire straight to her core. He bent and kissed her stomach. Her insides fluttered, and he made his way to her breasts. He licked the tops of them, bundled up by the underwire and padding, and peeled back the blue lace to reveal a pert nipple. His mouth latched around it, and Jasmine caught her breath.

"Do you want me to stop?" he asked. She started to answer, and he sucked her nipple into his mouth again, the hot tug sending her through the roof.

All she managed to do was moan.

Charlie reached to the headboard again, and this time he came back with a large pocketknife.

Jasmine's eyes widened as she focused on the red knife. At least it wasn't a cleaver. But still. "What's that for?"

He placed it beside them and swept the black silk blindfold across her lips. "Shhhh." He tied it around her eyes, blocking out the flickering candles, his intense gaze absorbing her reactions.

Suddenly her other senses leapt into a new acuity. She became more aware of the slide of satin beneath her body, the texture of his skin, the play of his muscles, the rhythm of his breathing, which was not as controlled as he wanted her to think. His fingers in her hair. His breath in her ear. The scent of his aroused male body, dominating her. The scent of her own arousal, succumbing to him.

His weight left her abruptly, and she nearly whimpered. "What are you doing?" She rotated her head, trying to dislodge the blindfold.

Something snicked, like a knife blade locking into place, and cool metal pressed on her chest. "What is it with you and knives?" she asked in a shaky voice. She wrapped her fists around the silken restraints and tugged.

"It's not me and knives, Jaz. It's you." He drew the blunt edge down her belly like a pen on paper, and she shuddered. A man with a knife had tied her to the bed and blindfolded her. A man with a knife could do anything he wanted with her.

He dragged her skirt down her legs. Two big, warm hands collared her ankles and spread them. "Don't move your legs or I'll bind them."

Jasmine tried to clench her legs together, and he yanked them apart, wider this time. "I mean it."

He shifted, and the blade pricked her inner thigh, briefly. She yelped but didn't twitch, unsure where the blade was. Her panties stretched and snapped off her body. He'd cut them off! Air kissed her wet pussy, alerting her to how damp she'd become. He palmed her before he smoothed the cold blade back up her body and underneath her bra. He cut the garment off her, tossed it, and she heard it hit the wooden floor of his bedroom.

"Were those Shae's?" he asked, his voice husky.

She shook her head. Where was the knife?

"Good. She'll be pissed enough about the blouse." Then he sighed, long and deep. His exhalation fluttered across her bare breasts, and her nipples tightened in anticipation. "You are so beautiful." His lips touched her forehead gently. Her nose. Her chin, but he didn't give her the soul kiss she craved.

"Charlie, why are you doing this?"

He laved the sensitive spot near her collarbone and then tugged her earlobe between his teeth. "Do you mean this?"

His hand slipped between their bodies and into her pussy, sliding through her hot juices. "Or this?"

She jerked against the sudden spear of pleasure as his finger rubbed her clit. "Yes," she said on a long breath.

"I'm giving you what you want."

She wished she could see his face. Was he mocking? Smiling? Glaring? Rolling his eyes? "You're nuts."

"Truth or dare, roughly five years ago." His body left her again, and his weight vacated the bed. She tensed. His voice sounded from across the room. "You picked truth, and Shae asked your naughtiest fantasy."

"I…" She remembered that night. They'd all been splitsville from their significant others and drunk. Or she and Shae had been drunk. What the hell had she confessed?

"You said you wanted to be tied up. Ravished." Charlie paused, and she heard the sound of fabric sliding on skin. Her nerve endings prickled. Was he undressing?

"Then you and Shae laughed, because you said any man who tied you up would just stick his dick in your mouth while he had the chance."

The mattress shifted and he crawled near her. The heat of his skin set her on fire, but he didn't touch her anywhere. She could sense him. Smell him. Hear him breathe. She could twist her legs and kick him, but then he might strap her down.

The arms were enough. More than enough. Her heart pounded in time with her pussy.

Something hot and hard brushed her hip. His cock. It was as silken as the blindfold. Jasmine swallowed. His arm brushed hers, then his hand cupped her cheek. "Shall I be like any man?"

"Just be yourself," she whispered, "and untie me. This isn't you." He shifted again, straddling her torso. The hair on his inner legs tickled her skin; his cock rested between her breasts. A dab of moisture leaked onto her chest. She smelled the tang of his body and her pulse quickened. Behind the blindfold, she squeezed her eyes shut.

"It's me you don't want." He cupped her breasts, his thumbs rubbing the tips, and brought them together to make a channel. Slowly he pushed and pulled his cock through her softness, pinching her nipples to aching beads. Each unhurried thrust swelled the head of his magnificent organ and brought it closer to her mouth. She brought her chin down and tried to taste him, and he expelled a long, drawn-out sigh.

"So it's true? You want a man to tie you up and stick his cock in your mouth?"

Jasmine clenched her legs together to reduce the desperate ache in her cunt. "Would you enjoy that?"

Charlie released her breasts and raised himself until his cock was inches away from her lips. The head brushed her cheek. She turned her face and licked him, and he shuddered. "Jasmine, I—"

She curled her tongue around and under the sensitive tip then enveloped the whole head with her mouth. He tasted of spice. Salt. A faint sweetness. He inhaled sharply but didn't move or thrust. Didn't grab her hair. Didn't force her up and down his shaft, like she was nothing but a rubber doll. Raising her head, Jasmine sucked him in halfway, learning his contours. She withdrew, her lips tight around him, until her tongue flickered his small opening. She exhaled across his moist flesh; he released a whistling breath of his own. With teasing strokes, she flicked the sensitive underside and tried to swallow him again, determined to unnerve him. Unman him.

Charlie withdrew and scrambled down her body. "Some other time."

Jasmine licked her lips, now slightly swollen from mouthing his cock. "I do better work with my hands free."

He pried her thighs apart and shoved two fingers into her cunt. Jasmine bit back a shocked cry. "So do I."

He dropped a thumb to her clit. With an expert contraction of his hand, he rubbed her bud and curled his fingers inside her simultaneously, almost like he was pinching her. Jasmine tightened her fists around the restraints and rolled her head to the side, gasping.

Not losing a beat, he slid her body closer to the edge of the bed and she heard his feet hit the floor. His hand continued its delicious assault, kneading her pussy until she trembled. Something clinked, something snapped, and he withdrew her fingers from her body. She whimpered in protest. He hopped back onto the bed and hovered over her. She could feel his arms bracketing her ribcage beside her breasts.

Almost hesitantly, he dropped a light kiss on her lips. Jasmine tilted her chin, and he parted her lips with his tongue. He tasted faintly of mint and her skin. He brought his nude body flush against hers, his eager cock parting her folds. She groaned into his mouth and wrapped her legs around his hips. He felt so phenomenal against her, so forceful and erotic, her anger at him dissipated, replaced by an almost painful craving.

Their tongues tangled as they explored one another's mouths, first delicate and then bold, tasting and learning. His unshaven chin and cheeks scraped her face; when he dropped his head to her breasts, the contrast between his soft, hot tongue and the scratch of whiskers made her head swim. He licked and nibbled and traced the centerline of her stomach, pausing to suckle next to one hip hard enough to leave a mark. The nip of pain shot her passion higher.

Jasmine chafed her legs against the satin sheets as Charlie's lips moved closer and closer to her core. He stroked her legs and spread them, murmuring compliments. Hands caressed her legs, brushed her knees. His weight transferred, and his hair tickled her inner thigh. Jasmine held her breath.

For a moment, nothing. Then he dropped a wet kiss on her swollen clit. The burst of pleasure was so intense, Jasmine's hips bucked. Charlie laughed.

"Patience," he whispered, his breath warm against her creamy folds. He began to tease her, suckling the tender skin at the join of her legs, the sweet spot near her hip. He brushed her pussy, tickling, not plunging the way she yearned for him to. He licked the inside of her leg, moving up and around until Jasmine was ready to scream.

Finally he spread her nether lips with his fingers and gave her clit and cunt a long, slow lick. If she hadn't been prone, her knees would have buckled. He licked her again, then flicked her clit with his tongue in a motion she could tell would bring her to orgasm shortly. He knew just what part of her to stimulate, and how hard, and how fast.

Something rigid and cool slid between her thighs and probed her. "What's that?" she said, her voice high.

"Something else from your list of truths." Charlie parted her inner flesh and entered her with a smooth, medium-sized dildo. He clicked it on; vibrations pulsed through her entire pussy. Not a dildo—a vibrator. Jasmine panted and tried to hold still. Delight poured over her in mounting swells. His slick tongue on her clit, his hair on her inner thighs, the vibrator deep in her cunt.

"Oh, God," Jasmine moaned. He pushed the vibrator deeper, then let it slide most of the way out, in and out, rocking her to bliss. She wished it was his cock, thicker and hotter. She wished he was mounting her, possessing her, pounding in and out of her. Taking her over the edge.

He clamped down on her clit, sucking and licking, and Jasmine crescendoed into an orchestra of sensation. Cream gushed from her body. Her inner contractions forced the vibrator out, and Charlie slipped two fingers inside her, blowing on her pussy as she clenched and released him. He continued stroking her clit until her orgasm rolled to a stop.

Behind the silken blindfold, Jasmine squeezed her eyes and tried to hold back sudden tears. Unexpected sentiment inundated her. Charlie rested his head on the curve of her stomach.

"Does this mean you'll untie me now?" she whispered.

"If I do, are you going to hit me?"

Jasmine sniffled, glad the blindfold concealed her foolish tears. One corner of her mouth tugged up in a reluctant smile. "Maybe."

"I can't take that chance." Charlie slipped to the head of the bed and fiddled with her restraints. His body pressed against hers, his chest near her face. Jasmine twisted, and one of her arms whipped free. She immediately whacked him in the ass. They tussled, giggling, until he grasped her wrists and lashed them together. She could smell the warm zest of his skin, so close to her lips.

"Okay, Charlie." When she opened her mouth, she could almost taste him. "You've made your point. It's time to untie me."

Charlie adjusted his position until his head was level with hers. His breath brushed her cheek, and his stiff cock prodded the tender area between her legs. "And that point is?"

Jasmine blushed. "I didn't want you to stop."

He pivoted his hips. His penis sliced her moist folds and stimulated her still-sensitive pussy. "I know."

What did he have in mind now? Jasmine bit her lower lip. "I swear I won't call the cops. Or hit you. You can untie me."

"You already hit me. I'm not finished."

Even though she'd just experienced an orgasm that brought her to tears, yearning flared as Charlie rotated against her. He pushed the head of his cock into her body, and she clasped him with her inner walls.

"So tight," Charlie murmured. "You feel so good." He nibbled her ear.

Jasmine drew her feet up the backs of his legs, widening her pelvis, until her heels dug into the curves of his muscular ass. He nudged in and out of her sheath, across her clit, taunting her, denying her his full impact. Compulsion built within her. Her body ached to take his shaft, deep and hard. She curved her hips upward, moaning softly, and he drew back.

"Ah, ah, ah." Charlie jerked the satin around her wrists toward the head of the bed, and her arms followed.

"No!" she protested. But Charlie swiftly knotted the rope to the headboard, this time with her arms together, and slid down her body.

Still blindfolded and tied, Jasmine tried to scrabble to the head of the bed and gain some leverage. Charlie grabbed her ankles and lifted.

"Charlie!" she exclaimed, suspended briefly in midair before he flipped her. She landed with a whump face down on her hair and the satin sheets, her legs pretzeled. Two strong hands untangled her and parted her thighs as she struggled to blow her hair out of her face.

Charlie smacked her lightly on the hip, just hard enough to sting. "Now I've got you where I want you," he said with a sexy growl.

Jasmine cringed. "Don't you dare!"

"Sweetheart, you can't stop me." He smacked her on the crest of her ass. Then the other cheek. He soothed the sting with soft strokes and then landed several blows, alternating sides.

"I don't like this." She clenched her teeth, the heat from the blows confusing her nerve endings. The sting of pain faded, replaced by a strange burn that was almost erotic. What would it feel like if he kept striking her? If he struck her pussy? If he paddled her while buried deep in her body?

"But I do. You're as pink as roses." One more time he spanked, low on her prickling cheeks. His broad hand struck dead center, and a jolt of unexpected sensation blazed into her cunt. She gasped, and not with pain.

"More?" he asked.

She had no answer. Her reaction frightened her; her vulnerability aroused her.

He leaned forward and stroked down her back, ending at her tingly ass. He massaged the small of her back, angling his weight on the curve until she groaned with pleasure, before shifting to her butt. He plied her cheeks like a chef making pizza dough, drawing them apart. She could feel the pull on her crevice and her wet labia. He worked her flesh until she melted. He caressed her and manipulated her. Against her will, she began to relax. Muscles she hadn't even known were tense released and stretched, all from his wonderful hands on her butt. She'd known a foot massage could have an all-body effect, but hadn't known an ass massage could do the same thing.

Only she wasn't entirely relaxed. When Charlie's finger wandered close to her rear opening, her cunt surged with interest.

"I love your ass. I could just eat it up." He sank his teeth into the curve of her derriere, and Jasmine whimpered.

It felt good. Too good. She shifted, her firm nipples rubbing against the satin.

Charlie kissed the beginning of her crack, running his slick tongue across her tailbone. With his hands, he continued to spread and knead her, his thumbs probing low, close to her folds. Juices seeped from her pussy. She longed to thrust her bottom in the air like a cat in heat and beg to be mounted.

One of his hands disappeared. Jasmine heard a click, like a bottle lid, and warm oil pooled in the small of her back. She turned her face to the side and inhaled—a combination of almond and something else, maybe sandalwood.

Charlie's touch on her ass, with the addition of the oil, turned blatantly sexual. Carnal. His fingers explored her rear crevice, and she barely suppressed a moan as a flood of sensation submersed her. It almost pained her, a knife edge of pleasure. His hands skated across her skin and woke every remaining nerve to a peak that had her pussy aching and frantic. The scent of the oil surrounded her in a haze of indulgence.

He smeared oil between her legs. This time she couldn't swallow her moan. She arched her back to allow him freer access. He laved her inner thighs and pussy with the sweet, silky oil, rubbing and whispering, his hands exploring every inch of her. A craving for something violent and feral built inside her like a looming storm. When he hoisted her hips into the air, she shifted her knees to expose her soaking pussy. Her thighs trembled with excitement.

"Perfect." He positioned himself between her widespread legs and curved oiled hands up and down the subservient slant of her back and thighs. He clutched her buttocks; his hips bumped hers. His cock slid between her legs and tapped her clit. She was so sensitized, if he pricked her too many times, she'd go off like a rocket.

"It feels too intense," she panted, wriggling her ass against him. "Quit playing with me."

"You're not in charge, Jasmine. Remember that." She heard another click and his hands, oil syrupy on the fingers, skimmed down her ass and across her cunt. He cupped his dick, oiling it, and fucked her labia. He pressed himself against her, his head almost slipping into her as she squirmed and gasped. Over her clit, her vagina, the slick heat initiated her rise to bliss.

"Please," she begged. "I want you inside me."

He palmed her ass and then smacked it. The oil, her state of arousal, turned it into a hot flash of pleasure almost instantly. "Do you like it better now?"

"Oh, God." Lust burned away coherent thought. "Please, Charlie. Please make love to me."

He fingered her rear opening, the tight, sensitive muscle slick with oil. "Are you mine? Can I do anything I want to you?"

Drums throbbed in her head, her veins, her pussy. He swiveled his thumb, entering her virgin ass with the tip. She nearly sobbed with frustration. "Anything, Charlie. Anything."

"Can I love you, Jasmine?"

Her throat tightened. She tried to think of a suitable reply, but his slippery cock prodded her anus, and she tensed, willing but frightened. Then he shifted and plunged into her cunt, the angle of their bodies sending him deep and hard. She cried out and nearly tumbled flat into the bed from the exquisite sensation.

He held her up by her hips. As she gasped for air, he pumped in and out of her, the wet sound of their bodies louder than her helpless moans. He let out a long, satisfied sigh as he pistoned, smacking against her with rhythmic force. His balls slapped her pussy. She gripped the rope at her wrists and shoved against him, meeting him with her own desire, finding his tempo.

"That's it, baby. Come with me." She felt an unusual pressure against her rear. A slick thumb entered her, raw and strange and wild. He began to work it in and out of her. She arched and shivered, wondering what his cock would feel like in that tiny, untried area. Charlie increased his cadence; his cock, somehow, swelled even larger as he neared his climax. The extra length took her beyond mere pleasure into a nearly agonizing joy.

He bent, breathing through his teeth, and wrapped an arm around her hips. His fingers sought her clit and pinched. "Now, Jasmine. Now."

Obedient to his will, she exploded in a hot torrent centered on her pussy. He groaned as she sobbed his name and rippled around his cock and his finger in her anus. The orgasm went on and on, waves that grew gentler, and then he climaxed. His cock leapt inside her. He grabbed her ass with both hands, riding her until he was fully emptied.

He continued to slide in and out, a contented growl capping the experience. She knew how he felt. Jasmine's limbs turned to jelly. If it hadn't been for his hands supporting her hips, she would have buckled to the bed and never gotten back up.

Was this her body, this satiated and numb? It had taken Charlie, her best friend Charlie, to finally show her what sex could be. Emotional. Overwhelming. Fulfilling in a way that was more that physical. He withdrew and cleansed her with a soft cloth. She let him flop her over like a rag doll, barely moving when he untied her hands. When he removed her blindfold, she didn't have the energy to raise her eyelids.

"Look at me."

She tried. Honestly. Her eyelids fluttered. His face was dark against the quiet, flickering light of the candles. The smell of the body oil embraced her senses. Charlie's sweaty body spooned her, and she lifted a newly freed hand to touch his face. The curls at his forehead were damp.

"It's too dark," she whispered. "I can't see you."

"You've never tried to see me."

She frowned. "I see you several times a week. Or I used to. Charlie…"

He placed a finger on her lips. "No talking. Go to sleep."

She struggled to wake up as weariness pulled her into a cocoon. "You'll leave me."

He laughed. "It's my house, Jaz. I'm not going anywhere."

When she woke, her body tender and tingly, Charlie sprawled on his stomach beside her. Satin covered the lower half of his body. Against the red sheets, he looked like a Greek god. Stubble darkened his chin more than the night before, and his breathing was deep and even. It was early.

His forearms were tucked beneath his pillow. Jasmine reached out to trace the muscular line of his back. The tattoo around his firm bicep was… actually, it was half missing.

A temporary tattoo?

Jasmine rubbed her eyes and frowned. She couldn't figure him out. The way he made love to her spoke of someone who cared deeply for her and her pleasure. He was amazing in bed, sexy as hell, taking her to heights she'd only dreamed of. But the way he treated her out of bed since last Friday night spoke of someone whose opinion of her was somewhat less stellar.

And he wouldn't talk to her.

God, she should have insisted he open up last night. Hopping straight into bed was a mistake. Again. They should have aired their feelings and frustrations. They were friends, dammit. Good friends. Best friends.

They could be better friends, even better lovers. Where had she heard that before?

He shifted in his sleep, his thigh coming to rest against hers. The crisp brush of his hair on her skin caused her libido to pulse with interest.

His leg hair made her horny.

This was pitiful. She'd never clear her head in bed with the world's hottest pharmacist. She had to figure this out, decide what her feelings were, how deep they ran. And what she wanted to do about it. This could be… serious. This could be it. The one. But he'd been so unpredictable and spiteful lately. He used to be wonderful. Steadfast and patient and a bit quirky. That little smile, when he looked at her. That was her Charlie. That was the Charlie she… Her breath caught in her throat. She hadn't seen that smile in over a week.

Did she have to trade one Charlie for the other? Couldn't she have both?

This time, Jasmine left Charlie asleep.

He supposed he deserved it.

He'd ripped off her clothes, tied her up, spanked her, and threatened to fuck her in the ass. No wonder she left as soon as he passed out.

It might be time to give up. Charlie tossed the melted candles into the trash and the beer cans into the recycling bin. He traced the mark Jasmine's finger had left in the dust on his television screen before cleaning it with a special cloth. The clutter in his apartment had been giving him twitches all week, but he'd wanted to be ready if she showed.

Charlie, not Charlie. A man like her others, who wasn't like her others.

In a pair of cut off sweats, he vacuumed and mopped the kitchen floor. The tomato sauce he'd blotted artfully on the tiles had turned black. What a relief! He was done with this part of his charade, and besides, it was driving him nuts.

After what happened, she wouldn't be brave enough to venture into his apartment for a long time. He knew Jasmine. She had awful taste in men, but anytime something about a relationship caught her by surprise, she split. When you always dated losers, you expected certain behaviors, few of them decent. Hell, he remembered one guy who'd brought her flowers and taken her somewhere besides beer joints—she'd broken up with him after a few weeks.

He'd given her something not even the baddest of her bad boys had managed. Smug machismo out of bed, irresistible orgasms in it. She'd loved every minute of being tied up and dominated. Pleasured. He had, too. In making her fantasies come true, he'd satiated himself, inside and out. All the planning and build up. Seizing complete control of the situation and her luscious body suited his fondness for order.

He threw the unread men's magazine in the trash as he remembered the tenderness in her gaze and touch afterwards. The way she'd begged him to talk to her.

Was she going to tell him they should just be friends? He'd been so immersed in his role and its effect on her, he'd opted to postpone conversation until he could thoroughly addict her. Force her off-balance, so she'd have to look at him with new eyes. Really look at him. It was his last effort before he gave up entirely—on their friendship, on any potential for a relationship. If Jasmine didn't love him, he could no longer suspend his life waiting for a miracle.

If she hadn't been about to give him the friends speech, what had she wanted to discuss? So many possibilities. Shae's blouse. His behavior. Sexual fantasies. The future.

He'd satisfied her body, but he didn't think she was ready for the truth. How long did you have to wait to ask a woman to marry you, anyway? Until she informed you the date was in June and you needed three groomsmen? Hinted about diamond rings? Cried at weddings?

Jasmine already cried at weddings.

The danger was if he'd performed his part too well. Maybe the only Charlie she wanted was jackhole Charlie. Someone erratic and superficial she could bitch about without getting serious. Could he continue that, just so he could have Jasmine?

No. It was fun to role play, especially in the bedroom, but he wasn't the man who didn't call. The man who kept a slovenly apartment. The man who disregarded his lover's wishes, even when he figured he knew better.

He finished in the kitchen and started in the bedroom. He stripped the sheets and shoved them in the hamper. The oil had been a nice touch. Smelled nice, too, and he'd loved the glide of his hands over her curves. He tucked his red box of tricks under the bed. Then the bathroom, his crowning achievement, and he didn't even know if she'd visited it. Scum and mildew smeared ugly patterns on his glass shower doors. Toothpaste hardened in the sink. He'd left toenail clippings and a stinky wet towel on the floor.

And still it was cleaner than Jasmine's bathroom. Charlie grinned, got out the disinfectant, and made quick work of his manly debris.

He'd just hung fresh towels when he heard his front door open. Who the hell? Probably Shae. She was the only person who barged into his house unannounced. He stalked out of his bedroom, rubber gloves on his hands. He didn't think it would be Jasmine so soon, and she always knocked.

But it was Jasmine.

Her eyebrows arced when he stomped into the living room. "That's something you don't see every day."

He looked down at himself. Bare feet, no shirt, scrappy shorts and yellow gloves. "Cleaning," he explained. Boy, this would ruin his new image.

She smiled. She had on—nothing special. Jeans. A T-shirt. No make up. Her hair was in a long, bouncy ponytail. She looked like she might have been on the way to garden.

Oh, he adored her this way. Shae-clothes were hot on her, but if she went around provocatively dressed all the time, he'd never get his brain out of his pants.

"What are you doing here?" He stripped off his rubber gloves and tossed them on the breakfast bar. He smelled of chlorine bleach and the massage oil from last night.

"I've been thinking." Jasmine shut the door behind her and twisted the deadbolt. Charlie instinctively tensed. "About some things you said to me. I've been trying to figure you out."

Though he loved her madly and longed to make multiple children with her, her tone set him on the defensive. It was that woman tone. The one that meant the female in question had reached a decision. And it never meant the upcoming discussion was going to be comfortable or wind up in bed.

He spread his hands and tightened his abdomen muscles, knowing how much she liked a man with flat abs. "I'm not a cipher, Jasmine."

"It was the temporary tattoo that clued me in."

"What? It's not... Oh." After mocking him for fearing permanent ink, the lady who'd helped him apply the design explained he could take it off with oil. He'd had plenty of oil all over his body last night.

"It was a test run." He flexed what was left of the tattoo. "It's this or a dragon. I can't decide."

"Oh, Charlie." Jasmine shook her head and advanced on him. "I need you to do something for me."

That gave him pause. "Women always want something," he answered, hoping he sounded asinine. Jasmine's lips tightened. He rubbed his chin and pretended to think. "Does it involve getting naked?"

She licked her full bottom lip, and he realized if he got a hard on in these sweats, it would tent up in a ridiculous fashion.

"Yes, it does," she purred. "In your bedroom, to be precise." She pulled a wad of money out of her pocket and peeled a bill off the outside. She scrutinized him with those big brown eyes. "I will give you twenty dollars to take off your clothes, shave your face, brush your damn hair, and dress in an outfit of my choosing."

Charlie frowned. "Is this a joke?"

She peeled off another bill. "Forty dollars."

What in the hell did she have in mind? Another sexual fantasy? Maybe she wanted him to don chaps and a gun belt and belly up to her bar. He could get into that. "Do I have to leave the house in this get-up?"

"Only if you want to." She peeled off another bill. "Sixty big ones."

He cocked his head. "What will you be wearing?"

She waved the bills down her body. "A stylish yet comfortable week-end ensemble."

"No pictures."

"Only mental ones," she agreed. "Shave first."

He decided to test her, as she was obviously testing him. "A hundred dollars."

She glared at him, then laughed and smacked the whole wad of dough onto his breakfast bar. "Done."

"I guess I'll shave, then."

"Thank God." Jasmine rubbed her left cheek, which was patched with red.

His face had done that to her. That settled it. He'd been longing to shave; his face itched like a mother. He went to the bathroom, and she followed, leaning against the doorjamb. She watched without comment as he splashed hot water on his cheeks and chin to soften the whiskers and lathered his face with cream. He took advantage of the water to clean off his hands and arms. If they did wind up in bed, he didn't find the odor of chlorine particularly seductive. Reassuring, maybe. But not sexy.

She'd watched him shave before, even hovered at his shoulder applying makeup at the same time. Today, however, her quiet regard made him nervous. He was performing, and she was evaluating. He didn't know the rules, so how could he excel?

He cut himself three times and went through two disposable razors before the thick scrub was finally eradicated. He splashed on a moisturizing aftershave, the burn mostly refreshing. He'd gotten an unusually close shave after growing it out for a week.

Jasmine nodded her approval. "Slick your hair back with water and comb it."

Charlie hesitated, but grabbed the comb in the end. He quickly dampened and styled his hair in the manner he normally did, noting it was time for a cut. He'd left the sideburns a little long. Uneven. He frowned, picked up his razor, and jimmied the left side until he was proportionate.

He turned to Jasmine, fully prepared for her to pull out some ridiculous outfit. Instead she crooked her finger, led him into his own closet, and tugged a pair of neatly pressed khakis and a blue dress shirt off their hangers.

"Put this on."

"These?" He held them up as if they were offensive. A week in jeans and T-shirts, even at work, and he'd become somewhat used to casual wear. "No black leather or maybe a mask? You know, Zorro?"

She shook the clothes. "These. Now."

"You can't watch."

Jasmine rolled her eyes. "It's nothing I haven't seen before."

"Get out, you voyeur." He pushed her, laughing, out of the walk-in closet, and shut the door.

Charlie yanked off his sweats and slid the familiar khakis up his legs. It was like putting his personality back on. He shrugged into the shirt, the starch crisp, and his urge to goad Jasmine dissipated. With the clothes came reason. What had he been thinking, acting like an asshole? If she didn't want him the way he was, he couldn't force her to change her mind. Yeah, she'd made some poor choices in boyfriends, but it wasn't his place to teach her any kind of lesson.

He tucked in the shirt and wound a black leather belt through the loops. Feeling oddly vulnerable, he stepped out of the closet.

Jasmine leapt up from the bed and clasped her hands. "Charlie! There you are."

He put his hands on his hips. "What's this all about?"

"Just stand there." She circled him slowly, twitching his khakis on his ass, running a hand up his bicep. She came to stand before him, close enough that he could smell her faint perfume, and touched his clean-shaven cheek with soft fingers.

"I thought I'd lost you," she said, her voice catching at the end.

Charlie studied her shining face for a moment, wondering what was going on in that brain. She seemed so pleased. Was it because she'd verified she could order him around, and he'd comply? Turn him back into—what was it she and Shae called him—Mr. Sensible?

Somebody who'd never tie her to his bed and have his way with her. Only, he, Charlie Sensible, had been the brain and libido behind that. The bastard he'd been emulating would never go to such lengths to please another person.

He hated himself for saying it, but he had to know. "What are you thinking?"

Jasmine slid her arms around his waist and sighed with contentment. "I need to tell you something. I've suspected for a while. I love you, Charlie. But I like this you better."

His heart stopped, started again. Painfully hard. "You mean that?"

Jasmine smiled. "I do."

"It's not just the sex?" Charlie held her away from him by the shoulders so she'd have to meet his eyes. "Do you love me, Jasmine?"

"I love you," she repeated, looking at him straight on. Then she blushed and dropped her gaze to a button on his shirt. "I hate all your girlfriends, and every guy I date isn't my type because nobody in the world can compare to you. I... I hope this doesn't pressure you. You don't have to say it back."

"Actually, there's something I've been wanting to ask you."

Charlie dropped to one knee in front of her.

Jasmine, he discovered, not only cried at weddings, but the mention of weddings, at least of weddings that involved her, and him, and three groomsmen and three bridesmaids and one maid of honor who was going to be very insistent about the name of their first child.

About the Author:

Ellie Marvel lives in the South and went to school for far too long. She likes her tea iced and sweetened and her pie homemade. She sometimes let men open doors for her—they need to feel useful, the darlings—and she definitely had relatives in the Revolutionary War. She used to teach English and work in the marketing department of a large software company, not at the same time. Now she concentrates on writing, child herding, cat petting, and stuffing her too-small house full of vintage clothing she never wears, antique dishes she never uses, books she often reads, and groceries that never, ever go to waste. You can read more about Ellie and her work at **www.elliemarvel.com**.

Intimate Rendezvous

❦

by Calista Fox

To My Reader:

Since the release of my first *Secrets* novella in July 2005, I have discovered how wonderful and devoted *Secrets* fans are. I hope you enjoy my erotic foray into the world of match-making, starting with this first story, *Intimate Rendezvous*.

To Alex and Cindy—Thank you so much for your continued support of my work.

To Judith—Your faith in my writing is greatly appreciated. I enjoyed working with you and will always remember the wonderful words of encouragement you imparted. Thank you.

Chapter One

Talk about looking for love in all the wrong places, Dean Hewitt thought as he passed through the tall metal doors of The Rage. It took mere seconds for his eyes to adjust to the hypnotic flashing of the multi-colored lights as he made a quick sweep of his immediate surroundings. It took a bit longer for his ears to adjust to the decibel level of the band's amplifiers.

Once acclimated, Dean stepped further inside the nightclub and let the sights, sounds and smells assault his senses, something he always did when entering a foreign environment. Dean had relied on his gut instincts and quick mental assessments when he'd been a part of the New York police force for five years. Those valuable traits had continued to serve him well over the past year, as he'd made the transition to private investigator.

The Rage was a trendy Upper West Side bar that showcased the hottest bands on the circuit, or at least that's what it stated on the flyer he'd been handed when he'd walked in. He dropped the flashy advertisement on a table as he stealthily moved through the throng of people. The décor of The Rage was an eclectic collision of art deco and industrial styles, with black furniture, glowing sapphire blue accents and stainless steel fixtures. Though Manhattan-chic, the club was a bit on the wild side. The rock and roll music blared loud enough to make his teeth rattle.

Had Cathy *really* said she'd been here last night?

Though the nightclub was neither seedy nor disreputable looking, Dean couldn't help but wonder if his little sister's quest for a husband had taken a turn for the worst. This didn't seem like her style. She generally preferred a more upscale dating scene.

Then again, playful Cat was always full of surprises. She was a fun-loving girl and a bit of a chameleon, capable of transforming herself from Upper East Side socialite to Midtown trend-setter with a change of wardrobe and hair color. This week, she sported fiery red curls and leather miniskirts. Last week, she'd been a sleek brunette in Versace.

She changed her mind like the wind changed direction, and she could even be considered a bit flighty. But Cat had the biggest heart of anyone he knew. She possessed a free spirit and a passionate nature.

The passion *du jour*, it would seem, was to have a good time with a heavy-metal head-banger at The Rage.

Mentally shaking his head at his younger sister's curious choice of Friday night haunts, Dean sidled up to the bar. He wedged himself between a Kid Rock look-a-like and a young gal who'd applied an excessive amount of makeup to her pretty face in what he suspected was an attempt to conceal her age.

His gut instinct told him she either hadn't been carded by the burly bouncer out front or she was carrying a fake ID. He wanted to check it himself, but that was no longer his gig. He'd left the police force to pursue his own path, preferring the more intriguing cases he took on as a P.I. versus the routine work he'd engaged in as a department detective.

The endless piles of paperwork had bored him senseless. He'd longed to be out on the street, tracking down bad guys, not saddled to his desk filling out reports. So he'd struck out on his own, much to his parents' dismay. They hadn't embraced his choice of career after he'd graduated from law school with honors, and they still weren't too keen on the path he continued to follow.

But Dean had finally found work that satisfied him. During his first year in business for himself, he'd helped the FBI to break up an international art theft ring, located two missing persons, and recovered nearly a million dollars in stolen jewelry for a popular Broadway actress.

Dean hadn't had much trouble finding exciting cases to occupy his time this past year. He had a good reputation, and it continued to grow with the successful conclusion of each case he was involved with.

He'd finally found his true calling.

Resting an arm on the stainless steel bar, Dean caught the bartender's attention. The lean-muscled, blonde-haired guy looked as though he'd walked right off the stage at a rock concert. He wore black leather pants and a black sleeveless T-shirt that said, quite simply, *Shut Up*.

"I'm looking for Slider," Dean announced over the bass-thumping music, thinking the nickname of the latest perp he was chasing sounded completely absurd. Maybe the kid was a *Top Gun* fanatic. He'd used the alias with Cat, who hadn't even known her designer wallet had been lifted until she'd gotten home.

The bartender made a quick assessment of him. Dean's relatively clean-cut visage helped the other man to deduce he wasn't a patron but a cop—or some derivative thereof. The bartender's gaze turned to minimal interest. "No one I know. My cousin might've heard of him, though." He inclined his head toward the entrance. "Upstairs."

Dean gave a curt word of thanks before backing away from the bar and fighting the crowd once again.

His first order of business was to locate this Slider fellow—he'd helped himself to all of Cat's high-limit credit cards. The second order of business was to take her in for a lobotomy.

He fought his way through the sea of bodies, back to the entrance of the nightclub and into the softly lit, small foyer of the contemporary building that housed The Rage. Earlier, he'd noticed the black wrought iron spiral staircase that led upstairs, but he'd dismissed it as leading to a second-floor office or apartment. Now he took note of the signage painted discreetly on the far wall, which read "Rendezvous" in elegant script. It was accompanied by a curvy arrow that pointed upward with a flourish.

Dean could only imagine what he'd find at the top of the stairs. A bar that was even rowdier than The Rage? Perhaps one teeming with illegal activity? His P.I. instincts kicked into high gear and a shot of adrenaline got his pulse racing just a bit quicker. He loved a good mystery.

As he ascended the winding staircase, Dean knew he should be a bit bent out of shape that he was spending his vacation working on a case. It was, after all, the first full week he'd taken off since opening Hewitt Investigations. He wondered now if the reason he'd opted not to leave town was for fear of missing out on any action.

He'd been resigned to catching up on some reading and maybe spending a couple of days doing target practice, but then Cat had called this morning to borrow money, something she never did. In addition to their own personal funds, they both had ample family money. So while Cat really didn't have an occupation to speak of, she never lacked for money. Their father kept her account well padded.

It had taken a stern interrogation for Dean to learn Cat had been robbed the night before. He'd loaned her three hundred bucks so she could enjoy lunch and shopping with her friends in SoHo, but the money came with a stipulation. He wanted a description of the thief and an exact accounting of what had transpired from the time she'd met Slider until the time she'd discovered her wallet had gone missing. In typical Cat fashion, she'd given feeble information at best. But it was still enough for Dean to work with.

As he reached the landing at the top of the stairs and traveled down a narrow hallway, the raucous din of The Rage slowly faded away, to be replaced by more enticing sounds. He pushed his way through a set of heavy metal doors, covered with a tufted layer of thick, dark red velvet.

He drew up short, taken aback.

It took a lot to throw Dean off kilter, but what he discovered at Rendezvous did just that.

Disappointment registered first.

So much for the tawdry, secret backroom he'd hoped to uncover. Instinct told him he'd be hard-pressed to find illegal activity in this place. Instead, Rendezvous was a stylish, upscale wine bar. Not at all the sort of establishment he'd expect to be housed in the same building with The Rage.

As he contemplated the scene, a sultry Jazz tune met his ears. Soft, enticing scents he couldn't even begin to identify, but which stirred his senses nonetheless, wafted under his nose. Slowly, relief washed over him as Dean realized *this* was the club Cat had visited last night, not the MTV video set downstairs.

Phew. He could scratch *Cat's lobotomy* off his To Do list.

The warm, inviting ambience of the lounge immediately drew him in. Though it was a large club, it felt cozy and intimate. The layout was a maze of nooks and private alcoves. Crescent-shaped sofas and high-backed, comfortable-looking chairs, all covered with crimson-colored, velvet upholstery, were strategically placed throughout the lounge. Coffee and end tables helped to create a living room-like setting. The diffused lighting added to the intimate atmosphere. The high-traffic areas were illuminated with a romantic, yellowish glow. The rest of the club was cast in a mixture of flickering candlelight and dancing shadows.

Dean's gaze swept the room. Toward the back of the lounge were tall bistro tables with barstools around them, along with two elegant, custom-made pool tables. Stretched along the back wall was a massive mahogany bar, as ornately designed as the pool tables. Dean headed in that direction, taking in the erotic scents and the seductive atmosphere along the way.

He passed attractive women draped provocatively over the wide arms of chairs and sofas, their soft, feminine laughter floating on the air, mingling with a curious sexual energy. In dark corners, couples swayed to the soulful wails of muted trumpets, their limbs and bodies entwined like lovers. Twosomes snuggled together on the plush sofas, deeply engrossed in private conversations, occasionally pausing to steal an intimate moment.

A sweep of hair from a cheek…

A kiss on the nape of a bare neck…

A hand creeping slowly up a shapely thigh…

The ambiance was clearly designed to inspire romance. Dean grew more intrigued by the second. He reached the bar and slid onto the only empty stool. Candles glowed in red-tinted glass votive holders, adding to the sensual environment. The air was just as sexually charged in this part of the club as it was in the lounge. His curiosity was already piqued…

And then he saw her.

A beautiful creature dressed all in red.

Suddenly, Dean felt sexually charged himself.

The woman was breathtaking. His gaze locked with hers as she made her slow, seductive approach. Her eyes were bright blue. Vibrant and sparkly, they practically glowed in the soft candlelight. Dean was instantly mesmerized.

A very peculiar sensation swept over him. He felt strange. Mellow, actually. As though he'd been drugged and was now moving about in a mind-tingling fog.

What was happening to him? He was usually disconnected from mind-altering scenes like this one. He was a man with razor-sharp focus and clarity. Not at all a sucker for a pretty face in an intimate nightclub, where the promise of sex lingered in the air, thicker than the scent of expensive perfume.

At the moment, however, Dean was deeply ensnarled. Definitely a sucker for *this* pretty face.

"Let me guess." Her soft, provocative tone mingled with the passion-induced haze that filled his brain. The erotic combination made his cock stand up and take notice.

Spellbound, Dean watched as the gorgeous bartender rested her elbows on top of the bar and leaned toward him. She tapped the pad of a long finger against her glossy lips in a contemplative way. Her nails were painted candy-apple red. Her lips were a deep crimson color. She was quite the siren.

"You look like a whiskey drinker. The good old-fashioned kind. Straight up. No frills." Her smile was soft, hypnotic.

"Good guess." Was that his voice he heard, so low and intimate?

"It's a gift." Her eyes twinkled playfully in the candlelight.

Thoroughly captivated, Dean knew he could sit on that barstool for hours, staring into her eyes, and never tire of looking at her.

Therefore, disappointment seized him when she pushed away from the bar and turned her back on him. She glided over to the mirrored wall behind her and reached for a bottle of Jack Daniels that sat on one of the glass shelves.

The disappointment he felt over her departure was quickly replaced by something else… a more primal reaction. Presented with her enticing backside, a slow rise of heat started in his groin. It spread slowly, deliciously throughout his body like some mood-altering drug flowing through his veins, creating a warm and molten feeling inside him. If he hadn't known better, he may have thought he actually had been drugged. But he hadn't taken a sip of anything yet.

No, the only way this feeling inside him could be blamed on illegal drugs was if some intoxicating scent was being piped in through the air vents.

Not an unlikely scenario… if he were James Bond.

But Dean wasn't the flashy Bond type. He'd never thought of himself as a ladies' man, and he preferred a subtle approach to everything he did. He wasn't into showboating.

Come to think of it, his current predicament seemed more reminiscent of Peter Gunn, hanging out at the stylish jazz club, Mother's. Gunn had always been Dean's favorite TV "eye," despite the fact that the show had aired in the late 50's, way before his time. He'd been hooked on reruns and, as a kid, had daydreamed about being the cool P.I. who swooped in to save the day.

Gunn had been a man's man. The kind of P.I. that could get the girl if he wanted to, but whose real focus was on solving mysteries. Hip and "in the know," Gunn was a man who got the job done in ultra-suave, low-key Bogie fashion.

Of course, Gunn probably hadn't entertained the kind of erotic thoughts about flame/jazz singer Edie Hart that Dean was currently conjuring up over the siren bartender before him.

Wicked thoughts. The kind that only seemed to dance into a man's head when he found the perfect female specimen with which to engage in the most carnal of activities.

She certainly had the body for those carnal activities, he noted as he took in every inch of her mouth-watering backside. The seductive bartender wore a red leather miniskirt that revealed a great ass and mile-long legs. Her red leather pumps were tall with spiky heels. Sexy as hell.

Visions of those toned, incredibly long legs wrapped around his waist drifted through his fuzzy brain. His groin tightened.

Reluctantly, Dean raised his eyes—just as the siren turned back to face him. She placed an intricately cut crystal glass in front of him and poured the amber liquid with precision. Dean's gaze swept over the gorgeous woman before him, settling on the red satin top that was knotted at her waist, leaving an inch or so of her toned midriff exposed. The first few buttons on her blouse were undone, revealing the hint of a red lace bra and the slightest glimpse of the full swell of her breasts.

Around her neck, she wore a red satin ribbon adorned with a small gold-and-ruby butterfly pendant, which rested peacefully in the hollow of her throat. The delicate ornament caught his attention for a moment, but then he was distracted by her movements. As she passed the drink to him, the candlelight caught the cut glass and, mixed with the hue of the liquor, created a prism of color. She noticed it too and smiled softly at the illusion. Warmth touched her eyes, making them glow in the soft light.

For a brief moment, Dean was rendered speechless. He was too entranced to even breathe.

But then a curious thought popped into his head. He pondered the situation, wondering what, exactly, he'd stumbled upon here. The sexy atmosphere, the intimate setting, the provocative bartender...

Were all these people really here for pool, cocktails and conversation? Or were there rooms to rent by the hour in the back?

Something was definitely going on. The attractive twenty- and thirty-some-things came to Rendezvous for some intriguing reason. Even the name of the club was suggestive.

He sat back in his barstool and sipped his drink. Of course, he knew what the allure was for the men. *Her.*

The siren before him moved away with grace and ease, a sleek tigress on the prowl. She turned her soft, sexy smile on a couple of guys at the end of the bar as she poured them fresh beers. Interestingly, she didn't engage in anything more than polite conversation. A quick visual sweep of the bar told him she had about a dozen beers on tap, but *she* clearly wasn't on the menu.

Dean felt oddly relieved by that observation.

When she made her way back to him, Dean's glass was empty. She'd been gone no more than five minutes. He'd needed that stiff drink to help take the edge off.

He set the glass back on the bar as she returned her attention to him. Her glossy blonde hair fell over her slender shoulders in big, loose curls. He imagined those thick strands felt as rich and luxurious as the red velvet on the sofas and chairs.

"Get you another one?" she asked. Mischief danced in her vibrant eyes.

Dean was certain he'd never met a woman who reeked of trouble the way this one did.

Better keep those hormones in check, pal.

No doubt a guy could easily fall prey to a woman who looked as sinful as this one did. She knew how to gaze seductively, suggestively into his eyes—doling out promises she'd never keep.

Dean found himself wishing they were the only ones in the club. Better yet, he'd like to get her alone, in his bedroom. Correction. In his *bed*. But he wasn't here to score with the sexy bartender, as appealing an idea as it was. He had business to attend to.

"I'll pass on the drink," he managed to say. He normally didn't trip over his own tongue when talking to a woman, but it seemed to have swelled to twice its normal size. He'd dated a bevy of beauties in his time, but she was more than beautiful. She was bewitching.

It would be a good idea, he decided, to stick to the issue at hand.

And, if he had half a brain left, he'd be able to recall exactly what that was.

Oh, yes. Cat, her stolen credit cards and cash, and the creep who'd availed her of them.

Focus, pal.

"I'm looking for someone." Again, that low, intimate voice sounded so foreign to him. They were speaking in tones that belonged in the bedroom, not a nightclub.

Trouble smiled wantonly at him, and he was momentarily mesmerized by her lush, full lips. *Her extremely kissable lips.*

"You've come to the right place if you're looking for that special someone." His gaze followed hers to the lounge. "Most of the patrons are members of my dating service. The pretty blonde over there in the corner," she said as she inclined her head toward the entrance, "will be more than happy to give you information about our services."

Dean had noticed the attractive woman at the sturdy wooden desk when he'd walked in. She was working diligently on her laptop. From time to time, she'd stop to converse with whoever slid into the seat across the desk from her.

No wonder there was so much sexual energy swirling about. They were all looking for love.

Like Cat.

Thinking of his sister, Dean turned his attention back to Trouble. "That's not quite what I meant."

Understanding registered in her eyes, but she still looked perfectly at ease. "You're a cop."

"Private investigator. Dean Hewitt's the name. Wanna see my ID?"

Her playful smile made his insides clench. "Clever. I'm usually the one carding."

Every fiber of his being wanted to follow this flirtation down its natural course, but he had business to take care of. He wanted to nail the guy who'd stolen his sister's wallet.

Why did he have to keep reminding himself of that?

"I'm looking for a guy named Slider. Smooth-talking, good-looking thief. Know him?"

She paused a moment before saying, "No." Her hesitation was just long enough to convince Dean that she was lying.

No problem. He could play that game.

He'd let her off the hook, for now. He reached for the wallet in the inside pocket of his black leather jacket, but she waved him off.

"It's on the house, Detective Dean." She gave him a contemplative look, then added, "Just don't share that little tidbit with your counterparts at the precinct. I don't want them loitering about, putting a damper on the party."

"You own this place?"

"Yes. I'm Cassandra Kensington."

He eased off his barstool and cast an appreciative look at Trouble. "Nice to meet you, Cassandra. Thanks for the drink."

He turned and walked out of her joint, knowing this wouldn't be the last he'd see of her.

Chapter Two

Cassandra let out a long, slow breath. Detective Dean was quite the tall, cool drink of water.

She grinned as she went about her business. It was nearing eleven, her standard closing time, and things were winding down with the "singletons," as she liked to call them. Some had hooked up for inevitable one-night stands. Some had left with high hopes of making a more permanent love connection. Some had simply collected phone numbers, wanting only to dip their toes into the dating pool rather than dive in head first.

Rendezvous wasn't the typical New York City meat market. It was classy and sophisticated. The singles who wanted to hook up here did it in a productive way by signing up for Cassandra's dating service. Ever optimistic about their chance for romance, they provided personal information about themselves and what they were seeking in a partner. A clever computer program matched them up.

Cassandra had hired a dating specialist to set up the whole process, as well as to conduct interviews and manage the dating service. With her patent-pending, state-of-the-art software, McCarthy Portman could match up the single men and women with potential dates that fulfilled their requirements and desires in all areas—physical appearance, income level, personal and professional interests, religions beliefs, *et cetera*.

Cassandra took pride in the fact that Rendezvous was a safe place for women to come alone. It was the perfect non-threatening, non-intimidating, elegant setting in which to meet and mingle with other singles. There were no outbreaks of violence in her establishment, no inappropriate behavior that wasn't immediately remedied or rectified.

It was Cassandra's own little utopia.

Despite the fact that the professional dating service was a thriving business, especially when conducted in such a trendy, sociable environment, Cassandra didn't quite believe in the concept of computerized compatibility. She was more the spontaneous combustion type. She wanted to experience the sparks and the electrifying jolts produced by two people sexually charged by the other. She didn't like to muck up chemistry with analyses of stock portfolios, levels of advanced degrees received, or personal incomes reported on the previous year's W-2s.

Good old-fashioned butterflies in the pit of her stomach and the flutter of her heart would alert her that she'd found Mr. Right.

If Mr. Right truly did exist.

It was hard to say. Cassandra had been in the business of love long enough to know it was a hit or miss game no matter how you played it. Sometimes, she saw the singletons hook up with the potential to live happily ever after—she and McCarthy had even been invited to several weddings. But more often than not, she saw hopeful dreams dashed when one party was more committed than the other, or some mistruths caught up to the relationship.

She'd seen some pretty devastating breakups. Enough to make her wary of that little thing called love.

Not that she didn't believe in it. She did. Wholeheartedly. But her idea of a great love involved not only truth and honesty, but raw, all-consuming passion. Something she had yet to experience in her twenty-six years.

As she went through her closing ritual of counting cash drawers and completing paperwork, her staff attended to their respective chores. One of the best things about Rendezvous, Cassandra thought, was that something different and intriguing happened every night. People fell in love or, at the very least, found someone to fill the void they felt, even if only for the night.

What had happened this particular evening intrigued Cassandra on a personal level. The visit from Detective Dean Hewitt had sparked her interest. She'd felt a curious flutter deep inside her. It fascinated her.

She'd been captivated by the sexy stranger who'd occupied one of her barstools for way too brief a period of time. And, as she completed the most tedious of her closing tasks—the paperwork—her thoughts were easily fixated on him.

Detective Dean. She nearly sighed with longing as his name flitted through her mind.

To say he was handsome didn't quite do him justice. He looked like a private investigator, she decided. Tall, dark and dangerous. Or, in her limited experience, what she *imagined* a clever P.I. would look like.

The man had an exceptional build. He'd worn a tight black T-shirt that accentuated the swell of his pectoral muscles and, had he not been wearing the black leather jacket, Cassandra was certain she would have discovered rock-hard biceps.

But the hunky build didn't stop there. His black-as-night jeans had conformed perfectly to him, encasing long, powerful legs. She'd gotten a great look at his butt, too, as he'd walked away, and it had confirmed what she'd suspected—Detective Dean had a great body all the way around.

His hair was as dark as his jeans and it was thick and wavy. So unlike the short, spiky 'dos she'd seen lately. Instead, it was the kind of hair a girl could tangle her fingers in.

The thought was an incredibly appealing one, and it elicited a soft sigh of longing from her.

Detective Dean had a handsome face, too, complete with a firm, square jaw line, well-sculpted cheekbones and mesmerizing eyes. They were sort of a silvery color. Not gray, that was too drab a word to describe them. No, silver was more fitting. And she imagined his gaze deepened to a smoldering smoky color when he was angry or aroused. She'd bet it was a dynamic transformation.

He seemed like the type who'd have a fiery temper, probably not easily sparked, but if the determined set of his jaw were any indication, she guessed he could be a formidable opponent when pushed to the breaking point.

And no doubt an incredibly passionate and imaginative lover.

In her line of work, the ability to quickly evaluate a man's sexual potency was an asset, and she was an expert at it. She'd lay odds that Detective Dean knew how to please a woman.

The thought sent an erotic thrill racing through her. She pulled in a ragged breath as she turned away from the bar to straighten the liquor bottles on the glass shelves.

She figured he was about thirty-two or thirty-three... and single. There'd been no ring on his finger and no tan line to suggest that he usually wore a ring.

He was some piece of work, that sexy P.I.

And she'd lied to him.

The thought sat like a rock in her gut. It had been the wrong thing to do, but damn it, she didn't want a P.I. or the police snooping around her club. She had a legitimate business, paid her taxes and was a law-abiding citizen. And, with the exception of Slider, she believed that went for her employees and patrons as well.

She didn't want the police to taint her perfect place or make her clients uncomfortable. She didn't want her utopia spoiled.

But that was wishful thinking. All good things got tainted in the end. She was experienced enough to know that being a good person did not preclude you from having bad things happen to you.

The fact that Dean Hewitt was hot on the trail of a thief, and that thief had darkened her doorstep, frustrated her. But she was even more annoyed by the fact that she'd lied to Hewitt. It wasn't her style.

Of course, there was more to the story than not wanting her special haven spoiled by an investigation. She didn't want to admit that she'd been suckered. She'd made a mistake hiring Slider a few weeks ago, but the little thief had disappeared two days later and—she'd thought—that had been that.

Apparently not.

"Damn it," she muttered out loud. It was a bad predicament all the way around.

"Kicking yourself in that pretty little behind for lying to me, aren't you?"

A spark of amusement warmed Cassandra's insides. Detective Dean Hewitt was quicker than she'd given him credit for. She should have known he'd turn out to be just as clever as he was hot.

She lifted her head and gazed at him in the mirror. Their eyes met and held. He was cool and nonchalant on the outside, but Cassandra could see he was simmering below the surface, ready to boil over at any point. Her little lie had bothered him.

But there was something else in those beautiful silver eyes of his. A smoldering expression that told her he may have come back to get some answers from her, but information wasn't all he was looking for.

Heat pooled between her legs and she felt that peculiar fluttering in her stomach that both intrigued and excited her. She suppressed a sigh of desire. She'd dispense with the business first, then find out exactly what else Detective Dean had on his mind.

She slowly turned and faced him, one hand planted on her leather-clad hip. "We're closed."

"Yeah, I know. I was waiting downstairs for the place to clear out."

"Wanted me alone?" She didn't bother to keep the flirtatious tone from her voice. And she suspected a hint of invitation was there in her eyes, too. How could it not be? He was one amazing-looking man, and she was responding to him like one of her love-starved singletons.

Well, she wasn't love-starved. But sex-starved?

Possibly...

He eyed her coolly as he divested himself of the black leather jacket he wore and dropped it on the bar. She'd been right about his biceps. They bulged under the hem of his tight shirt.

"I figured you knew more than you were letting on," he said. "But I understand why you wouldn't want to discuss a thief in the midst—at least, not in front of your 'discriminating clientele.'"

Oh, Josh. What did you tell the sexy P.I.?

He'd obviously had an informative visit with her cousin.

"I don't want any trouble." She crossed her arms over her chest in a defiant move.

The detective's look softened. "I know." He slid onto a barstool, clasped his large hands together and rested them on the bar in front of his impossibly wide chest. "I'm not here to cause any."

To distract herself from those well-defined muscles that she longed to touch—was his chest covered with soft, silky, dark-as-night hair, or was it gloriously smooth?—she reached for two glasses and set them on the bar. She took down the bottle of Jack Daniels from the shelf and then retrieved a bottle of vodka from the cooler. She made two drinks, handed him a cocktail and then sipped hers.

"If the police start snooping around, asking questions, it will upset my clients.

The women may feel their safety is threatened."

He nodded in apparent understanding. "From what I've learned tonight, this isn't the kind of place where drunken brawls break out or women get harassed. It's very respectable, despite the locale."

"The locale is fine," she said, albeit a bit defensively. "We're on the Upper West Side. Close to the park. It happens to be a high-rent area." Or *higher-rent*, as one may refer to it, considering all of Manhattan was now high-rent. Even the seedy areas.

But she knew to what he referred—The Rage. The bar downstairs didn't attract a bad element, just a wilder clientele than her own bar. Her cousin was a bit of party animal and liked rock-n-roll. "Don't be so quick to judge The Rage. That establishment has launched a number of successful music careers, and Josh makes the best martinis this side of the Park."

The detective frowned. "There was a minor at the bar. And the bouncer broke up a fight while I was down there. That makes it questionable in my book."

She sighed. Damn, he was sexy. But a tad annoying, especially with that stubbornly set jaw and those piercing silver eyes. He probably thought he was always right. Always knew what was best. Arrogant and obstinate. Totally not her type.

But damn it, he sure was gorgeous... And she'd bet a full years' rent those big, strong hands would feel like heaven on her body.

Cassandra forced herself to focus on the conversation, despite the sudden throbbing between her legs. "Josh is my cousin. And I assure you, he's quite respectable. So is his club. Now, how can I make you go away and conduct your investigation elsewhere?" Not that she wanted *him* to go away per se, but she certainly didn't want to get pulled into his investigation.

He cut right to the chase. "Look, I promise to be discreet and not bring in the cops—at this point. But only *if* you promise to tell me everything you know about Slider."

Cassandra weighed her options for a moment. Something about the hard glint in his steely gaze convinced her she shouldn't press her luck with Detective Dean Hewitt. With a sigh of resignation, she said, "There's really not much to tell."

She put him on hold for a few minutes while McCarthy and the other staff members said their goodnights. Cassandra locked the door behind them, then went back to the bar, returning her attention to the detective.

"Do you have a car?"

He nodded. "Parked up the street."

"Good. I'll tell you what I know about Slider, then you can give me a ride home so I don't have to wait for Josh."

"Sounds fair."

She hated to have this conversation, hated to admit she'd unwittingly let the little thief get the best of her. But what choice did she have?

With great reluctance, she said, "Slider came in a couple of weeks ago. We were slammed and a server and a bartender short. I was juggling the bar and the lounge. Even McCarthy was working the floor. We were having a hell of a time keeping up. We were at max capacity, maybe a little over." She eyed him a moment, wondering if he'd comment about that. Since he wasn't the fire marshal, he apparently didn't care about the risks of overcrowding the place.

She rested her elbows on the bar, leaned toward him. It occurred to her that this position gave him a phenomenal view down her shirt, but she suspected that wouldn't divert his attention from his investigation. Damn it.

She took a sip from her drink, then slowly lifted her eyes, just to see if he was looking. When his silver gaze caught hers, she felt a physical jolt pierce straight to the core of her being. His look was so hot it nearly seared her. She felt the muscles deep inside her clench and quiver violently.

Maybe he was a little more dangerous to her senses than she'd originally assessed. Her pulse quickened.

"You were saying, about Slider?"

Cassandra drew in a long, labored breath. The sexy P.I.'s look was a real scorcher. All sexual awareness mixed with subtle warning. What was he trying to tell her? That flirting with him was dangerous business?

And did he really believe she could think straight with him looking at her like that?

She tried to focus. Slider was becoming an even greater nuisance than she'd imagined. But if she wrapped up this discussion, then maybe they could get down to other business.

The naughty thought thrilled her. She wondered if Detective Dean was the adventurous type, then quickly decided he was. Private investigator... incredibly masculine, virile and confident, borderline cocky even. He radiated way too much heat and sexuality to *not* be a man who responded to chemistry—something they had in spades. Something she'd never experienced to this degree in her young life.

For a woman who owned a dating service, she was pathetically behind in sexual escapades.

"So it was a couple of weeks ago and I was in way over my head with drink orders," she recapped. "Suddenly, this attractive blonde-haired guy appeared at the bar, all friendly smile and cool temperament. He said he'd like to give me a hand and, well, I was too desperate to turn him down. He was a hard worker and a great bartender, so I asked him to come back the next night, just in case we had a repeat performance. Which we did. He more than pulled his weight."

"Sounds on the up and up."

"It was," she insisted.

"And that's it?"

"Yep." She ignored the sting of guilt that zipped through her at not telling the whole truth and nothing but... She'd left out a few pertinent details about her encounter with Slider. She categorized it as a minor error of omission, which eased her conscience a bit.

"Hmm," the detective mused, letting her know he wasn't quite sold on her story.

But the heated look he gave her told her he was as anxious to conclude this business as she was. Obviously, he was just as interested in exploring the intense sexual chemistry that sparked so easily between them. She'd give anything to know what he was thinking. Were his thoughts bordering on wicked, as hers were?

Unable to focus on Slider a moment longer, and much too curious to know if the gorgeous detective was feeling the sexual pull as strongly as she was, Cassandra rounded the bar, joining Dean on the other side. She stood next to him, her hip grazing his thigh. She dropped a hand on his powerful forearm and gave him a seductive look. "So, we're done with our little P.I. chat, right?"

Chapter Three

Dean had never felt such a strong physical pull. His gaze was fixed on her lips, and as badly as she seemed to want him to kiss her, he just as badly wanted to do so much more than that.

Her blouse pulled tight against her full breasts as she drew in a deep breath. Dean wondered how her bare skin would feel against his. Wondered if her nipples were tight behind the lacy cups of her sexy bra. Wondered how the puckered points would feel between his fingers, against his tongue, in his mouth.

His lips twitched, wanting to touch and taste her skin. It took all his willpower to keep his hands off of her. He longed to explore every inch of her luscious body.

When her long, slender fingers moved from his arm to his thigh, Dean knew he was a goner. He shifted his position. Clasping her narrow waist in his hands, he pulled her into the open V of his parted legs. Her dark eyes locked with his. He felt heat and desire flood his loins.

He wanted this woman more than anything else. She sparked his passion, stirred his soul. It was a strange and wonderful phenomenon. One he didn't analyze too carefully. He just knew he had to have her. Soon.

"There's something you ought to know about me," she said on a breathless whisper, as though she felt the pull as strongly as he did. "I may own a dating service, but I don't believe in computerized compatibility."

"What do you believe in?"

"This."

"Define '*this.*'"

She leaned into him, until their upper bodies just barely touched. Dean's pulse kicked up a notch and his erection strained against the fly of his jeans. His hands greedily moved from her waist to her hips and then around to her perfectly rounded ass. His mouth finally gave into its need to taste her.

"The butterflies," she whispered on a sigh as his lips explored the length and texture and taste of her long, graceful neck. Her head fell back, causing her hair to spill over his hands in soft silky waves as they moved to gently cup her heart-shaped face. His lips touched hers, softly at first, then with more pressure until his mouth fully covered hers in a possessive and demanding kiss.

He wanted all of her. And he wanted her *now*.

Need and desire gripped his body. She tasted like a mixture of her vodka and his whiskey, and apricots. The thought barely made it through the passion-induced haze that filled his head. *She tasted vaguely of apricots.*

His tongue tangled with hers for a moment, and a wicked thrill shot through him at her skillful dueling technique. She was neither too aggressive nor too passive. She seemed to want to touch and taste as much as he did, and was an active participant in the kiss, matching his passion and need. He felt as though his head and his cock were about to explode from the overpowering sensations that rocketed through him.

It was almost too much.

He broke the kiss, his mind reeling. His erection pulsed and throbbed in wicked beats that matched his pounding heart.

"That's what I'm talking about." Her voice was soft and sensual.

Dean's brain was scrambled. "What?"

She had a dreamy look on her beautiful face and her ultra-blue eyes glowed with fire and passion.

"The butterflies," she reminded him in a breathy voice. She cocked her head to one side, contemplated him with a mixture of amusement and immense satisfaction. "People just don't give fate, kismet, and good old-fashion chemistry a chance anymore. These days, dating and choosing a sex partner are all contingent on income levels, the type of car one drives, the designer labels hanging in the closet." She sighed contemplatively. "It's all about meeting the requirements on some pre-determined checklist. People so rarely toss their checklists aside and hook up on the simple basis of primal heat. Physical, subconscious awareness… and good-ole sexual stimulation."

All the things he was currently experiencing. They were obviously onto something good.

"The butterflies," she continued, "take flight when that awareness sets in. When that spark ignites. Your heart flutters, your breath catches. Do you know what I'm talking about, Dean?"

Oh, hell yes.

He tried to speak but his mouth had gone dry. Damn, she was beautiful. And sexy. If she felt a tenth of what he was currently feeling, they were proving good old-fashioned sexual chemistry was still a hell of a lot more reliable and fascinating than anything a dating service could drum up.

The thought struck him as odd.

"Why would someone who believes in fate and kismet and sexual chemistry own a dating service?"

She smiled at him, waved a hand absently in the air. "It's just a business. It's fun. And not everyone believes what I do, so why should I spoil their good time?"

Makes sense.

"You didn't answer my question," she said in a soft, coaxing voice. "About the butterflies."

He grinned at her. She was something else. "You really need me to talk about my heart fluttering and butterflies taking flight? Or can I just prove it's all happening inside me?"

Her smile grew mischievous. The vibrant blue pools glowed warmly, seductively. "What'd you have in mind?"

He wanted her, there was no denying that. But not on the edge of a pool table or propped on a barstool. He wanted her someplace comfortable, private, intimate. Someplace where they could be naked together... where he could see and touch and taste every inch of her.

He stood and wrapped his arms around her waist, holding her close. Their bodies melded together and an acute awareness arced between them as they swayed ever so slightly to the sexy music that drifted through the air.

He nuzzled her neck, his lips grazing her skin. "Who's playing?" he asked in a quiet voice.

"Gato Barbieri. Great saxophonist."

"Mm, good mood music," he whispered.

"Yes it is. Are you in the mood, Dean?"

"You already know the answer to that," he said as his erection pressed against the heart of her. She sighed into his ear. It was more erotic than anything Gato could belt out.

Her warm breath caressed his skin. So much of her body was melded to him that it created a dizzying effect. He was swimming in a sea of erotic thoughts, wanting more than anything to feel her bare skin against his, wanting to push his hard erection deep inside her.

In the distance, he heard a clock chime twelve times. It was officially the end of his first day of vacation. And, despite the fact that he'd spent most of it trying to nail a petty thief, it sure turned out to be more exciting than he'd anticipated.

"What's that?" he inquired.

"Midnight."

He smirked. "I got that part. Where's the chime coming from?"

She smiled against his neck. He felt her soft, full lips turn upward. "Across the street. The guy who owns the bookstore has a tower clock on top of his building. It only chimes at midnight, when his store closes."

"Interesting."

"He's very eccentric, but he has the most amazing book collection."

"You like books?" His hand eased over her backside, gently squeezed a cheek.

"You could say I'm a bit of a bookworm. You read books?"

"Only ones with pictures in them."

She laughed. The sound was so sweet, so genuine, it made him want to tell her every joke he knew just to keep her laughing.

"Dean?"

"Hmm?" Hearing her whisper his name was almost the death of him.

"Take me home."

Chapter Four

He was glad he didn't have to ask, "Your place or mine?" Asking that would have seemed too trite. Instead, he let her slip out of his arms and wrap up the last of her closing chores, which included turning off the sexy tunes. She dimmed the lights on this side of the club, then collected her purse from under the bar. They walked rather quickly to the door. She flipped off the rest of the main lights, leaving a few to softly illuminate the entire place for security purposes. She set the alarm and locked the double doors behind them.

Halfway down the stairs, she let out a soft curse as she stamped a spiked heel on the step.

"What?" Dean asked.

"Forgot my coat."

He chuckled as he draped his leather jacket over her shoulders. "We're not going back. That's a ten-minute ritual on the locks and alarm system alone."

"Eager beaver."

They made their way to the foyer of the building and she paused a moment to give the burly bouncer of The Rage a quick, chaste peck on the cheek. Dean heard her whisper that she had a safe ride home and asked the bouncer to relay the message to Josh. The beefy man eyed Dean up and down, apparently found him acceptable, and gave a quick nod of his bald head.

Cassandra turned to the entryway and shoved open one of the heavy metal and glass doors. The fact that she didn't expect Dean to open the door for her both intrigued and irritated him. She was obviously very independent. Accustomed to doing things for herself. Not comfortable relying on anyone else.

The characteristic was something he'd have to give some consideration to. He'd been raised on the premise of cultivating and executing gentlemanly qualities. A man opened a door for a woman before she passed through, held a chair out for her before she sat. Protected her chivalrously.

Hmm. Where had that latter thought come from? He wasn't looking to play knight-in-shining-armor. He was looking to get laid. Right?

When they reached Dean's car, she whistled under her breath at his 350Z. "Nice ride. Does it come in red?"

He laughed. "You would ask that." His version was all black. He opened the door and she slid gracefully into the leather bucket seat. She looked at him expectantly, and it occurred to Dean that she was a walking contradiction he doubted he would ever figure out. She was waiting for him to close the door. She would probably wait patiently for him to open it, too, when they reached their destination. It was a little confusing—hard to tell when being a gentleman conflicted with her fierce female independence.

But maybe she wasn't quite so fiercely independent. Just self-sufficient. A trait he admired.

As he circled around to the driver's side of the car and eased into the seat, he wondered vaguely why he was so fixated on her personal traits. It wasn't as though he was embarking on a major relationship. They were having sex. Plain and simple. It was lust that drove them both. They were acting on a sexual impulse. Nothing more.

He settled into his seat, a tight squeeze considering his six-foot-two-inch stature. He just couldn't imagine driving a sedan. He glanced over at Cassandra. "Where to?"

She directed him to a large, three-story brownstone several blocks away. He managed to find a parking spot relatively close. He shut the engine off and climbed out of the car. The siren next to him didn't reach for the handle on the car door, and he was oddly relieved. Maybe a little chivalry wouldn't bother her.

He opened her door, and she smiled seductively at him as she passed by. He followed her into the building, up the curving staircase to the top floor, then to a corner apartment. She unlocked the many deadbolts and let them in.

When she flipped the switch on the wall, he was both intrigued and amused by what he saw. The foyer opened into a large great room with tall windows on either side of an enormous fireplace. The windows were, not surprisingly, flanked by dark red velvet drapes.

A comfortable-looking, pristine white sectional filled the area in front of the fireplace. A vast array of pillows with gold and crimson patterns were piled high on the sofa. More pillows were scattered on either side of the fireplace and in front of it.

A large crystal chandelier cast a soft, yellowish glow over the room. Tables with fresh floral arrangements were scattered about. The only rug that covered the polished hardwood floor was under the sectional. Its ornate pattern was comprised of splashes of vermillion and gold.

Dean realized he'd stumbled upon yet another intimate living room this evening.

The corners of the walls that were closest to the front door housed tall, built-in bookshelves that were jam-packed with hardback books. On the floor in front of the shelving units were tall, disorderly stacks of books that looked as though they'd topple over at any moment.

"Sorry about the mess," she said as she crossed to the sectional. She carefully draped his leather jacket over the back of it.

"'Bit of bookworm' was an understatement."

She grinned. It was easy, natural. Sexy as hell. She stepped up to the open kitchen area and surveyed her fridge. "Beer okay with you?"

"Sure."

She pulled out two bottles of microbrew and opened them. She returned to the great room just as he was settling himself in the myriad of plump pillows on the sofa.

She settled in next to him. They clinked the longnecks of their bottles together and she giggled. It was a girlish sound, yet sexy at the same time.

He took a long pull from the bottle, desperately needing something to take the edge off. He was wound way too tight, consumed by thoughts of making love to Cassandra. One part of him wanted to rip her clothes off and have his way with her. The other part wanted to touch her slowly, explore her body intimately and eventually find his way inside her.

He wondered which side of him would win in the end.

She climbed out of the mass of pillows and walked to the tall fireplace. She flipped a switch and a fire suddenly roared to life.

Gas fireplace, he mused. Very modern. Very who-needs-a-man-to-light-my-fire?

Shit.

He fought his way out of the sea of pillows, set his beer on the large, sturdy coffee table. His brain was thinking long-term. His body was thinking short-term. The war waging inside him was maddening.

The object of his immediate desire was standing in front of the fire and that was exactly where he'd decided to have her. In front of that blazing fire, where the glow would illuminate her skin and the heat would keep her warm enough that no blanket would be necessary. She'd be gloriously naked, right there in front of him.

It was the perfect setting for their first encounter.

She kicked some of the pillows on the floor, seemingly arranging them for exactly what he had in mind...as though she knew what he'd been thinking.

"A little music would be nice, don't you think?"

The best Dean could do at the moment was nod. His eyes never left her incredible body as she strolled over to the kitchen counter and turned on an ancient boom box. A sultry jazz tune filled the apartment.

"I'm not very high-tech at home. No TV, no fancy stereo."

She returned to the spacious area in front of the fire and sank into the pillows. Dean eased down beside her.

"I get enough entertainment at the club." She sighed sweetly and smiled warmly at him. "When I'm here, I like quiet music, soft lights. And I've got a great view of Central Park, if you wanna see it."

"Maybe later," he said, his voice husky. His gaze continually drifted to her full, deep red lips. She was one hell of a kisser. Passionate. Sensual. She gave selflessly, took selfishly. It was an erotic contradiction.

"What do you do when you're not chasing bad guys, Detective Dean?" Her fingers glided over his forearm, up to his bicep.

"I sleep," he said, without really thinking about his answer. It was an honest one, though not nearly as sexy as hers.

A fingernail slid beneath the tight band of his sleeve, teasing his skin. His muscles flexed involuntarily under her touch. Her lips quivered slightly and her breath caught, as though the knowledge of what she did to him aroused her deeply.

Her voice was faint, breathless when she spoke. "You can do better than that." She shifted slightly on the rug, and settled herself more comfortably amidst the array of pillows.

Disappointment set in when she broke the contact with his arm. But then she tucked her legs underneath her, leaned close to him, and rested a hand on his leg. She stared up at him, her eyes smoldering beneath heavy lids.

"There has to be something that sparks your interest outside of work."

"Yeah," he said in a low, thick tone. "At the moment, it happens to be you."

"Mm, you're a real charmer, Detective Dean." She moved closer to him, leaning in for another mind-blowing kiss. Her lips brushed over his, ever so slightly. A whisper of a kiss.

Her eyelids fluttered closed and she sighed blissfully. "You smell nice. Crisp, clean. Like soap and..." She inhaled deeply. "Spice. Very masculine."

He was feeling pretty damned masculine.

Oddly, though, as much as he wanted to haul her up against him and kiss her senseless, this slow, subtle approach of hers was infinitely more arousing. He liked the way she touched him, with such intimacy and confidence. It stirred something inside him. More so than just a physical, sexual reaction.

Her hand moved over his thigh, up his tight abdominals to his chest. She lightly ran her fingers over one of his pectoral muscles, then sighed again. Her touch drove him wild.

"You lift weights. You're built quite nicely."

"So are you." Christ, she was doing crazy things to his head, and to his body. "Something tells me I ain't seen nothing yet, though."

Without breaking eye contact with him, Cassandra reached for the button on her red satin blouse and slipped the small disk through its hole. Dean's breath caught as his eyes drank in the erotic vision before him. Three more buttons followed, then she untied the knot at her waist. She shifted her position again, turning around so her back was to him.

Dean's fingers glided over the soft material on her shoulders before he gently eased the blouse down her arms. When he'd carefully discarded the garment,

Cassandra lifted the mass of blonde curls off her shoulders and back.

Holding the tresses in her hands, she said, "Mind unhooking my bra? The clasp is in the front."

Dean's jaw worked rigorously as he contemplated what this task would entail. As much as he wanted to touch her, he wondered if he could do it without completely ravaging her. He'd never wanted a woman as much as he wanted this one, and the desire building inside of him was all-consuming.

His hands rested in the dip of her narrow waist. As they moved upward, his fingers grazed her softly defined stomach. Over her rib cage and up to her lace-covered breasts. He was already having heart palpitations. He cupped the full mounds in his hands, gave them a gentle squeeze that elicited a soft moan from Cassandra. She leaned back against him, still holding her long hair off her shoulders. Dean's lips grazed her bare neck as his thumbs whisked over her tight nipples. He peeled the lacy cups back and tucked them under her breasts. His palms covered her plump flesh and he caressed her softly, with great restraint, as his mouth continued to tease and taste her warm skin.

He could feel her breathing quicken as her chest rose and fell in rapid beats. His cock strained against the fly of his jeans, desperate for attention, demanding release.

Soon.

His fingers worked the clasp on her bra. She dropped her hands and long, silky curls spilled over them both. He removed her bra and then swept all of her hair over one slender shoulder so he could continue to touch her bare skin.

A rush of excitement washed over him. Her peaches-and-cream skin glowed in the firelight. Her flesh was smooth and silky to the touch. His fingers grazed slowly up her spine, and he grinned with satisfaction when she trembled under his touch. She had a beautiful back, with softly defined muscles that proved she took good care of her body while still retaining her femininity.

Her neck was too tempting to resist. He couldn't stop himself from leaning forward and kissing her nape. His lips brushed over the skin. He nipped softly at the side of her neck and she gasped. As his lips once again swept over her skin, she moaned softly, leaned back against him.

His chest was pressed against her back. His hands returned to her breasts. He groaned as his fingers and thumbs skimmed over her hard nipples, gently pinching, teasing. He longed to taste her, to run his tongue over her smooth flesh and pull the taut nipples into his mouth.

He longed to be inside her, buried deep, while he discovered all the pleasurable gifts she had to offer. And not just once. He had a feeling one time with Cassandra Kensington would in no way fulfill this need he suddenly felt.

No, once would not be enough with this woman. He would want her over and over and over again, he was certain of that.

It was a heady sensation, knowing that he wanted more than just one night of mind-blowing sex. It was an enchanting, alluring feeling, actually. One he couldn't recall ever experiencing. And the fact that she seemed to be as entranced by the passion spiraling between them only served to heighten his arousal.

He burrowed his face in her hair, inhaling the fresh scent. His own reaction was explosive, and it took all the inner strength he possessed to keep his passion in check. He wanted to quickly strip away all of their clothes and plunge deep inside her.

Conversely, he wanted to spend endless hours touching and caressing her. He wanted to slowly remove what was left of her clothing and taste every inch of newly exposed skin. He wanted to take them both to dizzying heights then pull them back down. Then slowly push them up again, higher and higher, until they reached the point of no return with such fierce desire the explosive passion would consume them both.

Something told him he didn't have the patience for the latter—or the steely resolve to take it slowly with her. Besides, building the passion wasn't necessary. It was already there, tempting them both.

He turned her slightly so that his mouth could cover hers. Her lips were incredibly soft. His tongue slowly slid past her parted teeth and met hers. And then she was turning fully in his arms and pressing her bare breasts against his chest.

The thought of his T-shirt creating a barrier between them drove him crazy. He needed to feel her bare skin on his. Feel her heat. Feel her velvety-soft flesh. He tugged at the hem of his shirt, quickly yanking it out of his jeans. He broke the kiss just long enough to haul the shirt over his head. Tossing the garment aside, his mouth crushed over hers again.

Suddenly, her hands seemed to be everywhere, on his arms, his chest, his back. She moaned, low and needy, deep in her throat. The sound made him wild with want.

He fell back onto the pile of plush pillows and pulled her down with him. She landed on top of him, her lower body resting perfectly between his parted legs. His hands skimmed over her bare back, down to her leather-clad bottom. He cupped both cheeks and pressed her into him. His erection was strong and throbbing with need. But he found the restraint to keep his passion in check... for the moment.

Cassandra was not so self-disciplined. A small hand slipped between them and her long, lean fingers brushed the hard shaft of his penis as it strained against the button fly of his jeans. Patience wasn't even something she was striving for at the moment. That whole spontaneous combustion theory of hers was proving to be a worthy one. Lust was something she embraced, passion was one of her favorite emotions.

But in the far recesses of her mind, a curious thought formed. Yes, her attraction to Dean Hewitt was incredibly strong. But there was something else building inside her. A powerful emotion she couldn't quite identify. She quickly chalked it up to infatuation. After all, the detective was not only sexy, but also very clever and charming. It was no wonder she was losing all control with the man. She only wished he felt the same way. Instead, he seemed perfectly in command of his passion, perfectly capable of controlling his arousal.

She'd definitely have to do something about that.

Her fingers grazed his fly and then played absently with the top button, purposely not working it out of its hole, but giving the distinct impression that was exactly what she inevitably planned to do.

"Dean," she sighed seductively in his ear. Her lips grazed the outer shell, her tongue teasing the sensitive spot before she gently caught his lobe between her teeth. She held it for a breath before releasing it. Her breasts were pressed firmly against his chest, and the silky hair that covered his well-defined pectorals tickled her nipples, keeping them in a constant taut state. Pressure built in the heart of her, creating a dull ache. She hoped like hell he wouldn't leave her like this for too long...

Her palm caressed his tight, flat abdomen before she slid her fingers behind the waist of his jeans. He let out a low growl. If she moved her hand just the slightest bit south, her fingertips would slide over the smooth head of his penis.

She gauged his reaction to her touch, watched curiously as the pulse beat wildly at the base of his throat, and the cords of his neck strained slightly. She tilted her head just enough so that she could look up into his smoldering eyes, eyes that had deepened to an intriguing pewter color in his state of arousal.

The man had iron will, she had to give him that.

It occurred to her that perhaps he found it necessary to let her make the major moves. Given his line of work, and the fact that she was a virtual stranger—and they were alone in *her* apartment—he likely found it prudent to let her lead them, rather than find himself in a situation where he might be accused of wrongdoing.

Well, the only wrongdoing going on at the moment was his steel resolve. As far as she was concerned, they should have been making love ten minutes ago.

"I'm not going to get you all worked up and then leave you hanging," she whispered, "if that's why you're holding back."

"I'm holding back because otherwise I'll ravage you," he growled.

"Oh, God," she said on a lusty sigh. "*Please* ravage me."

Dean groaned. His hands plunged into her long hair as he pulled her mouth to his. He kissed her long and deep and with incredible skill. She heard a soulful moan escape her, one that was filled with need and desire. Her hand skimmed further into his jeans, beneath the band of his underwear and she touched the smooth head of his erection. Her fingers grazed the shaft, her thumb slid over the tip. She felt the jolt that rocked him. He tightened his grip on her.

Unable to contain her grin—or her enthusiasm for pleasing him further—she broke their kiss and moved slowly down his body, her tongue and lips blazing a trail over his hard muscles and smooth skin. Her hand retreated from inside his jeans just long enough for her to completely unbutton his fly. She ran a hand over the bulge in his sexy black underwear, and her breath caught.

She'd had no doubt back at her club that Detective Dean was well endowed. But being this close to experiencing that endowment was more erotic than she'd imagined.

She moved away just enough to drag his black leather boots off, followed by his socks. Then they were both working his jeans down his sinewy legs. The sexy black underwear quickly followed.

Cassandra felt her pulse rage out of control. *"Oh, my."*

She lifted her gaze for the briefest of moments and smiled appreciatively at Dean before returning her attention to the prize before her. Like a kid at Christmas, she anxiously surveyed the bounty, wondering how the hell she was going to let this man leave her bedroom when he was done with her.

Maybe, if she was really lucky, he wouldn't be done with her anytime soon...

The thought settled comfortably in the back of her brain. She didn't even know this man, not really. Yet she felt as though she did. She felt a sense of familiarity with him, a connection to him.

She stood slowly and watched his gaze as it followed her. Cassandra slid the side zipper on her leather skirt all the way down and let the garment fall to the floor. She stepped out of the pool of clothing and stood facing Dean in nothing more than a red lace garter belt and matching thong, stockings, and red leather high heels.

The look on his face was priceless. He groaned loudly, then announced, "You just gave me a small heart attack, sweetheart." His eyes swept over her, from head to toe, and he shook his head. "You're one hell of a sight, Cassandra."

She smiled at him as she absently played with a long strand of blonde hair, curling it around her finger. "Anything you'd like me to leave on?"

"The shoes and the necklace."

She laughed softly. "You got it."

She lifted a leg and rested a high heel on the top of the coffee table. Making a production out of stripping down to her shoes, she unfastened the back garter, then released the front one. Slowly, seductively, she rolled the stocking down her leg, all the while keeping her eyes on Dean. He was entranced. She slipped her shoe off just long enough to slide the stocking off her foot. She repeated the process of stripping off her stockings with the other leg. Then she unhooked the garter belt and tossed it aside. It landed on top of Dean's discarded shirt.

She hooked her thumbs in the slim waist of her thong and eased the material over her hips and down her legs. She bent at the waist, paused with the scant material at her knees and glanced up at Dean. He appeared to be having another small heart attack.

She smiled wickedly and let the panties drop to the floor.

The warmth of the fire caressed her bare skin, and the anticipation of what was to come burned low in her belly. She was already wet... fully ready to take him inside her. But that would come later.

She strolled back to where he was sprawled in a mess of pillows in front of the fireplace. She purposely crossed one long, lean leg in front of the other as she moved, making the short walk as sexy as possible. When she reached him, she nudged his foot with the tip of one of her high heels. He spread his legs for her and she sank to her knees between his parted thighs.

There was no way she was going to pass up the opportunity to enjoy his magnificent manhood.

Chapter Six

Cassandra bent her head to him, slid her tongue lightly over the tip of his rock-hard cock. A wicked thrill shot through Dean and he bucked under her touch. He groaned low and deep, and his hands reached for her, threading their way through her long hair.

He gathered the thick mass in his hands and held it away from her beautiful face. He wanted to watch her as she stroked him with her tongue and then drew him deep into her warm, lush mouth. Sharp pains of desire stabbed him in the gut and the groin as this gorgeous woman made love to him with her mouth.

Her technique caused his excitement to soar to all new heights. She knew exactly how to touch and stroke and suck, raising his pulse as he surged toward climax. She also knew how to bring him back down, just enough to keep him from coming. He helped her prolong the inevitable, fought to keep his passion from exploding as it so wanted to do.

As much as he longed for release from this exquisite pain, he wanted it to happen when he was deep inside her. He wanted her to come with him.

When he knew he couldn't bear another moment of her wicked tongue on his cock without exploding, he gently tugged at her, bringing her head up. Words wouldn't form in his head or on his tongue, and he was pretty certain that, even if they did, there was no way in hell he'd even recognize his own voice if he spoke. He communicated instead with his eyes. Beckoning her toward him. She smiled in turn and moved up the length of his body.

Swiftly, Dean rolled them across the pillows until they were both on their sides, face to face, legs tangled. A large hand swept over her bare shoulder then dropped to her breast. He cupped it in his hand, then lowered his mouth to tease the puckered nipple. He sucked hard, drawing the tight bud into his mouth. His teeth grazed it gently and she gasped. Her fingertips tightened on his bicep and her long nails dug into his skin.

He swept his tongue over the hard center, sucked again. As his mouth teased and pleased, alternately paying tribute to each gloriously full breast, his hand moved over the subtle curve of her waist, over her slim hip to her backside. His fingertips grazed the cleft of her bottom as his hand swept lower. He lifted a shapely thigh upward and draped it over his waist, thereby providing the perfect access to her. His fingers moved between her parted cheeks, easing forward until they brushed lightly over her swollen lips.

Cassandra moaned, settling herself a bit closer to him. Her head fell back as his fingers stroked her wet flesh. He continued to suck and lick her nipples as he pushed a finger deep inside her. She gasped as she arched into him, demanding more. Dean was happy to oblige. He plunged two fingers into her slick heat and pumped them in and out until she was panting loudly and writhing restlessly in his arms.

His mouth left her delectable breasts, skimmed over the long column of her throat and then covered her mouth. He kissed her passionately, skillfully using his tongue while his fingers continued to move inside her, pushing her closer and closer to climax.

As she wriggled beneath him, the tip of his cock brushed her nearly bare mound. It throbbed painfully, creating an almost blinding need for immediate release. But he wasn't done with the task at hand.

"Don't you want to be inside me, Dean?"

"More than you know. But not yet. I want to make you come."

She moaned, clutching at him.

He repositioned them so that he could bend his head to her opening. His tongue grazed the swollen nub as his fingers continued to plunge and retreat. He worked her from both sides, filling her with his fingers, stroking her most sensitive spot with his tongue.

His heartbeat raged so loudly in his ears he barely heard her cry out. But he felt her powerful orgasm, felt her buck beneath him as her inner walls clenched tightly around his fingers. He lapped up the moisture with his tongue, pushed deeper inside her as violent tremors continued to rack her body.

Before she had a chance to recover—her body still trembled beneath his—he repositioned himself and thrust his hard cock deep inside her, making her cry out again. He drew himself up on his knees, easing her legs further apart. His hands circled her small waist, holding her in place as he drove himself deeper and deeper into her.

Cassandra's legs created a wide V. She came up on her elbows, her back arched, her head tilted back. Her long, graceful neck was fully exposed, her blonde hair spilled over the pillows. Her full breasts were perfectly round and plump, and they bounced slightly as his body slapped against hers.

She was the most erotic vision he'd ever seen.

Her stomach was slightly concave, and it quivered as he pulled himself almost out of her and then thrust back into her. Over and over again, faster and harder. He forced himself to hold back for as long as possible. Enveloped inside her was a magnificent place to be. She was wet and warm. And so incredibly tight. Her inner walls squeezed him, milking him to the point of sheer ecstasy.

As he pushed her closer and closer to the edge, a visceral need took over his body. Her head thrashed from side to side as the overwhelming sensations gripped her as well. There was no staving off the intense need for release.

"Tell me you're close," he growled impatiently.

"*Yes, yes!*" The words escaped through her slightly parted crimson-colored lips.

"Now?"

"Oh, God, yes," she moaned. "Now... *Please*..."

He thrust inside her, felt his body slam against hers as he buried himself to the hilt. And then he felt the powerful explosion of her orgasm as her body convulsed violently around his cock. She cried out, then softly chanted his name. He couldn't hold back another second.

"Oh, Christ." Dean groaned as he came. His body trembled and shook as his cock pulsed and surged inside her. She held him tightly, squeezing him, milking him, making him damn-near forget his own name.

Nothing else registered except the incredibly erotic, sensational feeling of being buried deep inside her, feeling her all around him.

When his orgasm ebbed, he collapsed on top of her. They panted heavily in unison.

With a great deal of effort, Dean managed to roll off of her while still holding her tightly. They lay sprawled on the pillows. Cassandra was now nestled between his legs. Her head hit the hard wall of his chest, and she rested while dragging in ragged, unsteady breaths.

It seemed as though hours passed before Dean's heart rate slowed and the humming of his body dimmed. Eventually, the haziness in his brain cleared. He gently stroked Cassandra, running his fingertips languidly up and down the long, delicate line of her spine.

She lifted her head and said, "I feel paralyzed from the neck down."

Dean grinned at her. "That makes two of us."

She sat up. Pushing a hand through her mass of curls, she gave him a serious look. "We got a bit out of control. Just so you know, I'm on the Pill."

Christ, he hadn't even thought about using a condom. His brain really was scrambled tonight. "I'm not usually that careless."

"We were both careless, to a point. For the record, I haven't been with anyone in..." She paused a moment, seemingly giving this some serious thought. She shook her head and whistled under her breath. "Wow. Over two years."

Dean was shocked, yet damn relieved. He liked knowing she wasn't intimately involved with anyone else and hadn't been in a long while.

To be fair, he told her, "I was in a relationship for ten years. There were a few others before that, but no one after. We broke up a little over a year ago."

She nodded her head and gave him a look that suggested she was waiting for more details. But none were forthcoming. Dean didn't see the point in telling her about his on-again-off-again romance with socialite Bethany Carter.

Cassandra stood up, a bit shakily, he noted. She was still wearing those sexy red high heels—and nothing else. Her long blonde hair was a tangled mess of loose curls that fell over her shoulders and down her back.

She was incredibly sexy, a vision he'd remember the rest of his days.

He rolled onto his side so he could watch her as she made her way, swaying ever so slightly on her tall heels, toward the hallway that led to the bathroom.

She wagged a finger in the air as she went, saying, "I'm a bit light-headed at the moment. If I'm not back in five minutes, come get me."

He chuckled. He felt pretty light-headed himself. A bit delirious, in fact. He wasn't so sure he could even get to his feet without passing out. It seemed as if all the blood remained in his cock.

She returned a few minutes later, and Dean was pleased to see she hadn't found any clothes to put on. She was still gloriously naked, save for those red shoes. She was a siren, for sure.

He eventually hauled himself up and patted her lightly on the butt as he dragged his all-too-relaxed body past her. He felt as limp as an overcooked noodle. But good. Damn good, in fact.

He couldn't remember ever feeling this completely and utterly captivated by a woman. So turned inside out, so full of passion, desire and need. Still. Even *after* he'd made love to her.

Dean had certainly never wanted Bethany this much. In fact, last year when their relationship had hit the skids—*for what, the tenth time in as many years?*—he certainly hadn't lost sleep over the breakup.

Bethany had been the only steady female presence in his romantic life since law school. During his first year at Harvard, he'd met her in class. She was pretty, smart and sensible. The perfect wife for him, according to his parents. She came from a wealthy, well-established family, as he did. She belonged to the Junior League and sat on the boards of many charitable foundations. She taught Sunday school, was a gracious hostess and always looked as though she had just stepped out from underneath a hair dryer at the salon.

Perfectly coiffed, perfectly manicured, perfectly attired.

And perfectly dull.

As Dean cleaned himself up and then splashed warm water on his face, he found himself comparing prim and proper Bethany to wild and wicked Cassandra. He smiled at the thought of the latter woman.

Bethany was the picture of social decorum, a member of New York Society, while Cassandra was a creature of her own accord. From her sexy attire to her long, tousled locks, she appeared to be a free-spirited woman who believed in spontaneity and good old-fashioned fun.

He couldn't picture Cassandra Kensington at the country club, and that suited him just fine. Dean had never wanted a stuffy socialite for a wife, contrary to his parents' preference. Another source of contention between them.

The reason, he supposed, that he and Bethany had continued the lukewarm romance was because she was incredibly sweet and a really good friend. She was easy to be with and she was the only person, besides Cat, who supported his career choices. But eventually, Bethany had come to the realization that Dean didn't share her dream of a happily-ever-after between them. She'd decided to move on, and he was happy to know she'd finally found true love. She was getting married this fall.

Thank the lord, Dean was now off the hook.

Which led him back to thoughts of Cassandra. What an amazing creature, he mused as he shoved his fingers through his rumpled hair in an attempt to make it a little less post-sex messy.

Not much luck in that area.

He kept his hair on the longish side because he couldn't be bothered with regular trims. Besides, he liked it a bit unruly... it seemed to fit his job as well as his personality. A little mousse was all it took to get the thick locks to fall carelessly into all the right places. It wasn't country club hair, that was for damn sure. And his mother absolutely loathed the look. But it suited him, so he didn't see any reason to make a change.

It wasn't like he wore a suit and tie every day and hob-knobbed with the rich and affluent on a regular basis. In fact, he avoided that scene at all costs. With the exception of his mother's parties, which he wouldn't miss for the world because he truly did adore her, Dean no longer attended social events that required him to look as though he was a walking advertisement for Brooks Brothers.

He was his own man, which was all he'd ever wanted to be.

Until now.

At the moment, he wanted to be the kind of man Cassandra Kensington might keep around for a while.

But it sounded as though she wasn't into long-term relationships. She was independent, not exactly in need of a man.

What was her story?

To say he was intrigued by the beautiful woman he'd just made love to would be a monumental understatement. He was utterly fascinated.

He found her in the kitchen, standing before the patio door, which was cracked open to let in a slight breeze. He eased himself behind her and wrapped his arms around her small waist.

Nuzzling, her neck, he whispered in her ear, "I still want you."

She turned, wrapping hers arms around his neck. "I was hoping you'd come back and say something like that."

Their bodies melded together with intimate familiarity. "You're hot," he said in a soft voice.

"Hmm, thank you."

Dean chuckled. "In that way, too. But I meant your skin is hot."

"I'm burning up on the inside. Sort of a sexual fever, I guess."

Dean's ego got a hefty boost with that admission. Inspiration struck and he detangled himself from her, despite her soft protests. He wandered further into the kitchen.

"What are you up to?" she asked.

"Gotta find something to cool you down." He opened the freezer and inspected her ice cube inventory, pleased to find that her ice maker spit out crescent-shaped cubes. He removed one of her frozen beer mugs from the rack and plopped a half-dozen cubes into it. He headed back to the living room.

A cool breeze drifted through the apartment. To keep it from getting too chilly, Dean turned up the flame in the fireplace. He settled on the floor again and Cassandra joined him, her eyes aglow with curiosity—and anticipation.

Dean leaned over and brushed his lips over hers. Her palms covered his bare chest and then worked their way upward. She wrapped her arms around his neck. Dean kissed her long and slow. When he pulled away, she sighed against his cheek.

"Lay back." She did as he asked. He fished an ice cube out of the frosty mug and leaned over her, propping himself up on one elbow. He slid the tip of the ice cube over her full lips.

Cassandra sighed contently. "Hmm, that feels good."

Dean's mouth grazed hers again, his tongue gliding over her wet lips. He kissed the corner of her mouth as his hand moved downward, trailing the ice cube over her jaw line and then down the long column of her neck. The cold tip melted against her warm flesh.

Her eyelids fluttered closed. "Very creative, Detective Dean."

"I'm just getting started, sweetheart."

Chapter Seven

The sounds of the city drifted in through the open doors, mingling with the sexy music that flowed from the radio. A cool breeze caressed Cassandra's skin. By contrast, she was warmed by the heat emitting from the fireplace and her own quickly rising internal temperature.

As Dean glided the ice cube over her warm skin, she reveled in the contrasting sensations. Droplets pooled in the hollow of her neck and Dean bent his head to that very spot, lapping up the moisture with his talented tongue. He continued to sweep the ice cube over her skin, sliding it back and forth across her prominent collarbone. Then lower. He traced a line down to the valley between her breasts, then slowly brushed it across the inner slopes.

Cassandra's body began to tingle with anticipation. The dramatic variance in temperature heightened her arousal. Her heavy lids opened to narrowed slits as she watched him. The contemplative look in Dean's smoky eyes gave her goose bumps. He was up to something wicked, and she could hardly wait to find out what he intended to do next.

As though wanting to prolong her anticipation, he brought what was left of the ice cube to her lips. She drew it into her mouth, enjoying the crisp, cool taste. She crunched it with her teeth just before Dean's mouth covered hers. Their tongues mingled with the ice chips. Their heat mixed with the cold, creating a tantalizing sensation. When Dean drew away, Cassandra whimpered audibly.

Dean chuckled. He reached for another ice cube. Obviously, he was intent on driving her absolutely crazy. She closed her eyes again just as the frigid, sharp edge touched her hard nipple. She gasped at the shock of the ice cube on such a sensitive place. Her breasts ached for Dean's touch, her nipples were tight and highly sensitized, and a sharp throbbing built in the heart of her.

Dean continued his ministrations, tracing circles around the areola of one breast, then the other. Then he concentrated on the hard buds, using the tip of the ice cube to gently scrap against the peaks. Cold drops pooled and then spilled down the sides of her breasts. Dean swept his tongue along the outer swell of one breast, licking the water from her skin, while he continued to rub the cold cube over and around her nipple.

Cassandra squirmed and writhed beneath him. Even though he was making her crazy with desire, she didn't want the exquisite torture to end. She wanted more—more of Dean's creative ministrations, more of his mouth on her body. More of him, in general.

She moaned low and deep when his lips slid over her wet nipple. He drew the cold, hard bud into his mouth, instantly warming it. The sudden change in temperature was an overwhelming sensation. Cassandra threaded her fingers through his thick, soft hair and held his head in place. She arched into him, wanting him to take more. His tongue teased her nipple, his teeth gently grazed the hard point and she thought she would come right then. But he pulled her back. He lifted his head and smiled devilishly at her.

"Not yet," he whispered. As if he'd known how dangerously close to the edge he'd brought her.

His fingers were wet and cool from the melted ice cube and he used them to keep her nipples tight and hard.

"Dean, please…" She didn't think she could take much more of his teasing. She was wet and oh-so-ready for him. She wanted him to take her to that beautiful place only he seemed capable of taking her.

But he wasn't quite ready to oblige her. Rather, he selected another ice cube and continued his sensual assault on her flesh. Cassandra caught her lower lip between her teeth as Dean slid the cube down her belly. He circled her naval, then lapped up the water that pooled in the slight indentation.

"Spread your legs for me, sweetheart," he whispered.

She did as he asked, swallowing down a moan of need. Dean positioned himself between her parted legs and traced the cube lower, over her mound. With his finger and thumb, he parted the soft folds at the heart of her. His breath was warm against her flesh, and then suddenly, she felt the cold tip of the ice cube. Her body bucked in response to the erotic sensation, but he gave her no time to assimilate. He slid the ice cube over her sensitive flesh, moving it up and down in an intimate caress.

The cube was large enough to cover the targeted area, and wide enough to make her gasp as Dean slid it deep inside her. The cold cube mingled with her slick heat. She could feel the drops of water, mixed with her own moisture, trickling out of her. Dean's mouth covered her, and his tongue stroked her clit while he used the ice cube to push her closer and closer to orgasm. He slipped it out then slid it back in, over and over as the tension built.

Her nipples were still rock hard and begging for attention. Cassandra cupped her breasts with her hands as Dean discarded the nearly melted ice cube and used his fingers instead. Stroking her while she plucked at her own nipples, he took her to the very brink. And then a shattering climax took over her body and she cried out. She squeezed her inner muscles tightly, wanting so desperately to prolong the intense orgasm and savor every erotically delicious moment of it.

While her body still hummed like a livewire, Dean got to his feet. He bent down, scooped her up in his arms. She wrapped her arms around his neck, nuzzling close to him.

He carried her across the living room and down the hallway until she directed him to the room on the left. He crossed to the king-size bed that sat in the middle of the bedroom and gently deposited her on the upholstered bench at the foot of the bed.

He made no move to turn on the bedside lamps. Moonlight streamed through the partially open drapes that covered the floor-to-ceiling windows on the opposite side of the room. The silvery rays cast shadows across the bed, and across Dean's face.

He tossed pillows off her bed and then folded down the red velvet duvet cover. The crisp, white Egyptian cotton sheets followed. He fluffed the remaining pillows, then returned to her.

Dean scooped her up again and carried her to the bed. He settled her in before sliding in beside her, stretching out next to her.

The first time Dean had taken her, he'd been overcome by red-hot passion and intense need. This time, he intended to take his time with her, get to know every inch of her luscious body. Make love to her slowly, intimately.

It wasn't a desire he had imagined experiencing, especially not when he'd first met her. She was the type of woman who inspired erotic fantasies, drove a man to distraction with her long legs, full breasts, and wild mane. She was the kind of woman, he had originally thought, that a man had a wild, mind-blowing fling with before moving on to more suitable companionship.

He was currently rethinking that concept.

Although he had no doubt that Cassandra Kensington was a sexy, sensual, free-spirited woman with very few, if any, sexual inhibitions, he knew innately that there was much more to this woman than a sexual fantasy waiting to happen.

The problem was, when he was with her—his hands on her body as they were now, caressing, exploring, stroking—he conveniently forgot that he was a man who didn't like or need complications in his life. And that included complicated women. If his gut instincts served him as correctly in matters of the heart as they did while performing his job, he was certain this particular woman was as complex as they came.

Trouble. That's what he'd sensed when he'd met her, what he still thought of her. Because she was the type of woman who could make a man forget his own convictions, like the desire not to have complications in his life.

Yet he seemed incapable—and perhaps even reluctant—to break the spell between them. He was quickly becoming completely ensnared by her. He loved the silky feel of her smooth skin, was mesmerized by her incredible curves and lush body, and wanted to burrow his mouth against the side of her slender neck while deeply inhaling the fresh scent of her flaxen hair.

His lips touched the soft crook of her neck, then swept over her shoulder. He basked in the sensual tone of the soft moan that escaped her lips and was eager to discover every conceivable way of pleasing her.

Cassandra Kensington had the kind of body that made a man want to exhaust his knowledge of lovemaking, trying every single position under the sun and perhaps creating new ones. And the fact that she was so open with her sexuality, so comfortable with her body and the erotic urges it inspired, only served to make him absurdly crazed for her.

Her fingers were tangled in his hair as he continued to explore her soft flesh with his tongue and lips. Slowly, he kissed, licked and sucked. Tasting her, teasing her, making her sigh with a satisfying sound of lust, desire and pleasure. He found that he craved hearing her response to his ministrations. He wanted to make her sigh dreamily, moan erotically, gasp desirously. He wanted to make her writhe and wriggle beneath him, wanted to push her to the very precipice of desire.

His mouth reached the inner swell of her left breast and his own pleasure grew. Cassandra had breasts no sane man could resist. So full, so round, so perfect. He cupped one with his hand as his tongue glanced over the areola and then the taut bud. He drew her nipple slowly into his mouth and sucked gently, while his hand gave equal attention to her other breast.

"*Dean.*" She whispered his name on an erotic sigh.

He'd never felt so virile and manly as he did when he heard that sound. He was making her as hot for him as he was for her. It took all the willpower he possessed not to skim a hand down her body to feel how wet she was. How wet *he* had made her. He wanted to know how strongly he affected her.

He was relieved to find that her thoughts ran along the same lines. She withdrew her fingers from his hair and reached for one of his hands. Her palm covered the back of his hand and her fingers twined with his. She guided their hands downward to her most intimate area, and Dean's fingers, which burned to be inside her, slid over the swollen flesh between her legs.

A soft cry fell from her lips. She held his hand in place, obviously wanting him there, wanting him to bring her pleasure in the same way he so desperately wanted to. He reminded himself that he wasn't finished exploring her body with his mouth. But the way his cock throbbed so painfully, he knew he was still a long way away from having enough restraint for prolonged foreplay. As it was, he had serious doubts about his ability to make love to her slowly.

He continued to taste and tease her hard nipples, as his fingers explored her inner depths. The fact that her fingers were still twined with his increased his arousal. Just thinking of her touching herself, stroking her swollen flesh, pushed him close to the edge.

He maneuvered their positioning so that his hand covered hers and it was her fingers skimming over the protruding nub at the heart of her. He inclined his head just so, giving him a perfect view of their hands, a perfect view of her fingers stroking her clit. And then his hand eased away, until it was just hers at that precious spot. His fingers dipped inside her, pushing past the silky folds, plunging deep.

She gasped, then whispered erotic words that made it all the more impossible to keep his own passion in check. The pressure was building inside her, he could tell by the way she writhed beneath him. Her climax would be a powerful one, if he had any say in the matter. One that would take her breath away, one that would make her cry out his name. *His* name. God, how he longed to hear her scream in ecstasy...

Propped on his right elbow, he hovered slightly over her. He wanted to kiss her, but was so mesmerized by the vision of their hands between her legs that he couldn't quite tear himself away.

An overwhelming rush of want and need surged through him. He was more turned on than he'd ever dreamed possible. No other woman could ever make him *this* hard.

His jaw clenched tightly as he fought to keep his own orgasm at bay. Just watching her touch herself was nearly enough to make him come. But he was helping her to reach her climax, and that was all the more erotic for him.

He could sense the change in her when it came, could feel the tension in her body as she rushed toward that powerful release. He wanted to give her the ultimate pleasure. *Now.*

His fingers worked inside her as hers worked outside. His mouth went to the long column of her neck. Her breasts heaved against his bare chest, her breath coming in labored pants.

"Come for me, sweetheart," he whispered in her ear. "Come now."

She did. Her orgasm racked her body, as his fingers continued to plunge into her, prolonging her climax.

And she did scream his name. It tore from her lips with such pleasure and passion it made Dean desperate to make love to her. In a heartbeat, he removed his fingers from her and eased his rock-hard cock deep inside her. As she wrapped her long legs around his waist to hold him in place, he came instantly. He felt, through the dense haze of his own release, her second climax.

Her fingers were entwined in his hair again, her body bowed off the bed and conformed tightly to his. He wrapped his arms around her waist and held on as the spasms rocked both their bodies.

When the convulsions subsided, Cassandra's limp body eased back against the mattress. Dean's arms remained around her. He was up on his elbows and his head hung between his shoulders. Her legs slid away from his waist, but somehow managed to stay tangled with his.

Only one coherent thought formed in his mind. It was going to take years to reach a point where he could make love to this woman slowly, without losing all control ten minutes into the task.

He let out a short laugh at his own lack of control.

"What's so funny?" she asked as she sucked in a ragged breath. Her fingers dragged absently through his hair.

Dean glanced up at her. "Off the top of my head, I can think of twenty different ways I want to make love to you. But I can't seem to get past this first position."

She smiled, let out a puff of air. "Shall I take that as a compliment?"

"A compliment for you, an obvious weakness for me." He shook his head, sighing in frustration.

Cassandra giggled. "What you're failing to realize," she said in a matter-of-fact tone, "is that it doesn't matter *how* we make love. It's apparent that we both derive immense pleasure from each other, regardless of what position we're in."

"Agreed. But don't you think we'd derive even more pleasure if I could keep it together for more than ten minutes at a time?"

She laughed heartily now.

Dean frowned. "I don't find this particularly amusing."

"Did you not make me come twice just now?"

"I had help on the first one."

A wicked smile graced her plump lips. "But you were flying solo on the second one. And besides, I believe the assistance I provided was your idea to begin with."

"*Touché.*"

She stroked his cheek with a finger. "So we'll have to work on building up your tolerance."

The lustful look in her eyes made Dean's passion stir again. "That could take many, many, *many* attempts."

"I'm a patient woman," she assured him.

Dean grinned. "You are many things, Cassandra. In a word," he said as he stretched out beside her, "*incredible.*"

She sighed against his chest. "I knew that misguided charm of yours would eventually come around."

He held her tightly and she snuggled close, resting her head on his broad shoulder. Her fingers gently stroked his defined abdominal muscles. "You have a fantastic body," she whispered before stifling a yawn.

"So do you."

"How much rest do you need before Round Three?"

Chapter Eight

She extracted herself from his embrace in the late morning and he heard her bare feet pad across the hardwood floor. Dean opened an eye to watch her. He would have put the full effort into it—opening both eyes, sitting up and taking in the entire tantalizing view—but he was too damn exhausted. She'd worn him out.

His eye followed her as she ducked into the adjoining bathroom. He heard the water run for what seemed like forever, then she returned. Naked. Gloriously naked. Good God, she was a sight. All creamy skin and luscious curves. And breasts he was completely enthralled with. Like a teenager looking at his first *Playboy* centerfold, Dean was instantly aroused.

She dug around in a drawer and pulled out a lacy nightie.

"No," Dean protested in a weak voice.

She slipped the material over her head and shimmied into it provocatively, no doubt for his benefit. He groaned. If he could move, he'd grab her arm and drag her back to bed. As it was, his body felt like dead weight.

She turned to him, all thousand-watt smile and long wet hair. The red lace nightie had impossibly thin straps, a bodice that looked like a bra and which plumped up Cassandra's breasts in an enticing way. The material hugged her shapely figure, and the hem barely skimmed the middle of her thighs.

"God, you're beautiful." He all but drooled.

She laughed at him.

Okay, so he was probably a pathetic sight, burrowed deep beneath the sheet and comforter, his head resting in the deep grooves of a plump pillow. But his cock was already reminding him of the effect she had on him.

"Come here," he demanded.

She traced the pad of a finger over her full, soft lips. Contemplative. Playful. She was going to make him crazy—make his life hell, he could tell. Beautiful, wild women were good at making a man's life hell. He didn't care.

"Please?" He begged shamelessly.

She smiled. "I would, but I'm famished. And I bet you are, too."

Food was the last thing on his mind. "Ravenous. But not in the way you're thinking."

She giggled. "You can hardly move, let alone make love to me. How about I make us a nice spread? I'm a whiz at brunch. And then we'll see if your strength returns."

He groaned. Lord, when had he ever felt this completely satiated, this completely relaxed?

Never, that's when.

Bright-eyed and bushy-tailed, Trouble bounced around the room with more energy than a three-year-old hopped up on sugar. She put on a little bit of makeup, dried her hair with a hairdryer, then appeared at his side. She bent at the waist, gave him a kiss on the cheek.

"Hang in there, tiger."

Dean groaned. "I just need to know if anyone has died in this bed."

She laughed, a sweet sound he was becoming very fond of. "You're silly."

"I'm exhausted," he complained. Yet still looking forward to… what were they up to? Ah, yes. Round Six.

"Well, I think you have lots of potential. Don't give up yet. Just rest for a while. I need about an hour to get brunch ready, anyway."

"I can help." He shifted in the enormous bed.

"Not necessary," she said. "I've got it under control. Besides, I don't like to share my kitchen."

Dean settled back in the bed. She was on her way out the door when the phone on the night stand rang. He decided he'd catch a few more winks while she went about her business.

"Josh, what are you doing up so early?" Her sultry voice drifted into Dean's groggy brain. When her tone of voice changed, his eyes snapped open. "What do you mean someone broke into my club last night? The police would have called if someone tripped the alarm."

Tossing back the covers, Dean sat bolt upright.

"Of course I set the alarm." She shot Dean a quick look and he nodded in affirmation. "Oh, shit. This can't be happening."

She let out a distressed whimper that made Dean's heart wrench. He was out of bed and stalking down the hallway in the next instant. As she wrapped up her call with Josh, he located all of his clothes and quickly dressed. A few minutes later, Cassandra rushed into the living room, dressed in jeans and a red sweater. Keys already in hand, Dean ushered her out the door and to his car.

As they drove the short distance to Rendezvous, she told him, "Josh said the place is trashed."

Damn that Slider. If he was behind this, he had better pray the cops found him before Dean did. He had half a mind to strangle the little thief.

Shifting into third, Dean wove his way through light Sunday morning traffic and pulled up outside the club. Cassandra didn't wait for him to open any doors. She rushed through the foyer and straight into Josh's arms. A tinge of jealousy crept up on Dean, but he reminded himself they were family.

"The cops are upstairs," Josh said. "I told them everything I could, which unfortunately wasn't much."

"I want to go upstairs."

"Let me check it out first," Dean said, wanting desperately to protect her, but knowing innately it was impossible.

"I have to see the damage sometime, Dean," she reasoned with him. "The police will need to know if anything is missing."

He rubbed the back of his neck and gave her a compelling look. "Just be prepared for the worst. This is your personal space someone invaded, and that will make it all the more difficult to stomach."

She nodded her head, grateful for the advice. And the support. He followed her upstairs, muttered something about the lock on the doors not being jimmied.

When Cassandra entered her club, she drew up short, the breath escaping her in a hard rush of air. Even the worst scenario imaginable couldn't have prepared her for what she saw. She literally felt jolted to the core of her being, as though she'd just been dealt a physical blow. Her hand covered her mouth and her eyes grew wide as she took in the scene.

Behind her, Dean let out a soft curse.

The elegant, orderly nightclub was a shadow of its former self. The cushions on the expensive chairs and sofas were all slashed, their stuffing scattered about. Tables and barstools were overturned, their legs smashed. Large black "Xs" had been spray painted on the walls.

Cassandra took a few tentative steps inside, still reeling from what had become of her beautiful club. She slowly wound her way through the debris and piles of splintered wood. Shards of glass from broken lamps and wall sconces crunched beneath her booted feet. When she reached the back of the club, she let out a small, strangled cry.

Her beloved pool tables had the same spray painted Xs over the once-pristine red-felt tops. All of the pool cues had been smashed, along with the wall racks. The tall tables and the barstools had been reduced to rubble as well.

If her stomach weren't empty, Cassandra was pretty certain she'd have tossed the contents right then.

"My tables," she whispered in agony.

"We can fix all of this," Dean said in a soft voice. "I'll help. I'll do whatever I can."

She reached out to touch the smooth edge of one of her pool tables, but

Dean caught her hand in his.

"Don't touch anything, sweetheart. The cops are still dusting for prints."

She spared a glance at the two officers inspecting her club.

Her attention returned to the tables. Tears crested the rims of her eyes. "They were a gift from my uncle." Her heart sank as she regarded the mess before her. She felt personally violated.

Cassandra backed away from the tables and stood in front of her bar. The stools were no more than splintered wood. The mahogany bar wasn't severely damaged, but it was scuffed up a bit. The dozens of bottles of liquor on the shelves behind it were intact. Her eyes drifted to the shelves at the far end and her heart broke just a little more.

"Damn it." She groaned. "Not my glasses..."

She shuffled to the end of the bar, knowing she was a sad sight as she sank to her knees at the opening.

This was just plain cruel. Her delicate red-tinted wineglasses, which she'd bought from an estate in Tuscany, had been reduced to thousands of tiny shards. She lifted a triangular piece and stared it a moment, shaking her head in dismay.

"How could someone destroy something so beautiful?" she whispered to no one in particular, slipping a little out of the "here and now" as past pains crept up on her.

More tears stung her eyes. She'd been here before, which made it even worse for her. Though she stared at the ruined glasses, she saw something else she'd once loved, which had been smashed to bits as the glasses were.

Her father's beautifully crafted violin.

Cassandra had been just fourteen years old when her grandfather, in a moment of immense grief and fiery rage, had placed the exquisite instrument under the front tire of his Mercedes and backed over it. Cassandra had not forgiven him for destroying her father's prized possession, which had passed to her upon his untimely and tragic death.

She'd been devastated that day, as she was now, to lose something so special, something she'd held so close to her heart.

Getting to her feet, she approached the officers, who were speaking with Dean.

"I told them about Slider, sweetheart. These officers would like you to take a look around and see if anything is missing."

Cassandra wandered throughout the club and inspected her office. When she was done, she pulled Dean aside and said, "Nothing's missing. The band's instruments are still locked in the closet, all the expensive booze is still intact, the paintings on the walls are untouched." She considered this for a moment, then added, "The only stuff destroyed are personal items that meant some-thing to me. The pool tables, the glasses, the furniture. Those things have sentimental value."

"What about computer equipment?"

She shook her head. "Still locked in the safe with the cash. I've kept everything locked up since..." Her voice trailed off.

Oh, hell. Things were about to get ugly.

"Since what?" Dean eyed her with a suspicious look on his face, as though he knew he wasn't going to like what she had to say.

"Since the incident with Slider." She groaned. "Dean, I didn't tell you everything about him."

Crossing his powerful arms over his wide chest, Dean said in a terse tone, "Mind telling me now?"

Cassandra let out a long sigh. "He stole one of McCarthy's laptops and about eight hundred dollars from the till."

Dean's jaw clenched. "And you didn't call the police?"

"Dean!" She planted her hands on her hips. Hadn't she already explained her reasons to him? "I didn't want any trouble."

"Oh, you've got trouble, sweetheart. Whether you want it or not. Slider was here two nights ago."

She shook her head. "No. I would have seen him."

"How busy were you?"

"*Dean.*" She sighed in exasperation, conceding the point.

"He stole my sister's wallet. That's why I came looking for him."

"Oh, shit." As if she didn't already feel two-inches tall for lying to him. "Dean, I'm so sorry. I'll replace the wallet and any money Slider took from your sister."

"That's not necessary, nor is that the point. You should have contacted the authorities, Cassandra. Filed a report."

She'd been so worried about damaging her respectable reputation and now it was totally shot to hell. No way would her female clients feel safe here ever again. Once they found out the place had been vandalized, and that Cassandra had hired a thief...

Damn it. Things would never be the same at Rendezvous. And she'd lose a lot of business over this, she was sure.

Obviously angry with her, Dean stalked off to share this new information with the police. After answering all their questions, the officers informed Cassandra she could start cleaning up in a day or two. They'd let her know what they found out, but they told her not to get her hopes up on finding the culprit. With no witnesses, no surveillance tapes to capture the breaking and entering, and no real means of pinpointing a thief from prints because too many people came and went from the club, chances were slim they'd solve this mystery. Unless the vandal hit again and was more careless next time.

"I've got to call McCarthy," she said after the police left. Dean handed over his cell phone and offered to drive her home. She followed him out the door as she waited for McCarthy to pick up.

Once she'd explained the dire situation, she instructed McCarthy to contact all of their members via broadcast electronic and voice mail.

"Tell them we'll be closed for a month."

Dean shot her a quizzical look just as McCarthy asked, "A month? Are you sure we can get the place put back together by then?"

"I'll hire a cleaning crew, get someone in to paint the walls. I'm sure I can get everything replaced. It may not be as great as it was once was, but I honestly can't see us staying closed any longer than that. We'll lose our clients." She gave this some thought as she slid into the passenger seat of Dean's sports car. "We'll have to come up with a great promo to salve the sting of being closed for so long. We'll throw a big bash when we reopen. Members only. We'll also give everyone a free month of membership. You can continue to make matches, they'll just have to find somewhere else to meet."

"Christ, Cass. I'm so sorry."

"Me, too. But we'll get through it. Somehow." As an afterthought, she added, "Make sure your broadcast message mentions that we were broken into, but nothing of value was taken."

"Are you sure you want them to know that?"

"No. But what choice do I have? We need to be completely honest with them. The women who come here alone deserve to know what happened so that they can make an educated, well-informed decision as to whether they feel safe coming back. We can't lie to them, McCarthy."

She sighed. "I know. It's just… damn it. We've built such a great reputation."

"And we'll have to do everything in our power to keep it. Including being completely honest about this incident."

"You're right." She paused a moment, then asked, "Are you okay?"

Cassandra spared a quick glance in Dean's direction. He still bristled from her lie. "Sure. Don't worry about me. Just start thinking of some great way to keep all of our clients."

They said their goodbyes and Cassandra disconnected the call. Dean double-parked in front of her apartment building and left the engine running. A bad sign.

"I'm sorry I didn't tell you everything I knew about Slider," she said in a contrite tone.

"I'm not going to pretend it doesn't bother me, Cassandra." He raked a hand through his disheveled yet sexy hair. He looked over at her and said, "I want to help you. Right now, I need a shower and I need to make some phone calls."

She nodded. He got out of the car, then opened the door for her.

She placed a hand on his arm. "Dean, I really am sorry."

"I'll let you know if I hear anything." He climbed back in the car and drove off.

He'd said he'd help her, but Cassandra wondered if she'd driven a wedge between them too big to bridge.

Chapter Nine

Two days later, Cassandra made another thorough sweep of Rendezvous to determine if anything was missing. McCarthy was busy tracking down vendors to repair the damaged furniture, and Josh had offered to find a clean-up crew for her. Though she wasn't normally one to solicit help, Cassandra was infinitely grateful her friends had rallied around her. Even her waitresses had volunteered to help put the club back together.

Cassandra felt confident they could be up and running in one month, but she was less certain about the response they would get from their clients. She suspected they'd lose business when word got around about the break-in and vandalism, and the reality that her club and her reputation were now tainted broke her heart.

"Rule number one," Dean said as he came through the door. "Don't leave these doors unlocked."

His voice made her heart skip a beat and the sight of him, dressed in sinfully well-fitting, faded jeans and a tight navy-blue T-shirt, sent her pulse off the charts. Unfortunately, the stern look on his face made her scowl.

She placed a hand on her hip. "Josh is downstairs."

"Doesn't matter. Anyone can come in here when you're alone."

Cassandra tamped down the irritation rising inside her. "I have a cleaning crew coming. And the girls are in and out. I can't lock everyone out."

"It may be inconvenient, but when you're alone you need to—"

"Well that's odd," she interjected, suddenly discovering something amiss. Her attention diverted, she searched behind the bar for her missing notebook.

"What's odd?" Dean asked, his concern registering on his handsome face.

"My promotions book is gone."

"Maybe you misplaced it."

She shook her head. "No. I only make entries in it when I have some down-time. I keep it right here in this cubby hole behind the bar. I've never misplaced it in four years. And I know I didn't misplace it this time."

Dean's curiosity was piqued. "What's in this book?"

"Pretty much everything that helps to make Rendezvous a success. I log all the responses to the promotions we run. Whether they were successful or not, what we could do to improve on them, specific responses and requests from the members. I keep photos in it and ideas for the club and the dating service. It's basically the lifeblood of my business."

"Valuable information," he mused. He contemplated this a moment, then asked, "What's your competition like?"

"Non-existent at first. But a few clubs opened up last year. From what I hear, they're still struggling to stay afloat. We garnered the market when we opened. We've got a golden database and McCarthy's software is much more advanced and sophisticated than anyone else's."

Dean's jaw clenched for a brief moment. "So maybe one of your competitors hired Slider to steal your intellectual property. With the help of an accomplice, he easily could have lifted your keys while he was working here and had a dup set made. If he paid close enough attention, he could get the security code when you disengaged the alarm. That would explain how he got in here the other night without a forced entry."

The thought didn't sit well with Cassandra, but another one weighed even heavier on her mind. "Why would he trash my club?"

Dean smacked a hand on the bar. "That's the part that's tripping me up. If he could slip in and out without being detected, lift a few items that would help whoever hired him, why would he need to ransack the place?"

Cassandra shook her head. None of this made sense to her.

"We've got to change the locks and reset the alarm code," Dean said. "And I'd really like it if you'd consider installing surveillance cameras inside the club and in the hallway."

Cassandra closed her eyes and let out a groan. "Jesus, there goes my safe, respectable, non-threatening environment." She shook her head again. "One look at the massive security in this club and the women will be terrified to come here."

Goddamn it.

"Sweetheart," Dean said in a supportive tone, "Better safe than sorry, right?"

She'd had enough of this business for one day. She stepped around the broken glass and collected her purse and keys. "I'm going home."

"Not yet." Dean's expression softened. He slipped an arm around her and pulled her to him. "You need a distraction."

That was an understatement. His sexy grin held a mischievous promise. A smile tickled the corners of her mouth and heat flooded her veins. "What did you have in mind?"

"A date."

Cassandra felt some of the tension inside her ease a bit. "Sounds nice. I'm game."

"Good. Come on." With his arm around her waist, he walked her out. Once the entry was secured, he started across the street.

When he directed her to the bookstore she loved, Cassandra eyed him curiously. They entered the cavernous store, and Dean whisked them right past the owner, Walt Goodman. He took her down the long corridor and the narrow flight of stairs that led to what Cassandra had always thought of as a personal sanctuary. It was the room where Walt housed his impressive collection of first edition and extremely rare works, worth a small fortune. He kept the classics down here, under lock and key. Dean produced said key from the pocket of his jeans. Usually, Walt handed it to her as she passed by, but apparently Dean had made a prior arrangement with the bookstore's owner.

Cassandra couldn't help but smile as they stepped inside the small room, which smelled of old leather and dust. All of her troubles melted away when she was here.

"Pick one," Dean said in a soft voice.

Cassandra eyed him over her shoulder for a moment, then crossed to one of the tall shelves. She selected a rare edition of Shakespeare's poems. She settled on one of the large burgundy leather sofas, nestling herself in the opening of Dean's legs, which were stretched out on the long couch. He dropped an arm over her shoulders as she snuggled close to him.

"Read to me," he whispered in her ear.

Cassandra fell a little bit in love with him at that moment.

She opened the book and began to read.

Admittedly, Dean wasn't a fan of poetry or Shakepeare. But he was a fan of anything that would take Cassandra's mind off the ransacking of her club. He also loved to listen to her soft, sultry voice and to see the sparkle return to her bright blue eyes as she read to him.

They left the bookstore two hours later, and he drove them to her apartment. Finding a spot close to her building, he pulled in and cut the engine.

"Does this mean you're coming up?" She cast a suggestive, yet hopeful, glance his way.

Dean grinned. "If you'd like me to."

She leaned across the seat and gave him a quick but sweet kiss. "I was afraid, after the other night…" She shook her head, let out a soft sigh. "I'm really sorry about not telling you everything I knew about Slider."

He nodded. "I understand the reason why." He brushed a long finger over her cheek, gazed deep into her eyes. "Don't lie to me again."

"I won't."

He leaned toward her and grazed her soft, lush mouth with his. An erotic moan escaped her lips and he deepened the kiss. His tongue swept over hers, engaging her fully. The heat that flared inside him seared his groin. She sparked his passion so quickly, so easily, it almost alarmed him. But he knew he wasn't in this hot affair alone. She felt the intensity of their connection as deeply as he did, of that he was certain.

She broke the kiss and whispered, "Come upstairs and make love to me."

"Repeatedly," Dean said, wanting her even more tonight than he had the first several times he'd made love to her.

He climbed out of the car, then came round to her side. When she stood beside him, he gave her another long, slow kiss. Eventually, she eased out of his arms to head into her apartment. But something caught her eye and her attention shifted from Dean to some activity across the street.

"That's him," she said on a sharp breath.

"Him who?" Dean's brain was a bit foggy from her kiss. He shook his head as though that would help to clear it. Realization dawned. "Slider?"

"Yes. That's him across the street, under the tree."

Light from a nearby lamppost illuminated the area that held her attention. Leaning against the trunk of a tall elm, a cigarette dangling from his lips, was the blond-haired thief Dean had been chasing since Saturday.

"Go inside, sweetheart. Stay put until I come back, understand?"

She nodded. Dean moved around the front of the car and then sprinted across the street, dodging light traffic. Slider tossed his cigarette and took off, a move Dean had anticipated. He followed the thief down the narrow sidewalk then down a dark alley. Slider scrambled up a six-foot chain link fence, and Dean followed him. He dropped to the ground just seconds after Slider and hit a dead run. Closing in on the thief, he almost had him in his grasp. But then a delivery truck rounded the corner, and Dean had to jump out of the way, thereby losing his advantage.

He let out a low curse, but remained in hot pursuit. Dean took the tall steps of an apartment building two at a time and lunged forward, landing on the hard concrete. He was able to wedge his forearm in the doorway before the heavy door closed. He winced in pain, but quickly got to his feet, threw the door open and charged inside. Spotting movement on the metal stairwell, Dean raced up the three flights and down the hallway just as a door at the end of the corridor slammed shut.

Without a second thought, Dean's booted foot connected with the weak wooden door and it flew open.

"What the *hell*?" Slider demanded in a ragged tone. He stood in the back of the small apartment, by a partially open window, trying to draw in a full breath of air.

Dean was equally winded, but adrenaline pumped through his veins.

"This is breaking and entering!" Slider exclaimed.

"So call a cop." Dean planted his hands on his hips and pulled in some much-needed oxygen.

Wide-eyed and obviously alarmed, Slider demanded, "Who the hell are you?"

"I'm the brother of the woman whose wallet you stole on Friday night. I'm also the boyfriend of the woman whose club you trashed on Saturday night." Anger built inside him and he added, "And by the way, asshole, I'm also a private investigator."

Slider's jaw fell slack for a moment. He recovered quickly and said, "You can't prove I did any of those things."

"I'm not going to have to prove it. You're going to confess to the cops."

The thief let out a strangled laugh. "Yeah, right."

Dean narrowed his eyes at Slider, giving him a menacing look. He took several slow, measured steps forward—steps of a predator—nearly closing the gap between them. Dean could see the panic rise in the other man's eyes. His gaze scanned the immediate area, as though searching for a weapon. Dean wouldn't give him the chance to lunge for a knife or anything else.

As though realizing this, Slider caved a little. "I'm not the one you should be hassling. Jackson's the one who hired me. He wants information on Cassandra's business."

Dean's jaw clenched for a brief moment. "And what do *you* want with Cassandra?"

"I don't know what the hell you're talking about." But the flash of awareness in his hazel eyes told Dean that Slider knew exactly what he was getting at.

He crossed his arms over his broad chest, prepared to intimidate the hell out of Slider, if that was what it took to get him to talk.

Slider didn't stand much of a chance under Dean's hard, unwavering gaze. "Look, I don't want any trouble."

"Too late. Stealing her trade secrets was bad enough. Trashing her club has really pissed me off."

Slider's contrite disposition changed. His handsome face morphed into a mask of hard angles. Returning the menacing gaze, he said, "You don't even know her."

"And you do?" Instinct told Dean the direction in which this conversation was about to go. His stomach twisted in knots.

"She needs me. I understand her business and I can help her at the club."

"She doesn't want your help."

Slider's fists clenched at his sides. "Everything was fine until you came along."

Ah, shit. The kid was delusional. Hating this new turn of events, but knowing he had to discern Slider's intentions and the full extent of his fascination with Cassandra, he modified his approach a little.

Dropping his arms and assuming a less ominous stance, Dean said, "She's pretty hot, isn't she? Damn nice, too. I can see why you'd take an interest in her.

Hell, she got my blood boiling in record time."

"Don't talk about her like that," Slider said in a tight voice.

"Hey, I can see why you like her. She's got a great ass. Mile-long legs." He whistled under his breath.

Slider's agitation grew ever more apparent. "Shut up, man."

Dean knew he had the thief right where he wanted him. "If you want to help her, you'll tell the police everything they need to know."

"Bullshit. The best way for me to help her is to keep *you* away from her."

Dean wanted to tell the asshole in front of him that that was never going to happen. But said asshole, in a very unexpected move, practically dove out the window and landed on the fire escape. Dean crossed the room in three full strides, just in time to see Slider scurry down the ladder and drop to the sidewalk. Dean considered chasing after him, but it was too dark to see in which direction Slider had gone. He'd catch up with the delusional pervert soon enough, he had no doubt.

In the meantime, Dean had the perfect opportunity to better ascertain what Slider was up to. He started his search in the kitchen, rummaging through cupboards, drawers and the small pantry. He then moved into the living room/bedroom of the dinky studio. Settling himself in the rickety chair in front of a battered desk, Dean proceeded to search the drawers, looking for anything that would help him with this case.

His blood ran cold when he opened the bottom drawer. It was piled high with photos of Cassandra. Some had been taken recently with a Polaroid camera, others had been printed off the Internet.

Shit. Things had just gotten a whole lot worse for Trouble.

Chapter Ten

Cassandra was standing at the entrance of her apartment building when Dean climbed the steps. She rushed to the door and let him in. She threw her arms around him and held him tight, thankful he was okay. He returned the embrace for a few moments, then stepped away from her.

Taking her hand in his, he said, "Let's go upstairs."

Inside her apartment, Dean crossed to the kitchen in long, powerful strides. He pulled out two bottles of beer and popped the tops off. He handed her one before taking a long pull from his.

Cassandra's insides clenched. "Dean, you're scaring me."

He groaned. Dropping into a chair at her breakfast table, he reached out for her and pulled her into his lap. When she was settled comfortably, he asked, "Sweetheart, do you know anyone by the name of Jackson who'd want information about Rendezvous?"

Unfortunately, she did. "Bert Jackson owns a club in the theater district. Opened about a year ago. Very trendy, modern looking place, with a lot of bright lights. Definitely doesn't have the intimate feel we've captured at Rendezvous."

"He hired Slider."

Her eyes grew wide. "He said that?"

Dean nodded. "Among other things."

Cassandra studied him a moment. Suddenly, he eased her out of his lap and stood.

"Do you have a computer here? With Internet access?"

"In the guest bedroom. Why?"

He didn't answer her and was already stalking toward the hallway. Cassandra set her beer on the table and followed him. Dean waited impatiently as she booted up the computer and logged onto the Internet.

"Does Rendezvous have a web site?"

"Sure." She typed in the web address and smiled when her familiar site came up. "We attract a lot of new clients with this site. They can sign up online and search for potential matches."

Dean slid into the chair. He clicked on various links, pulling up photos of promotions at the club. "You're in a lot of these," he grumbled. "I've seen most of them."

She narrowed her eyes at him. "Where?"

Ignoring her question, he closed the site and opened up a search engine. He typed in her full name.

"You're *Googling* me? Why on earth…?"

A full page of links popped up and Cassandra gasped. She'd never entered her name in a search and was shocked by the amount of information there was on her and her family. She sat on the edge of the bed and gnawed her lower lip. Dean glanced at her over his shoulder.

"What is all of this?" The look he gave her was reminiscent of the one he'd given her at the club, when he'd found out she'd lied to him about Slider. He looked as though she'd betrayed him. Again.

Cassandra tried to make light of the situation. Waving a hand in the air in a dismissive manner, she said, "It's nothing. A past life."

Dean's attention returned to the screen. He clicked on a link and a magnified newspaper headline popped up.

"Violin Virtuoso and Wife Die in Prague."

Cassandra's insides seized up. The breath escaped her. This was a part of her life she'd tucked away many, many years ago. And she wasn't inclined to take a walk down memory lane. It was much too painful.

But Dean wasn't about to let this go. He turned in the chair, fixed her with a serious look. "What happened?"

Cassandra swallowed down a lump of emotion. She shook her head, knowing she couldn't possibly talk about this. She never did. Her past was dead and buried and she refused to relive it.

But damn it. Dean looked at her with such concern and empathy. *And the need to know.* The need for her to open up to him, to be honest with him. To share her past pains with him.

She felt him reaching out to her, felt herself retreating. She didn't want to talk about this, didn't want to remember…

Teardrops began to build in her eyes, but she fought them back. Drawing in a full, steadying breath, she simply said, "My parents died in a car crash when I was thirteen."

She hoped that was all she needed to divulge, but Dean's gaze remained on her, urging her to tell him more.

Urging her to let him in.

Cassandra didn't let people in. Not this far.

She'd had the perfect life growing up. Loving, doting parents who adored her *and* each other. A budding career that took her all over the world. The chance to touch people's souls with the beautiful gift God had given her.

She'd had everything she'd ever wanted.

But in one horrific evening, she'd lost everything.

How could she possibly explain this to Dean, especially when she could barely stand to think about it herself?

But something in Dean's silvery gaze made her fear that if she didn't share this part of her life with him, she'd lose him. Dean Hewitt was not the type of man to stand on the outside looking in. If they were going to build something together, she had to open her heart to him.

It was an incredibly painful thing to do, and she wasn't entirely sure she could accomplish it. Or come out of this emotionally unscathed. But the alternative—pushing Dean away—was even more difficult to bear. So she told him as much as she could without breaking down.

"My father was a famous concert violinist. I was his child prodigy. We toured together from the time I was old enough to play."

She couldn't stop the flood of memories even if she tried. "My mother would sit in the front row at every concert and watch us. She'd close her eyes while she listened and smile sweetly, as though she'd never heard anything quite so beautiful." The fat teardrops crested the rims of her eyes. Her parents had been so proud of her, so in awe of her talent. And Cassandra had loved them deeply.

She brushed a hand over the stream flowing down one cheek. She hadn't thought about her past in so long. She'd left it far, far behind her. It was heart-wrenching to suddenly recall it.

"They went out to dinner after a concert in Prague. It was their anniversary, so I stayed in the suite. You know, to give them some time alone. A tour bus hit them on the way back to the hotel. They both died instantly."

"Sweetheart, I'm so sorry," Dean said in a soft tone that tugged at her heart.

She nodded her head, no longer trusting her voice. Nor did she trust herself to continue to divulge such personal—such *painful*—information. Devastated didn't even begin to describe how Cassandra had felt following her parents' deaths. A huge part of her heart and soul had died with them. Were it not for the unwavering support and love of Josh and her Uncle Kent, Cassandra didn't know how she would have survived the ordeal.

Dean slipped out of the chair and sat next to her on the bed. He put a strong arm around her shoulders. "I didn't mean to evoke bad memories, Cassandra. I just needed to know where Slider got all the photos of you."

Her eyes grew wide, her mind shifting gears. "What are you talking about?"

Dean let out a low sigh and raked his hand through his thick hair. "He's got a drawer full of them."

Cassandra couldn't make heads or tails of this revelation, but that did not diminish the sinking feeling in the pit of her stomach. "What does he want with me?"

Dean stood and began to pace, which worried Cassandra all the more. Finally, he stopped and faced her. "I think he's stalking you."

"What?" She actually laughed, despite the potentially dangerous situation she could suddenly be in. "That's absurd."

"Yeah, that's exactly what the majority of the other one-and-a-half million stalking victims in this country thought. By the way, that's an annual figure."

She blanched. "Oh, God. You have statistics."

"Plenty of them. I saw a couple of cases when I was on the police force. None of them ended well."

Her stomach took a violent tumble. "I think I need that beer now." She shot passed him and headed straight to the kitchen. She guzzled her beer, sucking down half of it. Returning the bottle to the table, she turned to face Dean, who had followed her. "This doesn't make any sense to me."

"I know, sweetheart," he said as he gripped her upper arms in his strong hands, as though to help steady her. "But I think our thief has convinced himself the two of you belong together. Now," he said as he released her, apparently satisfied she could stand on her own without her knees buckling beneath her, "there are several classifications for stalkers. I think Slider falls into the delusional and vengeful categories. He's deluded himself into thinking he's an asset to you and Rendezvous. Likely, he's mistaken your benevolence for interest."

"Where does the vengeful part come in?" she asked, latching onto that little tidbit, unable to let it go.

Dean gave a noncommittal shrug. "My guess is that he saw us leave the club together Saturday night, and it set him off. He likely broke into your club just to steal your promotions book, but then his anger got the best of him. In my professional opinion, I'd say he wanted to get back at you for cheating on him."

"Cheating on him!" Her knees really were going to buckle. "Dean, that's ludicrous! It's downright... insane!"

Dean scratched his jaw, nodded his head. "Yeah, it could be. Slider could have a little brain malfunction. Who knows? Maybe he's bipolar. That would explain how he could go from suave and mild-mannered to delusional and vengeful."

"I think I'm gonna be sick," she muttered as she sank into a chair.

Dean knelt before her, clasped her hands in his. "Baby, don't let this freak you out too much. Slider's not getting anywhere near you. I won't let him."

She swallowed down a hard lump. "You can't protect me 24/7, Dean. You have a life... a family... a business to run."

"I can manage. I want you to come stay with me. I'd feel a hell of a lot better knowing you were out of his line of vision and someplace where I could keep you safe."

Anxiety welled inside her. "No, that's not possible," she said on a sharp breath. "Please don't ask this of me." She stood and did some pacing of her own.

Being confined, watched... *guarded*... was not something Cassandra handled well. She'd had too much of it as a teenager, under the protective and oppressive thumb of her grandfather following her parents' deaths. She'd lived a year in his house in London, virtually held captive. She'd barely escaped with her sanity. She couldn't—*wouldn't*—give up her freedom or be forced into captivity.

Okay, so maybe she was being a little overdramatic. Still, the anxiety was real, and so was the need to maintain her freedom.

"Dean, I can't just pack a bag and move in with you."

"Why not?" His jaw was set in that stubborn, determined way that told her he wouldn't give up without a fight.

"I have a life. I have responsibilities." She could feel the panic building inside her, bubbling up in her throat. "I have fish, for God's sake."

His eyes narrowed. "*What*? Where?"

"There!" She pointed to one of the corner units by the front door.

Dean let out a sharp growl. "Christ, Cassandra. They're goldfish. And they're in a *bowl*. We can take them with us."

"No," she said, shaking her head. "They like that bookshelf. They feel safe there. In fact, I once tried to move them to the kitchen counter, and they completely freaked."

As she was currently doing. She planted her hands on her hips, tried to grasp some semblance of control. "I can't move in with you, no matter how temporary. I just… *I can't*."

His jaw clenched then fell slack as her words seemed to spark some concern deep inside him. "Ever?"

Anxiety seized her. Why were they even having this conversation? It was *way* too early in their relationship to discuss living arrangements. Way, way too early.

"I'm just… I'm not *comfortable* with this, Dean." She tried to brush past him, but his hand clasped her upper arm and held her in place.

"Answer my question."

She could feel the tears sting her eyes once again. "I can't. You're pushing me too hard. Too fast." She turned to look at him, wanting him to know that she was very interested in pursuing an exclusive romance with him. But she wasn't at all capable of letting him take over her life.

Dean's eyes searched hers, looking for something that would salvage the moment. She knew there was only one way to convince him that she wanted to be with him. That she still needed him, despite her inability to fully let him in.

She took his hand in hers and pulled him toward the bedroom. As soon as they crossed the threshold, he hauled her up against him and kissed her. It was a demanding, possessive kiss. As though he needed to establish his claim on her as much as she needed to reconnect with him. It wasn't necessary. She didn't belong to anyone else, didn't intend to. But Dean obviously needed the reassurance.

Chapter Eleven

He knew he was being forceful. It was his nature. Dean was always in control, always relied on his gut instincts, and always held fast to his convictions.

These traits had saved his life on more than one occasion. Yet at the same time, they had the ability to be the bane of his existence. With his family, for instance. His need to pursue his own path had created a rift between him and his father that he still struggled to bridge. It had put the fear of God in his mother, knowing he was out on the streets in dangerous situations, risking his life. And with Cat… well, it had likely caused her to miss out on potentially good relationships because Dean had the uncanny ability to intimidate the hell out of any guy who got too close to her.

His need to help people—and particularly his need to protect people he cared about—had guided his actions his entire life. And though his work was rewarding and Dean truly did feel like he was making a small contribution to society, he could not deny the strife it created in his personal life.

Even now, with Cassandra, his need to protect her was driving a wedge between them. She obviously had a lot of painful memories tucked away. He wanted to know what haunted her. Hell, he wanted to help ease the pain if he could. But she had a lot of issues, and he didn't know her well enough yet to know how to deal with them.

She clearly didn't like authoritarians or high-handedness. She was independent and wanted to retain control over her life. He could certainly understand and respect that. Dean didn't want to squash her free spirit or keep her under lock and key. He just wanted to help her. And yes, he had the overwhelming desire and need to keep her safe.

Damn it. Just like with Cat, his overbearing nature was getting the best of him. He had to take a step back. Cassandra realized it too. And the fact that she'd dragged him into her bedroom—okay, yeah, he'd gone willingly—confirmed that she needed to find that happy medium as much as he did.

To prove he could back down a notch or two on the heavy-handed, domineering scale, he loosened his grip on her and instead of kissing her so possessively, altered his approach, turning the kiss into a slow, sensual one. His hands explored her body with familiarity and intimacy, but also in such a way that he hoped conveyed his intentions to turn over a new leaf.

He could hold her close without suffocating her or making her feel trapped and out of control. He could do this, he assured himself.

He *had* to do this. Or risk losing her.

That thought was unbearable. It didn't matter that he'd known her for only a short period of time. He did *know* her. In the most intimate, binding ways. The rest would come with time. But knowing the innate connection they shared, the bone-deep desire they had for one another, was all he needed to assure himself that Cassandra Kensington was the woman for him.

Now, if he could just keep his shit together and not blow it with her...

He slid his hands under her sweater and reveled in the feeling of her velvety-soft skin against his palms. She melded to him, responding to his touch. He broke their kiss long enough to divest her of the sweater and the lacy bra she wore. Her breasts filled his hands, and he dipped his head to lave a tight nipple with his tongue. She sighed into his hair as her fingers twined in the thick mass.

He would love her slowly tonight. Show her he was capable of taking a step back. Not pushing too hard, too fast as he'd done earlier.

He guided her to the bed and eased her down onto the mattress. His hands slid over her body. His mouth left feathery kisses on her quivering stomach. Unfastening her jeans, he worked the denim down her long legs, pausing only to remove her boots and socks. Her thong panties followed, and Dean took a moment to admire her lush, naked body.

His eyes drifted up to her beautiful face and his breath caught. She smiled softly at him, as though she knew his internal demons, knew the vow he'd silently made to not stifle her. *She knew.* Because she knew him on that visceral, mystical level that he couldn't explain, but which defined their innate connection.

"My God," he whispered. "You are so beautiful."

Her smile deepened. She reached for him and he settled between her parted legs. Her fingers caressed his temple, his cheek. She drew the pad of a long finger over his jaw.

"Not so hard-set anymore," she mused.

Dean grinned at her. "I may be a little thick-skulled, but eventually I catch on."

Relief flashed in her vibrant blue eyes. "Thank you."

He dipped his head, kissed her softly. She moaned low and sensual, making his already hard cock ache for her. It was more than that really. It wasn't just his body that ached for her. It was his heart. His soul. His very being.

He kissed her deeply, hoping to convey his desire as well as the breadth of emotion she evoked. Dean had never felt so entranced, so captivated by a woman. Nor had he ever felt the curious swell of his heart, the nearly breath-stealing sensation that came with the realization that he'd found his other half. The woman who would complete him.

His mouth left hers and traveled down her body, exploring the exposed skin. Moving lower still until his tongue slid over that ultra-sensitive, slick-with-desire spot. She moaned again, and this one held a near-desperate tinge to it.

Her desperation mirrored his own. But he wouldn't rush this. He would give her what she needed, everything she desired. But he would do it slowly and lovingly. He would take her someplace beautiful and ethereal, and when she came, his name falling from her lips, he would find the internal peace he sought.

Cassandra wasn't sure how the cosmic shift had come about, but somehow, the stars and the moon and the entire universe were now perfectly aligned. It was almost as though Dean had tapped into her soul and found the source of her consternation. He'd used that knowledge to find this perfect balance. And she loved him all the more for it.

As his mouth covered her most intimate area, his tongue teasing her swollen clit, his fingers easing deep inside her, caressing her, stroking her, taking her to dizzying heights, she knew she loved him. And in knowing, she was able to let loose of her own demons just a bit. The pain she held so close lessened a small degree as Dean slowly loved her.

There was nothing impatient or urgent or demanding about the way he touched her. Nothing that made her feel out of control of her own destiny. He pushed her closer and closer to the edge but in such a languid, sensual way, it made the sensations building inside her all the more erotic, all the more consuming. Raw passion collided with tender desire, and Cassandra felt herself surrender, just a tiny bit, to Dean.

He evoked emotions in her she'd never known existed. And he took her places she'd never gone before. The pressure building so slowly, so erotically inside her was delicious and warm and breathtaking. Her fingers twined in his thick hair and she gave herself over to the pleasure he gave her, so freely, so selfishly. As his fingers stroked her wet pussy and his mouth caressed and teased her sensitive clit, she felt everything inside her converge and explode.

She cried out. Her hips lifted off the mattress. Her fingers tightened around the strands they held. She came hard and fast, a powerful orgasm that rocked her to the core of her being. Little bursts of light flashed behind her closed eyelids, and her entire being seemed to ignite in a fiery inferno of need and desire.

"Dean," she pleaded, her breath coming in heavy pants. "Oh, God. Please, please make love to me. Now."

She needed him inside her. She needed to share this intense, exquisite sensation with him. She desperately wanted to envelop his hard cock in her warm, wet depths, wanted to squeeze him tight, hold onto him for as long as possible.

She didn't even open her eyes. She heard the rustle of clothing and a moment later, he was buried deep, filling her completely, stretching her and pulsing inside her.

"Oh, yes," she whispered. "Perfect."

She held him to her as he moved slowly inside her, not thrusting or pumping or hammering into her. Just slowly pushing deeper into her, fulfilling her every want, her every desire.

They found a steady, sensual rhythm that pushed them both toward the precipice with such intensity, it felt all-consuming.

"Oh, yeah," Dean whispered in her ear. "Just like that, sweetheart."

It felt so good. So right. This was the perfect place for her. Cassandra had found a new utopia that she could call her own. And this time, it wouldn't be taken from her. Nothing would mar this perfect moment, this perfect memory. She would hold it in her heart for the rest of her days, remembering the exquisite feeling, the love she felt for this man.

For this moment, all was right with the world. And Cassandra found her own internal peace.

Chapter Twelve

In the middle of the night, she reached for him. Her fingers tangled in the still-warm sheets and she let out a soft sigh as the memory of Dean and his amazing lovemaking flitted through her groggy mind. She pulled the sheet toward her, inhaled deeply. Reveling in the masculine scent that was his alone, she smiled and almost drifted back to sleep.

But then realization dawned on her and she opened her eyes. Dean was not in bed with her.

Cassandra sat up. Her attention was immediately drawn to the only source of light in the room. Dean stood at the window, with the curtain pulled partially back. She slid out of bed and eased behind him, wrapping her arms around his waist. Her cheek rested on his bare shoulder blade and she hugged him tightly.

He dropped the curtain back into place. "Didn't mean to wake you," he said in a low, hoarse voice.

"I missed your body in my bed."

He chuckled. His large hands covered hers. "You were sleeping so soundly. Otherwise, I would have woken you and made love to you again."

She smiled. "Next time, wake me."

His hands squeezed hers.

"What were you looking at?"

His muscles tightened. Curious about the vehement reaction, she worked her way out of the embrace and stepped around to face him. "Dean?"

She couldn't see him in the dark but she could tell his jaw was set in a hard line. She could *feel* it.

Dean drew in a breath, let it out slowly. "He's watching your apartment."

Cassandra's blood ran cold. "You *saw* him?"

"I saw the glow of his cigarette, under the same tree where he stood earlier."

"*Oh.*" That one word escaped her lips on a sharp breath. Her heart picked up a few extra beats. "Do you think this is the first time? Or do you think…?" She couldn't even bring herself to ask the question.

She didn't have to. "Yes. He's been watching you. Closely."

Fear gripped her like never before. To think this delusional, potentially dangerous person was a part of her life—someone she'd willingly let in. Worse, she'd unwittingly put other women's lives in danger by accepting Slider's help weeks ago. Maybe, she'd now put Dean's life in danger.

The thought sat so heavily in the pit of her stomach, it made her insides hurt. "Dean, what if…?"

His arms eased around her waist. "Shh. Don't worry about me."

That he'd known the direction in which her thoughts had gone was comforting. He knew her so well, and in such a short period of time.

"Yes, but—"

"Sweetheart, he's not going to hurt me," he said as his lips found hers and brushed over them. "And I'm going to do everything I can to keep him from hurting you."

She shuddered in his tight embrace. Suddenly, she felt foolish for her early protests. The man was trying to save her life, and she'd acted so petty and childish. Staying with Dean while this ordeal played out—and hopefully came to a successful and uneventful conclusion—wasn't exactly a hardship. What the hell had gotten into her earlier that she'd refused his help?

The need to tell him her fears, to explain her past, welled inside her. She eased out of his arms and said, "Dean, I'll do whatever you want me to. Whatever you think is best."

His fingers slid over her throat, up into her hair. His thumb grazed her jaw. "I don't want to smother you. You have to know that, Cassandra. One of the things about you that stirs my soul the most is your free spirit."

She nodded. Tears stung her eyes, but she kept them at bay. "I didn't mean to seem ungrateful earlier or to shun your help. It's just…" She swallowed hard, let out a sharp breath. Emotion welled inside her. "I had a hard time dealing with my parents' deaths, and when I went to live with my grandfather, after the funeral, things just really fell apart for me."

She pulled in a ragged breath. No longer able to hold back the tears, they flowed in a steady stream down her cheeks.

"Hey," Dean said on a soft whisper. "It's okay. You don't have to talk about this if you're not ready." He drew her close and kissed the top of her head.

His thumb continued to stroke her jaw and her cheek, bringing some measure of comfort to Cassandra, relieving some of the tightness in her chest.

"I just need to tell you… to explain." She fought back the need to let loose of this pain and give in to a really good, heart-wrenching cry. In his arms. But she didn't want to break down. She wanted to share this pain with him. Make him understand her need for independence and freedom.

"Two days after the funeral, my grandfather hired a violin instructor. He expected me to just pick right back up as though nothing had happened. He intended for me to continue touring, to continue playing concerts. I didn't want to disappoint him, but... I just... I couldn't play."

She shook her head, remembering how hard she'd tried to please her grandfather. She'd known his grief, it had mirrored her own. But what she hadn't known back then, what she'd come to realize just within the past couple of years, was that her grandfather had needed her to carry on in her father's stead. He had needed to hear the music as much as she had, had needed something to focus on so that his grief didn't consume him.

But Cassandra couldn't carry on. Her desire to make beautiful music had died with her parents. "No," she whispered, realizing it was more than that. "It wasn't that I didn't want to play. I did. It was all I'd ever wanted. But suddenly, I just... couldn't hear the music anymore."

She hadn't realized she'd voiced her thoughts until Dean's low, intimate voice filled the quiet room. "What do you mean?"

Unable to fully snap out of her reverie, she said, "God graced me with an incredible gift. The ability to make beautiful music. It was in my head from as far back as I can remember. I didn't need sheet music, I could just listen to a few bars of a waltz, pick up my violin and play it. With his meticulous French accent, my father would call me *ma petit miracle*. It means my little miracle. He thought I was the most gifted child he'd ever known, and he was just so..." She paused, drawing in an unsteady breath, "proud of me."

God, how she wanted to cry. Her heart ached. More so than it had in years. But she held it back. "My grandfather didn't understand the difficulty I had with continuing on, playing without my father. But it was more than that. I'd lost the ability to hear the music. It was like turning off a radio. One moment the music was there in my head, and the next, it was gone. Silence."

Dean moved away from her. A moment later, the soft glow from her bedside lamp filled the room. He sat on the edge of the bed and pushed a hand through his hair. "That alone must've been painful."

Cassandra nodded. "I wanted to please my grandfather, I just didn't have it in me. Things got worse. He hired tutors so I didn't have to go to school. Suddenly there was no reason for me to leave the house. He set strict rules and curfews. I felt... trapped. Imprisoned. And because I wasn't practicing, he grew agitated with me. Finally, about a year down the road, I'd had just about all I could take of being cooped up in his house for such long periods of time. I slipped out one afternoon to go to the mall. I didn't tell anyone where I'd gone or when I'd be back."

She recalled that day with vivid clarity. She'd felt so free! Losing track of time had been easy because she'd been so enraptured with the idea of being out without supervision, without someone ushering her back to the house.

She knew now that her grandfather had simply been afraid something tragic would happen to her, as it had her parents. He'd lost his beloved son and his daughter-in-law. He hadn't wanted to lose his granddaughter, too.

But his protectiveness was a bit misguided. So, too, was the way in which he'd dealt with his grief.

"When I finally went back home, my grandfather was beside himself. I'd never seen someone so angry. I realize now that he was scared and concerned about my disappearance, but it was like he completely lost touch with reality for a few minutes."

Cassandra considered the altercation. She absently wrung her hands as the memory of that fateful day flooded her mind. In a soft voice, she said, "He told me I didn't deserve the gift God had given me, that my father would be ashamed of me, that I was wasting my talent. And that seemed to spark an even bigger fit of rage. He went upstairs and I didn't think much about it. Until he came down with my father's violin. I just couldn't comprehend his intentions; or else maybe I could have done something to stop him. I don't know. I just sort of stood in the living room, frozen, not at all grasping what was happening."

But eventually, realization had dawned. Cassandra could almost feel the bone-chilling sensation that had crept up on her that day. "I finally knew something was wrong. I ran out to the garage just as my grandfather backed over the violin with his car. He crushed it. Reduced it to tiny splinters." In a very small, breathless voice, she said, "That beautiful instrument was gone in a heartbeat."

Like my parents.

She shook her head, swiped at the tears that wouldn't stop. "It was the one thing that made me feel close to my father. And suddenly, it was gone. My grandfather said I didn't deserve it. And maybe, in some ways, he was right. But still..."

Cassandra's fingers trembled as she pressed them to her quivering lips. What a sad day that had been. She'd felt an overwhelming loss that still lingered today. In fact, it made the destruction of her club all the more unbearable. "I just couldn't understand how someone could destroy something so beautiful."

Dean's head snapped up. He eyed her curiously. "That's exactly what you said at Rendezvous."

She nodded. "My Uncle Kent, the one who made the pool tables and the bar, also made my father's violin. He spent two years as an apprentice with a violinmaker. The process is complicated and time-consuming. It's not like making furniture," she said, a hint of awe creeping into her voice. "The design is infinitely more intricate because you have to capture the correct level of vibration. And the delicate curve of the C-ribs is a critical component to crafting an instrument." A sad sigh escaped her lips. "That violin was the most beautiful one I'd ever seen... destined to be a classic."

Cassandra had loved to watch her father play that gorgeous instrument, and she'd always considered it a special treat when he'd let her play it.

"Just like my father, Kent's hands were made to create beauty."

"Sounds like yours were, too."

"For a while."

Dean studied her closely. "Do you miss it?"

"No." She didn't even have to think about her answer. She'd asked herself the same question enough times over the years to know it. "My passion for playing died with my parents."

Dean moved close to her, wrapped his arms around her. She thought she would finally give into the need to cry, but that need had passed. Wrapped in Dean's warm and loving embrace, Cassandra felt stronger.

Endless minutes ticked by and she finally smiled. The past was the past. There was no changing it, no reconciling it. The fact that Dean held her so closely, waiting patiently for the memories to recede and the present to prevail, warmed her heart.

She glanced up at him, letting him see the smile on her face. "Thank you," she said in a soft voice.

His grin was slow and sexy. "Nothing to thank me for. If anything, I ought to be thanking you. For letting me in."

Her mouth quivered, but she was able to keep a new batch of tears from spilling. She *had* let him in. A monumental feat in her book.

She hoped he would stay.

Snuggling a bit closer to him, she asked, "So what haunts you, Detective Dean?"

He let out a soft chuckle. "The list is short but fraught with family strife."

"Ah. I'm sure I can guess one of the problems."

"I'm sure you can."

"Cat came to Rendezvous to find a match, Dean." She lifted her head, looked deep into his beautiful silver eyes. "It's what she wants. Someone she can connect with. Someone who will spark her desire and engage her heart. To deny her that…"

He let out a low groan. "I know. It's just… Christ. She's my kid sister. She's only twenty-five."

Cassandra laughed. "I'm only twenty-six."

"Yes, but you're different. More worldly and sophisticated. Cat is still naïve about so many things. I just don't want her to get hurt."

"You can't protect her forever. In fact, you have to let her make some mistakes on her own, Dean. She's a big girl, she can handle it. If you try to keep her under lock and key…"

"I know."

Cassandra could hear the resignation in his voice, mixed with uncertainty. It made her love him all the more that he was so concerned about his sister's wellbeing. He was kind and compassionate, and he wanted to take care of the people he loved.

She knew she was fortunate to be included on that distinguished list. She had a feeling Dean did not give his love easily, and knowing his emotions ran deep for her made their relationship all the more meaningful to him. And to her.

She wouldn't let him feel at a loss when it came to her safety. She would do what he asked of her, let him protect her. He had already bestowed some very precious gifts on her... she would return the favor.

Chapter Thirteen

Turns out, captivity was a great place to be.

Cassandra settled into the comfy, worn leather sofa in Dean's living room as she perused another furniture catalog. She'd yet to find replacements for her bistro tables, barstools and glasses, but she had high hopes. After all, the rest of the club was coming along nicely. It had only been three weeks since the break-in, yet she and her friends and family had made excellent progress. The debris had been whisked away, the sofas and chairs had been sent to an upholsterer for refinishing, and Cassandra had located coffee and end tables, plus some very elegant lamps and sconces to replace the broken ones.

She still needed the painter to finish the walls, but all in all, things were moving along at a better clip than she'd anticipated.

Spending most of her days and all of her evenings at Dean's wasn't quite the prison she'd envisioned. Though he preferred she stay in while Slider was still on the loose—the slippery little sucker had disappeared without a trace—Cassandra didn't mind.

Dean had a gourmet kitchen that he let her have full run of. His twenty-CD, high-def stereo was a bit too complex for her to manage, so he'd loaded it up with some mutual favorites and left it running for her. He was currently whistling along to a sexy Gato Barbieri tune as he searched for his missing boot, which had been quickly discarded when he'd come through the door last night.

Ah… nights with Dean Hewitt were infinitely more erotic than anything she'd ever imagined. Their lovemaking just got more creative and sensual and seductive as time went on.

Fact was, Cassandra was perfectly at home in Dean's apartment. Even her fish had settled in, after a mild protest of frantic swimming and maybe a half-day of fasting.

The phone rang and Cassandra was distracted from her furniture search as Dean's deep, sensuous voice filled the room. God, she could listen to him talk all day. He didn't even have to say anything of importance, although when he talked dirty to her, it really set her pulse racing.

And lord, did the man know how to talk dirty! Cassandra let out a wistful sigh as she wondered how long he'd be on the phone. She contemplated moving her reading material into the bedroom, stripping down and waiting for him to join her. But when he told whoever was on the other end of the line that "they" would be "there" shortly, she dropped her catalog on the coffee table and cast a quizzical look his way.

Dean disconnected the call, located his black leather boot in the front entry-way and slipped it on. "Shoes, babe."

She eyed him curiously. "Where are we going?"

"Rendezvous."

Cassandra gnawed her lower lip. She hadn't been there in two weeks. Admittedly, as much as she wanted to reopen, she was also dreading it. The club would never be the same. She wouldn't be able to recapture the elegance and the intimate feel because it had been desecrated.

Dean reached a hand out to her. "Trust me."

She glanced up at him, taken aback. "I do. Of course, I do. It's just…"

"Trust me," he repeated.

Cassandra let him pull her off the sofa. She slipped on her shoes and followed him out the door.

When they arrived at Rendezvous, her stomach clenched. This place meant so much to her. Helping the singletons hook up meant so much to her. But it would never be the same.

As she and Dean ascended the spiral stairs, she felt less than enthusiastic about returning. Sure, she'd worked frantically to put the place back together. But she'd done it from Dean's apartment. Josh and Dean had been her "on the ground" people. She'd handled the furniture repairs herself, but Josh had supervised the clean-up crew. McCarthy had continued to work matches, and Dean had created an entire security plan that actually looked inconspicuous. Once implemented, her clients would be hard-pressed to see the surveillance cameras. They wouldn't feel as though they were walking into a heavily monitored club. Cassandra would assure her members that the club had beefed up security, but it wouldn't be so conspicuous as to make them feel uncomfortable or overwhelmed.

When they reached the door to Rendezvous, Cassandra paused. Memories of stepping inside to find her club trashed assaulted her mind. She felt at odds, standing on the threshold of a place she'd considered home, but which now held bad memories.

Damn it.

Dean squeezed her hand, gave her a sexy smile. "Come on."

He pushed open one of the metal doors and she followed him in. Cassandra drew up short and let out a soft gasp of surprise.

"Oh!" She couldn't believe her eyes. The club, though certainly not completely put together, was further along than she'd ever imagined. The repaired sofas and chairs had been returned to their original places, a week early. The walls had received a fresh coat of paint. The hardwood floor had been buffed to a glossy finish.

All of the damaged furniture had been replaced. The coffee and end tables. The bistro tables and barstools. They were magnificent, all intricately crafted like the pool tables her uncle had made for her.

And speaking of… Kent and Josh stood toward the back of the club, gauging her reaction. She rushed in their direction and threw her arms around her uncle. "You did all of this!"

He gave her a tight squeeze, then released her. "I had a lot of help. I owe favors all over town now." But he looked damn happy to have been able to help her.

She turned to Josh. "The place looks great."

"I really didn't do that much. Just made a few calls, let a few people in."

She kissed his cheek. "You're the best."

She hugged McCarthy and thanked her as well. McCarthy whispered in her ear, "Actually, Dean did a lot of the heavy lifting."

She glanced at him over her shoulder. He shrugged noncommittally.

"I love it," she said. "It's perfect. I can't thank you all enough." A thought occurred to her and she said, "We're a few days early. We could have our re-opening this week."

The look that crossed Dean's face made her falter. Her stomach instantly twisted in knots. "Dean?"

He shook his head. "I don't think that's such a good idea, sweetheart."

"Not with Slider still on the loose," her uncle added.

She glanced from one man to the other, sensing there was something they knew that they weren't telling her. "Spill."

Dean raked a hand through his hair. "We have a new lead on Slider."

She stood a little taller, ignoring the sudden tremble in her legs. "Oh?"

"Sweetheart," Kent said, "He could be planning something."

Her gaze shifted back to Dean. She crooked an eyebrow, awaiting an explanation.

Dean seemed disinclined to give one, but did so anyway. "He recently purchased a substantial amount of camping gear. And," Dean said, shaking his head and letting out a short puff of air, "he mentioned to the sales clerk that he was planning a long, secluded getaway with his girlfriend."

"He means you, sweetheart."

She eyed her uncle. Her stomach turned. "You can't be serious."

Kent nodded. Her gaze shifted back to Dean. He looked pretty damn dismal, enough to convince her they were deeply concerned about her wellbeing.

"So what does this mean?"

Dean rubbed the back of his neck. "Just that you still need to lay low for a while. Until we can nail him."

She knew the police were involved. But the fact that Slider eluded them…

eluded *Dean*... made her nervous as hell. Obviously he knew he was a wanted man. He was hiding out somewhere and though Cassandra felt supremely confident that Dean would track him down, she hated this waiting game.

But she'd promised to do as he asked, and she wouldn't sacrifice his peace of mind for anything. "Okay. I still have some work to do. Glasses to find and whatnot. I don't have to reopen just yet. But..." She spared a quick glance at McCarthy before she cast a compelling look on Dean. "Much longer and I don't know if I'll even have a business to reopen."

He nodded in understanding. "We're doing our best, baby. And this new lead is a good one. It means he's finally come out of hiding. We'll track him down."

She knew he would. She gave him a hug and thanked him for his efforts, for wanting so desperately to keep her safe. She pulled away and said, "Since we're all here, why don't we at least celebrate our accomplishment? Drinks are on the house!"

"They damn well better be." Josh smirked.

Cassandra linked her arm with his and stared up at him, batting her long lashes. "Will you make martinis, Josh?"

"Oh, Christ," he grumbled. But she knew he recognized her request as a compliment to his skill as a bartender, and that no doubt boosted his ego.

As she slid onto a barstool next to Dean, she was warmed by the presence of her family.

Chapter Fourteen

"This is a true needle-in-a-haystack situation, partner."

Eddie Wilson eased his large frame into the chair across from Dean, who was studying a map spread out before him. They were actually *former* partners, but Wilson never made that distinction. They'd been close when Dean was on the force and still remained tight friends.

"Christ. Did you know New York had so many camping sites?"

Dean groaned. "Unfortunately, no." He tapped the capped turquoise-colored highlighter on the map he'd laid out on Wilson's desk. He'd marked all the campsites within a hundred-mile radius of Manhattan. Problem was, there weren't enough resources or manpower to cover all the territory he'd noted as potential hiding places for Slider. Particularly if they wanted to find him soon.

"Damn it," Dean muttered under his breath. "This guy could be anywhere."

Wilson's phone rang. After listening to whoever was on the other line, he covered the mouthpiece with his hand and said, "Sorry, partner. I've got to take this call. Carjacking near Central Park."

Dean shook his head. "It's never-ending in this city." He went back to studying the map, hoping a brilliant strategy would strike him. When none was forthcoming, he pulled out his cell phone and called the clerk Slider had purchased all the camping gear from.

Ten minutes later, Dean didn't really think he had any new information, except that he now felt pretty certain that the stuff Slider had bought indicated he was hiding out in a cabin or travel trailer, rather than living out of a tent. That narrowed the options a bit. Dean could rule out all the campsites that didn't offer hook-ups. Still… that left several dozen potential areas that were developed, and an infinite number that weren't.

Christ. This really was a needle-in-a-haystack situation.

He leaned back in his chair, contemplating the current predicament. As much as he'd hated leaving Cassandra, she'd insisted she needed to put the finishing touches on the club and plan for the reopening party so it could be thrown at a moment's notice. Josh was with her, so Dean had agreed to let her stay while he came to the police station.

He wasn't particularly pleased with himself for caving. He should have brought her with him. But she'd given him that look, like he was suffocating her again, and he'd conceded. He couldn't help it, really. He would do anything to make her happy.

He'd also do anything to keep her safe.

He flipped open his cell phone and called Cassandra. He told her he'd wrap up his work with Eddie in a few minutes and then he'd pick her up for dinner.

"Cass, you are not going to *believe* what I just found!" McCarthy said excitedly.

Cassandra cradled the cordless phone between her ear and her shoulder as she unwrapped the new red-tinted votive holders from their Fed Ex packaging. "Do tell."

"I'm in the Village, and I was talking to one of the shop owners about some of the glasses he carries. I mentioned the ones you'd purchased in Tuscany, and he actually has a source there who sells an almost identical style."

As much as she wanted to, Cassandra didn't get her hopes up. Over the past few weeks, she'd had the same conversation with other vendors. Problem was, she needed a vast quantity and she needed them carefully packaged so she didn't lose half the shipment on the trip over to the States. The vendors she'd talked with earlier couldn't promise her either. "Did you tell him how many we need?"

"Yep. He's got four dozen on hand and can deliver another six dozen by the middle of next week."

Cassandra set aside her votives. "You're shitting me."

"Nope!"

McCarthy was clearly beside herself with excitement, a good sign. She knew Cassandra's discernible taste, knew exactly what she was looking for. If McCarthy was excited, Cassandra knew she should be, too.

"You have to come see them," McCarthy said.

"Dean just called. He's on his way over from the police station. As soon as he gets here, I'll have him drive me over."

She jotted down the name of the shop and the address. As she disconnected the call, Josh came upstairs, carting a long, narrow box with him.

"What have you got there?"

He wagged his blonde eyebrows. "The good stuff. Pool cues, I suspect. Special delivery."

She followed him over to the pool tables. He set the package on one and used the box cutter she supplied to open up the parcel. Cassandra clasped her hands together. "Wonderful!"

As Josh pulled out the cues and carefully placed them in the racks her uncle had crafted, he said, "You know, I'm really proud of you, Cass."

She eyed him as she inspected a stick, rolling it over the red-felt top of the pool table to check its balance. "What for?"

"For letting everyone help you."

Ah, that. She propped a hip against the edge of the table. "I'm not *that* bad."

He crooked an eyebrow at her before reaching for another stick.

"Okay, maybe I am. *Was.* Actually, I think I've made a lot of progress lately. I like being part of a team."

"That's another thing," he said as he racked two more sticks. "You're pretty serious about Dean, aren't you?"

She nodded. It didn't faze her to discuss her personal life with Josh. After the debacle with her grandfather, she'd moved to New York to live with her uncle and cousin. Her aunt had died when she and Josh were toddlers, so she'd become the female presence in the family.

She contemplated his question, then gave him an honest answer. "I'm crazy about him."

Josh grinned at her. "Good for you."

She tested another stick before handing it to him. "So what about you?"

"What about me?"

"Well, you're not getting any younger, you know."

"Yeah. Twenty-seven is *so* old, Cass. What's your point?"

"My point is, you could use a nice girl in your life. Someone to go home to at the end of the day. Have a romantic dinner with, make love to. You know. Break up the monotony of club life."

"First, club life is not monotonous to me. Second, what the hell would *I* do with a nice girl? I don't date nice girls, Cass. I date women. Preferably ones who don't mind their hair getting messed up when they ride on the back of my Harley. Women who order *real* martinis, not the frou-frou girly kind. Women who understand how sublime the symphonic range of a classic Les Paul guitar can be."

"Christ. No wonder you're still single."

His grin returned. "I like my life, Cass. It may not be for everyone, but it works for me. I'm married to The Rage. It wouldn't be fair to turn it into a love triangle with a woman."

"Yeah, well. You can't go on like this forever."

"Hey," he said in a jesting tone, "stick to hooking up your singletons and leave me alone."

"Okay, okay." She held her hands up in the air. "Fine. But don't come crying to me when you're past your prime and can no longer score a hot date."

His grin widened. "I've got a lot of good years left in me, cuz."

She didn't doubt that. Josh was extremely handsome, in that really sexy, bad boy way. But would he ever settle down? Find what she'd found? More than a bedmate, a soul mate?

Speaking of… she gave Josh a quick peck on the cheek and told him she had to meet Dean downstairs.

She unlocked the entrance doors and slipped out when she saw Dean's car pull up to the curb. Unable to contain the smile that instantly graced her lips, she bounded across the sidewalk and slid into the passenger seat.

"McCarthy found glasses. Can you take me to—" Cassandra gasped and fear gripped her heart as she stared at the man next to her.

It wasn't Dean.

Dean finished up a couple more calls, then flipped his phone shut. He waited for Eddie to conclude his call. When his former partner turned back to him, Dean's gut took a tumble.

"I know that look."

Wilson's sharp-angled face was scrunched up in consternation. "Got some bad news, pal. The dispatcher put that call through to me because the carjacker matched the description of your perp."

"Shit," Dean growled. He shook his head, then said, "Well, at least we've got another lead. He's still in town and he's mobile."

"Yeah, well it gets worse," Wilson said as he hauled his six-foot-five-inch frame out of the chair. "The car Slider stole is identical to yours."

"*Son of a bitch!*" Dean shot out of his chair. He flipped open his phone as he stalked down the long corridor to the front entrance, Wilson close on his heels. He hit the speed dial number for Rendezvous. Five unanswered rings and he disconnected the call. He punched in the number for The Rage. No answer. Where the hell was everyone?

"I've got an ABP going out on the car. Slider won't get out of town."

Dean drew up short, a thought striking like lightning in his brain. "Maybe he doesn't intend to get out of town. He knows we're looking for him and surely he'll know the stolen car will tip us off." Dean let the thought form more fully in his mind, then said, "He stole the car around Central Park. There are plenty of service roads winding through heavily wooded areas in the park. Lots of unused outbuildings shrouded by trees and foliage."

"He could hide out there unnoticed for a while. Until he gets his plans to-gether."

Dean's stomach wrenched. That was likely where he planned to ensconce Cassandra.

Not if I have any say in the matter.

Dean knew he had to get to Cassandra first.

He called The Rage again. When Josh picked up, Dean demanded, "Where is she?"

"Dean? She ought to be with you. She left ten minutes ago."

"Damn it!" Dean growled, his heart constricting, a bad feeling settling deep in his gut.

"She said you were picking her up out front. She needed to go to the Village," Josh said in a hesitant tone, realization obviously dawning.

Dean made the final confirmation for him. "It wasn't me. The car she got into wasn't mine."

"Oh, shit. What the hell are we going to do?"

"You stay put. She may call there if she gets away." He disconnected the call.

"We'll take the cruiser," Wilson said as they exited the building.

Cassandra reached for the door handle but Slider had engaged the electronic locks. She reached for the one on her door, but he grabbed her arm and pulled her toward him.

"This is kidnapping," she said, hoping she really didn't sound as terrified as she thought she did. Or as terrified as she felt.

"Not really." He released her as he shifted into second and began to weave through traffic. "It's more like an intervention."

She eyed him closely, startled. "*What*?"

"Yeah. You can thank me later."

She let out a sharp, slightly strangled laugh. "Oh, my God. Are you on some kind of medication?"

Slider's head snapped around and he glared at her, wide-eyed, alarmed. "Who have you been talking to?"

Oh, shit. He truly was delusional… and obviously completely off his rocker. Cassandra reached for the door handle again but when Slider produced a gun from under his seat and pointed it at her, her hand fell away.

Her heart jumped into her throat as she stared at the barrel of the gun.

Be brave. Don't fall apart.

Do not fall apart.

"Okay, look. This is getting a little out of hand, don't you think?" Reasoning with him had to work. *It had to.* "Why don't you pull over, Slider? Then we'll discuss this whole thing."

"No. The only way I can help you is to get you away from him."

"Him?"

"I know what he's doing, Cassandra. He's trying to keep us apart. He's turned you against me."

Oh, God. Her blood ran cold as she suddenly understood exactly what was happening. Slider thought he was saving Cassandra from Dean. And maybe from herself.

Shit. How was she supposed to reason with him when he was a complete nut job?

Okay, think.

If he wanted to "protect" her, did that mean he'd actually shoot her if she tried to escape the car? She couldn't be sure, and she wasn't exactly inclined to find out. There had to be another way. As she contemplated her perilous predicament, Slider maneuvered the car through evening traffic. He made last-minute turns when street lights turned red, avoiding stopping or down-shifting. He didn't take his eyes off the road…or his finger off the trigger.

Did he really have bullets in that thing?

Christ. Calling his bluff was too damn dangerous.

He drove through the same neighborhood twice, making her wonder if he even knew where he was going. Did he have a specific plan in mind for this hideous *intervention*, or was he making it up as he went along? Had he anticipated she would get in the car—having tapped into her phone line? Or had he simply been waiting, hoping fate would deliver her to him?

Cassandra felt violently ill as all the questions swirled in her mind.

Goddamn it. Why did she have to be so impulsive and spontaneous? She hadn't spared a glance at the license plate or even poked her head in the car before she'd plopped down in the seat. She'd just assumed she'd find Dean sitting next to her.

How incredibly foolish.

Gnawing her lower lip, she wondered how Dean would ever find her.

As Slider pulled into the entrance of Central Park, it dawned on Cassandra that she was going to have to *help* Dean find her.

Slider drove through the park toward a thick patch of woods, and she recalled what Dean and her uncle had said about Slider purchasing large quantities of camping gear. He meant to keep her locked away somewhere, she was certain of it. And when he turned up a steep hill that led into the dense forest, she knew she had better do something. Fast.

They crested the hill and a small outbuilding came into view.

Oh, hell no! He couldn't keep her locked up in there!

Panic seized her insides. Her heartbeat thundered in her head.

Do something! Now!

When Slider set the gun in his lap so he could downshift, Cassandra hit the button to release the door lock and then yanked on the handle. She shoved open the door and tumbled out of the car, rolling several feet down the hill.

The car came to a screeching halt and she jumped to her feet. She sprinted through the woods, dodging branches and leaping over rocks and tree stumps.

She heard Slider's heavy footsteps behind her. He yelled at her, demanding she stop running, telling her she couldn't possibly get away. She ran faster. Thin tree limbs scraped her cheeks and forehead. Her feet slipped on the damp foliage that covered the ground. She tripped and slid down the hill, but quickly recovered near the bottom.

Scanning the immediate area, she got a good fix on the entrance of the park. There was no one around that she could see, no one who could help her.

But then the flash of red and blue lights caught her attention as several police cars rounded the corner of The Plaza Hotel, near the front of the park.

"Dean!" She cried out as she hit a dead run.

Her lungs burned and her legs shook, but Cassandra focused all of her energy on reaching the cops, knowing in her heart Dean was with them.

She sprinted across a paved roadway and cut through the park. She was so close! She waved her arm in the air, hoping someone would see her. She hurdled a small boulder, but landed unsteadily. Her ankle twisted and Cassandra cried out as she went down, hitting the ground hard.

Nothing would stop her from getting away from Slider, though. She scrambled to her feet, but before she could move, Slider toppled her. Cassandra's body pitched forward and her head slammed against a sharp rock. Light burst before her eyes and she let out a shrill cry of agony. Blood flowed down her temple and dripped into her eye. She tried to brush it away, but couldn't lift her arm. Her body went limp and blackness descended.

No! She screamed inside her mind. *No!*

But there was nothing more she could do. The darkness consumed her and Cassandra lost consciousness.

"Cassandra!" The car Dean was in came to a screeching halt and he was out of it and running toward Cassandra a second later. He'd seen her emerge from the woods. His heart had nearly leapt from his chest when he'd realized she'd gotten away from Slider. She'd raced toward him, waving her hand in the air. Dean had never felt so relieved in his life. But then he'd caught a glimpse of Slider and he'd watched, utterly helpless, as the other man lunged at Cassandra and took her down.

He towered over her now, pulling on her arm as though to get her to stand. But Cassandra didn't move.

Dean's heart sank and his insides seized up.

Shit. She was hurt.

His long, powerful legs took him across the grassy plain with speed and agility. Before Slider could react or counter the move, Dean tackled him. They hit the ground and Slider struggled beneath him, his fist connecting with Dean's jaw. The impact jarred him, and Slider used the opportunity to roll away.

Dean recovered quickly and grasped Slider's leg. They exchanged blows, but Dean wasn't letting the asshole get the best of him. In two swift wrestling-type moves, he had Slider on his stomach, sprawled facedown on the ground. A knee to the small of his back and a quick jerk of Slider's left arm behind him, and Dean had rendered his prey defenseless.

Eddie, who hadn't been far behind Dean, swooped in to cuff Slider.

Dean moved away and collapsed next to Cassandra. As carefully as he could, he pulled back the bloodied strands of blond hair from her face.

He winced at what he saw. The gash along her hairline looked serious. And she was unconscious.

Dean's heart sank.

Goddamn it.

Was he too late?

Chapter Sixteen

Cassandra's throbbing head felt like a soccer ball being kicked around by a bunch of rambunctious tots. With her eyes still closed, she lifted her hand and gingerly fingered the bandage that covered a large portion of her forehead and temple. She felt woozy and light-headed. Her throat fell raw and tight, as though she'd done some major screaming. Or hadn't had anything to drink in a week.

She cracked open an eye and assessed her surroundings. Hospital. How long had she been there?

Trying to swallow, but having limited moisture to work with, she closed her eye and prayed a nurse would arrive soon.

When she heard footsteps, Cassandra opened both eyes and tried to sit up in bed. She winced in pain, feeling as though a bolt of lightning had just pierced her brain.

"Oh, God," she mumbled in a tight, hoarse voice as she fell back against the stacked pillows, her eyes closing.

"Hey, hey. Just lay still."

The deep, familiar voice instantly soothed Cassandra's frayed nerves. Her eyelids fluttered open just as Dean carefully eased onto the edge of the bed. A finger lightly grazed her cheek, and she smiled weakly.

"What happened?" she asked, having only a vague recollection of the events following her initial escape from the car.

Dean swept his lips over her cheek and, in a tone laced with pride, he said, "You got away, sweetheart."

"No," she whispered. "I didn't. He had hold of my ankle. And then... I don't know what happened after that."

"You lost consciousness. But Cassandra, you did get away." He reached for one of her hands, gave it a gentle squeeze. "You got out of his car and out of the woods so I could find you. You did good, sweetheart."

A weak smile touched her lips as she recalled how happy she'd been to see the flashing lights on the cop cars. Knowing, just knowing, in her heart, that Dean was in one of them.

"You found me."

"Yeah, I did." He lifted her hand to his mouth, gently kissed her fingers, then brushed her knuckles over his lightly whiskered jaw. He returned her hand to the bed and gave her one last peck on the cheek. "Get some rest, sweetheart. We'll talk later."

Cassandra frowned. Something about the hard edge of his voice sent up warning signals in her head, but her brain was just too fuzzy to fully process its meaning.

She sighed as weariness consumed her, then slowly drifted off to sleep.

"You look like hell."

Dean eyed his younger sister and grimaced. "Thanks, kid. I really needed a second opinion on that."

Cat frowned. "Don't call me that. And don't be so damned grumpy. Everything's fine now. The cops got the bad guy and your girlfriend is going to be okay. Once again, you saved the day." She gave him a kiss on the cheek, ever the staunch supporter.

But Dean didn't feel the least bit optimistic. Kent, Josh and McCarthy were in with Cassandra, and the doctor had assured them all she was going to be just fine. Still…dread sat in his gut like a heavy rock.

He glanced across the hospital waiting room and watched as his parents held a private conference by the coffee machine. They'd arrived less than a half an hour after he'd called them. He'd told his father over the phone that he was okay, nothing to worry about. He hadn't wanted them to freak out if they heard the news on TV or if it leaked in some other fashion. Martin Hewitt was well connected and very "in the know." Dean had made it a habit to keep his parents abreast of his comings and goings. It helped to ease some of the guilt he felt over not following the path they'd wanted. Attorneyville had never been his destination, never would be.

He'd explained about Cassandra when Cat and Crew had shown up. His mother, of course, had wanted full details about the woman he was so obviously ensnared by that he'd risk life and limb to save her. The woman that made his heart ache at the mere thought of something bad happening to her. The woman that had his stomach in knots and his jaw set in a hard line because he just couldn't get the image out of his head of her taking a tumble and nearly cracking her skull on a boulder.

Yes, she was fine. And yes, Slider was behind bars. But damn it…Dean knew the situation could have been much worse. She could have been trapped by Slider, still in his clutches, unable to get away. Dean could have missed the signs that led him to her. This whole ordeal could have turned out to be a horrific nightmare.

He knew what Cassandra would say at this moment. Fate had intervened.

Kismet had brought them together, and it had helped them to stay together.

And maybe it had. He wasn't above believing in a cosmic force at this point. Not after all he'd been through with her.

The thought made him want to smile, but he just didn't have it in him.

Part of him blamed himself for her predicament. He never should have left her alone.

But if he attached himself to her side, she'd pull away.

It occurred to Dean this was a no-win situation, regardless of how much help kismet lent them.

The truth of the matter was that Cassandra was a whimsical, free spirit. He was an overbearing bodyguard. He didn't want her out of his sight for two minutes.

But that was absurd and unrealistic. He had a job to do, a life to lead. And so did she.

As he scratched the fresh whiskers lining his jaw, he knew he was in trouble. The happy medium he'd thought they'd struck really didn't exist.

He'd tried to make it work between them.

Unfortunately, he'd failed.

Chapter Seventeen

"The place looks amazing," McCarthy said as she sidled up to Cassandra and gave her a gentle hug, mindful that Cassandra was still incredibly sore from the trauma she'd suffered last week.

"I can't believe we pulled this together. And so quickly." She looked around the crowded lounge and prayed the fire marshal wouldn't drop by, because the place was packed. "And it's even better than before."

The furniture her uncle had crafted for her added to the sophisticated ambience. The entire club radiated a new warmth and intimacy. Cassandra believed it was because of the love and devotion that had gone into restoring the place. Her friends and family had rallied around her, and she was pretty sure the spirit of their selfless, giving natures had been captured within the walls of Rendezvous.

Everything had come together perfectly. Cassandra had even purchased enough wine glasses from McCarthy's vendor to make do this evening.

"They all came back," McCarthy mused. "I know you weren't expecting that."

"We handled the situation well. I couldn't have done it without you."

McCarthy grinned. "We make a great team, Cass."

"Yes, we do."

The only thing missing... correction, the only *one* missing... was Dean. Cassandra hadn't heard from him in a week. Not since their brief visit at the hospital. He hadn't even returned her phone call the other day when she'd told him that, at the very least, she needed to pick up her fish.

She was no fool. She knew he was avoiding her. What she didn't know was why.

Frustration consumed her. Everything was okay now. The club had been put back together. Slider no longer posed a threat. All was right with her little world.

Except... Dean wasn't speaking to her.

Emotion welled in her throat and she fought it down. She'd thought about him every minute since the last time she'd seen him. She'd even put a little extra effort into her appearance this evening, on the off-chance he'd show up, heart in hand. She wore red leather pants and a red satin bustier, infused with thin strands of gold in an intricate pattern. Her long hair fell past her shoulders in loose curls, the way Dean liked it.

But as she glanced around the club for the hundredth time, she didn't catch a glimpse of him.

Cassandra sighed. She really couldn't afford to let her melancholy infringe on tonight's festivities. She was blessed with a fresh start. And despite the fact that Dean Hewitt didn't want to be a part of that fresh start, she had to go on.

Carefully lifting a tray full of cocktails, she wound her way through the club, offering the free drinks to her members. This hurrah was going to cost her a small fortune, but she knew it would be worth it in the end. If her reputation had been slightly tarnished by the vandalism, she was pretty sure it would gleam like a shiny new penny come morning. Everyone was having a great time. And some of the singletons were already hooking up, despite the early hour.

"Please tell me there's at least *one* man in this sea of hunks that would make a good match for me."

Cassandra handed over her empty tray to a passing waitress before facing Cat Hewitt. Dressed head-to-toe in burgundy, looking as sleek and sophisticated as an Oscar-nominated actress on the red carpet, Cat was utterly breathtaking.

Cassandra had met her the night she'd signed up for Rendezvous' dating services. She'd thought Cat was attractive enough—not to mention vivacious enough—to land the man of her dreams in record time. But Cat was still on the prowl. No doubt, she needed to sample a few more men before she settled down.

Cassandra smiled at her then gave her a quick peck on the cheek. "You look fabulous. And I assure you there's not a man in this room that would disagree."

"God, you're sweet," Cat said as she carefully returned an affectionate kiss. "And looking fabulous yourself. You feel okay?"

Aside from a broken heart?

"I'm fine. Thanks for asking."

"Well, don't thank me too soon. You may be cursing my name in a minute."

Cassandra eyed her curiously. She opened her mouth to inquire about Cat's peculiar remark, but in the next instant, a very elegantly dressed, distinguished couple descended upon them.

"Cassandra," Cat said with all due grandeur, "meet the parents."

Cassandra's stomach took a quick dive south. Of all the painful things for her to experience right now... *Holy shit.* Did she *really* have to meet the parents of the man she loved? The man who wanted nothing to do with her?

There was no time for an internal debate. Cat introduced Cassandra to Martin and Bridget Hewitt. Bridget swept her up in a motherly embrace that instantly brought tears to Cassandra's eyes.

She hadn't had a maternal presence in her life since she was thirteen. And to be held so tightly in Bridget's arms... it made a wealth of emotion rise within Cassandra.

When Dean's mother released her, his father swooped in for a quick, paternal hug. Though it was fleeting, it certainly packed a wallop. She could feel the unity of this family, could feel its strength. No matter what their issues, the Hewitts were devoted to each other.

Cassandra fought back the fat tear drops stinging her eyes, but one escaped despite her effort. "I suffer from an overactive emotional state," she quipped. "Don't mind me."

Bridget gave her a warm smile. "You're in good company. Cat has a flair for the dramatic."

"Oh, Mother," Cat said on, yes, a dramatic sigh.

Cassandra laughed.

"This is a lovely club you have," Bridget said. "So stylish and... intimate."

"I had a lot of help putting it back together."

"And now would you *please* help me find a man?" Cat all but begged.

"I doubt that's going to be a problem," Cassandra assured her.

"Cat," her father said. "A little propriety, hmm?"

"Oh, Daddy. I don't have time for propriety. I'm aging as we speak."

Cassandra's stomach tightened. She'd fallen instantly in love with Dean's family. It was a damn shame she'd never be a part of it.

As though his mother had read her thoughts, she asked, "Where is Dean?"

"Oh, well..." Cassandra swallowed hard. Time to tell the clan she and Dean were splitsville. Christ, she couldn't even joke about it. The mere thought of their falling out brought a whole new batch of tears to her eyes. She swiped at them, annoyed. "Apparently he didn't explain to you that we're no longer...involved."

"Oh, *that*." Cat made a soft "tsking" sound. "Here's a little tidbit about the Hewitt men. They have hard heads and, yeah, it takes a sledgehammer to break through sometimes, but eventually they do come around. For instance, Daddy has admitted that Dean's job has merit and that he's actually doing something good for society. So he's agreed to get off Dean's back and not badger him incessantly about joining his law firm."

"That's not exactly what I said," Martin commented, his brow furrowed.

Ignoring him, Cat continued. "And Dean has agreed to stop running background checks on all the men I'm interested in, *and* he's agreed to stop scaring the shit out of them so that maybe one or two of them might call me back for a second date."

"That's not exactly what *I* said."

The familiar rumble of Dean's low, intimate voice made Cassandra's insides flutter. Her heart soared and she knew his family caught the flash of excitement that no doubt lit her eyes. Turning slightly, her gaze met Dean's over her shoulder.

Cassandra couldn't keep the smile from her face. "You came."

He gave a noncommittal shrug. "It's a big night for you."

Her smile faltered. Was that the only reason he was at the club? Hadn't he come to profess his unwavering, undying love for her?

"Well," Martin said as he linked an arm with his wife's. "I'd like to see more of Rendezvous. Shall we take a tour, maybe get a cocktail?"

"Lovely idea," Bridget agreed. "Come along, dear." She latched onto Cat's hand and nearly dragged her away.

Cassandra turned fully to face Dean. "That's some family you have."

He nodded. "They seem to have taken an instant liking to you. Not that I'm surprised. Anyone who wreaks havoc in my life, or on my heart, is fine by my father."

He'd meant it as a joke, and she knew it. But Cassandra frowned, her heart sinking. "Dean, I don't want to wreak havoc on your heart."

He let out a low sigh. "That's inevitable, sweetheart." A large hand cupped the side of her face and his thumb skimmed over her jaw. "Because I love you."

Cassandra's breath caught. "You do?"

He grinned at her, slow and sexy. "Yeah, I do. And that means trouble for my heart. But damn it, a week without you is even more torturous."

She shook her head, her own grin coming to fruition. "That misguided charm of yours has returned."

Dean chuckled. "I never claimed to be a poet or a Cassanova." He reached for her and pulled her into his arms, "I do, however, promise to love and honor you for the rest of our days."

"Oh, damn it," Cassandra whispered as tears sprang to her eyes once again. "I'm so freakin' sentimental."

Dean laughed. "Does that mean you forgive me for being a horse's ass this past week?"

Her gaze connected with his. "I never thought that. I just…need to know something."

"I can't promise I won't worry about you all the time, Cassandra. Don't even ask it. I love you too much to not want to protect you."

She nodded. She lifted a hand to his face and smoothed his furrowed brow. "I'm okay with that. All I need to know is that you're never going to shut me out again. No matter what."

She'd opened her heart to him, after all. Let him in. All the way in. She needed that in return.

Dean's arms tightened around her. "I promise."

His head dipped and his mouth captured hers in a sweet, erotic kiss that chased out all doubt, all dread.

She belonged to him. The realization mended her broken heart, repaired her damaged soul. Cassandra knew exactly what she was gaining tonight. A lover. A soul mate. A family.

Dean's tongue tangled with hers, delivering a kiss that caressed her soul… and made the butterflies in her stomach take flight.

About the Author:

Award-winning author Calista Fox resides in Arizona. She is the author of several erotic romance novellas and short stories, the author of romantic suspense novels, and the recipient of the 2005 Over The Moon Award of Excellence for Best Erotic Sci-Fi Short Story. Calista also writes erotic romances as Ava McKnight.

Visit the author at **www.calistafox.com** *or email her at* calista@calistafox.com.

Men you've been dreaming about!

Secrets

Satisfy your desire for more.

*F*eel the wild adventure, fierce passion and the power of love in every **Secrets** Collection story. Red Sage Publishing's romance authors create richly crafted, sexy, sensual, novella-length stories. Each one is just the right length for reading after a long and hectic day.

Each volume in the **Secrets** Collection has four diverse, ultra-sexy, romantic novellas brimming with adventure, passion and love. More adventurous tales for the adventurous reader. The **Secrets** Collection are a glorious mix of romance genre; numerous historical settings, contemporary, paranormal, science fiction and suspense. We are always looking for new adventures.

Reader response to the **Secrets** volumes has been great! Here's just a small sample:

> *"I loved the variety of settings. Four completely wonderful time periods, give you four completely wonderful reads."*

> *"Each story was a page-turning tale I hated to put down."*

> *"I love **Secrets**! When is the next volume coming out? This one was Hot! Loved the heroes!"*

Secrets have won raves and awards. We could go on, but why don't you find out for yourself—order your set of **Secrets** today! See the back for details.

Secrets, Volume 1

Listen to what reviewers say:

"These stories take you beyond romance into the realm of erotica. I found *Secrets* absolutely delicious."

—Virginia Henley,
New York Times Best Selling Author

"*Secrets* is a collection of novellas for the daring, adventurous woman who's not afraid to give her fantasies free reign."

—Kathe Robin, *Romantic Times* Magazine

"…In fact, the men featured in all the stories are terrific, they all want to please and pleasure their women. If you like erotic romance you will love *Secrets*."

—*Romantic Readers* Review

In *Secrets, Volume 1* you'll find:

A Lady's Quest by Bonnie Hamre

Widowed Lady Antonia Blair-Sutworth searches for a lover to save her from the handsome Duke of Sutherland. The "auditions" may be shocking but utterly tantalizing.

The Spinner's Dream by Alice Gaines

A seductive fantasy that leaves every woman wishing for her own private love slave, desperate and running for his life.

The Proposal by Ivy Landon

This tale is a walk on the wild side of love. *The Proposal* will taunt you, tease you, and shock you. A contemporary erotica for the adventurous woman.

The Gift by Jeanie LeGendre

Immerse yourself in this historic tale of exotic seduction, bondage and a concubine's surrender to the Sultan's desire. Can Alessandra live the life and give the gift the Sultan demands of her?

Secrets, Volume 2

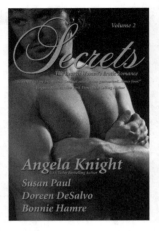

Listen to what reviewers say:

"*Secrets* offers four novellas of sensual delight; each beautifully written with intense feeling and dedication to character development. For those seeking stories with heightened intimacy, look no further."

—Kathee Card, *Romancing the Web*

"Such a welcome diversity in styles and genres. Rich characterization in sensual tales. An exciting read that's sure to titillate the senses."

—Cheryl Ann Porter

"*Secrets 2* left me breathless. Sensual satisfaction guaranteed… times four!"

—Virginia Henley, *New York Times* Best Selling Author

In *Secrets, Volume 2* you'll find:

Surrogate Lover by Doreen DeSalvo

Adrian Ross is a surrogate sex therapist who has all the answers and control. He thought he'd seen and done it all, but he'd never met Sarah.

Snowbound by Bonnie Hamre

A delicious, sensuous regency tale. The marriage-shy Earl of Howden is teased and tortured by his own desires and finds there is a woman who can equal his overpowering sensuality.

Roarke's Prisoner by Angela Knight

Elise, a starship captain, remembers the eager animal submission she'd known before at her captor's hands and refuses to become his toy again. However, she has no idea of the delights he's planned for her this time.

Savage Garden by Susan Paul

Raine's been captured by a mysterious and dangerous revolutionary leader in Mexico. At first her only concern is survival, but she quickly finds lush erotic nights in her captor's arms.

Winner of the Fallot Literary Award for Fiction!

Secrets, Volume 3

Listen to what reviewers say:

"*Secrets, Volume 3*, leaves the reader breathless. A delicious confection of sensuous treats awaits the reader on each turn of the page!"
—Kathee Card, *Romancing the Web*

"From the FBI to Police Detective to Vampires to a Medieval Warlord home from the Crusade—*Secrets 3* is simply the best!"
—Susan Paul, award winning author

"An unabashed celebration of sex. Highly arousing! Highly recommended!"
—Virginia Henley, *New York Times* Best Selling Author

In **Secrets, Volume 3** you'll find:

The Spy Who Loved Me by Jeanie Cesarini

Undercover FBI agent Paige Ellison's sexual appetites rise to new levels when she works with leading man Christopher Sharp, the cunning agent who uses all his training to capture her body and heart.

The Barbarian by Ann Jacobs

Lady Brianna vows not to surrender to the barbaric Giles, Earl of Harrow. He must use sexual arts learned in the infidels' harem to conquer his bride. A word of caution—this is not for the faint of heart.

Blood and Kisses by Angela Knight

A vampire assassin is after Beryl St. Cloud. Her only hope lies with Decker, another vampire and ex-mercenary. Broke, she offers herself as payment for his services. Will his seductive powers take her very soul?

Love Undercover by B.J. McCall

Amanda Forbes is the bait in a strip joint sting operation. While she performs, fellow detective "Cowboy" Cooper gets to watch. Though he excites her, she must fight the temptation to surrender to the passion.

Winner of the 1997 Under the Covers
Readers Favorite Award

Secrets, Volume 4

Listen to what reviewers say:

"Provocative… seductive… a must read!"

—*Romantic Times* Magazine

"These are the kind of stories that romance readers that 'want a little more' have been looking for all their lives…."

—*Affaire de Coeur* Magazine

"*Secrets, Volume 4*, has something to satisfy every erotic fantasy… simply sexational!"

—Virginia Henley, *New York Times* Best Selling Author

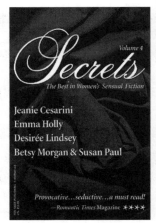

In *Secrets, Volume 4* you'll find:

An Act of Love by Jeanie Cesarini

Shelby Moran's past left her terrified of sex. International film star Jason Gage must gently coach the young starlet in the ways of love. He wants more than an act—he wants Shelby to feel true passion in his arms.

Enslaved by Desirée Lindsey

Lord Nicholas Summer's air of danger, dark passions, and irresistible charm have brought Lady Crystal's long-hidden desires to the surface. Will he be able to give her the one thing she desires before it's too late?

The Bodyguard by Betsy Morgan and Susan Paul

Kaki York is a bodyguard, but watching the wild, erotic romps of her client's sexual conquests on the security cameras is getting to her—and her partner, the ruggedly handsome James Kulick. Can she resist his insistent desire to have her?

The Love Slave by Emma Holly

A woman's ultimate fantasy. For one year, Princess Lily will be attended to by three delicious men of her choice. While she delights in playing with the first two, it's the reluctant Grae, with his powerful chest, black eyes and hair, that stirs her desires.

Secrets, Volume 5

Listen to what reviewers say:

"Hot, hot, hot! Not for the faint-hearted!"

—*Romantic Times* Magazine

"As you make your way through the stories, you will find yourself becoming hotter and hotter. *Secrets* just keeps getting better and better."

—*Affaire de Coeur* Magazine

"*Secrets 5* is a collage of luscious sensuality. Any woman who reads *Secrets* is in for an awakening!"

—Virginia Henley, *New York Times* Best Selling Author

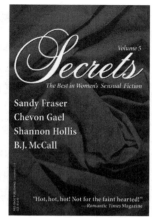

In *Secrets, Volume 5* you'll find:

Beneath Two Moons by Sandy Fraser

Ready for a very wild romp? Step into the future and find Conor, rough and masculine like frontiermen of old, on the prowl for a new conquest. In his sights, Dr. Eva Kelsey. She got away once before, but this time Conor makes sure she begs for more.

Insatiable by Chevon Gael

Marcus Remington photographs beautiful models for a living, but it's Ashlyn Fraser, a young corporate exec having some glamour shots done, who has stolen his heart. It's up to Marcus to help her discover her inner sexual self.

Strictly Business by Shannon Hollis

Elizabeth Forrester knows it's tough enough for a woman to make it to the top in the corporate world. Garrett Hill, the most beautiful man in Silicon Valley, has to come along to stir up her wildest fantasies. Dare she give in to both their desires?

Alias Smith and Jones by B.J. McCall

Meredith Collins finds herself stranded overnight at the airport. A handsome stranger by the name of Smith offers her sanctuary for the evening and she finds those mesmerizing, green-flecked eyes hard to resist. Are they to be just two ships passing in the night?

Secrets, Volume 6

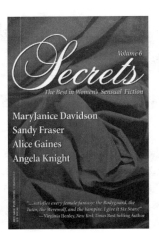

Listen to what reviewers say:

"Red Sage was the first and remains the leader of Women's Erotic Romance Fiction Collections!"

—*Romantic Times* Magazine

"*Secrets, Volume 6*, is the best of *Secrets* yet. ...four of the most erotic stories in one volume than this reader has yet to see anywhere else. ...These stories are full of erotica at its best and you'll definitely want to keep it handy for lots of re-reading!"

—*Affaire de Coeur* Magazine

"*Secrets 6* satisfies every female fantasy: the Bodyguard, the Tutor, the Werewolf, and the Vampire. I give it Six Stars!"

—Virginia Henley, *New York Times* Best Selling Author

In *Secrets, Volume 6* you'll find:

Flint's Fuse by Sandy Fraser

Dana Madison's father has her "kidnapped" for her own safety. Flint, the tall, dark and dangerous mercenary, is hired for the job. But just which one is the prisoner—Dana will try *anything* to get away.

Love's Prisoner by MaryJanice Davidson

Trapped in an elevator, Jeannie Lawrence experienced unwilling rapture at Michael Windham's hands. She never expected the devilishly handsome man to show back up in her life—or turn out to be a werewolf!

The Education of Miss Felicity Wells by Alice Gaines

Felicity Wells wants to be sure she'll satisfy her soon-to-be husband but she needs a teacher. Dr. Marcus Slade, an experienced lover, agrees to take her on as a student, but can he stop short of taking her completely?

A Candidate for the Kiss by Angela Knight

Working on a story, reporter Dana Ivory stumbles onto a more amazing one—a sexy, secret agent who happens to be a vampire. She wants her story but Gabriel Archer wants more from her than just sex and blood.

Secrets, Volume 7

Listen to what reviewers say:

"Get out your asbestos gloves — *Secrets Volume 7* is… extremely hot, true erotic romance… passionate and titillating. There's nothing quite like baring your secrets!"
—*Romantic Times* Magazine

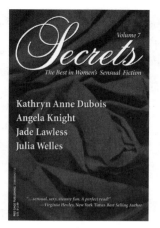

"…sensual, sexy, steamy fun. A perfect read!"
—Virginia Henley,
New York Times Best Selling Author

"Intensely provocative and disarmingly romantic, *Secrets*, *Volume 7*, is a romance reader's paradise that will take you beyond your wildest dreams!"
—Ballston Book House Review

In *Secrets, Volume 7* you'll find:

Amelia's Innocence by Julia Welles

Amelia didn't know her father bet her in a card game with Captain Quentin Hawke, so honor demands a compromise—three days of erotic foreplay, leaving her virginity and future intact.

The Woman of His Dreams by Jade Lawless

From the day artist Gray Avonaco moves in next door, Joanna Morgan is plagued by provocative dreams. But what she believes is unrequited lust, Gray sees as another chance to be with the woman he loves. He must persuade her that even death can't stop true love.

Surrender by Kathryn Anne Dubois

Free-spirited Lady Johanna wants no part of the binding strictures society imposes with her marriage to the powerful Duke. She doesn't know the dark Duke wants sensual adventure, and sexual satisfaction.

Kissing the Hunter by Angela Knight

Navy Seal Logan McLean hunts the vampires who murdered his wife. Virginia Hart is a sexy vampire searching for her lost soul-mate only to find him in a man determined to kill her. She must convince him all vampires aren't created equally.

Winner of the Venus Book Club Best Book of the Year

Secrets, Volume 8

Listen to what reviewers say:

"*Secrets, Volume 8*, is an amazing compilation of sexy stories covering a wide range of subjects, all designed to titillate the senses. …you'll find something for everybody in this latest version of *Secrets*."

—*Affaire de Coeur* Magazine

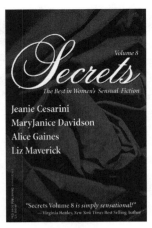

"*Secrets Volume 8*, is simply sensational!"

—Virginia Henley, *New York Times* Best Selling Author

"These delectable stories will have you turning the pages long into the night. Passionate, provocative and perfect for setting the mood…."

—*Escape to Romance* Reviews

In *Secrets, Volume 8* you'll find:

Taming Kate by Jeanie Cesarini

Kathryn Roman inherits a legal brothel. Little does this city girl know the town of Love, Nevada wants her to be their new madam so they've charged Trey Holliday, one very dominant cowboy, with taming her.

Jared's Wolf by MaryJanice Davidson

Jared Rocke will do anything to avenge his sister's death, but ends up attracted to Moira Wolfbauer, the she-wolf sworn to protect her pack. Joining forces to stop a killer, they learn love defies all boundaries.

My Champion, My Lover by Alice Gaines

Celeste Broder is a woman committed for having a sexy appetite. Mayor Robert Albright may be her champion—if she can convince him her freedom will mean a chance to indulge their appetites together.

Kiss or Kill by Liz Maverick

In this post-apocalyptic world, Camille Kazinsky's military career rides on her ability to make a choice—whether the robo called Meat should live or die. Meat's future depends on proving he's human enough to live, man enough… to makes her feel like a woman.

Winner of the Venus Book Club
Best Book of the Year

Secrets, Volume 9

Listen to what reviewers say:

"Everyone should expect only the most erotic stories in a *Secrets* book. ...if you like your stories full of hot sexual scenes, then this is for you!"

—Donna Doyle Romance Reviews

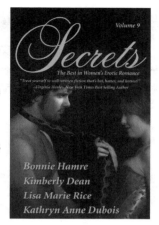

"*SECRETS 9*... is sinfully delicious, highly arousing, and hotter than hot as the pages practically burn up as you turn them."

—Suzanne Coleburn, Reader To Reader
Reviews/Belles & Beaux of Romance

"Treat yourself to well-written fiction that's hot, hotter, and hottest!"

—Virginia Henley, *New York Times* Best Selling Author

In *Secrets, Volume 9* you'll find:

Wild For You by Kathryn Anne Dubois

When college intern, Georgie, gets captured by a Congo wildman, she discovers this specimen of male virility has never seen a woman. The research possibilities are endless!

Wanted by Kimberly Dean

FBI Special Agent Jeff Reno wants Danielle Carver. There's her body, brains—and that charge of treason on her head. Dani goes on the run, but the sexy Fed is hot on her trail.

Secluded by Lisa Marie Rice

Nicholas Lee's wealth and power came with a price—his enemies will kill anyone he loves. When Isabelle steals his heart, Nicholas secludes her in his palace for a lifetime of desire in only a few days.

Flights of Fantasy by Bonnie Hamre

Chloe taught others to see the realities of life but she's never shared the intimate world of her sensual yearnings. Given the chance, will she be woman enough to fulfill her most secret erotic fantasy?

Secrets, Volume 10

Listen to what reviewers say:

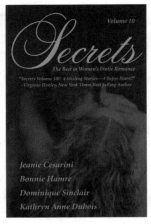

"*Secrets Volume 10*, an erotic dance through medieval castles, sultan's palaces, the English countryside and expensive hotel suites, explodes with passion-filled pages."

—*Romantic Times BOOKclub*

"Having read the previous nine volumes, this one fulfills the expectations of what is expected in a *Secrets* book: romance and eroticism at its best!!"

—*Fallen Angel Reviews*

"All are hot steamy romances so if you enjoy erotica romance, you are sure to enjoy *Secrets, Volume 10*. All this reviewer can say is WOW!!"

—*The Best Reviews*

In *Secrets, Volume 10* you'll find:

Private Eyes by Dominique Sinclair

When a mystery man captivates P.I. Nicolla Black during a stakeout, she discovers her no-seduction rule bending under the pressure of long denied passion. She agrees to the seduction, but he demands her total surrender.

The Ruination of Lady Jane by Bonnie Hamre

To avoid her upcoming marriage, Lady Jane Ponsonby-Maitland flees into the arms of Havyn Attercliffe. She begs him to ruin her rather than turn her over to her odious fiancé.

Code Name: Kiss by Jeanie Cesarini

Agent Lily Justiss is on a mission to defend her country against terrorists that requires giving up her virginity as a sex slave. As her master takes her body, desire for her commanding officer Seth Blackthorn fuels her mind.

The Sacrifice by Kathryn Anne Dubois

Lady Anastasia Bedovier is days from taking her vows as a Nun. Before she denies her sensuality forever, she wants to experience pleasure. Count Maxwell is the perfect man to initiate her into erotic delight.

Secrets, Volume 11

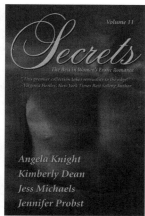

Listen to what reviewers say:

"*Secrets Volume 11* delivers once again with storylines that include erotic masquerades, ancient curses, modern-day betrayal and a prince charming looking for a kiss." **4 Stars**

　　　　　　　　　—Romantic Times BOOKclub

"Indulge yourself with this erotic treat and join the thousands of readers who just can't get enough. Be forewarned that *Secrets 11* will whet your appetite for more, but will offer you the ultimate in pleasurable erotic literature."

　　　　　　　　—Ballston Book House Review

"*Secrets 11* quite honestly is my favorite anthology from Red Sage so far."

　　　　　　　　　　　—The Best Reviews

In *Secrets, Volume 11* you'll find:

Masquerade by Jennifer Probst

Hailey Ashton is determined to free herself from her sexual restrictions. Four nights of erotic pleasures without revealing her identity. A chance to explore her secret desires without the fear of unmasking.

Ancient Pleasures by Jess Michaels

Isabella Winslow is obsessed with finding out what caused her late husband's death, but trapped in an Egyptian concubine's tomb with a sexy American raider, succumbing to the mummy's sensual curse takes over.

Manhunt by Kimberly Dean

Framed for murder, Michael Tucker takes Taryn Swanson hostage—the one woman who can clear him. Despite the evidence against him, the attraction between them is strong. Tucker resorts to unconventional, yet effective methods of persuasion to change the sexy ADA's mind.

Wake Me by Angela Knight

Chloe Hart received a sexy painting of a sleeping knight. Radolf of Varik has been trapped for centuries in the painting since, cursed by a witch. His only hope is to visit the dreams of women and make one of them fall in love with him so she can free him with a kiss.

Secrets, Volume 12

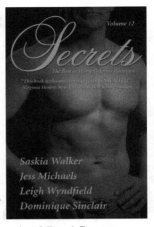

Listen to what reviewers say:

"*Secrets Volume 12*, turns on the heat with a seductive encounter inside a bookstore, a temple of naughty and sensual delight, a galactic inferno that thaws ice, and a lightening storm that lights up the English shoreline. Tales of looking for love in all the right places with a heat rating out the charts." **4½ Stars**

—Romantic Times BOOKclub

"I really liked these stories. You want great escapism? Read *Secrets, Volume 12*."

—Romance Reviews

In *Secrets, Volume 12* you'll find:

Good Girl Gone Bad by Dominique Sinclair

Reagan's dreams are finally within reach. Setting out to do research for an article, nothing could have prepared her for Luke, or his offer to teach her everything she needs to know about sex. Licentious pleasures, forbidden desires… inspiring the best writing she's ever done.

Aphrodite's Passion by Jess Michaels

When Selena flees Victorian London before her evil stepchildren can institutionalize her for hysteria, Gavin is asked to bring her back home. But when he finds her living on the island of Cyprus, his need to have her begins to block out every other impulse.

White Heat by Leigh Wyndfield

Raine is hiding in an icehouse in the middle of nowhere from one of the scariest men in the universes. Walker escaped from a burning prison. Imagine their surprise when they find out they have the same man to blame for their miseries. Passion, revenge and love are in their future.

Summer Lightning by Saskia Walker

Sculptress Sally is enjoying an idyllic getaway on a secluded cove when she spots a gorgeous man walking naked on the beach. When Julian finds an attractive woman shacked up in his cove, he has to check her out. But what will he do when he finds she's secretly been using him as a model?

Secrets, Volume 13

Listen to what reviewers say:

"In *Secrets Volume 13*, the temperature gets turned up a few notches with a mistaken personal ad, shape-shifters destined to love, a hot Regency lord and his lady, as well as a bodyguard protecting his woman. Emotions and flames blaze high in Red Sage's latest foray into the sensual and delightful art of love." **4½ Stars**

—*Romantic Times BOOKclub*

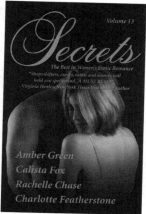

"The sex is still so hot the pages nearly ignite! Read *Secrets, Volume 13*!"

—*Romance Reviews*

In *Secrets, Volume 13* you'll find:

Out of Control by Rachelle Chase

Astrid's world revolves around her business and she's hoping to pick up wealthy Erik Santos as a client. Only he's hoping to pick up something entirely different. Will she give in to the seductive pull of his proposition?

Hawkmoor by Amber Green

Shape-shifters answer to Darien as he acts in the name of the long-missing Lady Hawkmoor, their hereditary ruler. When she unexpectedly surfaces, Darien must deal with a scrappy individual whose wary eyes hold the other half of his soul, but who has the power to destroy his world.

Lessons in Pleasure by Charlotte Featherstone

A wicked bargain has Lily vowing never to yield to the demands of the rake she once loved and lost. Unfortunately, Damian, the Earl of St. Croix, or Saint as he is infamously known, will not take 'no' for an answer.

In the Heat of the Night by Calista Fox

Haunted by a century-old curse, Molina fears she won't live to see her thirtieth birthday. Nick, her former bodyguard, is hired back into service to protect her from the fatal accidents that plague her family. But *In the Heat of the Night*, will his passion and love for her be enough to convince Molina they have a future together?

Secrets, Volume 14

Listen to what reviewers say:

"*Secrets Volume 14* will excite readers with its diverse selection of delectable sexy tales ranging from a fourteenth century love story to a sci-fi rebel who falls for a irresistible research scientist to a trio of determined vampires who battle for the same woman to a virgin sacrifice who falls in love with a beast. A cornucopia of pure delight!" **4½ Stars**
— *Romantic Times BOOKclub*

"This book contains four erotic tales sure to keep readers up long into the night."

— *Romance Junkies*

In *Secrets, Volume 14* you'll find:

Soul Kisses by Angela Knight

Beth's been kidnapped by Joaquin Ramirez, a sadistic vampire. Handsome vampire cousins, Morgan and Garret Axton, come to her rescue. Can she find happiness with two vampires?

Temptation in Time by Alexa Aames

Ariana escaped the Middle Ages after stealing a kiss of magic from sexy sorcerer, Marcus de Grey. When he brings her back, they begin a battle of wills and a sexual odyssey that could spell disaster for them both.

Ailis and the Beast by Jennifer Barlowe

When Ailis agreed to be her village's sacrifice to the mysterious Beast she was prepared to sacrifice her virtue, and possibly her life. But some things aren't what they seem. Ailis and the Beast are about to discover the greatest sacrifice may be the human heart.

Night Heat by Leigh Wynfield

When Rip Bowhite leads a revolt on the prison planet, he ends up struggling to survive against monsters that rule the night. Jemma, the prison's Healer, won't allow herself to be distracted by the instant attraction she feels for Rip. As the stakes are raised and death draws near, love seems doomed in the heat of the night.

Secrets, Volume 15

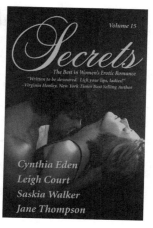

Listen to what reviewers say:

"*Secrets Volume 15* blends humor, tension and steamy romance in its newest collection that sizzles with passion between unlikely pairs—a male chauvinist columnist and a librarian turned erotica author; a handsome werewolf and his resisting mate; an unfulfilled woman and a sexy police officer and a Victorian wife who learns discipline can be fun. Readers will revel in this delicious assortment of thrilling tales." **4 Stars**
—*Romantic Times BOOKclub*

"This book contains four tales by some of today's hottest authors that will tease your senses and intrigue your mind."

—*Romance Junkies*

In *Secrets, Volume 15* you'll find:

Simon Says by Jane Thompson
Simon Campbell is a newspaper columnist who panders to male fantasies. Georgina Kennedy is a respectable librarian. On the surface, these two have nothing in common... but don't judge a book by its cover.

Bite of the Wolf by Cynthia Eden
Gareth Morlet, alpha werewolf, has finally found his mate. All he has to do is convince Trinity to join with him, to give in to the pleasure of a werewolf's mating, and then she will be his... forever.

Falling for Trouble by Saskia Walker
With 48 hours to clear her brother's name, Sonia Harmond finds help from irresistible bad boy, Oliver Eaglestone. When the erotic tension between them hits fever pitch, securing evidence to thwart an international arms dealer isn't the only danger they face.

The Disciplinarian by Leigh Court
Headstrong Clarissa Babcock is sent to the shadowy legend known as The Disciplinarian for instruction in proper wifely obedience. Jared Ashworth uses the tools of seduction to show her how to control a demanding husband, but her beauty, spirit, and uninhibited passion make Jared hunger to keep her—and their darkly erotic nights—all for himself!

Secrets, Volume 16

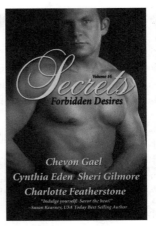

Listen to what reviewers say:

"Blackmail, games of chance, nude beaches and masquerades pave a path to heart-tugging emotions and fiery love scenes in Red Sage's latest collection." **4.5 Stars**

—*Romantic Times BOOKclub*

"Red Sage Publishing has brought to the readers an erotic profusion of highly skilled storytellers in their Secrets Vol. 16. … This is the best Secrets novel to date and this reviewer's favorite."

—*LoveRomances.com*

In *Secrets, Volume 16* you'll find:

Never Enough by Cynthia Eden

For the last three weeks, Abby McGill has been playing with fire. Bad-boy Jake has taught her the true meaning of desire, but she knows she has to end her relationship with him. But Jake isn't about to let the woman he wants walk away from him.

Bunko by Sheri Gilmoore

Tu Tran is forced to decide between Jack, a man, who promises to share every aspect of his life with her, or Dev, the man, who hides behind a mask and only offers night after night of erotic sex. Will she take the gamble of the dice and choose the man, who can see behind her own mask and expose her true desires?

Hide and Seek by Chevon Gael

Kyle DeLaurier ditches his trophy-fiance in favor of a tropical paradise full of tall, tanned, topless females. Private eye, Darcy McLeod, is on the trail of this runaway groom. Together they sizzle while playing Hide and Seek with their true identities.

Seduction of the Muse by Charlotte Featherstone

He's the Dark Lord, the mysterious author who pens the erotic tales of an innocent woman's seduction. She is his muse, the woman he watches from the dark shadows, the woman whose dreams he invades at night.

Secrets, Volume 17

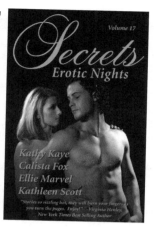

Listen to what reviewers say:

"Readers who have clamored for more *Secrets* will love the mix of alpha and beta males as well as kick-butt heroines who always get their men." **4 Stars**

—*Romantic Times BOOKclub*

"Stories so sizzling hot, they will burn your fingers as you turn the pages. Enjoy!"

—Virginia Henley, *New York Times* Best Selling Author

"Red Sage is bringing us another thrilling anthology of passion and desire that will keep you up long into the night."

—*Romance Junkies*

In *Secrets, Volume 17* you'll find:

Rock Hard Candy by Kathy Kaye

Jessica Hennessy, the great, great granddaughter of a Voodoo priestess, decides she's waited long enough for the man of her dreams. A dose of her ancestor's aphrodisiac slipped into the gooey center of her homemade bon bons ought to do the trick.

Fatal Error by Kathleen Scott

Jesse Storm must make amends to humanity by destroying the computer program he helped design that has taken the government hostage. But he must also protect the woman he's loved in secret for nearly a decade.

Birthday by Ellie Marvel

Jasmine Templeton decides she's been celibate long enough. Will a wild night at a hot new club with her two best friends ease the ache inside her or just make it worse? Well, considering one of those best friends is Charlie and she's been having strange notions about their relationship of late... It's definitely a birthday neither she nor Charlie will ever forget.

Intimate Rendezvous by Calista Fox

A thief causes trouble at Cassandra Kensington's nightclub, Rendezvous, and sexy P.I. Dean Hewitt arrives on the scene to help. One look at the siren who owns the club has his blood boiling, despite the fact that his keen instincts have him questioning the legitimacy of her business.

Secrets, Volume 18

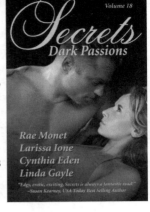

Listen to what reviewers say:

"Fantastic love scenes make this a book to be enjoyed more than once." **4.5 Stars**
>   —*Romantic Times BOOKclub*

"*Secrets Volume 18* continues [its] tradition of high quality sensual stories that both excite the senses while stimulating the mind."
>   —CK²S Kwips and Kritiques

"Edgy, erotic, exciting, *Secrets* is always a fantastic read!"
>   —Susan Kearney, *USA Today* Best Selling Author

In *Secrets, Volume 18* you'll find:

Lone Wolf Three by Rae Monet

Planetary politics and squabbling over wolf occupied territory drain former rebel leader Taban Zias. But his anger quickly turns to desire when he meets, Lakota Blackson. Focused, calm and honorable, the female Wolf Warrior is Taban's perfect mate—now if he can just convince her.

Flesh to Fantasy by Larissa Ione

Kelsa Bradshaw is an intense loner whose job keeps her happily immersed in a fanciful world of virtual reality. Trent Jordan is a laid-back paramedic who experiences the harsh realities of life up close and personal. But when their worlds collide in an erotic eruption can Trent convince Kelsa to turn the fantasy into something real?

Heart Full of Stars by Linda Gayle

Singer Fanta Rae finds herself stranded on a lonely Mars outpost with the first human male she's seen in years. Ex-Marine Alex Decker lost his family and guilt drove him into isolation, but when alien assassins come to enslave Fanta, she and Decker come together to fight for their lives.

The Wolf's Mate by Cynthia Eden

When Michael Morlet finds Katherine "Kat" Hardy fighting for her life in a dark alley, he instantly recognizes her as the mate he's been seeking all of his life, but someone's trying to kill her. With danger stalking them at every turn, will Kat trust him enough to become The Wolf's Mate?

The Forever Kiss
by Angela Knight

Listen to what reviewers say:

"*The Forever Kiss* flows well with good characters and an interesting plot. ... If you enjoy vampires and a lot of hot sex, you are sure to enjoy *The Forever Kiss*."

—*The Best Reviews*

"Battling vampires, a protective ghost and the ever present battle of good and evil keep excellent pace with the erotic delights in Angela Knight's *The Forever Kiss*—a book that absolutely bites with refreshing paranormal humor." **4½ Stars, Top Pick**

—*Romantic Times BOOKclub*

"I found *The Forever Kiss* to be an exceptionally written, refreshing book. ... I really enjoyed this book by Angela Knight. ... 5 angels!"

—*Fallen Angel Reviews*

"*The Forever Kiss* is the first single title released from Red Sage and if this is any indication of what we can expect, it won't be the last. ... The love scenes are hot enough to give a vampire a sunburn and the fight scenes will have you cheering for the good guys."

—*Really Bad Barb Reviews*

In *The Forever Kiss*:

For years, Valerie Chase has been haunted by dreams of a Texas Ranger she knows only as "Cowboy." As a child, he rescued her from the nightmare vampires who murdered her parents. As an adult, she still dreams of him—but now he's her seductive lover in nights of erotic pleasure.

Yet "Cowboy" is more than a dream—he's the real Cade McKinnon—and a vampire! For years, he's protected Valerie from Edward Ridgemont, the sadistic vampire who turned him. Now, Ridgmont wants Valerie for his own and Cade is the only one who can protect her.

When Val finds herself abducted by her handsome dream man, she's appalled to discover he's one of the vampires she fears. Now, caught in a web of fear and passion, she and Cade must learn to trust each other, even as an immortal monster stalks their every move.

Their only hope of survival is... *The Forever Kiss*.

Romantic Times Best Erotic Novel of the Year

It's not just reviewers raving about *Secrets*. See what readers have to say:

"When are you coming out with a new Volume? I want a new one next month!" via email from a reader.

"I loved the hot, wet sex without vulgar words being used to make it exciting." after *Volume 1*

"I loved the blend of sensuality and sexual intensity—HOT!" after *Volume 2*

"The best thing about *Secrets* is they're hot and brief! The least thing is you do not have enough of them!" after *Volume 3*

"I have been extremely satisfied with *Secrets*, keep up the good writing." after *Volume 4*

"Stories have plot and characters to support the erotica. They would be good strong stories without the heat." after *Volume 5*

"*Secrets* really knows how to push the envelop better than anyone else." after *Volume 6*

"These are the best sensual stories I have ever read!" after *Volume 7*

"I love, love, love the *Secrets* stories. I now have all of them, please have more books come out each year." after *Volume 8*

"These are the perfect sensual romance stories!" after *Volume 9*

"What I love about *Secrets Volume 10* is how I couldn't put it down!" after *Volume 10*

"All of the *Secrets* volumes are terrific! I have read all of them up to *Secrets Volume 11*. Please keep them coming! I will read every one you make!" after *Volume 11*

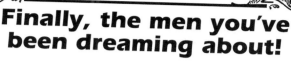

Finally, the men you've been dreaming about!

Give the Gift of Spicy Romantic Fiction

Don't want to wait? You can place a retail price ($12.99) order for any of the *Secrets* volumes from the following:

① **Waldenbooks and Borders Stores**

② **Amazon.com** or **BarnesandNoble.com**

③ **Book Clearinghouse (800-431-1579)**

④ **Romantic Times Magazine** Books by Mail (718-237-1097)

⑤ Special order at other bookstores.
Bookstores: Please contact Baker & Taylor Distributors, Ingram Book Distributor, or Red Sage Publishing for bookstore sales.

Order by title or ISBN #:

Vol. 1: 0-9648942-0-3 ISBN #13 978-0-9648942-0-4	**Vol. 7:** 0-9648942-7-0 ISBN #13 978-0-9648942-7-3	**Vol. 13:** 0-9754516-3-4 ISBN #13 978-0-9754516-3-2
Vol. 2: 0-9648942-1-1 ISBN #13 978-0-9648942-1-1	**Vol. 8:** 0-9648942-8-9 ISBN #13 978-0-9648942-9-7	**Vol. 14:** 0-9754516-4-2 ISBN #13 978-0-9754516-4-9
Vol. 3: 0-9648942-2-X ISBN #13 978-0-9648942-2-8	**Vol. 9:** 0-9648942-9-7 ISBN #13 978-0-9648942-9-7	**Vol. 15:** 0-9754516-5-0 ISBN #13 978-0-9754516-5-6
Vol. 4: 0-9648942-4-6 ISBN #13 978-0-9648942-4-2	**Vol. 10:** 0-9754516-0-X ISBN #13 978-0-9754516-0-1	**Vol. 16:** 0-9754516-6-9 ISBN #13 978-0-9754516-6-3
Vol. 5: 0-9648942-5-4 ISBN #13 978-0-9648942-5-9	**Vol. 11:** 0-9754516-1-8 ISBN #13 978-0-9754516-1-8	**Vol. 17:** 0-9754516-7-7 ISBN #13 978-0-9754516-7-0
Vol. 6: 0-9648942-6-2 ISBN #13 978-0-9648942-6-6	**Vol. 12:** 0-9754516-2-6 ISBN #13 978-0-9754516-2-5	**Vol. 18:** 0-9754516-8-5 ISBN #13 978-0-9754516-8-7

The Forever Kiss: 0-9648942-3-8 · ISBN #13 978-0-9648942-3-5 ($14.00)

Red Sage Publishing Mail Order Form:

(Orders shipped in two to three days of receipt.)

Each volume of *Secrets* retails for $12.99, but you can get it direct via mail order for only $9.99 each. The novel *The Forever Kiss* retails for $14.00, but by direct mail order, you only pay $11.00. Use the order form below to place your direct mail order. Fill in the quantity you want for each book on the blanks beside the title.

—— *Secrets* Volume 1	—— *Secrets* Volume 8	—— *Secrets* Volume 15
—— *Secrets* Volume 2	—— *Secrets* Volume 9	—— *Secrets* Volume 16
—— *Secrets* Volume 3	—— *Secrets* Volume 10	—— *Secrets* Volume 17
—— *Secrets* Volume 4	—— *Secrets* Volume 11	—— *Secrets* Volume 18
—— *Secrets* Volume 5	—— *Secrets* Volume 12	—— *The Forever Kiss*
—— *Secrets* Volume 6	—— *Secrets* Volume 13	
—— *Secrets* Volume 7	—— *Secrets* Volume 14	

Total —— *Secrets* Volumes @ $9.99 each = $——————

Total —— *The Forever Kiss* @ $11.00 each = $——————

Shipping & handling (in the U.S.) $——————

US Priority Mail: UPS insured:
1–2 books .... $ 5.50   1–4 books $16.00
3–5 books .... $11.50   5–9 books $25.00
6–9 books .... $14.50   10–19 books $29.00
10–19 books $19.00

SUBTOTAL $——————

Florida 6% sales tax (if delivered in FL) $——————

TOTAL AMOUNT ENCLOSED $——————

Your personal information is kept private and not shared with anyone.

Name: (please print) ————————————————————————

Address: (no P.O. Boxes) ————————————————————————

City/State/Zip: ————————————————————————

Phone or email: (only regarding order if necessary) ————————————————

Please make check payable to **Red Sage Publishing**. Check must be drawn on a U.S. bank in U.S. dollars. Mail your check and order form to:

Red Sage Publishing, Inc.   Department S17   P.O. Box 4844   Seminole, FL 33775

Or use the order form on our website: **www.redsagepub.com**